Blood Sea Tales
Book Two

The Pirate's Truth

I0658001

Chris A. Jackson

This is a work of fiction. Names, characters, places, and incidents are the products of the author's imagination. Any resemblances to actual persons, living or dead, events, or locales are coincidental.

Copyright © 2019 by Chris A. Jackson

All rights reserved. No part of this book may be reproduced or used in any manner without written permission of the copyright owner except for the use of quotations in a book review.

Published July 2019 by Jaxbooks Publishing

Cover design by Fiona Jayde
Images for interior from Pixabay have been altered for use

ISBN 978-1-939837-22-6 (paperback)
ISBN 978-1-939837-23-3 (ePub)
ISBN 978-1-939837-24-0 (Mobi)

jaxbooks.com

Acknowledgements
As always, thanks to my wife, Anne, for her
help, patience, and passion for the sea.

This novel is dedicated to my mother,
Shirley Louise Jackson,
December 14, 1930 -
October 14, 2018
who infused me with her love of books.

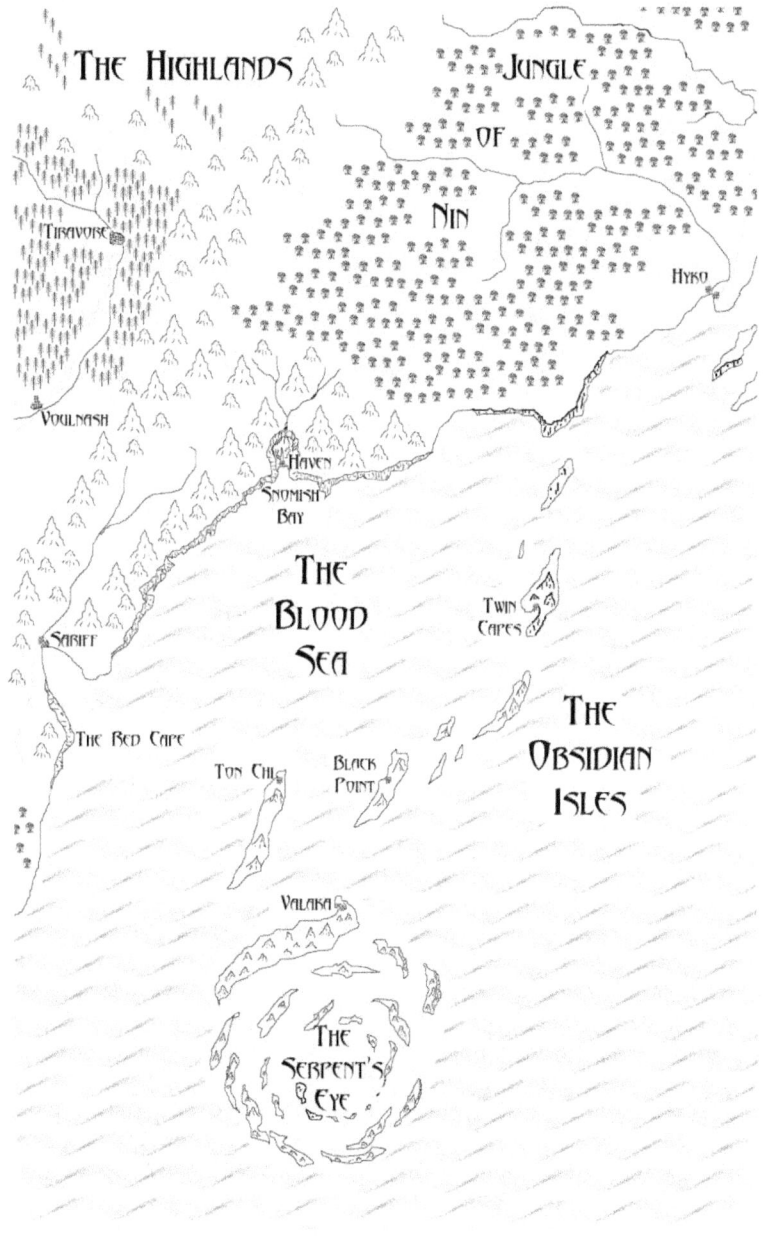

Chapter One
A Pirate True

Nothing is more seductive than knowledge.
The Lessons of Quen Lau Ush

From the diary of Kevril Longbright –
There is a danger in having all of your most pressing questions answered. I can understand how wielding this strange power could drive one mad, but there is one thing that keeps me sane. This truthsayer, this dove who lays diamond eggs, means so much more to me than her preternatural gift. Seeing her experiencing freedom for the first time changed me. I feel reborn. But I'm still a pirate at heart.

"They're dumping cargo, sir!"
Boxley's shrill call from the foretop brought my spyglass up to my eye. With a deft twist, my view focused on *Honor Bound*, a big four-masted junk flying the black and red crescents of the Mati flag from her mizzen. Her full-battened lugsails were flying to their fullest, dangerous in these conditions, but not surprising, considering they

were being chased by pirates, namely us. Then something heavy splashed over the leeward rail. A barrel.

"Bugger!" I snapped my spyglass closed and tucked it away. "They're lightening ship."

"They must be delusional," Miko scoffed. "They couldn't outrun *Scourge* sailing with an empty hold *and* using sweeps!"

"True enough." I bit a nail and cursed under my breath. "So why dump cargo?"

A hand touched my arm, and I turned to Preel. She held out her notebook, the page scrawled with her elegant hand. She couldn't speak because she wore her enchanted gag; an incautious question now, like my careless inquiry regarding *Honor Bound*'s tactics, would put her out cold for a day and ruin our secret advantage on this mission. Employing her truthsayer's talent to the best effect was one of our most difficult challenges.

I read the note aloud for Miko's benefit. "Perhaps to lessen their value as a prize, to make our pursuit less profitable?"

"Could be," Miko nodded. "Or maybe they know what we're *really* after, and the ambassador commanded them to take every measure to escape."

"That could be, too. But they're cutting into our profit margin with every barrel they pitch over the side." I gritted my teeth. "We've got to close on them quickly and convince them that they can't get away."

"Topgallants?" Miko cocked an eyebrow at me.

I looked aloft, gauged the wind, our heading, the strain on the shrouds, and the feel of the ship. I'd served in and captained *Scourge* for thirty years, and knew her better than I knew any living soul on the planet. We were already pushing hard, spray flying from our bow, though not quite dipping our leeward rail. The swell wasn't bad for the open sea north of the isle of Twin Capes, barely ten feet, but the wind was freshening. *Honor Bound* was still a mile off our bow, her greater size and full hold stiffening her rig against the wind. We were closing, but not fast enough, and every minute cost us money.

But so would a shattered topmast.

Decisions like this were my job, but that didn't make them any easier. "Yes, topgallants, but with one reef. We can't afford to carry away a spar."

"Aye, sir!" Miko shouted orders, Wix relayed them with his usual sprinkling of epithets, and my topcrew scrambled aloft.

I watched with some trepidation as Boxley clambered down to the foretopsail crosstrees to get out of the way. One slip at that height was a death sentence. Thankfully, no one fell, and the small square sails billowed, snapping taut as the sheets were drawn tight. Two squares barely the size of bedsheets, but so high that their force on the ship was greatly amplified.

Scourge responded, surging and heeling hard, pounding into the foaming seas. Immediately, the helmsman called for help, and my sailing master, Rauley, lent a deft hand at the wheel.

"She's griping like a bitch, sir!" he shouted. "Permission to ease the mizzentop a trifle?"

"Aye, do that!" As the orders were passed, I added a few of my own. "Run the log! Mister Kivan, go forward and ready that contraption of yours. I want to convince *Honor Bound*'s captain that it would be in his best interest to heave to."

"Aye, sir!" She dashed forward with a grin.

"You just made her day, sir," Miko chided.

"True enough." Kivan used to be my laziest midshipman, but she'd found a comrade in Boxley, and the two energized one another in a way that all the cajoling, ranting, and outright threats from a higher officer never could have.

Seemingly from nowhere, Kivan had demonstrated a passion for machinery that I hadn't even known she'd possessed. She'd bought plans for a small siege engine—a ballista—with her own money, and begged me to allow her to build it. I'd given her free rein, and she'd surprised me once again. Not only did the ballista work, but it scared the shit out of merchantmen and, when the bolts were tipped with tar-soaked rags and ignited, dissuaded other pirates from considering *Scourge* an easy target.

"Twelve knots, sir!" Quiff, my third midshipman, shouted from the middeck. "We're cracking on!"

"Aye, that we are!" *Scourge* capped a swell and fairly flew down the back side, the foredeck awash.

On the bow, Kivan swore a blue streak, her voice barely audible over the wind as she fought with the canvas covering her contraption.

A hand gripped my arm, and I turned to find Preel looking worried. She held up her notebook, and I read the smeared ink, "Permission to go below?"

"Of course, love. Sorry." I couldn't suppress my grin. Preel might be a pirate's lady, but she'd never developed a liking for rough seas and wet decks. "Morelie, there! Give the lady a hand down the steps. It's a bit trouncy for her."

Preel squeezed my arm in thanks and took the sailor's arm, sure-footed as a cat, but white-knuckled as the two crossed the quarterdeck. Hemp passed her on the way, wearing a weather cloak and hunched over a bundle. He made a face as we capped another swell and spray lashed aft.

"Sir! Bert's compliments and ain't you comin' down fer lunch?" Hemp cradled the cloth bundle like a newborn babe.

"No! Tell her I'm sorry, but we're on the chase!" I pointed to *Honor Bound* now barely half a mile off. "We should be on them in half a glass or less. Tell her to feed Preel if she's hungry and put mine aside."

"Aye, sir, I thought that'd be the case, so I brung you up a spot of blackbrew and a biscuit." He unwrapped a pot and held it out. "A bit rough fer cups, sir. You'll have to drink out the spout."

"Odea bless you, Hemp!" I took the pot, downed a mouthful of the blistering-hot brew, and handed it off to Miko. "Pass it around!"

Hemp looked like I'd docked his pay. "But that was fer *you*, sir!"

"I know, and it hit the spot!" I accepted two rock-hard biscuits and gnawed off a bite. "Bring up my cutlass and a brace of daggers, would you?"

Hemp muttered an oath, snatched back the now-empty pot, and shuffled off, ducking the spray that came aft.

A ship's brat dashed up the steps and slid to a stop before me, pressing a knuckle to his forehead. "Mister Kivan reports all ready, sir, and begs permission to fire when they're in range."

"Permission granted, Twik." I tossed him my second biscuit, and he caught it like a bat picking off a fat moth.

"Thank you, sir!" He dashed off, nibbling happily.

"You old softie," Miko muttered at my shoulder.

I glared at her. "What did I tell you about that?"

"That you're a right bastard, and don't forget it, sir!" Her grin remained undaunted.

"Damn right." I produced a dagger and pared a nail. "But it was the *old* part that I took exception to."

Miko's grin faded. "Oh, um...right, sir. You don't look..."—she tried not to break into a smirk—"...a day over...um..."

"I hear that the bilges need scrubbing..."

"Thirty! Not a *day* over thirty!" Her attempt to hide her smirk failed. "Maybe thirty-five."

Considering that that was a solid decade below my real age, I let it go and sheathed my dagger. Miko knew I wouldn't stab her for calling me old. Well, not lethally. She was my only senior officer, though both Kivan and Quiff were close to passing for lieutenant. If they did, I'd have to repopulate the midshipman's berth, either from the lower decks or by bringing on a stranger. With the secret of our own truthsayer still tightly kept, I didn't like the idea of bringing on new people, though I knew I'd have to eventually.

But not today, Kevril...

A sharp crack snapped my attention to the foredeck. Either we'd parted a stay or Kivan had fired a ranging shot. We were still a good quarter mile from our target, and I opened my mouth to tell her not to waste ammunition. Then I saw the arm-thick shaft of iron-tipped hardwood slam into *Honor Bound*'s high transom.

A cheer rang out from the foredeck, the ballista crew pounding my young midshipman on the back.

"Bugger me, but she's good with that thing," Miko commented.

"That she is. I just hope she doesn't kill the captain, or worse, the *ambassador.*"

"That *would* be bad," Miko agreed.

Jhavika's directive had been explicit; we were to abduct Ambassador Fawahah and deliver him to her. She hadn't told me why, but it didn't take a truthsayer to figure it out. The king of Mati was sending Fawahah to the god-emperor of Toki to negotiate a cooperative effort to control piracy in the Blood Sea. How Jhavika learned this, I have no idea, but abducting the ambassador meant she wanted a spy. She'd lash him with the same enchanted scourge that had enslaved me, and he would thereafter follow her every command. Through him, she'd drive a wedge between Toki and Mati, our two most powerful neighbors to the north and south, thereby increasing her value to Haven's Council of Lords, and putting her one step closer to her goal of ruling Haven.

Despite my hatred for that scourge of hers, I approved of her tactics. Haven was my home port. If Toki and Mati united to subdue the city states of the Blood Sea and Obsidian Isles, we would be beaten into submission like a piece of hot iron between anvil and hammer.

"Messenger!" I barked, and Twik dashed up. "Tell Mister Kivan to aim for her sails. We don't want to kill anyone important."

"Aye, sir!" He dashed off, and I watched him deliver the message.

Kivan waved to me and increased the angle of her contraption, her crew fitting another bolt into the mechanism. We were still closing fast, but veering a bit to leeward. *Honor Bound*'s sails were no longer in a line, which would reduce the impact of Kivan's shot. Also, our leeward slide would relinquish the weather-gauge advantage to the junk. Not that it would do them much good, other than to delay the inevitable, but I'd learned long ago never to surrender an advantage.

"Master Rauley, bring her up a point. We're making leeway. Line us up right on her transom."

"Aye, sir! Right up her ass!" He hauled on the wheel with his mates, and *Scourge* fought her way to windward.

Kivan and her crew hauled on the blocks that moved the ballista to the windward side of the foredeck, thus avoiding putting her shot right through our own jib. I watched her line up the shot, my interest not only tactical, but technical. I knew little of siege weaponry and, as I said, a pirate never surrenders an advantage. If the political situation went bad, I'd need every advantage I could get.

My midshipman bent down to aim along the ballista bolt, called for adjustment, waited for *Scourge* to crest a swell, and pulled the release. The siege engine's carriage jumped back against its restraints as the long shaft flew. Another cheer went up as the missile holed all four of the junk's sails, though it did little real damage. With all the reinforcing battens in the junk-rigged sails, there was far less stress on the canvas, so nothing tore or gave way. The shot fractured one batten in the mizzen, which might diminish its efficiency slightly, but not enough to make a difference. The winner of this race had been decided the moment we sighted our quarry. The only question was how long it would take us to overtake *Honor Bound*, and how much cargo she'd toss before we reached her.

Then Boxley's shrill call cut through the howling wind. "She's veering to leeward, sir!"

Finally! It was the maneuver I'd been anticipating.

"Rauley, cut her off! Wix, rig for a port-side broad reach! Topcrew, shake the reefs on those t'gallants!" This was where my well-honed crew shone. A junk is easier to handle than a square-rigged ship, but my people leapt to their duties, and *Scourge* veered to cut off the larger ship, quickly closing the gap.

Rauley called for preventers to be rigged on the mizzen boom in case we jibed unintentionally, a wise precaution and a testament to his seamanship, despite his youth. Making him my sailing master had been one of my best decisions. Miko bellowed for Quiff to take a boarding party forward, and for Wix to ready grapples.

Straight downwind was the one point of sail where a junk might give *Scourge* a run for her money, but we had a few minutes before the much larger ship built up speed. We had to close and board quickly. The only danger to that tactic was if they tried to ram us. *Honor Bound* massed four times our tonnage, and a collision could leave us foundering with cracked ribs and sprung seams or worse.

"Sharp eye on their helm, Miko! If they veer toward us, don't wait for my order."

"Damn straight, sir!" Miko raised her spyglass and took up station on the forward corner of the quarterdeck.

"Fenders out on the starboard side, Mister Quiff. Archers to the tops! Hemp, where's my bloody cutlass?"

"Comin' right up, sir, and I brung your patched jacket, too. No sense in havin' the good one cut to ribbons." Hemp held out a baldric, two daggers, and my patched jacket, as always, far more concerned about the damage to my clothes than my skin.

"About damned time!" I doffed my good jacket, clipped on the baldric and daggers, though I already wore two in my boots, and accepted the patched jacket. "Now arm yourself and—"

"Captain! They've got—"

I missed the rest of Boxley's warning cry as something jerked the tricorne from my head. I ducked reflexively at the distinctive hiss of arrows buzzing through the air. Hemp swore a blue streak at the damage to my hat, though I was grateful it hadn't pierced my skull. A cry from aloft and the thud of a body hitting the deck told me that at least one arrow had found its mark. I muttered a prayer to Odea under my breath that it hadn't been Boxley.

Wix's voice boomed across the deck. "Return fire, you fookers!"

Crossbows cracked from aloft as our archers raked *Honor Bound* in response. Risking a quick look, I confirmed that we were still a good hundred yards away, so a hit would be sheer luck. *So how the hell did they hit one of my topmen and nearly kill me on the first salvo?*

I reached for my spyglass, but another flight of arrows flew from *Honor Bound* before I could raise it to my eye. Cries rang out as this volley found multiple marks. One of those marks was my first mate.

"Miko!" I dashed for her as she fell, her chest transfixed by a long black arrow. My knees hit the deck beside her, and I steadied her before she could roll onto the arrow. "Can you breathe?"

"Breathe?" She grimaced as I helped her sit up. "Yeah, but I'll never play the flute again!"

I laughed. If she could joke, she could breathe. With luck, her lung wasn't flayed. Then I took note of the arrow and realized why the archers had such uncanny accuracy.

The arrow, a bamboo shaft fully four feet long, sported hawk-feather fletching and a notch carved of ivory and banded with silver. It was a *ya*, used exclusively by one class of Toki warrior, the komei, the god-emperor's finest. This one had a peculiar Y-shaped head, generally used for unarmored foes. Wearing armor at sea was a quick way to drown if you fell overboard, so the komei had assumed correctly that we wouldn't be. They, of course, *would* be; legend stated that the komei slept, bathed, and fucked in their armor, though I had my doubts about the bathing.

I drew a dagger and cut open Miko's shirt. The shaft pierced her just below her left breast, exiting on the same side. "Hold still, I've got to cut this short."

"Mind the *ship*, Captain," she growled.

"Shut up." I cut the shaft protruding from her back close to her skin, and helped her to sit up against the bulwarks. The butt of the arrow I also cut, but left a couple of inches still protruding, which would give Bert something to grasp when she pulled it out. I knew better than to do that now. "You're not coughing blood, so you'll probably live, but stay down until I can get Bert to have a look at you."

Miko grimaced, but nodded. "Aye, sir."

I stood just in time to duck again as another flight of arrows zipped past. The komei were renowned for their archery skill, often shooting geese in flight for practice. They were using pirates for practice today, and four of the six arrows hit their marks. Our return volley, more accurate now that we were closer, bristled from their armor, but they stood firm, holding their tight formation. Our light crossbows couldn't punch through their laminated bamboo plates or gilded full-mask helms.

We had one thing, however, that would.

"Kivan! Fire amidships!"

"I'm on it, sir!"

As her crew repositioned the ballista, I watched the six komei draw their asymmetrical bows and take aim. *Come on, Kivan...*

"Cover!" I bellowed just as they loosed. My warning might have saved some lives, for only two arrows found flesh on that salvo.

Then Kivan fired her ballista.

The bolt tore through the rank of komei, felling two and momentarily breaking the poise of the others. The komei recovered quickly, however, and reached for arrows, now aiming at our foredeck and the ballista crew. We had only a moment's advantage, and I intended to make the most of it.

"Kivan, take cover! Rauley, put us alongside! Wix, grapples! Quiff, board her bow!"

Even as the last command left my mouth, the komei fired. Fortunately, the ballista framework offered cover, and only one of the four arrows struck home. A young man named Penrick had been peering over the framework, and he took an arrow squarely in the forehead.

I gritted my teeth and drew my cutlass; this mission was costing far more than I'd bargained for. Unfortunately, when we left Haven I asked Preel only where to find our quarry, not whether *Honor Bound* had any special defenses against piracy, or if the god-emperor had sent bodyguards to protect the ambassador. My lack of foresight was costing lives.

Rauley steered us in at a steep angle, then veered sharply at the last moment. Our bowsprit swept over the junk's lower foredeck, our bobstay chain raking splinters from their cap rail, and sending *Honor*

Bound's armed sailors scrambling for cover. My sailing master was cutting it very close indeed. Thirty iron grapples flew in unison, pirates hauling and cleating off the lines. The ropes snapped taut with a horrendous jerk, more than one parting. Sailors aboard *Honor Bound* fought to cut the grapples free, but our archers were making them pay for their efforts.

"Slack sheets! Scourges, with me!" I jumped to our starboard rail just as the komei fired another volley. A black arrow creased my ribs, but, at that moment, nothing short of a killing shot would have stopped me. The ships smashed together, and I leapt, fifty screaming pirates at my side.

I kicked a sailor in the teeth as he raised a boarding axe, and deflected a pike-thrust with my cutlass before my feet touched the deck. I rolled low and cut the pikeman across his legs. Pirates surged aboard, knocking the Mati sailors away from the rail and securing the grappling lines. Our front line—myself, Wix, and nearly a dozen of our best fighters—faced the remaining four komei. Like a deadly wall they stood: bows discarded in favor of fine katanas, armor bristling with our crossbow bolts, dark eyes glinting from the eyeholes of their hideous masks.

One would think that three-to-one odds would secure a quick victory, but no. Two of my pirates went down before I even crossed swords with my opponent. Despite their armor, the komei wielded their katanas with a speed and grace that I'd never seen. I parried the cut that would have cleaved my skull, but the impact numbed my hand, and the fine blade sliced the epaulet off my right shoulder. I stabbed low with my dagger and nearly lost a finger to my foe's lightning parry. Tansy, to my right, exploited the opening my attack had provided, and her cutlass cut a deep furrow in the komei's breastplate. His backstroke creased her brow in turn. That strike, however, gave me the opening I needed, and my cutlass bisected his left arm at the elbow.

I made the mistake of thinking that my cut had ended the fight— I mean, who in their right mind keeps fighting after their arm is cut off?—and nearly missed parrying the komei's next strike. I deflected two more lightning blows before his severed arm hit the deck, then spun under the third strike, parrying high with my dagger and sweeping a foot at his ankles. He leapt like a dancer over my kick, using all of his momentum for a downward slash. Though I deflected the blow, my sword snapped an inch from the hilt.

"Fuck!"

I dropped the hilt, parrying again with my dagger and rolling with the force of the blow. Snatching my boot dagger, I threw it at his face. The blade merely clanged against his mask, but the distraction gave Tansy an opening. She feinted high and drove her dagger into the komei's groin.

This, too, should have dropped him, but didn't. My blood chilled as I considered that this foe might not be alive at all, but some necromantic animation. As Tansy parried yet another slash, I stepped in and sheathed my last dagger in the eye hole of his mask. The komei stiffened and fell twitching to the deck.

Finally!

I scooped up his katana—not my best weapon, but I needed a sword—and whirled to find another opponent. Thankfully, the fight was over. Six pirates were down, but so were all the komei. Wix, missing a patch of scalp and his left ear, grinned horribly down at his fallen opponent. The komei's mask was crumpled in, sporting four bloody holes from the spikes of Wix's dagger guard. The rest of *Honor Bound*'s sailors had dropped their weapons, her captain and officers standing unarmed around the helm, surrounded by pirates.

"Quiff, cut their sheets, take a detail forward, and find the ambassador! I'll search from aft. Wix, secure the deck and find your ear. Maybe Bert can stitch it back on."

"Bah! It's just a fookin' *ear*, sir."

"That's why the gods give you two, I suppose. Tansy, bind up your head and see about our wounded." I glanced back at *Scourge*'s quarterdeck. Miko stood at the rail, leaning heavily on Boxley's shoulder. "Mister Boxley, secure my first mate and take her below! I want Bert to have a look at her. Sit on her if you have to."

"Aye, sir!" Boxley and Bert would take care of Miko better than I could.

"Master Rauley, heave us to."

He snapped a salute. "Aye, Captain!"

"Kivan, the deck is yours!"

"Aye, sir!"

I climbed to the helm station and saluted *Honor Bound*'s captain, a tall, dark-skinned man wearing the red robe of a lesser Mati noble. That didn't surprise me. There were as many lesser nobles in Mati as there were common folk, with more begat every day. The king alone has two dozen wives, over a hundred grand-children, and thousands of cousins. I wondered how anyone managed more than one spouse.

"Captain, I'm Captain Longbright, a privateer for the city-state of Haven." A bald-faced lie, but a reasonable one. Jhavika was due to rise to the Council of Lords soon, and as Haven's only governing body, the Council could hand out letters of marque. They hadn't *yet*, but they could if they wanted to. "I understand you were only following orders to protect your charge, but I truly wish you hadn't resisted. It only accomplished unwanted deaths and injury for both your crew and mine. My orders were only to secure Ambassador Fawahah. *Now*, however, I'll be relieving you of the best of your cargo to compensate for our losses." That wasn't exactly true either—I would have pillaged his ship regardless—but it seemed a fair argument. "Now, please bring me the ambassador."

He glared at me without a twitch. "Who?"

I knew he was lying. "Come now, Captain. Mati merchantmen don't have komei aboard unless they're sent by the god-emperor to protect something. Cough him up and there won't be any need for further unpleasantness."

"I assure you, Captain Longbright, there is no ambassador aboard this ship." The captain folded his arms over his chest, his features expressionless.

I sighed and gritted my teeth. "Bugger off, then. We'll find him ourselves." I ordered my pirates to secure the captain and his officers, and we started searching.

An hour later, we'd found nothing.

Swearing a blue streak under my breath, I stepped back aboard *Scourge* and went aft. I had only one more option.

I opened my cabin door and staggered back under the onslaught of an enthusiastic truthsayer. It's nice to know someone cares about you. Of course, Hemp had already told Preel that I was fine, but still, her concern warmed my piratical heart.

"I'm fine, love! Really. Just a few scratches." Actually, the arrow crease would probably take a few stitches, but it wasn't a dangerous wound.

Preel released me, glared down at the blood on my clothes, and tapped the ivory silk gag that kept her from speaking.

"Yes, of course." I untied the binding, and she promptly kissed me hard, her fists nested in my hair.

"A few scratches?" She glared and kissed me again. "Kevril Longbright, you're a lying pirate!"

"Well, true, but I'm afraid I need to ask you a question, love. We can't seem to find the ambassador, and the captain insists he's not aboard."

Preel sighed and nodded. "Of course." She went to our bunk and lay down without preamble. "You're sure Jhavika was telling you the truth?"

"Well, to the best of her knowledge, though she could have been wrong. Still, there were komei aboard, which is kind of a giveaway; they were guarding something the god-emperor wants protected. They're hiding the ambassador, I'm sure. I just need to know exactly where."

"Then make sure to be specific with your question."

"I will be." I leaned down to kiss her once more. "Ready?"

"Ready."

I asked her, "Where exactly is Ambassador Fawahah of Mati?"

Preel's eyes rolled up and her back arched. She drew a ragged breath and said in a raspy voice, "Floating in a barrel, three-point-two-three nautical miles south-southeast, at a bearing of one-six-three degrees true." She collapsed, breathing heavily.

"Well, bugger me! The bastard was telling the truth!" I kissed Preel again, replaced the gag for her safety, and dashed back up on deck. My crew was busily plundering *Honor Bound*, but stopped when I hailed my quarterdeck. "Kivan, plot a course for a spot three-and-a-quarter miles at one-six-three degrees true, and make all ready to get underway. We're leaving!"

She gaped at me for a heartbeat. "What about the ambassador, sir?"

"That's where we're going." I grinned. "He was in one of the barrels they threw overboard."

"What?"

"They were obviously planning to scoop him up after we'd given up searching their ship. Make all ready." I crossed to *Honor Bound* and shouted down into the hold for my crew to finish up quickly. If we were going to find the ambassador before dark, we'd have to crack on. Lastly, I thanked the Mati captain for his hospitality and assured him that I meant nothing personal by our attack. This was just politics, Blood Sea style.

He called me a bloody pirate, which I couldn't deny. I am a pirate, and my lacerated ribs had bled all over my clothes.

In less than thirty minutes, we were underway. I checked on Miko and found Boxley doting on her. Bert had extracted the arrow and covered the chest wound with a strange dressing that flapped when Miko coughed. I told Boxley to assign a crewman to watch over Miko and to see to her own duties, then checked on Preel. She was sleeping soundly.

Hemp insisted I change clothes, and applied a bandage and salve to my ribs, since Bert was busy with the seriously wounded. He also told me our butcher's bill: six dead and eleven wounded badly enough to keep them off duty. I swore under my breath.

Two hours later, we scooped up the ambassador and opened his barrel, which was padded and stocked with food and water. I locked him in a cabin under guard and set sail for Haven. The mission had been a success, but the cost had been high.

Chapter Two
A Necessary Evil

Power is a drug more addictive than opium.
The Lessons of Quen Lau Ush

From the journal of Jhavika Keshmir –
I know now that I'll never be satisfied. Is this a curse or a blessing, a bane or a boon, providence or my inevitable demise? I don't know and don't particularly care. I do know that I can't stop, that I don't want to stop. If I can't have it all, I'll die trying.

Ty-lee held the carriage door open for me and bowed. "Please be careful, mistress."

Whether his concern was genuine or impelled by the scourge, I didn't know or care. I found his fawning both welcome and bothersome. "Just another gods-be-damned summons from the Council of Lords, Ty-lee." I boarded the carriage. "See that the new recruits are ready when I return."

"Yes, mistress." He bowed again and closed the door.

I sighed and settled back as the carriage rumbled into motion. I couldn't very well refuse the summons, but I had better things to do than listen to the Council's endless questions, arguments, insults, and jibes. It would be easier if I could simply slaughter the lot of them while they slept. That, too, I couldn't do; at least, not yet. They were too valuable, their fingers in too many plots and plans that I still didn't know enough about. No, they would make far better vassals than corpses. Or *most* of them would. I would be one of them soon, which would mean closer access to the ones who weren't already enslaved to my will. The only question in my mind was whose flesh should my scourge taste next.

The scourge wouldn't let me rest until everything was mine. I hadn't consciously realized it was controlling my desires until Kevril told me, but there was nothing I could do about it, even if I wanted to. I shifted irritably in my seat, unsure if my discomfort was real or imagined. *Damn you, Kevril!* The desire for power—*My desire? The scourge's desire?*—pressed me day and night, even plagued my sleep with dreams of conquest, riches, empires... Only victory gave me brief respite.

With nothing better to do, and desperate for a distraction, I pulled my notebook from my satchel and started studying my notes on the other council members. I'd devised a code for my personal journal; I couldn't afford to have anyone learn its contents.

I already had three members of the Council under my sway: Getashi Temuso and Ursilla Roque, who didn't know yet of their slavery; and Lord Tambris Matesh, who did. Matesh had been my first, and I must admit I'd been clumsy in recruiting him. Luring him into an intimate encounter had been simple enough—I have many weapons at my disposal and I use them all—but he'd refused my attempt at painful play, which I had planned to lead into a playful lash with my scourge. He'd told me of some foolish tradition from his Marathian homeland about women being submissive. Angry and impatient, I'd lashed him, only then realizing the danger of my impulsiveness. I spent hours indoctrinating him, assuring that no one would ever learn what I'd done to him. Since that day, Tambris had given me everything I asked for; he could never betray me, never harm me, and never rebel. I'd even kept up a secret romance with him, our dalliances a convenient cover whenever I needed to impart orders.

I've since refined my technique. Recruiting Temuso and Roque had been carefully planned and executed, their randy natures more conducive to a playful flick of the scourge. The only adverse consequence of that evening had been Kevril's discovery that I also had him under my control. I'd pushed him too far, and he rebelled.

Damn you, Kevril! Though nearly six months had passed, and he still served as my partner and pirate captain, my blood boiled at the thought of his escape from my control. Forcing myself back to task, I returned to my notes.

Of all the lords, Balshi was foremost in wealth and power, owning a significant fleet of merchant ships and half the warehouses in Haven. He hated me even before I sank his precious *Hymoin*. Now, he truly despised me. Lashing him with the scourge wasn't an option; nobody would believe a sudden shift in his attitude toward me. His sister, Brilla, however, was a different story. She'd actually approached me first, promising to use her influence over her brother if I arranged her husband's death. Brilla hated both of them—Balshi for forcing her into marriage, despite knowing her preference for women, and her husband for being a misogynistic boor. Getting close to her had been simple, and a discreet scratch with one of the tiny barbs that tipped the thongs of the scourge had made her mine. She had no inkling that she was under the sway of my scourge; I'd learned that it was less risky that way. One day I'd suggest to Brilla that putting a dagger in her brother's heart would result in her inheriting all his power and money. But not yet.

That left eight other possibilities for my next conquest.

I had two more open enemies on the Council: Lord Fa-Chen, an exiled shipping magnate from Chen, whose ship, *Yellow Rose*, I'd recently had Kevril pillage and burn; and his sycophantic comrade, Lord Reginald Malchi, formerly of Tsing. I'd already set the gears in motion to usurp Malchi's domain—*Thank the gods for disgruntled children!*—by suggesting to Ursilla Roque that a liaison with Malchi's youngest son would be both politically and physically fulfilling. The young Maurice Malchi had a reputation with the ladies, and secretly loathed his father.

Of the remaining lords, most were either neutral or willing to approve my ascent to the Council. Lady Hatsu, an exiled distant cousin to the god-emperor of Toki, was nigh unassailable; old and wise, cautious and well protected, her only weakness was money. She was in the slave trade, and we'd reached an agreement: she gave me good prices on slaves, and I assured her that no ships carrying her cargo would fall to piracy from me. I could count on her vote. Nevertheless, I had a few spies in her household, and would have more soon.

Lady Hashi Severn frankly scared the hell out of me. Whereas my scourge was a subtle and secretive weapon of power, the fell blade she wore openly for all to see was neither. Few soul-bonded weapons are. The obsidian dagger, Soul Drinker, is said to have been forged in a volcano and imbued with the soul of a necromancer. My sage had been unable to confirm this, but I didn't want to find out firsthand. I did know that virtually anyone who opposed her ended up mysteriously dead. Fortunately, we had no animosity toward one another. She specialized in smuggling antiquities, and we'd also cut a deal so that none of her baubles were targeted by Kevril. Conversely, several of her competitors hadn't been so lucky, their cargoes stolen and sold to Hashi's merchants at a discount.

I hadn't dealt much with the other four council members. All were either non-human or of mixed blood and so harder for me to read. Of course, that didn't mean that I hadn't set spies to discover anything and everything about them. Blinth Tinworthy, a gnome, controlled the formerly abandoned mines of Haven. Though largely played out, he still managed to eke out a profit. He employed a lot of people, mostly gnomes or dwarves, since the mines were cut to their proportions. His dwarven nemesis, Lady Ingrid Brickhammer, controlled most of the stonemasons in Haven, and had been trying to secure her own mining interests. For years I'd run a careful game of protection and information by bartering between the two.

Tori Blackbriar, a northerner with some distant elvish blood, was a charismatic rake with fingers in more pies than any baker in Haven. His spy network rivaled my own, though some were double agents who also reported to me.

The last council member, Nahli Twince, was more fae than human, rumored to be a shape-shifter, and eerily uncanny. She had fled the jungles of Nin to evade the god-emperor's truthseekers and enslavement. Her fae magic might counter the scourge's, so I couldn't rely on it. Her paranoia of the god-emperor, however, might be useful. Siccing a truthseeker on her might be an option if I needed to eliminate her.

Decisions, decisions...

"You," I tapped Tori Blackbriar's name with one finger, "will be my next conquest."

Once I was admitted to the Council—and there were not enough dissenting votes to keep me from it anymore, despite Lord Balshi's best efforts—an enslaved Lord Blackbriar would give me five irrevocable votes of thirteen. Swinging two more to my side wouldn't be difficult, giving me a majority on all votes.

Yes...things were coming together nicely.

I tucked the notebook back into my satchel as my carriage pulled into Lord Balshi's courtyard. He allowed the Council to use his estate for their meetings, not out of the goodness of his heart, but to exert a measure of control over the proceedings. A liveried footman opened my door, and I stepped out, my eyes scanning the assemblage of carriages and entourages. I wasn't late, but it looked as if I was the last to arrive. Had Balshi called everyone else in early to oppose my ascendance? I'd gotten my hopes up before, only to have them dashed. Instinctively, my hand sought the soft leather of the scourge's handle, and my nerves eased.

My escort dismounted, and Captain Vakna took his place at my side, his looming bulk a comforting presence. Of all my warriors, he was the most formidable, both skilled and preternaturally tough due to his part-ogre heritage. He could take a blow that would kill two men and still fight on.

"Miss Keshmir." The footman bowed and waved me to the stairs leading up to the impressive keep. Balshi, the petty git, had instructed his people to only address council members as Lord or Lady. "The Council of Lords awaits you."

"Of course." I followed dutifully, girding my ire.

Balshi's keep is the finest in all of Haven, overlooking the entire harbor and Snomish Bay from its perch high above the city. It's said to have belonged to a gnomish king centuries before. If so, it had undergone some serious refurbishing over the years. The original spare, utilitarian gnomish design had been embellished with gilded doors, vaulted chambers, and ornate appointments. Buttressed balconies jutted out over the waters of Mirror Lake, the balustrades dripping with verdant growth and colorful blossoms. Snowmelt from the impassable coastal mountain range roared over White Rock Falls into the lake, then swirled and clashed down steep and roaring rapids to the city. Mist hazed the air, glinting like diamonds on the high stained-glass windows. The ground itself trembled with the pounding water.

A nice place, I considered, *though the constant roar of the falls will take some getting used to.* It might be a few years, but this would be my home one day. A castle fit for a queen.

We crossed a foyer the size of my estate's gardens, ascended a stair wider than any of the streets of Haven, and strode down a carpeted hallway to the designated council chamber. The second dining room had been set aside for the purpose. I knew from Brilla that the keep had seven dining rooms, so I guess the Council should have felt privileged that they got number two, not number seven.

I didn't.

The footman ushered me in, announcing to the room, "Miss Keshmir has arrived, your lordship."

Lady Keshmir, soon enough, I thought. *I like the sound of that.*

The buzz of conversation died as the footman bowed to the seated assemblage.

Again, I didn't.

None of the lords or ladies rose from their seats, but all turned to regard me with knowing smiles, blank miens, or clear disdain.

"Jhavika, good of you to come. Please, have a seat." Lord Balshi gestured to the one empty chair at the long table. He sat at the head, of course, two armored bodyguards at his shoulders.

I was grateful for Captain Vakna at my back. Most of the lords and ladies also had bodyguards. The most notable were Lady Hatsu's armored komei, standing like statues, their grim masks gilded and snarling. Only two council members were unaccompanied: Nahli Twince, looking tiny, vulnerable, and alien, her over-large golden eyes wide and pupilless; and Hashi Severn, who looked about as vulnerable as a coiled viper, tall and seemingly carved from a pillar of obsidian, Soul Drinker sheathed prominently upon her chest. The leather wrapping the hilt was said to be human skin; I didn't doubt it. Just looking at that weapon gave me chills.

Power... my conscience whispered greedily. *The soul of a necromancer, invulnerability, magic, immortality... This, too, will be mine, in time.*

I snapped out of my reverie, nodded to my host, and took my seat. "Thank you, Lord Balshi."

Never one to mince words, Balshi dropped the other shoe even before my ass touched the plush cushion.

"You'll be delighted to know that our vote on your membership to the Council has been decided in your favor."

I was in.

I caught my breath and settled into my seat. "I *am* delighted." *And about damned time, too*, I seethed silently, longing to slice the sneer of distaste from his face. I had to accept with grace. "Thank you, Lord Balshi. I know we can—"

"Don't thank *me*, Jhavika. The vote came out with three against, eight in favor, and one abstaining, meeting the required two-thirds margin...barely. *Mine* was one of the dissenting votes. Oh, and in council, we do away with the pleasantries of titles. It's...tiresome."

"Of course." I gauged the others, wondering who the abstaining vote had been. No matter, really, but I was curious. "I know we can put our differences behind us for the good of Haven and the Council."

Ingrid Brickhammer snorted and scoffed, "Not bloody *likely*, lass." She tugged her fiery red muttonchops and winked at me. "Just because we sit at the same table don't mean we don't still hate the livin' fook out of each other."

Several of the others chuckled or frowned at the dwarf's comment. Hashi Severn grinned like a snarling wolf. Only Nahli Twince didn't respond in the slightest, her uncanny eyes unreadable.

"Admittedly, loving each other isn't part of our job description." Balshi favored Ingrid with a respectful nod. "We must, however, see to the business of governing, however *dreary* it may be."

Gods and devils, I hate your pompous ass, I thought. And I wasn't the only one. I sensed a hidden hostility between Balshi and Brickhammer, and filed it away for future exploitation. But I had to show that I was ready to work, at least ostensibly, and that I wasn't intimidated by any of them.

"Then, in the interest of utilizing our valuable time in *governance*, please bring me up to speed. What's on the Council's agenda?"

"Sea defenses," Balshi replied with a tight smile. "We've contracted Ingrid to refurbish the stonework on the harbor fortifications, and Blinth to supply the stone. We need to find someone with engineering skills to see to the siege engines themselves, and...*perhaps* secure some offshore defenses as well."

"Offshore defenses." I grinned. *So that's why my vote went through.* Even though there were shipping magnates on the Council and independent pirates aplenty on the Blood Sea, only I commanded an actual fighting ship and had nautical experience. "Well, if we can draft up a letter of marque, we'll have one privateer, at least, the *Scourge* under the command of Captain Longbright. We can spread the word to other pirates and offer the same."

"That's a beginning," Balshi admitted.

"More than a *beginning!*" Ursilla Roque cocked an immaculate eyebrow at me, blissfully unaware that she was under my control and doing exactly as I'd suggested, coming to my defense in council. "Privateers are a perfect solution. They cost us nothing and will put our neighbors on the defensive."

"But we're not at war, and we shouldn't *want* to be!" Fa-Chen pounded his fist on the table top. "If we antagonize the other city-states, *especially* Mati, we could make problems we're not ready to deal with."

"Which is precisely the difference between using privateers versus pirates, Fa-Chen." I kept my tone neutral, biting back the impulse to call him a fool. "It's a win-win, don't you see? If we bring the pirates of the Blood Sea to our flag and make them privateers for Haven, we *stabilize* the region, decrease the overall threat to our *allies'* shipping, and have a formidable force to deal with any city-states—or *empires*, for that matter—that might consider subjugating the entire region."

The budding alliance between Mati and Toki was no secret. If Kevril's mission went well, I would have a spy in the god-emperor's palace, but I couldn't use that as a lever in this milieu...yet.

"And what assurance do we have that your pet pirate won't continue to prey on *our* shipping?" Fa-Chen shot back.

24

I waved off his concern. "Now that I'm a member of the *Council,* that won't be an issue." That earned me a few glares, but the point was made.

"I call for a vote," Tambris Matesh, my reluctant devotee, interjected, following my long-standing instruction to back my plays once I rose to the Council. "Two votes, actually. The first to draft a letter of marque to Jhavika's business partner, Captain Longbright, and the second to begin making offers to recruit other pirates. They'd all have to agree to forego open piracy upon Haven shipping interests and only target merchants from city-states and empires seeking to curtail our independence."

"A good start!" Getashi Temuso agreed. "I'll second both of those. We vote!"

Good little slave, I lauded silently.

"It's not that simple." Malchi protested. "Why would pirates agree to this?"

"No, it's *not* that simple, but it *can* be." I nodded to Malchi respectfully. "We offer privateers a safe harbor in exchange for ten percent of the net proceeds from their operations payable directly to council coffers. Fighting ships moored in Haven will serve as a deterrent to our enemies, and will be good for every business in Haven. Their cargoes of plunder will be sold and resold here, and their crews will spend their money ashore *here,* rather than elsewhere. Lords and ladies, let me assure you, we will *all* gain from this." Of course, I'd gain more than most, but I wasn't about to announce that little detail.

"A vote has been called for and seconded," Balshi said with barely a hint of derision. He might hate me, but he knew a good deal when he saw it. "First, all in favor of drafting a letter of marque, with the provisions Jhavika has stipulated, to Captain Longbright of the *Scourge.*"

The motion passed with only Fa-Chen dissenting. He was still sore over the loss of *Yellow Rose,* no doubt.

"Excellent! I'll inform Captain Longbright of the Council's offer when he returns."

"And secure our percentage?" Fa-Chen asked with a frown.

"The deal won't actually take effect until *after* he receives his letter of marque," I countered, and then smiled and nodded, "but, to show good faith, I'll donate the inaugural ten percent from my cut of his most recent conquest."

"And what conquest might *that* have been?" Balshi asked pointedly.

"No ship from Haven, I promise you." I wasn't going to give him any more than that, and he knew it.

"Very well. The next vote is to make offers to other Blood Sea pirates for the same deal: a letter of marque, safe harbor, and free rein to prey on shipping of non-allied city-states, kingdoms, and empires, in exchange for ten percent of their net proceeds to the Council of Lords."

The vote passed unanimously.

The rest of the meeting passed quickly. I had to admit that Balshi was good at ushering issues along with alacrity; we all had better things to do. After we all agreed to finance the refurbishment of the sea defenses, which made Ingrid and Blinth happy, he called for adjournment. As we rose from our seats, several of the other council members approached to congratulate me on my ascent.

"Well done, Jhavika!" Getashi embraced me with a kiss, and Ursilla did likewise.

Tambris shook my hand as I'd instructed him to, his swarthy smile intact and seemingly genuine. It wasn't, of course, but he had no choice in the matter. Tori Blackbriar joined in with a handshake and a wry smile. Squeezing his hand firmly, I gave him my best sultry look along with my thanks. *I'll be seeing you soon,* I promised silently as he strode away.

Turning, I was startled to find Nahli Twince standing barely a step away. "Congratulations," she said with apparently honest good will.

Trying to avoid looking into those fathomless golden eyes, I thanked her and shook her dainty hand.

She looked down at our conjoined hands, her smooth brow furrowing. "There is magic about you, Jhavika." She squeezed my hand for a long moment, then released it. "Have a care, lest it consume you."

"Oh, don't scare the poor woman with your prophesizing, Nahli!" Hashi Severn stepped through the group, and everyone else edged away as if physically repelled by her presence. She held out a hand. "Congratulations, Jhavika. You've earned this."

26

"Thank you." Her chill grasp elicited an involuntary shiver, as if ice water trickled down my spine. I wondered if she was actually undead. Despite my repulsion, my gaze was drawn to the dagger strapped to her chest. It fairly smoldered with power. A visceral hunger welled up in me, the desire to possess it. I knew I couldn't...yet, and released her hand, regarding all of my peers. "Thank you all."

The group broke up, and we all followed our escorts out of the keep. As I boarded my carriage, a call stayed my foot on the step. Tambris approached and addressed me quietly. No doubt anyone observing us would have heard the rumors of our affair and dismissed our encounter as a quick exchange between lovers. I knew better.

"Be careful of the fae," he whispered. "She sees everything and senses more. If she learns of the scourge, there'll be trouble."

I'd ordered him to warn me of any danger, so this didn't surprise me. I nodded and smiled. "Thank you, Tambris. Perhaps you'll come by my estate tonight and we can discuss this." It wasn't exactly a command, except that I'd already conditioned him to agree to any suggestion I made.

A fleeting struggle raged behind his eyes, his jaw briefly clenched, then he asked through gritted teeth, "What time?"

"After dinner. We'll have a drink and chat." His jaw clenched again. He knew there would be more than chatting.

"I'll be there." He turned away without another word and hastened to his own carriage, undoubtedly hating me with every stride. I hadn't yet commanded him to love me as I had Brilla, and being enslaved by a woman affronted his Marathian masculine superiority. I took great pleasure in twisting that knife at every opportunity. I boarded my carriage with a smile, considering how I would have him debase himself for me tonight.

As the carriage lurched into motion, I sighed happily, content with my victory for a moment. I knew this peace of mind wouldn't last, but I reveled in it while I could, caressing the haft of the scourge and letting fantasies of conquest run through my mind.

But with every minute, the fantasies faded, and my satisfaction ebbed. There was work to do.

At home, I stepped out of my carriage to be greeted by Ty-lee's usual smile. "All went well, mistress?"

"Perfectly, Ty-lee. I'm now officially *Lady* Keshmir, member of the Haven Council of Lords." I strode toward the steps without pause.

"Excellent, milady!" Ty-lee followed dutifully.

"Call me 'your ladyship' from now on, and spread the word. Are the recruits ready for me?"

"Yes, your ladyship. Fifteen of them. They await your attention in the cellars. Please follow me."

"And send for wine, Ty-lee." I pulled on the leather tie that secured the scourge to my belt, the familiar haft caressing my palm, and gave the thongs a preliminary *snap*. "This will be thirsty work."

"Yes, your ladyship!" He snapped his fingers at a hovering footman.

Lashing and indoctrinating fifteen new slaves would take time and concentration. Long practice had made the process easier, but I had to be careful. Never could I allow the secret of the scourge to get out. Except it already had.

Damn you, Kevril!

Kevril Longbright and the crew of the *Scourge*...my privateers. They were an invaluable asset, one that I couldn't afford to lose...yet. In the future, however, I would have an entire navy of pirates. One more or less wouldn't matter in the slightest.

Chapter Three
The Dove Takes Flight

Release the dove from the cage.
If it returns, it is truly yours; if it doesn't, it never was.
The Lessons of Quen Lau Ush

From the journal of Preel Longbright –
Freedom, love, friends, luxury... I have more now than I ever
wished for, ever dreamed of. I have only one fear, and that is
losing this new life I have. That which we gain can be taken
away. I fear that I am still a slave, if only to my own fears.

"All secure, love."

I glanced over at Kevril as he came into our cabin, still salty from
his watch and needing a shave. I caught his eye and nodded, but
continued my exercises. I couldn't answer verbally; wearing the gag,
even though it had been five days since my talent was last invoked,
had become my habit of choice. There would be another question
soon—there was always another mission, another quarry, another
question that would save lives or cost them—and we dared not lose
the opportunity to a slip of the tongue. Kevril was still depressed about

our losses in taking *Honor Bound,* and I couldn't blame him. The komei warriors had been a grim surprise.

Kevril forced a smile and started for the quarter gallery, doffing his shirt on the way. "I've got to take Jhavika her prize money. Hemp will bring your share down as soon as Quibly gets all the cargo sold."

I smiled beneath my gag. As a member of *Scourge's* crew, not just the captain's wife, I earned a percentage of the plunder. I take great pride in my contribution to our success, and greater pleasure in spending my money on things I desire. I'd bought some pretty clothes and jewelry, certainly, but that's more disguise than luxury. Freedom has given me much, most importantly the ability to pursue my own interests. More than anything, I thirsted for knowledge, which seems ironic for a truthsayer, but knowledge is power. There are booksellers and sages galore in Haven, and I spent a good deal of my prize money there.

But not yet. I forced myself to concentrate on my yamshi, every move, every twist, every placement of my hands and feet. The discipline is more than exercise for me, and since I've learned its origins, more than even mental well-being.

As it turned out, Kevril was right in his surmise that yamshi evolved from martial disciplines. It's Chen in origin, devised by sects of monks trained in unarmed combat as a means to focus their inner strength and defend themselves from imperial subjugation. Yamshi actually means 'mind and body as one', which is apt.

In the months I'd been with Kevril, he'd taught me some basic fighting with daggers, but I preferred yamshi. I'd been experimenting with the moves, studying ancient texts and drawings of the warrior monks of Chen. I found this new knowledge empowering. Once I saw the parallels between my exercises and the martial arts, I felt like I'd cracked some kind of secret code. Every move was a block, a strike, a trip, or a feint. I was learning to defend myself with one goal in mind.

I would never be a slave again.

I held the last pose—*sun low in sky*—for several heartbeats longer than usual, reveling in the precision, the balance, the oneness of mind and body. Finally relaxing, I performed the closing move, hands pressing down, inhaled a deep cleansing breath, and exhaled, feeling whole, serene, powerful.

"I could watch you do that forever."

I turned to find Kevril watching me from the quarter gallery door, a towel around his waist, freshly shaven, his hair damp, the stitched wound along his ribs still livid. The sight of him thus always gave me a shiver of longing combined with a pit of dread in my stomach. Every time he was injured, every time he went into battle, and every time he went to see Jhavika, I invoked the same prayer: *I won't lose this... I can't...please.*

I bit my lip beneath the gag, purging my dread. *Don't ruin this...* I tapped the gag and went to him. He untied it—*sailors are so good with knots*—and I could speak.

"How are you feeling?" I brushed the stitches with my fingertips. The wound was cool and dry, and he didn't wince.

"Well enough." He bent down to kiss me. "Are you planning to go ashore?"

"Yes, just some shopping. I can wait for you to return if you'd like to go with me."

"Hours traipsing through bookshops?" he smiled. "No, thank you."

"Then I probably won't see you until this evening." I bit my lip and fingered the edge of his towel, tugging just hard enough to loosen it. "Will you miss me?"

He smiled down at me. "Every moment."

"Well, then, I better give you something to remember me by, hadn't I?" I tugged harder, and the towel fell away. I caressed him gently. "I promise to be careful of your stitches."

He caught his breath as my fingernails teased him. "You're going to make an old man out of me, Preel."

"Now you know my evil plan! I have a penchant for older men, you know." I tugged him to the bunk and pushed him backward onto it. This time he did wince. "Oh, I'm sorry."

"I'm fine, love."

"But I *hurt* you." I unwound my sweat-damped halter and wiggled out of my pantaloons, enjoying his eyes watching me, then leaned down over him. "How can I make it up to you"?

"I'm sure you'll think of something."

And I did.

I was gentle and took my time, teasing him relentlessly before finally coupling fully. When we were both sated, we lay skin against skin, breathing deep, reveling in the afterglow.

"I'm afraid you need another bath," I said as I climbed off. Retrieving his towel, I tossed it to him, then stepped into the quarter gallery, flashing a grin over my shoulder. "Join me?"

"A swipe with a towel will do." He rose and did that, returning my smile before reaching for the clothes that Hemp had laid out for him. "Besides, I like your scent."

"Suit yourself." I closed the door and sponged myself clean, suffused with a warm satisfaction. Toweling dry, I peeked to make sure Hemp wasn't in the cabin before venturing out. Kevril was just clipping on a cutlass and shooting his cuffs. I sidled up to him and looked at his reflection in the mirror, reaching around to finger his shirt. "You look nice."

"And you look..." He sighed and turned to run his hands over me. "How did I get so lucky?"

I grinned up at him. "Well, there was this evil pirate who rescued a slave girl..."

"Evil?" He kissed me. "*Nice.*"

"Well, she *made* him nice, with a little coaxing." I fondled him again, just for fun.

"You..." He grabbed me suggestively, but I laughed and spun out of his grasp.

"Go see Jhavika, you pirate, before I can't resist and have my way with you again!" I went to my locker, stepped into some silk scanties, and threw on a matching camisole.

"Yes, Lady Longbright." Kevril bowed, then strode to the door. Pausing, he said, "Make sure you take a proper escort, love."

"Oh, that reminds me!" I retrieved the silken gag and handed it to him. "Please." Kevril had kept his word, and would never put the gag on me unless I asked him to.

"Such a shame to cover that lovely mouth..." He complied, however, then kissed my brow and left the cabin.

From the hanging locker that Kevril ordered built for my clothes, I chose what I would wear ashore: a crimson sari, matching veil, and a headpiece with a dangling pearl pendant. I took them to the starboard quarter gallery, which had been converted from storage into a dressing room for me, complete with a vanity and full-length mirror. I applied makeup to hide my tattoo, added dark kohl to my eyes, donned the sari, brushed out my hair before arranging the ornate headpiece and veil, then slipped a couple of bracelets onto my arm.

I smiled at the exotic creature in the mirror. The makeup hid my distinctive Toki tattoo—the Flame of Truth, symbol of the truthsayer—and the Marathian veil rendered my enchanted gag invisible. My outfit mingled the traditions of several cultures: Fornician sari and headpiece, the pearls of a type revered in Hyko, Marathian face veil, and jewelry with the Chen flair for dragons. Thankfully, Haven was a culturally diverse city, and its more affluent inhabitants appropriated all manner of garb. I fit right in.

Lastly, I strapped a dagger to my thigh, hidden beneath the sari, but accessible. A handbag, my notebook, a pencil, and some money, and I was ready.

I found Hemp lounging in the galley, as usual, mooching tidbits from Bert. I wrote a note in block script—he couldn't read very well—and showed it to him. "Going ashore."

"Need an escort, Miss Preel?" He lurched up and brushed biscuit crumbs from his threadbare shirt. Though Hemp kept Kevril and my clothes in fine trim, he cared little for his own appearance.

I wrote, "No, thank you. Kivan and some crew are going with me."

"Very well, then! Keep your shoes clean, now." He sketched a salute and grinned at me.

Waving, I made my way to the wardroom where I found Kivan and Boxley together leaning over a book.

Kivan jumped up and tugged her midshipman's jacket straight. "Ready to go, Lady?"

I sighed. The crew had taken to calling me 'Lady' for lack of anything better. They'd previously called me 'Miss Preel', but when Kevril and I married, Hemp had proclaimed me "First Lady of the *Scourge*", and the moniker stuck. It seemed pretentious, but there was no changing a sailor's mind once they'd latched onto a notion. Even Kevril had taken up the title, teasing me with his 'Lady Longbright'.

Kivan wore a wide sash instead of her usual belt, a komei katana tucked through the cloth. She had earned it by felling two of the warriors with her ballista, and Miko was training her in its use. I often wondered at these boys and girls Kevril was forging into officers, so young and seemingly innocent, but pirates under the skin.

I nodded to Kivan and wrote a note for Boxley. "How is Miko?"

"Oh, she's fine. Just a little stiff. Bert said she'll be right as rain in a few days. Dumb luck that arrow didn't flay a lung, it was." She looked suddenly distraught. "Oh, that reminds me; she gave me a letter for you to pass on to Illian. Figured you'd be goin' up top, and *Fancy's Folly*'s only few blocks up."

I nodded and took the letter. Miko's girlfriend, Illian, lived and worked at the social club, *Fancy's Folly*, singing for her wages. I'd met her a few times—elvish, graceful, and beautiful—and liked her. We had something in common; we both loved pirates and worried about them constantly.

Miko couldn't go ashore and was chafing at her enforced bedrest. Boxley had made the first mate a pendant from the arrowhead that had nearly taken her life, and Kevril had given her one of the komei's katanas as her bonus, but neither had improved her mood. The least we could do was to deliver her letter to Illian.

We left Boxley with her book and went on deck. The ship was a beehive of activity. Rauley worked alongside the carpenters to replace some kind of fitting on the side of the ship, and the air buzzed and thumped with the sound of their saws and hammers. Wix's usual stream of foul language encouraged his riggers, the bandages swathed about his head doing little to impede his uncouth enthusiasm.

"Tansy!" Kivan called to one of the bosun's mates.

The dour woman hurried over, pressing a knuckle too the headscarf that covered the bandage on her forehead. "Ready to go, Mister Kivan?"

"Yes. I think we can do with four more this time. We're going up top, so pick a couple of topcrew with sharp eyes. Issue cutlasses."

"Aye, sir." Tansy dashed off.

I looked around at the workers while we waited, puzzled as always by the cat's cradle of lines, blocks, and spars. There is much about ships and sailing that I don't know, even though I lived on one and was married to a pirate. How it all worked together without getting tangled was a mystery to me, and sometimes it seemed as if sailors spoke an entirely different language. I asked Kevril once about the tradition of addressing officers as Master, Mister, or sir regardless of their sex, and he'd just shrugged. "Why are there no women sultans in Marathia or no male rulers among the fae? Why won't dwarven women ever use edged weapons? Why do elves prefer bows to crossbows? Customs are different all around the world."

Wisdom from a pirate; who would have guessed it?

I knew better, of course. I considered my piratical spouse as our small party descended the gangplank, crossed the stone quay to the warehouses that loomed over the docks, and boarded the first available cargo lift. Kevril was an atypical pirate; educated by his former captain at the end of a lash, he took to knowledge like a fish takes to water. His grasp of mathematics astonished me, and his love of poetry and philosophy set him apart from the average rapacious scoundrel on the Blood Sea. A peaceful, educated man who used violence to make his way in the world... He loved his freedom even more than me, I thought, and I often saw parallels between us.

We were both slaves. He freed me, and I helped to free him.

I snapped out of my musing as we arrived at the highest level of the waterfront buildings. Haven is a dangerous and most curious city, but I've come to love it a little. It's a bit like a big, dirty, vicious dog; if you treat it with caution and care, it can be a wonderful asset. Ignore its dangerous side, and it'll bite your hand off. So, we proceeded into the bazaar with caution.

"The *Folly* first, Lady?" Kivan asked.

When it came to excursions into Haven, I was more than happy to follow Kivan's lead. I nodded and followed her through the maze of tents, stalls, and shops.

With armed pirates glaring at anyone who came within six feet, no one accosted us. Hawkers just smiled and waved, some of them calling my companions by name. For now, we ignored them all and made a beeline for *Fancy's Folly*. Haven's bridges unnerved me, and we had to cross two to get there. As Kevril said, cultures are different everywhere, and gnomes evidently never saw the need for guardrails. There was a good bit of foot traffic today, and we closed ranks to cross. I kept one hand on my bag and the other inside the slit in my sari that allowed me to pull my dagger quickly.

We arrived at the *Folly* without incident. It's a private club, and non-members don't get in without an invitation. Kivan passed the letter to the door guard, telling him that it was for Illian.

"Of course." He handed the letter off to a boy in a white coat. "Will you wait for a reply?"

"Not necessary," Kivan said before turning to me. "Now where?"

I handed her another note.

"Teriwill's Bookshop," she read. "Right." Grinning, she led the way.

Part of the reason Kivan had volunteered to escort me was her newfound love of mechanical contrivances. While I looked for books on philosophy, history, and mystical Chen martial arts, she delved tomes on engineering, most of them translated from gnomish or dwarvish. Unfortunately, our escort of four pirates were not book lovers—I wasn't sure if they could even read. They stifled yawns and fidgeted as we spent hours perusing. I bought several books on varied subjects for myself, and one of poetry that I thought Kevril would like. Kivan bought two thick tomes on engineering that I would probably only ever read if I needed something to help me sleep.

More than anything, I enjoyed my freedom. Even with four grim pirates looming nearby, hands on their weapons and glaring at anyone who got too close, I was free to go where I liked and see whatever I wished. My escort carried our books without complaint, packing them carefully into cloth backpacks to keep their hands free. In recompense for taking their time and boring them to distraction, I suggested to Kivan that we stop for refreshment.

"You needn't, Lady," Kivan said, perhaps regretting it when the other sailors' eyes lit up. "I mean, it's not like you can...um...partake."

She was right, of course; I couldn't remove the gag in public. Still, I wanted to pay them back for their time. I wrote, "True, but I want to. One round won't take long."

So we found a rooftop establishment and sat beneath a colorful awning for a cool drink. Or rather, *they* all had a cool drink. I sat back and watched people.

The variety was infinite and endlessly fascinating—short and tall, fat and thin, of every color, race, and heritage. For too long, I'd lived my life hidden away. With my newfound freedom, I reveled in opportunities to be part of the flow and diversity, even if I had to do it in disguise.

Drinks finished and smiles all around, we picked up our parcels and started back to the ship. I walked along with a hidden smile, flushed with quiet contentment. Never had I imagined that freedom could be so sweet. Bridge after bridge we traversed until we were only a block from the waterfront warehouses.

As we crossed the final span, a man walking in the opposite direction dodged suddenly between two of my escorts to snatch my handbag. The stout cord around my wrist prevented him from simply jerking it out of my grasp, but a small hooked blade flashed in his other hand.

Without thought, my countless hours of yamshi training kicked in. I planted a foot, twisted—*willow bends in wind*—and pulled hard on the cords of my bag. The edge of my other hand struck the wrist of my assailant's knife hand—*hawk strikes serpent*—deflecting the stroke that would have cut my purse free. He yelped in surprise, his eyes wide, even as I continued my pivot, tearing my bag from his grasp.

If he had simply let go of the bag, he might have survived, but he was overbalanced already. When Tansy's blade caught him in the ribs, he cried out, flailing at the edge of the span, his terror-filled eyes locked with mine. Then he fell.

Kivan and the others clustered around me, blades in hand, facing outward. Far below, the cutpurse's scream ended in a horrifying crunch. Passersby backed away from us, as if we might push them to their deaths, too.

One fellow glanced over the side. "Guess he chose the wrong target."

"Won't be making that mistake again!" Another agreed.

"Lady, are you all right?" Kivan asked, glancing back at me.

Nodding, I showed her my bag and gestured for us to move on. There were no authorities here to ask questions or levy charges, so we hastened off the span without anyone's interference. Safe atop the warehouse roof, I looked back over the edge, down the eighty-foot drop to the filthy street below. A crowd milled around the body, scuffles breaking out over his boots and clothes.

I felt sick. *Why didn't I just let the bag go?* There was nothing in it but a few coins, my little notebook, a pencil, a pen knife, and a pot of makeup, hardly worth fighting over. Yet now a man was dead.

"We should get back, Lady." Kivan tugged at my arm. "There's nothing for it. The lout chose poorly and paid the price. Wasn't your fault."

I knew she was right. Kevril had warned that the bridges of Haven were often choice spots for assassination attempts, but this had evidently been a simple attempted robbery. I noticed little as we hurried back to the ship, my mind's eye haunted by the shocked look in the man's eyes as he realized that he was going to die.

And I killed him.

Chapter Four
Mission Accomplished

The difference between friendship and business is money.
The Lessons of Quen Lau Ush

From the journal of Jhavika Keshmir –
Every time I meet with Kevril I'm filled with a curious mix of
longing for him and the desire to have him murdered. If I'd
played him differently, I might have had everything. Now he
is both the perfect business partner and a threat to everything
I have planned. He and his crew know my secret. My knee-
jerk reaction to such a threat is to kill, but I know I can't. The
risk is too great, and I still need him. Someday, that will
change.

"Captain Longbright is here, your ladyship."
I turned from my garden windows to find Ty-lee ushering my
pirate captain into the room. In turn, Kevril guided a tall, manacled
figure wearing fine Mati-style clothes and a burlap sack over his head.
His mission had obviously been a success.
"Kevril! Wonderful to see you." I beamed at him. "And this is
Ambassador Fawahah, I presume."

"Hello, Jhavika. He denies it, but I'm pretty sure this is the ambassador, yes. They took far too elaborate an attempt to keep him from us for him not to be."

I stepped up and pulled the sack off Fawahah's head. Gagged, the man's dark features were cast in a dangerous scowl. Well, one lash with the scourge would change that. "Escort the ambassador to the second-floor guest quarters, Ty-lee, and put him under guard. I'll speak with him shortly."

"Yes, your ladyship." Ty-lee led the ambassador out, and I turned to my breakfast table.

"Tea or blackbrew?" I poured blackbrew for myself and lightened it with cream.

"No, thank you." From his hard tone and narrowed eyes, I could tell Kevril was in a mood.

I sighed and leaned back against the table. "Well, go ahead and tell me what went wrong."

"I lost six crew on this mission, Jhavika. The god-emperor sent an escort, six komei warriors. Miko took an arrow and will be in bed for another few days."

I didn't care in the slightest for Kevril's losses, but I had to feign concern. "That *is* unfortunate. I had no idea they would have komei aboard, Kevril, but that *does* speak well for the importance of our prize."

"True. The god-emperor must want this alliance badly. He's going to be pissed when he learns his komei were killed."

"No more pissed than he already is. We aren't the only ones preying on his shipping. Blood Sea pirates have been picking off Toki trade ships with increasing frequency, and it's only going to get worse for him. That's why I need the ambassador. Which reminds me, I have something for you." I pulled the letter of marque from inside my jacket and held it out. Kevril's hand never left the hilt of his cutlass as he reached out with his off-hand for the letter. "The Blood Sea's about to change, and Haven is going to be the naval power at the center of that change."

His eyebrows rose as he read. "A letter of marque?" He looked up with an odd expression that I couldn't interpret. "You did it. You're on the Council of Lords."

"I am." I raised my cup to him. "And you're our first privateer. We're going to start recruiting other pirates as well, and I'll need your help for that. You know the situation at sea far better than anyone on the Council, myself included. We want people who will see the end game in this and play by the rules."

He looked suddenly worried. "The other city-states will pitch a fit. Sariff will send ships here, Jhavika."

"I hope they do! We're refurbishing the coastal batteries. The gnomish siege engines will be working within a fortnight."

"And if they blockade the harbor out of range of the engines?"

"That's why I need you to recruit other captains quickly, Kevril. We may convert one of Fa-Chen's smaller ships into a proper fighting vessel—Captain Tan's volunteered to command—but we need more ships with experienced captains and crews. Six, at least, within the month."

Kevril folded the letter and tucked it away. "That's a tall order, but I know a few captains who might be interested."

"I thought you might." I turned and took in the view of my gardens. "But the offer we make to the other city-states won't be all stick and no carrot. Once we have a navy, we're going to send emissaries. If they want to ally with Haven, we'll guarantee that their shipping won't be touched by our privateers. If they don't, they're fair game. The threat of Mati and Toki teaming up to annex the Blood Sea should bring them into line."

"So...I'm going to be taking assignments from the Council now?" He still sounded dubious.

"Technically, yes, but only through me." I turned back and smiled. "Cheer up, Kevril, you'll be an admiral in no time!"

"Or a glorified tax collector," he countered.

"Privateer is better than pirate, Kevril, admit it. And admiral is better than captain. You're moving up in the world. Quit bitching and enjoy it!"

He snorted in open disgust. "And you're on the Council now. How many of them are your slaves?"

Well, it didn't take him long to bring that *up*. I didn't understand why he couldn't just focus on the end game and leave the means to me. I dismissed the question with a casual wave of a hand.

"You don't need to know that, but rest assured that I'll be supplanting Balshi as foremost councilor within months." Little did he know that he'd already helped me toward that goal by killing Brilla's husband. That, of course, had been before he'd broken the scourge's hold on him. With that thought, a question that had plagued me for months came to mind. I'd never asked it, but now might be the right time. "You know, Kevril, I've been thinking a lot about what you told me about the scourge, and I don't mind telling you that I'm troubled with the notion that this...thing is controlling me." I patted the scourge at my hip, enjoying the sudden tension in his shoulders. *He still fears it. Good.*

He frowned, his knuckles white on the hilt of his cutlass. "But you can't give it up, can you?"

"No, but perhaps there's a way to...mitigate its effects on me. Magic is a fickle thing." I began to pace slowly before the windows. "*You* broke the enchantment, after all. If you were able to, perhaps I could."

"I can't tell you how I broke the enchantment, Jhavika."

Kevril was no fool, and had already figured out where I was going with this. "Why not? It might be my only way free of the scourge."

"Because I can't. My relationship with the...person who helped me ended poorly. That bridge is burnt."

"That's unfortunate." I considered him, suspicious at his obvious evasion. Why would it matter if his relationship with this person was ruined? Whoever it was probably didn't know *me*, so there was no good reason why I couldn't consult them on my own. He was being evasive for another reason. I played my fingers along the soft leather handle of the scourge, wondering if it would be possible to lash him again to find out. The risk was significant; if I failed, and he made good on his promise to spread my secret far and wide, I'd have a serious problem. I wasn't yet ready to move openly against my adversaries. There was also the not-insignificant threat of his cutlass. I'd felt its sting before, and Kevril was in fine fighting trim, hard as nails. Weighing the odds, I moved my hand away from the scourge. *Better to keep him off guard for now.* Besides, there was one other thing I'd been wanting to know. "How the hell did you find out about the enchantment in the first place? I was very careful with you, Kevril."

His features darkened. "Until the night with Roque and Temuso."

"Ah, so *that* was it." I sighed despondently. "I went too far."

"Yes, you did."

"And the next day?" I cocked an eyebrow at him. "That was all an act?"

"Yes, it was, and it confirmed that you had some kind of control over me. I came very close to putting a dagger in your back that day, but I didn't know what would happen if I did." He shrugged. "It doesn't matter. Water under the bridge. We're business partners, and that's all."

"That's enough, I suppose." Kevril was lying to me, that much was clear, and I had to know why. A plan started to form in my mind, but I needed some time to put it into motion. "Give Miko a few days to get on her feet, then take a cruise to contact your pirate friends. Recruit as many as you can. We can offer a safe harbor and special rates on repairs and provisions, and the privateers will only have to donate ten percent of their net profits to the Council."

His eyebrows rose. "That's a better deal than I have!"

I knew he'd say that and was ready. "Until today. From now on, you work for the Council, not me. You'll pay us ten percent of your profits, and I'll continue to hand you the fattest prizes."

Kevril considered for a moment, then nodded. "Fair enough. We should be fit to sail in a few days."

"Good. Safe journey, Kevril."

He nodded and left without another word.

I paced some more, gestating my embryonic plan to discover the root of Kevril's lies. Truth be told, I *wasn't* easy with the thought of being controlled by the scourge, but the benefits far outweighed whatever drawbacks there might be. I didn't want—didn't *need*—a cure to the scourge, but *damn*, I wanted to know how Kevril had managed to find one, if only to prevent anyone else from doing the same.

I'd researched far and wide for information about my enchanted lash, and had come up empty. Not even the sage in my employ could tell me anything about its origins or workings. So how could a simple pirate discover a cure to such an obscure enchantment in less than a month?

I had to know, and there seemed to be only one way to find out.

Kevril tended to play his cards close to the vest, but there were a few people he trusted implicitly. Miko would have been my first choice, but with her sequestered aboard *Scourge* recovering from an injury, she'd be hard to get to.

The question was, who knew Kevril better than anyone?

Chapter Five
Privateers

No one is more attuned to the sound of distant thunder than a sailor.
The Lessons of Quen Lau Ush

From the diary of Kevril Longbright —
Call me a suspicious old cynic, but I don't trust Jhavika any
farther than I could throw an ogre. She does nothing out of
altruism. There is always an ulterior motive. She cares for no
one but herself. She can't. That gods-damned dragon coiled
at her hip won't let her.

"Come in, come in, and for Odea's sake sit down, Miko, before
you fall down." I waved them to the table already set for our
celebratory feast.

"I'm not going to bloody fall down." Miko walked stiffly, leaning
on Boxley more than a little, but made it to the nearest chair without
trouble. "Just a little weak is all. Everybody's treating me like a gods-
damned invalid."

"'Cause you kinda *are* an invalid, sir!" Boxley scowled at her
superior officer. "Gettin' stuck through the chest with an arrow'll do
that to you!"

"But you got some nice new jewelry and a new sword outta the deal!" Quiff chuckled along with the rest of us at Miko's expense.

"Boxley's started a new fashion trend aboard, you know." I gently flicked the arrowhead pendant—a razor-sharp Y of tempered steel struck with the Toki character for death—that dangled from Miko's neck. "Everyone who was hit with one of those and survived is wearing them as pendants or earrings now."

"Consider it a badge of honor!" Kivan raised her wineglass to my first mate.

"I can't recommend it." Miko grimaced as she shifted in her seat.

She looked a little gray still. Although the arrow had missed the lung, it had cut several of the small arteries between the ribs, and Bert couldn't cauterize them without risking damage to the lung. A lot of blood had pooled in Miko's chest, and it hurt like hell to breathe, but she would recover in time. I'd offered to let her off the hook for our celebratory dinner, but she'd told me she wouldn't miss it for half a dozen arrow wounds.

The starboard quarter gallery door opened, and the last of our party arrived. Preel looked amazing, dressed in an emerald green sari that hugged her like a glove. She still wore the magical band of silk that kept her from speaking, but that would come off for the meal. She'd been quiet since her incident in town, and I honestly didn't know how to help her. Everyone deals with killing differently; some aren't bothered by it, while others are utterly crushed. Everyone remembers the first life they took. It's something we carry until our dying day.

My three midshipmen lurched to their feet. Miko started to stand, but I put a hand on her shoulder.

"Sit down, Miko. You're exempt from pleasantries this evening." I pushed her down firmly and pulled out the chair beside her for Preel. "Here, love." Preel sat, and my midshipmen followed suit. Lastly, I loosened the knot securing the silken gag and took it off. "I know I don't have to remind you all to watch your tongues tonight, but I'm going to anyway. No questions of any sort unless you're asking someone to pass a dish or fill a glass. Our conversation's likely to delve into the new political situation and our place it in, so be cautious."

"Aye, sir," they all agreed.

I finished pouring the wine and took my seat at the head of the table, raising my glass. "Let me be the first to toast you all and our new status. We're pirates no more, but privateers lawfully appointed by Haven's upstanding Council of Lords."

The last bit earned a few scoffs, but everyone lifted their glasses and drank.

"So, Jhavika's plan is to create her own private navy." Miko swirled her wine with a grim smile. "And you're going to be her admiral."

"So she says." I shook my head. "And maybe she is, I don't know. It's not a bad strategy, really. The city-states who join our alliance will benefit, the others will suffer. It could start a war, but that's less likely if we recruit enough privateers quickly."

"She won't be satisfied." Preel stared into her wine, her lips set in a thoughtful pout. "She'll never be satisfied. She can't be. The scourge won't let her be."

"Exactly." I matched gazes around the room. My midshipmen looked worried, Miko grim, and Preel frightened. "What we have to consider is how best to survive this storm. We could just batten down and continue to ride Jhavika's coattails, stormy though the ride might be. I think that she'll eventually rule the Council. Or she may simply murder all her peers and proclaim herself queen."

"The other council members won't just let that happen," Quiff argued. "That bloody scourge don't make her immortal."

"True, but none of them know about it yet," Miko countered. "We could tell them, but I don't think that'd be in our best interest."

"I don't think so, either."

The door opened, and Hemp came in with a large silver platter mounded with tasty morsels. "First course, Captain!" He placed the platter on a serving table and started distributing smaller plates mounded with canapés, shrimp, tiny legs of fowl, and deviled eggs. "Bert's gone full sail tonight. Yer all in fer a treat!"

He bustled about the table, topping off glasses and seeing to everyone's needs. Hemp might be a scallywag, but he was a damn fine steward. I thanked him as he left, and we all began sampling the various dishes. Kivan, Quiff, and Boxley ate like ravenous wolves, grinning and commenting on everything, chasing every bite with my wine. I didn't mind; they deserved it. They were used to basic crew fare, so this was a real treat for them. Preel ate sparingly, and Miko barely touched anything. I ate some of each, savoring each bite and thanking all the gods of sea and sky that I'd found Bert.

"So, we can't interfere in Jhavika's plans, but riding the wave all the way to the rocks could likely get us crushed. Jhavika's cravings for power won't end with Haven, or even the Blood Sea. I wouldn't be surprised if we ended up at war with Mati, Sariff, or even Toki." I dipped a shrimp in one of the sauces and sampled it carefully. Sometimes Bert's sauces left blisters on my tongue.

"With you as the admiral of her navy. A lee shore if ever there was one," Miko agreed.

"So, the question is," Preel said, "at what point do we abandon her?"

"Aye, that's it. Not if, but when." I quenched the fire of the spicy shrimp with a sip of wine. "Just like a lee shore, you have to pick the right time and tide to claw off. We just don't know when that'll be."

"Pardon me, sir, but we can just ask Preel when would be best." Quiff looked from me to Preel with a furrowed brow. "Then we *know*."

"Unfortunately, that's not the way my...talent works." Preel sighed. "It can't pierce the future or predict what someone intends to do. It can only reveal what's already come to pass."

Boxley snorted a laugh. "So, you could tell us if she's *already* plannin' to have us all murdered, like, but not if she doesn't know when she's gonna do it."

"Yes, if she already has a specific plan to do so."

"Might be nice to know who exactly she's got control of," Kivan said, reaching for the wine.

"It would be, but that answer would press Preel harder than I'd be willing to risk." Preel and I had already talked about this. "Jhavika's enslaved at least dozens, probably hundreds, of people. Her entire household staff, guards, slaves, spies, assassins, and probably by now this ambassador we snatched for her. That would be too much for Preel to answer in one go."

"Correct. Questions that yield long answers, like when we asked what materials went into the making of Jhavika's scourge, tax me. We'd have to be more specific in our query."

"Like who on the *Council* she controls," Miko suggested.

"Or who, if anyone, aboard *Scourge*," Quiff added.

A silence fell over the table as we all exchanged glances. Thankfully, the awkward pause was broken by Hemp coming in with the second course, a salad of greens, mango, tangerine, and sweet onion. He served it out and removed the previous course, though Boxley loaded her plate before he whisked the dishes away.

"Waste not, want not, ya know." She stuffed a canapé into her mouth and grinned.

"Just don't make yourself sick," I warned. Boxley was still learning the rudiments of officer-like behavior, and table manners were coming slowly. I couldn't complain. She'd taken to basic navigation and seamanship like a duckling to water. I sampled my salad with bliss, fresh greens and citrus a treat for any sailor.

When Hemp had topped up everyone's glasses and opened two more bottles of wine, I continued the conversation where we'd left off. This was exactly the reason for this dinner. I needed all my officers thinking about options.

"So, yes, Quiff, we can ask that question, and have. So far, nobody aboard is under Jhavika's sway. But we need options in case this situation goes against us."

"Sail away," Preel said flatly.

We'd also had this discussion between us several times, and I knew her thinking. Unfortunately, this was one point where we disagreed.

"We certainly could, but if we do, we can never come back to Haven, and there's no guarantee that anywhere else will be safer than here."

"In Jhavika's mind, if we're not with her, we're against her," Miko agreed. "And that'll be a dangerous place to be when she has all of the Blood Sea under her control."

"Not gonna happen, sir." Boxley shook her head. "Like Quiff said, that scourge don't make her immortal. Somebody'll put a blade through her heart before she gets it all."

"Then there's the possibility that whoever kills her will take up the scourge and try to follow in Jhavika's footsteps." I speared a slice of mango and ate it, the tangy dressing offsetting the sweet fruit perfectly.

"There will be no end to it until that vile scourge is destroyed." Preel pushed her plate away. "Whoever created the thing was insane."

"Or just a greedy bastard who already wanted everything for himself." Miko raised her wine glass to the table with a wry grin. "World's full of greedy bastards, present company excepted, of course."

That brought a laugh, and I blessed her for breaking the somber mood. I raised my glass. "Here's to all the greedy bastards we know and love!"

Preel shook her head with a rueful smile, but drank to my toast.

Hemp came in with the soup course, a rich bisque that I'd been smelling all day. He exchanged the salad plates for soup bowls, then opened two bottles of red wine, decanting them into a crystal carafe.

"But the question remains of what our strategy should be." I sampled the soup and nearly forgot the conversation. Everyone voiced their appreciation, some coherently, others with moans of gastronomic bliss. When the comments died down, I continued. "I'm afraid I can't offer anything better than to bide our time and keep a weather eye on the horizon for squalls."

"But we should ask Preel *somethin'.*" Quiff downed the last swallow of his white wine, refilled his glass with the red, then offered the decanter around. "I mean, there's gotta be *somethin'* we need to know."

"Therein lies the quandary, Mister Quiff." Preel put her hand over her glass at the offer of wine, but smiled at my midshipman. "That's *always* the quandary. What question to ask. How best to employ this advantage we hold. Whether to use it or hold it in reserve for urgent need. If you ask me today if anyone aboard *Scourge* is under Jhavika's spell, and the answer is no, that doesn't mean that someone who *isn't* aboard may not be enslaved, or that she won't enslave someone five minutes after the question is answered."

"Good point." Quiff raised his glass to Preel and smiled. "I'd like to propose a toast, with the captain's permission, to Lady Longbright, our secret weapon."

"I'll drink to that!" I raised my glass to my love. "No sword shown so brightly or cut me to the heart so deeply."

My officers cheered and drank. Preel blushed, her dark eyes cast down.

"You mentioned we're gonna be on the dock for some days, Captain." Kivan said, and I wondered if she was changing the subject on purpose.

"Until Miko's rated for duty, at least." I wondered at that concession; Jhavika gave nothing away. If she gave us time ashore, it was for her own benefit, not ours.

"And until she has a chance to go see Illian," Preel amended, smiling at my first mate. "She's got to be worried about you."

"Why not invite her to come down to the ship for a visit?" I suggested. "We can give her an escort."

Miko's countenance brightened. "If you wouldn't mind, Captain, thank you. She doesn't get out of the club much, and a change of pace would do her good."

"Of course! We could even have a dinner for her," I gestured to the table, "assuming we've recovered from this one by the time you're well."

That elicited a round of laughter and a toast to Bert, to which we all, even Preel, drank.

"The reason I asked, Captain," Kivan continued after the toast, "is I was thinking about building a few more ballistae. They're not that expensive, and we've room for another on the foredeck, and maybe one on the poop. We could even rig some ballista bolts with grapples. They use them like that during sieges for scaling walls. The potential applications are really interesting!"

"Consult with Rauley and Wix before you do, but yes. The one has already shown its usefulness." I ate more soup and considered, picturing the placement of the contraptions. "My only concern is they'll clutter up the deck."

"They are ungainly things," Miko said.

"But they're good for skewering komei!" Boxley chirped, raising her glass to Kivan.

"I'll get with Rauley about it, sir. Don't you worry." Kivan grinned. "Thank you."

"Thank *you* for coming up with the notion!" I raised my glass to her as well.

The door opened, and two scullery swabs entered bearing a positively massive platter that barely fit through the door. Atop sat three huge dishes: a full-sized roast goose, its skin golden brown; a saddle of mutton as long as my arm; and a roasted snapper that probably outweighed Boxley. The serving table groaned under the weight, and Hemp took great pleasure in serving out the course.

"Odea's green garters, there's enough to feed the entire ship's complement here!"

"Not after I'm done with it, sir!" Boxley picked up her knife and fork, eyes wide as Hemp served.

Juices filled the platters as the goose and mutton were sliced, and the fish came apart in great slabs of white flesh, its skin spiced with pepper and citrus and cooked to a crispy sheen.

"And don't forget to save room for the sweets!" Hemp crowed with glee as he served everyone. "Bert's done one of her tartberry pies. You don't want to miss it!"

"I think Bert's trying to make us all rival her in stature. She's been trying to fatten me up for months." I sampled the mutton and rolled my eyes.

"She can fatten me up as much as she likes!" Quiff stuffed a huge bite of goose into his mouth and moaned blissfully.

"Just remember," Kivan took a much smaller bite and chased it with a sip of wine, "a fat pirate is a slow pirate, and a slow pirate is a dead one."

"Only we're privateers now!" Boxley crowed, already decidedly giddy from the wine.

"Which raises yet another point." I tried the fish, flaky and delicious. "Tell me what the crew's saying about our change in status, Hemp. You've got your ear cocked to every complaint aboard *Scourge*."

"Aye, that I do, sir, and not everyone's happy about bein' suddenly all legal and proper." He pulled a cork with a resonant pop and topped up the carafe. "Wix especially, though he's still pissin' and moanin' that we didn't have time to plunder *Honor Bound* good and proper."

"Oh, he's just sore that he lost an ear," Quiff muttered around a mouthful of mutton.

"Aye, maybe that, too, Mister Quiff, but some ain't happy with us startin' up a proper navy." Hemp shrugged and directed the swabs to take out the serving platter. "Most of us has already had more'n one run-in with navies, and ain't too fond of 'em."

Hemp left, and I considered the unforeseen effect on crew morale. Come to think of it, I wasn't in as high spirits as I pretended. I'd always cringed at Jhavika's promise to make me an admiral, and now that future seemed more likely than not. I didn't really want to command a navy. Maybe simply sailing away wasn't such a bad plan after all.

The question isn't if, but when, I reaffirmed. *And sooner might be better than later.*

Chapter Six
The Unwilling Accomplice

Words can murder as readily as swords.
The Lessons of Quen Lau Ush

From the journal of Jhavika Keshmir –
The scourge imbues a most interesting enchantment. It not only allows me to control people's actions, but gives me power over their desires, feelings, fears, and even their loves. It cannot, however, alter their memories. Experimentation has yielded variable results. I can order a slave to slaughter their own children, and to even enjoy it, but I cannot obliterate the memory that they loved those children. Down that road lies madness, and a witless slave, I have found, is a much less useful one.

The city of Haven is nothing short of a rabbit's warren above ground. Fortunately, through my network of spies, I had accurate maps of the entire city from the street level up: every bridge connecting one building to the next; every passageway, hallway, and corridor; every stair, ladder, and disused trap door. Whoever renovated these gnomish buildings to accommodate humans must have smoked black lotus.

We progressed through the warren like a pack of invisible weasels, silent and deadly. I strode in the middle of my six best nokitu, dressed as they were in close-fitting black clothing, black silk scarf wrapped around my head and lower face. I couldn't match their stealth, of course—nokitu are trained from childhood in the arts of silent assassination—but a hundred nighttime boarding actions in my years as a pirate served me well. We passed largely unnoticed through the nighttime shadows of the seedier levels of the city: the taverns, inns, flophouses, lotus dens, and brothels that catered to less-discerning tastes. Our goal, on the third level a block from the waterfront, was a brothel by the apt name of *Rolly Molly's* that attracted clients with a taste for the robust.

We reached the store room of a rug merchant and paused. I studied the diagram on my map with a red-hued glow crystal, then pointed to a rug in the corner. "There." Under the rug, just as my map indicated, we found a disused trap door.

One of my nokitu picked the lock, and, one by one, we dropped down into the cramped dark space of a broom closet. We were in. I expected the rest of the mission to proceed just as smoothly. My spy had given me the exact location of our quarry, right down to which trollop he preferred, what room she used, when they would be occupied, and how long their business transactions usually took.

There was enough noise from both the brothel's common room and behind closed doors to mask the passage of a contingent of armored knights, much less me and my silent escort. We crept through the hallways like a breath of night wind to the designated door. From the grunts and squeaks coming through the thin wood, the trollop and her client were well engaged. The senior of my nokitu, Busashi, tried the latch, and it turned easily. He nodded, and the rest drew their weapons. Hopefully there would be no need for killing, but it's best to be ready and not need, rather than to need and not be ready.

I drew the scourge, eased open the door, and slipped inside, my nokitu as silent as shadows behind me.

Hemp stood at the foot of the bed, gripping both bedposts, his skinny ass bucking hard. The trollop's ankles were locked around his neck, her toes clenching his long pigtail, copious curves undulating in waves at his every thrust. From her cries, she was either a consummate actress or genuinely enjoying the romp. Her eyes focused upon me for an instant, her mouth opening to scream as my scourge lashed out.

In one deft stroke, the barbs creased both Hemp's ass and the woman's thigh. A thrill of pleasure shot up my arm, the familiar rapture when the scourge tasted flesh.

"Quiet!" I whispered, and the woman's scream cut off. Hemp whirled to face me, but froze in place when I commanded, "Don't move! Either of you! No noise, not a word, not a scream, not a sound!"

I glanced toward the door. Busashi gave me a hand signal: all quiet. The brief scream had not drawn any attention from outside. In a place like this, screams and cries were common enough. He closed the door and stood in front of it, my other nokitu spread out at the ready, weapons in hand. I turned to examine my two new slaves.

Neither of them moved a muscle. They couldn't. The woman's legs stuck straight up, her ample loins glistening with sweat. Hemp stood like a horrified statue, utterly still save for the pulsing of his engorged manhood. I quashed a cruel impulse to apply the scourge to the thing—I was here for business, not pleasure—and told them, "Both of you, sit on the edge of the bed."

They complied, the woman struggling slightly to right herself, and Hemp folding his hands over his groin. I hadn't told him he could do that, but then, I hadn't told him he couldn't. Another foible of the scourge; my command to sit had rescinded the command not to move. I had to be careful, but I had long experience at this.

"Now, both of you sit there quietly and listen to every word I say. You're under my command, so don't try to fight it." I lowered my black silk scarf and smiled at Hemp. "You may both speak, but only quietly, and only to answer my questions. You will answer truthfully. Hemp, you know me, yes?"

He nodded, his motions jerky, fear filling his eyes.

I raised the scourge. "And you know what this is, what it does."

He nodded again.

"Good." I turned to the woman. "Your name?"

"Lola Marie Tonce," she said, her jaw quivering.

"Lola, my name is Jhavika Keshmir. Do you know that name?"

She nodded.

"Good. Are you a free woman, indentured, or a slave?"

Her multiple chins jutted out slightly. "I'm a free woman."

"Not anymore. You're mine. You serve me. You will never harm me in any way. You will take great pleasure in serving me. You will relate to no one in any way that I was here, that my people were here, that I lashed you with this scourge, or that you are under my command. Nod if you understand."

She nodded again.

"Excellent. Now, if anyone asks, you'll tell them in your own words that you transacted your business with Hemp to his satisfaction. If anyone sees the marks on your thigh, you'll say that he was enthusiastic and left the marks, for which you received a bonus. If anyone comes to you and says the phrase 'Queen Keshmir's Servant', you will answer their questions truthfully, remember everything they tell you, and follow their orders. Other than that, you'll go about your business and your life as you would normally, and you'll let no one discern from your mood, actions, words, or deeds that anything is amiss. If anyone presses you about this subject or about me, you'll throw yourself from the highest bridge adjoining this building. Do you understand?"

"Yes."

"Good. Now get dressed, stand quietly in the corner, and disregard everything I'm about to say to Hemp here. After I leave, you'll go about your business."

Lola got up and reached for her clothes.

I turned to Hemp. "Hemp, you will never harm me in any way, by word or action. You'll relate to no one in any way that I was here, that I lashed you, or that you're under my command. You'll go about your life, your job, and your recreation as you normally would with no outward sign that you're enslaved. Nod if you understand me."

He nodded stiffly, quivering with fear and rage.

"Good, now *relax*, for fuck's sake, and listen."

Hemp visibly relaxed, but his eyes still shone with terror.

"All right, then. You'll answer my questions truthfully. How did Kevril break the scourge's enchantment?"

His jaw clenched for a moment. "He didn't break the spell."

"Then how in the name of..." I realized my mistake and almost laughed. Hemp was being evasive. His answer had been truthful, but not what I obviously wanted. "How was the scourge's enchantment on Kevril broken?"

"By a magical oil."

"And how did he get this oil?"

"He got it from an alchemist."

"Where?"

"Valaka."

Now we were getting somewhere. "And what is this alchemist's name?"

"Brekka."

"And why do you think Kevril wouldn't want me to know about this Brekka?"

"Because she knows things Kevril doesn't want you to know."

That made sense. "And what *specifically* does this Brekka know that Kevril doesn't want me to know?"

"Preel," Hemp said through clenched teeth.

That took me aback. "What's that?"

"Not a what. A who."

"Then—" I stopped mid-thought. *Preel...* That name struck a chord, the young woman I'd met in Kevril's cabin the day after the party with Temuso and Roque. "Wait, Miko's girlfriend? The truthseeker?"

"She's..." He fumbled for words. "No."

I gritted my teeth. "What do you mean 'no'?"

"She ain't neither of those things."

Something wasn't right. Hemp couldn't lie to me, but he sure as hell was trying not to tell me the whole truth. I knew how to solve that. "Tell me exactly who this Preel woman is!"

"She's...the captain's lady."

"His *lady*?" That didn't make much sense either. "Tell me what it is about this Preel that Kevril doesn't want me to know."

"She's...his wife. They're in love."

I considered that revelation. That couldn't be it, though true as far as it went. Kevril wouldn't want me to know about anyone he loved for fear I'd use them against him. But there had to be something more Hemp wasn't telling me. No matter; I'd work around his evasions. "Tell me specifically what this alchemist Brekka knows about Preel that Kevril doesn't want me to know."

"That...she's...a...truthsayer," he hissed through clenched teeth.

Every nerve in my body tingled. "Truth*sayer*? Not a truth*seeker*?"

"Yes." Hemp hung his head, a sob escaping his mouth.

"Oh, stop that sniveling!" He did, and I considered. *A gods-damned truthsayer!* It was as if a light suddenly illuminated the darkness; I could see everything clearly, and it all made perfect sense. That was how Kevril learned of the enchantment, how he found a cure to it, and how he knew so much about the scourge. *Hells, he probably knows more about it than I do!* A cold finger chilled up my spine. He'd told me the truth about what the scourge was doing to me. I looked down at the weapon in my hand. *It's controlling me, manipulating me...but the power...* Shaking off the specter of magical slavery, I focused on the real potential of this revelation. *A truthsayer...* That was nearly as great a boon as the scourge. With both, I'd be invincible.

I paced the tiny room, considering my next move. I could kidnap the truthsayer, but there would be repercussions. Kevril had threatened to spread the secret of the scourge far and wide if I ever crossed him, and he was not one to make idle threats. I had to consider this carefully before putting anything into motion, but right now my thoughts were anything but calm. *Oh, what questions might I ask! What mysteries I might learn!* All of the council members' weaknesses would be laid bare. I'd have Hashi Severn's Soul Drinker in my hand, Fa-Chen's fleet at my command, Balshi's keep as my home, and Nahli Twince's magic all for my own. I'd be Queen of Haven in a matter of days!

Slow down! I forced myself to stop pacing, relax my grip on the haft of the scourge, think clearly. *Consider. Be careful.* I hadn't gotten where I was by being hasty.

I turned back to Hemp. "Listen to me carefully, Hemp. When I'm done speaking to you tonight, I want you to get dressed, pay Lola a nice bonus for her services, and go back to the ship as you normally would. You'll perform all your duties as if nothing unusual happened tonight. You'll act perfectly normally. If anyone asks, you'll tell them in your own words that Lola was exceptionally fine and earned her bonus. You'll listen to and remember everything Kevril says to Preel that you can overhear. You'll be as careful as you can about eavesdropping to avoid raising suspicion and getting caught. You'll *especially* try to discover when Preel will go out in public again. When you learn when this will be and where she will go, you'll return to this room and contract Lola's services." I succumbed to a cruel impulse. "After fucking her until she can't stand, you'll tell her that you're Queen Keshmir's Servant, and then tell her everything you've learned about Preel and Kevril. Nod if you understand."

The pirate cast a glance at Lola standing silently in the corner, then nodded sullenly.

"And lastly, Hemp, I know you're loyal to Kevril, but I can't have you cheat me by killing yourself. You'll take care to stay healthy and alive...*unless* anyone presses you for information about me or suspects that I've lashed you. In that case, you'll cut your own throat with a straight razor. Do you understand me?"

Hatred smoldered behind his eyes. "I understand you perfect, you sadistic fuck."

I laughed and leaned down to pat his stubbly cheek. "Not wise to insult someone who can command you to cut off your own cock, Hemp."

His eyes widened.

"But I won't do that...*today*." I chuckled at his terror, returned the scourge to my hip, pulled the silk scarf up to conceal my face, and nodded to my enslaved nokitu. "Time to go, Busashi. Back to the keep, the usual precautions."

He nodded once, waved his team forward, and we left the room. Glancing back, I saw Hemp reaching for his trousers, his shoulders quivering, and reveled in my victory.

A truthsayer... All the world lay at my fingertips, ready for the taking.

Chapter Seven
Love and Loss

All good things come to pass.
The Lessons of Quen Lau Ush

From the diary of Kevril Longbright –
What is love? Nothing in this world has fulfilled me more, and nothing has cut me so deeply. Would it be better to never have loved at all? That is one question I don't want the answer to.

I tapped a finger on my chart of the Obsidian Isles. "I guess the question is where to start." I'd been poring over the chart for half an hour, trying to decide which of the pirates I knew might consider signing on as Haven privateers. "I know several pirates who shelter in coves around Twin Capes, Black Point, Ton Chi, and some of the smaller islands."

"And Valaka?" Preel asked from the stern gallery windows. She stood watching the sun rising over the bluffs that surrounded Snomish Bay.

"I don't think so." I gulped my blackbrew and grimaced; it had cooled while I reviewed my charts. "Brekka will likely hold a grudge until she dies, and maybe even after. We don't dare return to Valaka."

"How about Hyko? That's a rich city. Aren't there pirates there?"

"Too far north for pirates. Toki warships patrol there."

"And you think the pirates will listen to you?" Preel didn't like the idea of dealing with unpredictable criminals, even though that description fit her husband well enough.

I shrugged. "Approaching them *will* be dangerous, but a white flag will generally elicit a parlay." I stood, stretching my healing wound. "We'll move *Scourge* to the quay today for provisioning and be ready to leave day after tomorrow."

"Will you want to ask me your question tonight then?"

"No, actually. I can do that when we leave harbor. That way you're only sleeping through a day of boring sea travel instead of missing out on our last day in port."

I didn't hear Preel sigh, but her shoulders shrugged in that familiar way. She hadn't been ashore since her encounter with the thief, and I knew she missed the freedom. I had a cure for that, however.

"I think we deserve a night out!"

"Out?" Preel turned to face me then, one dark eyebrow arched. "Out where?"

I shrugged and went to her, running my fingers down her silk-clad shoulders. "Your choice. We'll likely be at sea for weeks, so let's live it up. Whatever you'd like."

Preel pursed her lips and considered. "Well, no restaurant, considering..." She pointed to the silken gag lying on the table. Though she now freely ate among company aboard ship, it was too risky for her to go without the protection in public.

"You're not missing much. Few chefs in Haven can top Bert's cooking anyway."

Her eyes suddenly lit up, and she smiled. "Let's go watch Illian perform tonight! That would be fun."

"Perfect!" We'd gone to *Fancy's Folly* before to watch Illian. She had a voice like a goddess, and Preel had enjoyed her company after her performance. Also, the *Folly* had enough security to ensure the safety of their well-heeled patrons, a significant asset given Preel's recent anxiety. "Miko can swing an invitation, and I'm sure she'd like to go with us." I kissed her brow, then called for my steward.

Hemp was through the door in a heartbeat. "Sir?"

"Send for Miko. We'll be warping the ship into the quay this morning for provisioning. Tell Bert to stock fresh stuff for at least two weeks at sea, and the crew that we'll set sail in forty-eight hours."

"Aye, sir!"

"And lay out some clothes for Preel and me. We're going out to the *Folly* tonight."

Hemp froze. "The *Folly*? The both of you?"

His response took me aback. "Yes. If you have a *problem* with that, tell me."

"Oh, no, sir, I just..." His hands clenched at his sides. "I just thought, with what happened in town, you might want to have a care for the lady's safety."

I gritted my teeth. "I *will* be taking care for the lady's safety, Hemp! Lay out clothes and ask Wix to round up some volunteers for an escort. Six should do." I'd be damned if I'd let my steward remind me of my responsibility to keep the woman I loved safe.

Hemp looked immediately abashed. "Aye, sir. Sorry, sir." He ducked out.

"Go easy on him, Kevril," Preel said. "He's just concerned."

She was right, of course; the whole crew was concerned for Preel. They idolized her. "I know, but I feel bad enough about what happened. I don't need lessons on security from my steward."

"Well, just be *nice* about it, okay? Hemp's a dear."

"Hemp's a scallywag, love." I took her in my arms. "He just dotes on you."

"Well..." She pouted prettily, looking up at me with those bottomless dark eyes. "It's nice to have *someone* doting on me..."

"Oh, you *little*..." I poked the ticklish spot just below her ribs.

Laughing, she whirled away, shooting me a sultry look.

I took a step toward her, but a knock on the door stopped me. "Yes?"

Miko came in looking much better and walking without strain. "Hemp said we're warping ashore and you wanted to see me."

"Yes! We'll be going to sea on the morning tide day after tomorrow, and I thought it would be nice to have an evening out. How about a visit to the *Folly* tonight to see Illian?"

Miko grinned. "Sounds perfect! It'll give me a chance to kiss her goodbye."

"More than *that*, I hope! I won't expect you back aboard until tomorrow morning. Captain's orders." I waved her out. "Now, get us ready to unmoor ship."

"Thank you, sir!" She flashed a wider grin, threw me a salute, and ducked out.

The door hadn't even closed before Hemp was back through. "All's well, sir. Just need to pick out your jacket and trousers." He hurried to my locker. "And if Lady Preel could pick out a gown, I'll see it's ready."

It was still early, only just past breakfast. "There's no rush, Hemp."

"Well, I was hopin' to get it done by midday." He picked out a deep crimson jacket and trousers, brushing at the fabric. "With yer permission, I'd like to take a few hours ashore. Last minute goodbyes and such, you know."

I snorted a laugh. "Meaning you've still got gold in your pocket and intend to spend it on trollops and tots."

"Kevril!" Preel scowled at me. "Be *nice*!"

"Oh, he's right enough, Lady." Hemp grinned as he headed for the door. "Money to spend and a lady I figured I'd give a proper send off to. Give her somethin' to remember me by, ya know!"

"Have fun, Hemp." I waved him out and locked the cabin door behind him.

"I thought you were going to move the ship." Preel looked at me with hooded eyes and an innocent smile. "Why lock the door?"

"Because Miko won't have us ready to haul anchor for an hour, and I've been informed that I'm not doting on my lady properly. I mean to rectify the situation." I advanced on her with my best piratical swagger.

"Oh?" She backed up against the stern gallery windows, fingering the tie of her robe. "And how do you plan to do that?"

I dropped to one knee before her and raised my hands in supplication. "Just tell me what I must do to win your favor, fair lady."

"Hmm, let me think." She leaned back on the window sill with a pensive look, and drew her robe open. "What*ever* could you do to make amends for your bad behavior?"

"I'm sure something will come to mind." I leaned forward, and she ran her fingers through my hair. "Now let me think...it's on the tip of my tongue..."

Preel caught her breath, her hands clenching into fists.

I looked up at her. "Am I amending properly, milady?"

"Shut up and keep amending."

I may be the captain, but I know when to follow orders.

We arrived at *Fancy's Folly* just as evening darkened to night, Miko, Preel and myself decked out in our finest. Unfortunately, at the door we had to part ways with our escort; the club didn't allow private security inside.

"Stay sober," I told Tansy, nodding across the way to an open-air establishment. "No more than one tot apiece. We'll stay for two sets. Probably three hours."

"Aye, sir." She touched a knuckle to her forehead and grinned. "No more'n one."

Fancy's Folly is as flamboyant from the outside as its entertainment is inside. Its circular outer wall is festooned with colorful murals, and towers above the rest of the rooftop establishments. The roof is a massive tent of waxed and painted canvas that soars even higher. Two bruisers roughly the size of orcas stood guard beneath the colorful awning that sheltered the main entrance. They obviously knew Miko and greeted her warmly.

"Evening, Miko. Got yer note. Yer usual table's ready. Illian's on shortly." Bruiser One eyed me, then Preel, and nodded. "Two guests?"

"Just the two." Miko slipped him a coin, and he grinned. He had teeth like an orca, too.

"Have a nice time." They waved us through, Bruiser Two motioning for a white-coated attendant to escort us to our table.

Preel squeezed my arm as we were immersed in the cacophony of sound, motion, color, and aromas, her eyes alight with excitement. One thing about the *Folly*: they catered to all tastes. Their acts included singers, dancers, comedy teams, jugglers, acrobats, and some entertainers that defied description. Currently, a team of rainbow-clad trapeze artists were daring the heights of the big top.

"This way, please." Our escort beckoned us to follow.

The club was larger than its outward appearance suggested, built down into the top two floors of the building. Four concentric circles connected by short flights of gleaming, gilded stairs descended to the main stage. On the uppermost level, dim, cozy booths, perfect for romance or private business, lined the curved outer wall. Next was a ring of white-clothed tables and polished mahogany bars where patrons imbibed exotic beverages and ate prime cuisine from around the world. Down the next stair, the circle of gaming tables resounded with laughter and the clatter of dice. We followed our escort past all these to the central floor of small tables surrounding a star-shaped stage. Generally, the lower-level tables were reserved for the well-heeled or politically powerful of Haven, but Miko's relationship with the *Folly*'s star performer conferred her special status. We took our seats only one row back from the stage.

68

"Something from the bar?" our escort asked, bending low to be heard over the roars of the crowd and the cries from the performers over our heads.

Preel shook her head, eyes rapt on the high-fliers. I differed to Miko, since she was technically our hostess.

"Nothing right now. We'll wait for Illian."

"Of course." The waiter bowed and left us.

The trapeze act crescendoed with a series of twists and flips that left us gaping in awe and brought the entire club to its feet. The acrobats descended on long silken ropes to each of the six points of the stage, then performed perfect summersaults to the floor below and trotted away, waving to their cheering fans.

As the applause faded, the club went dark save for a few dim glow crystals around the periphery. It was time.

"And now, ladies and gentlemen," boomed a disembodied voice, "our evening's star event, the incomparable Illian!"

Bright lights flared to life around the periphery of the stage, shining inward toward the center. To frantic applause, Illian rose like a pillar of alabaster: hair like spun silver, skin of polished marble, and a flowing gown of ivory silk. A willowy elvish beauty with upturned brows, high cheekbones, and a pointed chin, almond-shaped eyes of vivid lavender, and the graceful curve of pointed ears peeking out from her platinum tresses, her simple grace contrasted the previously boisterous atmosphere. She hailed from the Northlands, Miko had told me, though Illian had never said exactly where. How she came to Haven, we had no idea, and Illian only ever said that it wasn't important. Someone, evidently, had just as many secrets as we did.

The applause and general racket from conversations, music, and games faded to silence. Everyone in the place watched spellbound. Then Illian began to sing.

Swaying like an ice-shrouded tree in the wind, her voice filling every corner of the huge club, at once throaty and pure, full and subtle, every note perfect, Illian began with 'The Ballad of Azrael.' There wasn't a dry eye in the house as all gazed upon her in rapt attention.

The singer, however, had eyes for only one person, every note, every word crafted especially for Miko.

A finger tapped my hand, and I looked down to read Preel's note. "Illian's in love."

I smiled at Preel and nodded. I dared not answer aloud, but I borrowed Preel's pen and scrawled, "Lucky Miko."

She poked my leg under the table and wrote, "You're just begging to make more amends, aren't you?"

I grinned and wrote, "Yes, please, milady."

Preel closed her notebook and squeezed my hand, her smile crinkling the corners of her eyes above the veil. We settled back and enjoyed the performance. Throughout Illian's entire set, the club remained quiet, only the faintest clink or scuff as the staff saw to the needs of their patrons. When the set was done, Illian curtsied gracefully, and the packed house erupted in applause.

As Illian descended the steps from the stage, the master of ceremonies climbed up from the opposite side, clapping wildly. "Have you ever heard such a voice? The incomparable Illian!" Even before the applause subsided, he waved his arms wide. "The lovely Illian will return in an hour for another set. In the meantime, enjoy the death-defying antics of Reginald and his Ribald Rascals!"

Jaunty music filled the air as a team of scantily clad male tumblers bearing swords and daggers vaulted up to the stage, leaping and filling the air with steel. I was glad we were one row back.

We all stood as Illian approached our table, grace in motion, her lips drawn into a subtle smile.

"You were fantastic, love." Miko greeted her with a kiss. "I'm the luckiest sailor in the world."

"Oh, you make me blush." Illian did, then turned to greet us. "Captain Longbright, you're looking as dashing as ever."

She extended a hand, and I bent to kiss it. "A pleasure, as always, Illian."

"And your lady is lovely tonight." Illian greeted Preel with a light embrace and a kiss to her cheek. "You're well, I trust, Lady Longbright?"

Preel nodded and immediately began writing in her notebook as we sat down. Illian had readily accepted that Preel was mute. Most people never asked us why, and those who did were told that we simply didn't want to talk about it.

Our waiter arrived to take orders for refreshment. With Miko and Preel competing for Illian's attention—the former gripping her hand and the latter dashing off notes—I took the liberty of ordering a bottle of sparkling ice wine. Sitting back, I watched the three for a while, warmed by Miko's obvious affection for her lady and Preel's eager engagement. This, more than anything, was the freedom my lady loved.

Their conversation continued until the wine arrived. When four glasses had been poured out, I toasted Illian, complimenting her performance. Preel raised her glass, too, pretending to sip from under her veil.

"And where are you sailing off to this time, dearest?" Illian asked Miko.

"No specific destination on this trip, love." That was true enough, since we'd be scouring most of the Obsidian Isles. "We'll be gone for at least a couple of weeks, however."

"So long?" Illian pouted and ran her fingertips down Miko's cheek. "I'll miss you so..."

"Oh, but think about the homecoming!" Miko laughed and returned the gesture. "And the captain isn't expecting me aboard until morning, so I can give you a proper send-off."

"I might not let you go, you know." Illian leaned in to whisper in Miko's ear.

Miko's coloration was dark enough to hide a blush, but her eyes widened and she shifted in her chair.

I felt a bit like we were intruding, but knew we weren't unwelcome, and raised my glass again to them. "Here's to homecomings and send-offs. May our absence only make your hearts grow fonder for each other."

We sipped, and Preel casually tipped her glass into mine. The conversation shifted to the *Folly* and Illian's increasing popularity. Miko joked that she'd soon have to fight off hoards of adoring fans, and Illian admitted that some had already become too persistent in their adoration.

"Truly, I don't understand it." She shook her head and sipped her wine. "Can people not conceive that there is a difference between *singing* of love and engaging in...well...amorous activities?"

"I hope this isn't anything serious." I cocked a questioning eyebrow.

"No, just bothersome. I'm not the only performer with adoring fans." Illian gestured to the stage and a small cluster of women gazing devotedly at the Rascals. "But the *Folly*'s security people see to our safety."

Preel scrawled a note and passed it to Illian, who read it and nodded. "Yes, it is comforting. We're allotted living space right here, in fact, just one floor down, and our rent is—"

A flicker of motion caught my eye, and something hit the table and shattered. My hand came up reflexively as tiny shards of glass pricked my face. At first, I thought someone might have thrown a bottle or glass, one of Illian's jealous fans, perhaps. Then, a billowing cloud of noxious vapor enveloped us. I shouted a curse, but couldn't manage anything else as the gas seared my throat and stung my eyes.

Amidst the shouts and screams erupting throughout the club, I heard more shattering glass and Miko bellowing for Illian. I lurched out of my chair and lunged for Preel. Her reflexes were as good as mine, however, and she was already up. We collided, and my hand found hers, though I could barely see through my streaming eyes. Pulling her with me, we blundered away from the table even as more gas bombs detonated around us. We crashed into overturned tables and stepped on fallen patrons as I fought to see, to breathe, to escape.

I pulled Preel along as fast as I dared through the panicked crowd. My hands and feet were numb, my head spinning, everything ablur. A dark shape dropped down right in front of us. Blinking hard, I discerned black cloth covering their head and face, hands wielding twin kamas.

Nokitu! my mind clicked, and my cutlass sang free, slashing to clear our path. This was obviously more than a simple brawl—perhaps a grudge feud between the crime lords who owned most of the businesses in the city—but I didn't have time to sort it out. Steel struck steel, and I swept my arm back for another strike. Then something jerked my ankle out from under me, and I went down, cracking my head on a fallen chair. My cutlass clattered away, and I lost my grip on Preel.

Panic surged up, burning away the rising darkness for a moment. "No! Preel! Here!"

And she was there, kneeling at my side, clutching me, her dark eyes wide and streaming with tears, a dagger in her free hand.

The darkness edged in again. I tried to stand, failed, and swore. "Run! Get out! Get to Tansy!"

She blinked at me and shook her head.

Another dark shape loomed out of the mist behind her, a short tube raised to their lips, and the truth hit me like a lightning bolt.

They're after Preel!

I gasped a breath to warn her—*Run! Get away!*—but gas burned my throat, and I could only emit a hacking cough. My vision narrowed as the blackness encroached again. The last thing I saw was Preel's face, her expression curiously blank, before I descended into a dark pit where my screams of rage died of loneliness.

Chapter Eight
A Prize Like No Other

Information, not swords or soldiers, is the key to victory.
The Lessons of Quen Lau Ush

From the journal of Jhavika Keshmir –
I have many beautiful things, but the moment I beheld my
truthsayer, I knew I had a treasure that surpassed all others.
Here lay my victory, my triumph, my destiny. With the answer
to any question I asked, and the scourge to enforce my will,
the world lay at my feet for the taking.

My nokitu delivered Preel with silent efficiency, drugged but
undamaged, just as I'd ordered. She lay upon a padded table, the tiny
dart that had rendered her unconscious still lodged in her neck. Other
than the one prick from that dart, she appeared to be unharmed, her
breathing slow and regular. I strode slowly up to the table to look
down at my prize, savoring my moment of victory.

"Were there any difficulties?"

"None, your ladyship." Busashi bowed stiffly.

I brushed the truthsayer's fine silk gown with my fingertips, just
to make sure she was real. "Was anyone killed?" Not that I really cared,

but deaths would complicate things. However unlikely, the operation might be traced back to me, and invading another lord's territory to abduct someone was a serious breach of our tentative truce.

"No one, your ladyship."

"Very good. You and your people performed well, Busashi. You're dismissed."

He bowed again and left the room.

"Ty-lee, summon my physician and my sage." I had to make sure my prize was healthy and genuine.

"Yes, mistress." He hurried out.

Guards flanked the table upon which my prize lay, but I waved them back. There was no danger. Busashi had assured me that she would remain unconscious for at least two more hours.

"A truthsayer," I whispered as I leaned down to examine her, wondering at the disguise Kevril had garbed her in. Was this, in fact, the same woman I'd met in his cabin?

Her pearl headdress lay askew, but her veil still hid most of her features. I remembered the tattoo etched between her brows and ran a finger over the spot. Makeup smudged my fingertip. Picking up a cloth from a tray of supplies, I wiped it away, revealing the stark black ink beneath. Yes, this was the same woman.

"But why the veil?" I unclasped it and drew it aside, receiving my first of many surprises.

A band of white silk embroidered with golden runes girded the woman's mouth. I dropped the veil and took a half-step back, wary of curses or enchantments. Was this some kind of defense or trap? It would be just like Kevril to garb his treasure in something that would render it useless if stolen or perhaps even kill the thief. I would leave that for Master Lewin to decipher. In fact, it would be wise to allow Doctor Yiv to examine her first, too.

I bridled my eagerness and walked around the table slowly, inspecting my prize by eye. Her finger and toe nails were painted and manicured, and she wore rings on both. There might be magic there, also. Lewin had been researching truthsayers since I'd learned about

Preel, though he'd discovered relatively little. Their powers to answer any question were legendary, but not limitless; they couldn't locate powerful magic or magical beings, for example. There were also many tales of truthsayers mysteriously dying, which was worrisome. Did the magic they bore weaken or strain them? Care seemed prudent.

Finally, my physician and sage arrived. Yiv looked bored, her dark eyes hooded, her hands hidden in her voluminous sleeves. Lewin, however, looked intrigued, this unique discovery infusing his ancient face with youthful vigor.

"So, this is the truthsayer, your ladyship?" Lewin stepped forward to peer down at her tattooed brow. "Yes, that is the Toki character for the flame of truth, a mythical fire that burns away all falsehoods. It's the traditional marking of the truthsayer."

"What of the binding on her mouth?" I asked.

He shrugged. "Magical runes, certainly. Let me see." Drawing a notebook from an inner pocket, he leaned close to examine the binding. "It'll take me a moment to decipher."

"Why am I here, your ladyship?" Yiv frowned at me. "I'm no magician."

"Examine her physical condition and tell me all you can about her." Yiv was perpetually surly, angry that I'd taken her from a profitable practice to be my personal physician. Of course, being magically enslaved probably had something to do with her mood, as well. Even though I'd commanded her to enjoy serving me, she remembered her former life and what it was to be free.

"Very well." She began her examination, reciting her findings as she went. "Young human Fornician female, probably in her twenties. No apparent head trauma." She pulled the tiny dart from Preel's neck and dropped it on the floor, then withdrew a glow crystal and shown it in the truthsayer's eyes. "She's drugged, but her eyes react normally and equally to light. She's well-nourished and seemingly healthy." Loosening the neck of Preel's gown, she picked a listening trumpet from the tray of supplies and pressed the fluted end to the truthsayer's chest, her ear to the opposite end. "Breathing and heart appear normal." Laying aside the instrument, she examined one arm, then the other. "Few calluses on her hands, so she does no manual labor. She has old scars on her wrists that suggest a history of wearing restraints."

"She was a slave?" I asked.

"Quite possibly, but there could be other explanations." Yiv turned over the arms and stopped. "There are scars on the inside of her wrists that suggest repeated attempts at suicide."

"What?" I stepped forward to look. There were three long scars on the inside of her left wrist and two on her right. "Can you be sure they were self-inflicted?"

"No, but it's probable." Yiv continued passionlessly. "Her legs are well muscled, feet well formed."

"Your ladyship, if I may interrupt my learned colleague," Lewin interjected.

"Pause for a moment, Yiv. Proceed, Lewin."

"The silk binding on her mouth is indeed magical. It has two enchantments: one restrains the wearer from speech, and the other prohibits the binding from being donned or removed by the wearer. Why she would wear such a thing is beyond me."

"Interesting. Well, I suppose I'll have to ask her when she wakes. Do you know if it's safe to remove the gag?"

"Safe for her or us?" Lewin shrugged. "I don't know, your ladyship."

"And her other jewelry?"

"Mundane, mistress."

"Then step aside and let Yiv finish her examination. Yiv, continue."

My sage stepped aside, and Yiv promptly and efficiently opened the truthsayer's luxuriant gown and gave her a thorough examination, rattling off the details as she went. "The subject is fit, with good muscle tone and mass, and doesn't appear to be pregnant, malformed, ill, or mistreated. There are no other scars, whip marks, or obvious signs of abuse, though she has a faint bruise across both buttocks. It's straight and new, but not serious. She likely fell backward onto something hard." Her deft fingers poked, prodded, and explored. "There are no signs of previously broken bones. She's had sexual intercourse with a male recently."

I remembered what Hemp had told me. *Kevril's wife.* "How recently?"

Yin shrugged. "Within twelve hours or so. There's a minor discharge of seminal fluid." She stepped back from the table and wiped her hands on a towel.

"Is that all?"

"With the gag on, I can't do an oral examination, so that's all I can determine at this time."

I considered and rejected the idea of removing the gag. Not until I knew more. "Fine. Dress her exactly as she was before. I don't want her to wake up knowing she was examined."

As Yiv did so, I turned to Lewin. "Research truthsayers with regard to that magical binding. I want to know why she'd be wearing such a thing."

"Yes, your ladyship."

I dismissed them both and regarded my treasure, my very own truthsayer. It bothered me that she'd tried to kill herself more than once. I had to make damned sure Preel couldn't try again and succeed. The easiest way, of course, would be to lash her with the scourge and command her not to, but there was always a risk with employing the scourge's magic openly. The greatest danger was the slave knowing they were enslaved and rebelling in some way. Some of the more drastic cases had even taken their own lives. Slaves who had no idea they were under my control, as Kevril had been, and Ursilla Roque and Getashi Temuoso were now, were much more malleable and useful. With the truthsayer, I didn't want to take any risks I didn't have to, but the control the scourge gave me was far too effective to disregard. So, the question wasn't whether to use the scourge on Preel or not, but how to do so without her knowing.

I pulled the weapon from my hip and flicked out the lashes, resisting the visceral urge to lay it across that pristine flesh. Instead, I picked out a single lash, held the tip between two fingers, and pressed one barb into the tiny wound on Preel's neck. Pleasure thrilled up my arm, a sure sign of the scourge's magic being invoked. It had tasted her flesh.

The truthsayer was now my unknowing slave.

I dabbed the wound with a handkerchief, replaced the scourge on my hip, and beckoned Ty-lee with a crooked finger. I'd ordered the entire household to follow his orders to simplify things, freeing me for more important matters.

"Have her taken to her new quarters. Be *careful* not to injure her. Post guards outside her door day and night. Have Nala and Binsh report to me. They're from Fornice. Perhaps their familiarity would put her at ease. They can attend to her needs, but I want to instruct them personally first."

"Yes, your ladyship."

"Oh, and make another search of her rooms. There's to be nothing she can make a weapon from or injure herself with. Nothing breakable, no glass mirrors, no razors, scissors, or anything sharp. And nothing she can hang herself with. Be as thorough as you can."

"Yes, your ladyship."

"Also, no one is to speak to her or...take liberties with her. When she wakes, have me summoned."

"Yes, your ladyship."

"Go." I waved him on, then left the room. It was late, and I was tired, but the excitement of my new treasure thrilled me. I knew I wouldn't be able to sleep. I considered summoning Yiv to mix me a sleeping draught, but discarded the notion. I had planning to do and could go one night without sleep.

I'd barely sat down at my desk and begun jotting notes when a knock sounded. "Yes?"

Nala and Binsh, the two Fornician slaves I intended to use as Preel's attendants, entered. "You summoned us, your ladyship?"

"Yes. Come here and stand in front of my desk."

They did so, and I leaned back to examine them. Siblings, they were two of the most beautiful and talented dancers I'd ever seen. I'd used them to seduce Roque and Temuso, but until now had found few applications for their talents other than my own personal enjoyment. I had to take great caution in their instruction if they were to care for my most prized possession.

"I have a special assignment for the both of you. I have a new slave. Her name is Preel. She's a truthsayer, which makes her more valuable than all of the rest of my slaves combined. You two will attend to her every need. You'll sleep in the sitting room of her chambers and do whatever she asks, except to harm her in any way. She currently wears a magical binding over her mouth that she can't remove herself. You'll only remove it if I tell you it's okay to do so. You'll not allow her to harm herself in any way or attempt to escape, and will protect her from any harm with your lives if necessary. You'll not speak to her at all or write messages to her. Your only response to her questions will be a nod of affirmation or a headshake of negation. You'll do whatever else she asks you to do if it doesn't risk her safety or go against any of my previous or subsequent commands. If she asks if you're treated well by me, you will reply in the affirmative in all respects, and that you're never punished unjustly or severely. If, in the future, I rescind the order not to speak to her, you'll tell her in your own words that you take great pleasure in serving me, and that I'm a kind and gracious mistress. You'll never in any way let her discover that I've used the scourge on her, or that she's a slave to me. Do you understand these instructions?"

"Yes, your ladyship," they replied in unison.

I considered for a moment any potential loopholes in my commands, but couldn't think of any. "See to your duties."

They left without a word, and I returned to my work. I had a world to conquer, after all, and now I had the perfect tool to facilitate my victory.

Chapter Nine
Wrath

The ability to think clearly in crisis is the most blessed gift.
The Lessons of Quen Lau Ush

From the diary of Kevril Longbright –
A large part of a sea captain's job is to deal calmly with crisis situations. That holds even truer for a pirate captain, since we tend to create crisis situations. I'm good at it. Analytically assessing damage and injuries comes easily for me. Never once in the command of my ship, any boarding action or shore-side battle, have I lost my head. The day I lost Preel, that changed.

I woke with my mouth tasting of vomit and my head ready to explode. The air reeked of harsh chemicals, and people were groaning and retching all around me. I fought to my hands and knees, choked, spat, and blinked hard to clear my blurry vision.

Memory returned—the *Folly*, gas bombs, running, falling, dark shapes, Preel...

"Preel!" I lurched up, found my cutlass, and squinted into the haze. The club was a shambles, with tables overturned, patrons fleeing, and heavy-set bouncers prowling the perimeter looking for someone to blame for the mess. People were sprawled all around, but Preel was nowhere. "PREEL!" My head pounded with my bellow, but I got no reply.

Remembering figures dropping from above—black clothes, nokitu weapons—I looked up. There were several large slashes in the tent fabric. I couldn't imagine even nokitu escaping the same way they'd come in. Someone must have seen where they went. I needed answers.

I strode toward one of the beefy bouncers. "You! Where did the bastards go?"

"Just calm down and put the sword away." The man stood head and shoulders taller than me and hefted a heavy truncheon like he knew how to use it.

I leveled my cutlass at him and didn't break stride. "Tell me where the *fuck* they went, or I'll carve you up for dog meat, fat boy!"

He grinned and pointed the club at me. "Shut up and drop the sword before I—"

I pitched a boot dagger underhand into his gut and took his hand off with my cutlass. Screaming, he dropped to his knees. I kicked him under the chin, sending him sprawling back. With my boot to his neck and my cutlass pricking his nose, I asked again. "Where did they *go*, dog meat?"

He spat blood at me. I considered removing his other hand and asking again when a familiar voice rang out.

"Captain!" Miko dashed up, katana in hand, Illian not far behind. My first mate stared at me wide-eyed. "What the holy fuck—"

"Drop the swords and stand away!" another bouncer bellowed.

I looked up to find half a dozen of them closing in, truncheons at the ready. Behind them stood a truly massive woman, taller than me and almost as wide as tall, two short tusks jutting from her lantern jaw. This was Gurt, the manager of the club, and her eyes were fixed on me like I was to blame for all of this. Maybe I was. I didn't care.

"Tell me where the fuckers went who took my wife or I'll hand you this asshole a piece at a time!"

The bouncers started to close in, grim and angry.

Miko put a hand on my arm. "I'm with you, Captain, but is this really smart?"

"What?" I looked at her stupidly. "Smart? Who the fuck cares!? They took *Preel*!"

"I know, sir, but it wasn't *them*!" Miko nodded toward the closing ring of bruisers.

I tried to make sense of what she was saying, but I just couldn't. All I could think was that Preel was gone and these people must know where she'd been taken. I gritted my teeth, struggled to think this through, and failed. Cutting a swath through these bastards until someone told me what I needed to know seemed my only option.

Deliverance came from an unexpected quarter.

"Captain Longbright, *please*." Illian stepped between us and the advancing bruisers, her empty hands out, imploring. "This is not helping you *or* your lady. I saw them take her. They retreated the same way they came, one of them carrying her over his shoulder."

I lowered my sword, my rage melting away, trying to understand what she'd said. "They climbed a *rope* carrying her? That's impossible!"

"Nevertheless, that *is* what I saw. They were nokitu. Their abilities are preternatural." Illian looked to the bouncers and her rotund boss. "Please, Gurt, Captain Longbright is not at fault here. He's the *victim*! He's only concerned for his lady."

"Then tell him to put his weapons away." Gurt ambled forward, jostling her beefy bouncers aside. "Our security was breeched and your lady abducted in *my* club, Captain. I'll do all I can to find her, but cutting my people into pieces is *not* going to engender my goodwill *or* my help."

"Fine." I wiped my cutlass on my jacket and sheathed it, then removed my boot from the bouncer's throat and retrieved my dagger from his gut. "I know your boss personally. I expect results."

Gurt nodded, her chins wobbling like jelly. "I'll tell Lady Roque what happened here, Captain. The reputation of my club has been harmed, so rest assured, I want answers as much as you want your lady back."

"I *doubt* that!" I wiped my dagger and put it away. "I'll be aboard my ship. Miko, we're leaving."

"Aye, sir." She stopped to give Illian a kiss, thanked her for intervening, and followed me to the exit. Our escort stood there, blades in hand, prevented from coming in by another dozen bouncers.

"Captain?" Tansy's eyes flicked around, searching for something that wasn't there. "Where's the lady?"

"Gone." The word felt like a knife in my gut, but my mind was starting to function again. "But I'm going to get her back if I have to burn this entire fucking *city* to the ground to do it."

"Not a far stretch to figure out who took her, Captain." As we stepped out of the club, Miko put a hand on my shoulder and squeezed hard. "My money's on Jhavika."

My teeth chirped like crickets as I ground them together. "I know, Miko, but we've got to be *sure* before we burn a bridge we can't rebuild." I was really thinking now. The repercussions for murdering one of the Council of Lords and burning her keep to the ground would be significant.

"True enough, but it's even more complicated than that."

"How can it be *more* complicated?" I glared at her. "Threatening Jhavika will do no good, and starting a war will get us all killed. Even if I tell the whole council about the scourge, she'll just use her influence to call me a liar or have me murdered."

Miko shook her head. "Not that. *Think*, Captain! If Jhavika's got the scourge *and* a truthsayer, what's the first thing she's going to do?"

"Ask Preel how best to use the scourge to further her plans, I guess." I didn't understand where she was going with this. Maybe my brain wasn't working so good after all.

"No. Think about how Preel helped you! How much more *effective* her help was when she was on your side, helping you ask the right questions, *willingly*."

"Willingly..." It hit me so hard I stopped in my tracks. "She'll use the scourge on her."

"Exactly."

"Fuck." The thought of Preel under Jhavika's complete control sickened me. Images of what Jhavika might do just to manipulate me or for her own sadistic pleasure ran through my head like a school of sharks, each one tearing off a piece of my soul. "Come on, Miko. We've got to find out if Jhavika's behind this and figure out what to do."

"Aye, sir!"

We hurried back to the ship, eight grim pirates with blood in their eyes and steel at their hips. Even Haven's worst lowlives weren't stupid enough to get in our way. When we arrived at the ship, however, we were met by Wix at the gangplank. He held a sealed envelope in one hand, his other clenching and flexing at his side.

"What?" I snatched the envelope. "What is it?"

"Messenger said it was from Lady Keshmir." His eyes swept our group. "Wait! Where's Preel?"

"Nokitu took her." Murmurs swept the deck around us as I tore open the envelope and read.

Kevril,

By the time you read this note, Preel will be mine. It will be best for everyone, Preel included, if you simply forget you ever knew her. I value our partnership and would like your help in carving out the future for Haven, the Blood Sea, and the world. I don't, however, require your help. I now have everything I need.

If you choose to continue our partnership, you'll be rich and powerful, and Preel will be happier, healthier, and safer than you could ever make her. If you oppose me, I'll use the scourge and Preel's talent to rain death and destruction down on you and everyone you care about. Trust me when I tell you that I will never let any harm befall her; she's far too valuable. But consider, please, what I can command her to do if I use the scourge to control her...much as I commanded you.

The choice is yours, Kevril. Don't let your heart dictate your actions, or you will perish and Preel will suffer.

With my deepest sincerity,

Lady Jhavika Keshmir

I crumpled the fine parchment in my fist as my heart pounded in my head. "Shit, shit, *shit!*"

"She's got Preel, don't she?" Wix asked.

"Yes."

The murmurs escalated into a dangerous rumble of epithets and curses, then speculation, oaths, and accusations of treason. For Jhavika to have learned about Preel, someone aboard had to have talked. The crew wanted to know who had betrayed us and string them up. The answer, however, was simpler than treason. None here would have betrayed Preel intentionally.

"The *scourge*," I growled, silencing my piratical family. "She must have used it on someone. We have to find out who, but I don't want them killed. No one leaves the ship! Wix, you and Tansy strip-search every single member of the crew down to the last ship's brat! Anyone refusing to be searched or sporting fresh whip marks is to be brought to me unharmed. Got it?"

"Got it, sir!" Wix barked orders.

"Miko, with me. Send word for Bert, Quibly, and my midshipmen. We've got to figure out what the *hell* to do." I started aft while Miko rounded up my most trusted and sharp-witted people. Together, we would figure out some way to get Preel back.

"Sir?" Hemp poked his head out of the galley door as I strode past. "Heard a..." His eyes widened, sweeping the passage. "Where's Lady Preel?"

"Jhavika took her. Bring a big pot of blackbrew to the cabin, and tell Bert to come in, too."

I didn't wait for an answer, but opened my door and threw my jacket in the general direction of my locker. My mouth still tasted of vomit, so I poured a measure of whiskey into a tumbler and tossed it back. I had to think, and a little alcohol and a lot of blackbrew was a potent mixture. Too much alcohol, however, would be counterproductive, so I put the bottle away. While hanging up my cutlass and daggers and kicking off my boots, I considered my bleak options: fight, run, or do as Jhavika had suggested and try to forget the woman I loved.

That last one wasn't going to happen.

I turned back to the cabin, empty for the first time in half a year, though traces of Preel were evident here and there—a book she'd bought, a handkerchief, her nightgown draped over the airing rack—and clenched my fists to keep despair from overwhelming me. *Think, Kevril! There has to be a way to get her back.*

A knock at the door snapped me out of my downward-spiraling thoughts, and Miko entered with everyone I'd summoned.

I motioned them to the table. "Everyone sit down. By now you've probably heard that Preel was abducted by Jhavika." I tossed the crumpled note onto the table. "She admitted it. The one thing we couldn't let happen has happened. The question is, what do we do?"

"You mean other than kill the maniacal bitch?" Quiff passed the note to Kivan.

"Not as easy as you might think, Quiff." Miko still wore her finery, but her expression was anything but festive. "She has some very impressive forces at her disposal." She related what had happened at the *Folly*, how the nokitu had stolen Preel literally from my grasp and escaped with her.

I paced.

"More'n one way to kill that don't need soldiers." The cold fervor in Bert's voice chilled me.

I considered the source and frowned. With what Bert knew about food, she probably meant poison, but that was a chancy prospect in this situation. "Killing Jhavika *is* an option, but a dangerous one. What else?"

Kivan passed the note to Boxley. "Do you think she's telling the truth about...what she would do to us *and* Preel if we betrayed her to the Council?"

"Knowing what we know about the scourge, and what it's made her into, yes, I think she'd rain hell and damnation down on us if we outed her secret."

"Are we sure this is genuine, sir?" Quibly asked, eyeing the note. "Could be a forgery. One of her competitors setting her up."

That was a possibility I hadn't considered. "It's possible, but I don't think so. The note sounds too much like her, and it refers to the scourge. I might use that to get close to her, however, tell her I want proof that she actually *has* Preel and that she's okay." Hemp entered the cabin bearing a huge tray with two pots of blackbrew, cups, and a plate of biscuits and cheeses. "Thanks, Hemp. You may as well pull up a chair, too. You've got just as much at stake here as the rest of us."

Hemp put the tray on the table and backed away. "If it's all the same to you, sir, I'll just...see to my duties." He turned for the door.

Hemp's tremulous tone struck me like a discordant note. "What duties?"

"I...uh..." He looked around and spotted my dress jacket on the floor next to my boots. "Just figured I'd spruce up yer fine jacket and shine your boots, sir. There's blood that'll never come out if I don't get to it quick."

Under normal circumstances I'd have believed him, but he doted on Preel almost as much as I did, fairly worshiped her. He was also a devious rascal and might well conceive of some strategy that none of the rest of us came up with. "Forget the bloody clothes, Hemp. I need your *help* here. Sit down."

"I...got nothin' to say, sir." He started for the door again, boots and jacket in hand. "I'm...sorry...but I gotta...go."

"Captain!" Miko caught my eye and shook her head sharply. She'd spotted Hemp's unease, too.

Something wasn't right. I'd only seen him this upset once before, when Preel had been assaulted in this very cabin. Now he wouldn't help us get her back?

I beat Hemp to the door and slammed it shut before he could pull it fully open. His hand trembled on the latch. "Hemp. What's wrong?"

"*Nothing*, sir. I swear." His voice shook. "I just...need to go."

"Bullshit! You know something. Tell me what's wrong!"

"I *can't*, sir!" He backed away, clutching my boots and jacket with white knuckles. "*Please* don't ask me nothin'!"

The sheer terror in his eyes told me something was very wrong indeed, but I had to know for sure what it was. Miko and the others were out of their chairs. Hemp had nowhere to go.

"Hemp, just relax." I held my hands out, empty and unthreatening. "I just need you to tell me what's wrong. You know something about Preel's abduction, about Jhavika's part in it. Just—"

A mournful wail like nothing I'd ever heard from Hemp's throat filled the cabin. He dropped my clothes, whirled, and dashed to my cabinet. By the time I had taken a step, he had my straight razor out of the drawer. He whirled to face us all, his eyes wide, the razor gleaming in his hand.

"Hemp! Wait!" I still held my hands out. My steward knew something, and I had to know what. Preel's life depended on it. "We're not going to hurt you."

"I'm...sorry, sir, but I've got to do this." Hemp brought the razor to his throat.

"NO!" I lunged, but too late. The razor scored a line of blood before my hands closed around his wrist. My momentum smashed Hemp against my cabinet, splintering the wood.

The razor clattered to the floor, and Hemp shrieked in protest. "Wait, sir! Please!"

"What?" I pinned him against the cabinet, wondering how he'd just spoken through a cut throat. Then I saw that the line of blood was just that, barely deep enough to part the skin. "What the *hell*?"

"I *had* to, sir! I didn't have a *choice*!"

"Sir!" Miko put a restraining hand on my arm. "The *scourge*."

But I already knew. "Help me with him, Miko, Quiff." I hauled him away from the cabinet and pinned him facedown to the floor. He yelped and struggled, but with three of us, he had no chance of escaping. "Cut away his shirt, Miko!"

"Aye!" Her dagger parted his shirt from collar to hem, but his back was clean. Miko didn't stop there, however, and while I put a knee between Hemp's shoulder blades, she parted his belt and the seat of his trousers. Five livid marks marred Hemp's left buttock.

"Bind his hands, Miko! Use his belt."

In short order, we had Hemp bound to a chair and Bert was examining the cut across his throat.

"Barely a scratch." Bert shook her head and swabbed the cut with a rum-soaked cloth.

"But *why*?" I glared down at my steward, though I knew I couldn't fault him. He'd been lashed by the scourge; he'd had no choice. "Hemp, I know what happened now, so you don't have to say anything about who ordered you to betray me, but why did you cut yourself?"

"I had to, sir. I was...told to, if anyone asked...things."

"Jhavika told you to cut your throat if I asked you about her." I stared at him for a moment and felt like laughing. "And you did, but only deep enough to draw blood."

"Didn't say how *deep*, just to cut."

"You're *brilliant*, Hemp!" I clapped a hand to his shoulder. "And you've got a deft hand with a razor!"

"I...um..." He looked up at me, startled, but no less miserable. "I'm sorry, sir. I wanted to tell you, but...couldn't."

"I understand." I went to my cabinet, poured a finger of rum into a tumbler, and brought it back to him. "Here. Drink this down. It'll steady your nerves."

He drank while I considered what we'd discovered and what we might learn from this.

"We can't let him go, Captain." Quibly said. "We can't trust him."

"He's *right*, sir!" That came from Hemp, and surprised us all. "You *can't* let me go!"

"No, we can't," I agreed, clenching my fists at my sides. "Not until Preel's safe and Jhavika's dead."

Chapter Ten
The Gilded Cage

Simple lies are always easier to believe than difficult truths.
The Lessons of Quen Lau Ush

From the journal of Preel Longbright –
What is the truth? For a truthsayer to ask herself that, I must
be insane. There is nothing in this world I can trust now, not
even my own thoughts. I am a slave once again. Perhaps I
always was.

I woke with a splitting headache, light piercing my closed eyelids
like knives into my skull. *Too much drink?* I threw an arm over my eyes
and reached out for Kevril.

My hand encountered nothing, and heavy clothing covered my
arms all the way down to my wrists. *No nightgown? What in the name of...*

I blinked my eyes open and squinted into the blinding light. *Not
the cabin? And I'm wearing my gown from...* Memories of the *Folly*—Illian
singing; shattering glass; my eyes stinging; Kevril's hand in mine,
pulling me through the fog; dark shapes with weapons; a prick of pain
at my neck—all flooded into me in a scalding torrent.

I bolted upright, seized by panic. A lavish bedroom with ornate appointments surrounded me. I still wore my gown from the night before, even the pearl headdress. I rolled off the bed's soft white coverlet, wobbling on unsteady legs. My head still blazed with pain, but I had to get out of here, wherever *here* was. Dashing to the window, I pulled aside the gauzy drapes. The portal was barred with white-painted iron, the view outside dark. It was still night. I recognized Haven, but from a vantage I'd never seen. Instead of looking up at the bluffs from the harbor, I saw the harbor below me in the distance, anchor lights atop ships' masts like fireflies atop toothpicks beyond the buildings. *Kevril...* I wondered where he was, if he was even alive. I needed to go to him, but even if I could get through the bars, the sheer drop of several floors to a cobbled street would probably kill me.

I looked around for some kind of weapon, but the room was utterly bereft of any knickknacks. There was no glass to break, no lamps—the light that had plagued me blazed from several wall-mounted glow crystals—nothing to smash into something sharp. Even the furniture was heavily built; I might break a door off the sturdy clothespress, but the wood was an inch thick, impossible to smash into sharp splinters with my bare hands. My dagger, of course, was gone.

There was only one door, and so, only one way out.

It'll be locked, I thought, edging toward it as if the brass latch would transform into a serpent and bite me. *Come on, Preel, you're being foolish!* I swallowed my fear and fought to think rationally. I felt the tiny wound in my neck and remembered the dart. I'd been abducted, but whoever had done it didn't want to hurt me. *Of course not; you're a truthsayer!* If they didn't want me damaged, that might give me an edge.

I gripped the latch and turned it slowly. *Unlocked?*

I pulled the door open just a crack. A man stood beside it, dark-haired, dusky-skinned, with smooth features that reminded me of my father's. He turned his head to look at me with dark eyes, untroubled, his features handsome.

I slammed the door, jamming my foot against the bottom to keep it from opening.

The man's voice reached me through the door. "She's awake."

"Obviously," a woman replied. "Go tell her. I'll stay in case she comes out."

"Okay." I heard another door close.

I waited, but there was no knock, no calls, and no attempts to break down the door. *Come on, Preel, you've got to open the door sometime.* Moving my foot, I edged the door open far enough to peer out into a larger room. A woman, also dark-haired and dusky-skinned, stood to the other side of the door. Only slightly taller than me, she might have been the man's feminine mirror image. She smiled at me and gestured to the room, welcoming, but didn't say anything. I couldn't speak with the binding over my mouth, and she seemed unwilling to talk.

Warily, I stepped into the room and looked around. It was large, well furnished with a dining table, several chairs, two divans, and a full bookshelf, but the same lack of ornamentation or knickknacks as the bedroom. No glass, porcelain, or easily splintered wood. There were windows on two walls, the drapes open to show white-painted bars, and two other doors. The silent woman was unarmed, dressed in ivory-hued servant's garb, and didn't interfere as I opened the nearest of the two doors. Beyond it, I found a well-appointed bathroom with tiled floor and walls, a mirror of highly polished silver rather than glass—I saw in it that the makeup covering my tattoo had been scrubbed away—and heavy porcelain tub, sink, and commode, each with its own drain that ran right through the floor. Gnomish ingenuity, expensive and uncommon in most human cities.

Everything here spoke of affluence and great effort to keep me from escaping or hurting anyone, but where the hell was I?

I tried the other door, also miraculously unlocked, and found a long, carpeted hallway beyond, two armed and armored guards barring the way. They, too, seemed disinclined to speak to me, but the crossed halberds spoke volumes. I was a prisoner. Closing the door, I regarded my confines once again.

I needed information.

Removing my headdress and veil, I motioned to the woman to remove the silken gag. She frowned and shook her head. I glanced around, but there was nothing in the room to write with. I gestured imploringly, begging her to take off the gag, to speak to me, but she just shook her head with that same sad frown. Desperate, I slapped her hard, but even that provoked little response. With my handprint livid on her cheek, she cast her eyes down submissively, frowned, and shook her head.

My face warmed with shame. She'd obviously been ordered not to speak to me, and I'd abused her. I touched her chin to lift her eyes to mine and gestured in apology. She just shook her head.

Well, this is gods-damned infuriating! Living with pirates had broadened my vocabulary considerably, and even though I didn't curse much, if ever there was a valid excuse to start, abduction and imprisonment fit the bill. I turned away and started to pace.

I'd only made four passes back and forth when the hallway door opened and Jhavika Keshmir walked in.

Smiling at me, she said, "Hello, Preel."

I should have known.

I glared at her. There was little else I could do. She was flanked by the two guards from the hall, and the dark-haired man I'd seen earlier stood behind. Attacking her would be worse than pointless. My eyes were drawn to the scourge on her hip; one lash with that and I'd be her slave forever.

"I apologize for the way I brought you here, but Kevril wasn't likely to give you up willingly." Her smile deepened. "You see, I know what you are. But let me assure you that I have no desire to hurt you in any way. You're far too valuable to risk, and you're safer here, by far, than in the clutches of a pirate."

Fuck you, you maniacal bitch, I thought, and made a gesture that said exactly that.

Jhavika laughed hard and shook her head. "Really? That's the thanks I get for rescuing you from that scoundrel?"

Rescue? I stared at her, stunned that she would seriously expect me to believe her. Whirling away, I strode to the window and glared out at the city, the distant masts of ships. Somewhere out there, Kevril was already planning how to get me back. That I believed with every fiber of my being.

"Preel, please. Here."

I turned to find Jhavika only a step away holding out my notebook and a short stub of pencil, too short, unfortunately, to stab her with. I glared down at the notebook, knowing that she'd read every word written in it, the notes Kevril and I had passed in the *Folly*. I felt violated.

"I need to ask you some questions and I don't want to risk your safety. You obviously wear that magical binding to keep you from speaking, but I need to know why."

I snatched my notebook and the pencil, flipped to a blank page, and scrawled, "Fuck off!", then shoved the page at her.

"Still?" She sighed as if bored. "Just because I don't want to hurt you doesn't mean I can't make your life here a living hell, Preel. Nala, Binsh, come here."

The man and woman in servants' clothes hurried over.

"I've assigned Nala and Binsh to serve you, Preel. They're brother and sister, from Fornice, like you, which I thought would be comforting." She turned to regard them. "They're my slaves. Let me show you what that means. Nala, strike your brother as hard as you can."

Without hesitation, the woman struck her brother open-handed, hard enough to send him reeling.

Jhavika produced a short dagger and held it out to Binsh. "Should I order him to skin his sister right here and now? Believe me when I tell you he would do it. He would even *enjoy* it if I commanded him to. I can command them to do anything I wish. Or I could send my nokitu out to fetch someone you care about, lash them with the scourge, and order them to commit any number of atrocities. Are a few answers to some harmless questions too much to ask to stay my hand?"

I wondered why she didn't just lash me with the scourge and ask her questions, but I wasn't going to tempt fate. Resisting her would only cause others pain, and I couldn't have that on my conscience. I scribbled on the page—"I wear the gag to protect myself. Questions that invoke my talent tax me. Ask too soon, and I'll die."—and handed her the notebook.

Jhavika put the dagger away, read my note, and frowned. "Interesting. And how soon is too soon?" She handed the notebook back to me.

I considered lying, but it seemed pointless. I wrote, "Four days," and showed her.

"And how many days has it been since your talent was last invoked?"

"Nine."

"So long? Why would...oh, never mind. Nala, remove Preel's gag." The servant deftly untied the knot behind my head and took the gag.

I licked my lips and asked, "Is Kevril alive?"

"Tell me first if all questions invoke your talent."

I saw no point in refusing. She'd find out soon enough. "No. Only ones I don't know the answer to. Now, tell me if Kevril is alive."

"Yes, he's alive, and I'm sure he's quite angry with me, but let me assure you, you're safer here with me." She took the gag from Nala and strolled back to her guards. "Don't you think you should *thank* me for getting you away from him after what he did to you?"

"What he *did* to me?" I glared at her anew. "He *freed* me! He *loves* me, and I love him!"

"Freed you?" She barked a laugh. "Freed you to live as a captive in that squalid ship, only able to go out under guard? Freed you only to answer questions and feed his lust?"

"It's not *like* that!" I screamed.

She laughed again. "*Believe* me, Preel. I know Kevril Longbright *far* better than you do. I've known him for better than two decades. I fought with him, drank with him, and fucked with him. Kevril only loves Kevril. He *seduced* you into believing he loved you, that you were free. Hells below, he seduced *me* into believing that he cared for me, then tried to kill me to take the *Scourge!* He lives for nothing but his own gain. Having your talent at his fingertips, *and* you in his bed, gave him *exactly* what he wanted."

"You're *wrong!*" I raged, though I had to admit to myself that she probably did know Kevril better than I did. Twenty years beat six months no matter how close you were to someone.

I considered what I knew, or thought I knew. Kevril had told me he and Jhavika were shipmates together, and that they had a physical relationship that was more recreation than anything approaching affection. But could he have lied? *Could* our entire relationship have been a seduction so he could have me as both his willing truthsayer *and* bedmate? It didn't seem possible.

I remembered too much tenderness from him for it to be true, too much love. I remembered what he'd done to the man who violated me, all the nights when I wanted him to touch me, hold me, kiss me, and his gentle refusals. Even when I'd kissed him, he'd repeated his assertion that it wouldn't be right, that he was captain, and if he took me as a lover, he would be no better than the crewman who had raped me. But what motive could Jhavika have for telling me this if it wasn't true? She needed nothing from me but my talent, which I couldn't deny her, and she could make me her willing slave with a single lash of that scourge at her hip.

Why hadn't she? I wondered silently. Then I wondered if she actually had while I was unconscious. I felt no wounds, but I hadn't really checked myself over.

Jhavika must have seen the war raging behind my eyes, the suspicion tumbling end over end with my memories of Kevril.

She shook her head once again and sighed. "You poor thing. He really has you wrapped around his finger. Think about what he did, Preel, what he *really* did. You were a slave, and he promised you freedom. You were alone, and he promised you companionship. You were in danger, and he promised you safety. Now, think of what you were actually *given*." She counted off on her fingers. "You live in a tiny ship's cabin with him, only as free as he allows, always under guard. You share his bed, satisfy his lust whenever he crooks his finger at you. And he failed *completely* to keep you safe! My nokitu abducted you with little difficulty!"

I whirled away from her, hating the rising doubt in my mind. I loved Kevril. I knew it as well as I knew my own name. But did he truly love me? Was it all a lie, all manipulation? If I could have asked myself that question, invoked my talent to learn the truth, I would have. I wracked my brain, but could think of no motive for Jhavika to lie. One lash, and I'd be her slave.

I wiped away tears and cursed my very existence.

"Preel, please consider what I'm offering you here," Jhavika implored me. "You'll be truly safe and want for nothing. With your help, in a matter of weeks I'll be queen of Haven, then the Blood Sea, then empress of the west. You'll have everything you ever wished for: servants, concubines, riches..."

I wanted none of those things, but Jhavika had no understanding of what it was to be a slave. "Everything but freedom and love."

"Freedom is an illusion and love is a lie, Preel." A harsh bitterness edged her tone. "We're all slaves of one sort or another. If you believe otherwise, you're naïve."

Maybe I was naïve, but I knew for a fact that I loved Kevril. Whether he truly loved me or not didn't change that fact. I stood there trying to think through the tornado of emotions raging through me. This was my worst nightmare come true. I had once asked Kevril to kill me rather than let Jhavika take me. I had little doubt that she would use me to take the whole world for her own; the ruthlessness and avarice of a dragon ran through her veins.

But even dragons could be killed.

I had few options: cooperate, rebel and be enslaved, try to take my own life, or stall and hope for rescue. If someone or something managed to put an end to Jhavika Keshmir, I might gain a chance at freedom. If Kevril loved me, he would find a way to free me. If he didn't, I was lost. But I remembered his tenderness and knew there was a chance. I had something to live for.

I turned to face Jhavika Keshmir. "So, ask me a question."

Her smile returned. "I'm in no rush. You've been through a lot. It's still hours before dawn, but you should freshen up, bathe, eat something."

Largesse from her felt like a lie, but I couldn't deny that I was hungry and could use a bath. Still, a slave with my gift is not without power. "What does it matter? I'll be out cold for half a day, anyway."

"All the more reason you should eat." Jhavika waved toward the adjoining rooms. "There's plenty of hot water, clothes in the bedroom, and I'll have food sent up. I've ordered Nala and Binsh to care for you. They'll do whatever you ask, but they won't speak to you. I can't have someone asking you a question that'll invoke your talent."

"Of course." That explained their silence. It also posed interesting possibilities, though I didn't yet know enough about my new attendants to try to use them against my captor.

Jhavika turned toward the door. "I'll be back after you've eaten. Take your time."

I didn't thank her.

She left, taking the guards with her. Nala and Binsh looked at me expectantly. I didn't want them.

"I can bathe and dress myself." Striding to the bedroom, I flung open the clothes press. A rainbow of colors greeted me: dresses, robes, even the halter-pantaloon combinations that I'd grown accustomed to. The small dressing table hosted a similar overabundance of grooming supplies: brushes, blunt nail files, polishes, pumice stones for calluses, even makeup. It seemed ridiculous; who did I have to dress up for?

Kevril...

I stripped off my clothes, picked out a robe, and wrapped myself in its silken folds. Turning around, I found that Nala had already picked up my fallen gown.

"You don't need to do that."

She smiled and nodded, gathering up my sandals and discarded scanties as well. She had obviously been ordered to care for me whether I wanted her to or not.

I sighed and strode for the bathroom. There I found Binsh filling the tub from a curious spigot set into the wall. I'd never seen water supplied to rooms through pipes before, and stared as he turned the spigot handle to cease the water's flow.

"That's amazing." The words were out of my mouth before I could stop them.

Binsh turned and smiled, nodding before pouring hot water from a huge copper kettle into the tub and testing the temperature with one hand. Apparently satisfied, he put the kettle on a little iron stand and gestured me forth, showing me the array of oils and soaps on another little table. He held out a hand, looking expectant.

"I don't need help. Please leave and close the door behind you."

Nodding, he showed me the stack of towels and wash cloths, then backed out of the room. The latch clicked as he closed the door.

"No, that's not creepy at all," I muttered.

There was no lock on the door, which was no surprise—slaves didn't get privacy—but my desire to be alone had nothing to do with modesty. I shrugged out of the robe and examined myself thoroughly in the silver mirror, head to foot, front and back. I found not a scratch save for the prick of the dart that had knocked me unconscious. *Jhavika's scourge hasn't tasted my flesh yet.* I was a prisoner, but not yet her slave.

I bathed thoroughly, even washing my hair. Why not? I took my time, submerging myself to my chin in the warm water, willing it to sooth my roiling nerves. Only when the water started to cool did I emerge. Pulling the plug in the bottom of the tub, I watched the water swirl away. If only I could escape so easily.

Once again wrapped in the robe, a towel around my damp hair, I returned to the main room to find a variety of food arrayed upon the table. Nala and Binsh stood like solicitous statues, ready to attend to my every need. *Worse than Hemp*, I thought.

I sat and filled my plate from the varied dishes. Binsh offered blackbrew and tea, and filled a glass with orange juice from a silver pitcher. I sipped the juice and considered the glass. If I broke it, I'd have a makeshift weapon, but my attendants had probably been ordered to keep me from hurting myself. I sighed and ate the food without tasting it.

Nala tapped my shoulder and showed me a hair brush, gesturing to my wrapped head, her meaning obvious.

"Oh, all right." I continued to eat while she brushed my hair, and realized that my headache was gone. When I was full, I pushed my plate away, but sat for a time sipping tea and considering the servants. They seemed too eager, too solicitous for slaves. I thought about testing Jhavika's claim that they had been ordered to do whatever I asked, but thought better of it for now. I had time, and picking apart what they would and wouldn't do at my behest required some forethought. They would probably tell Jhavika every word I said, every move I made, and the last thing I wanted was to let her know I was testing my bonds.

Binsh took the dishes out, while Nala continued to brush my hair, her hands sure, never tugging or pulling. I caught my eyes closing, my mind wandering with the pleasant sensation, the simple peace. Then the door opened, and Jhavika returned.

"Feeling better?" The guards came in with her and took station by the door.

"Yes." I stood. The pink of predawn lightened the sky outside my prison. "Do you mind if I lay down for this?"

"Not at all." She gestured to the bedroom.

"Also, you should put the enchanted gag back on after I pass out. Even unconscious, my talent will be invoked if someone asks an incautious question." There was no point in risking my life if there was a chance of rescue.

"A reasonable precaution." She followed me into the bedroom.

I lay down atop the coverlet still in my bathrobe, my damp hair spread out on the pillow. Closing my eyes, I took a deep breath. "Ask."

"What magical effects does my scourge grant to me?"

I opened my eyes and looked at her standing beside the bed. "Kevril already asked that."

Jhavika shrugged. "So, tell me."

I considered lying, but yet again it seemed pointless. She no doubt already knew much about the scourge, and Kevril had warned her about how the thing was affecting her. Was she testing me to see if I'd tell her the truth?

The truth is complicated.

"Fine. Anyone you lash with it must follow your commands, it bestows upon you the ruthlessness and avarice of a dragon, and it will be yours alone until you die."

Jhavika nodded, her smile twitching, possibly strained. "All right. Let's try another: How did Kevril break the enchantment of the scourge?"

Again, I knew the answer, but this seemed a more legitimate question. Was she really looking for some way to escape the thing's influence? If so, telling the truth might benefit me.

"I already know that answer, too. An alchemist in Valaka named Brekka brewed an oil that, when spread over his skin, dispelled the enchantment. I wouldn't advise asking her to do the same for you. Their relationship didn't end well. She threatened to kill Kevril if he ever returned."

"Thank you for the warning."

"Are you really interested in being free of the scourge?"

"Well, not exactly yet, but perhaps someday." Jhavika shrugged. "It's useful, but I don't like the idea of anything controlling me."

I narrowed my eyes at her. "I know *exactly* what you mean."

"I suppose you do." She gave me a sympathetic smile, which I knew for a lie. Jhavika enslaved people with the flick of her scourge, hundreds probably. I doubt she felt sympathy for her minions. "Which brings up my next question. How can I escape the control of the scourge?"

I gave her a disgusted look. "That one's easy. Die or destroy the foul thing."

"Well, those aren't very attractive options." Jhavika folded her arms, her expression pensive, as if she was putting more thought into the next question.

That, too, rang false. Surely she'd thought ahead. The questions she'd already asked were those logically asked by Kevril in his quest to break his enslavement. Now, if she asked how to destroy the scourge, she might or might not get an answer, but I'd be damned if I'd help her craft a question to circumvent my talent's limitations.

"All right, time for a new subject." Jhavika looked down at me, her smile turning suddenly cold. "Is Kevril Longbright currently planning to take you away from me by force?"

I wanted to scream, "Of course he is!" but the curse took hold of me. The power of it never ceases to take my breath away, like a demon rising up from within. My muscles clenched, my vision blackened, and the voice that was not my own tore from my throat. The truth scored my soul like a glowing hot blade.

"No."

Chapter Eleven
Victory

Knowing when you have won and when you have not is the key to true victory.
The Lessons of Quen Lau Ush

From the journal of Jhavika Keshmir —
I remember the moment I won. Victory over Preel burned in me like nothing I'd ever felt. Yes, I could have commanded her, revealed to her that she was my slave, but how much sweeter when she capitulated of her own free will. I could see the seeds of doubt growing in her, all because I had said two simple words that she could not resist: believe me.

For an instant, panic flashed across Preel's face as the double-edged sword of my question pierced her soul. Then her eyes rolled up, she went rigid, and her back arched until only her heels and shoulders touched the bed. I thought at first that she might be having some kind of seizure, then her voice issued forth in a most unsettling guttural croak.

"No."

She collapsed, breathing hard.

"Well!" I checked her, worried that I might have damaged my prize, but her breathing soon slowed, and the pulse at her neck eased to a steady cadence. Ever suspicious, I tested to make sure this wasn't a ruse, but even when I slipped a hand under her robe and pinched one nipple hard, she didn't stir. She was truly unconscious. Heeding her caution, I replaced the silken gag over her mouth and considered the answer she'd given. "Well, well indeed! The good captain must have taken my warning to heart."

It was exactly the answer I'd hoped for. Not only did I not have to worry about an imminent attack, but Preel would wake knowing her lover had forsaken her, and all the seeds of doubt I'd sown would take root and grow. My first victory with my new truthsayer. I ran a thumb over the tattoo etched into her brow and felt a swell of satisfaction. When she woke, Preel would beg me to help destroy the man she had loved.

That would be an even sweeter victory.

"Watch her in shifts," I ordered Nala and Binsh. "The moment she wakes, send word for me. See to her every need, every desire, unless it interferes with my previous orders. I'm rescinding the order not to remove the enchanted binding over her mouth. If she wants you to take it off, do so."

"Yes, your ladyship," they said in unison.

I considered the two slaves for a moment, so lovely and compliant. My victory smoldered in me like post-coital heat. I suppressed the urge to indulge myself, to quench that heat with these two. I had work to do, resources to deploy, spies to consult with, plans to make.

Maybe later.

I left Preel's rooms and found Ty-lee waiting outside where I'd left him. "Ty-lee, call my nokitu back from the waterfront. There will be no need to assassinate Captain Longbright."

"Yes, your ladyship."

I strode past him toward my office. "Keep at least three spies in place to watch the ship. If Kevril goes anywhere, he's to be followed.

In fact, keep eyes on Miko, too, and if Hemp shows up at the brothel, let me know."

"At once, your ladyship."

"Good. Report to my office when those orders have been relayed. I'll have more for you. Go."

He bowed and ran off.

In my office, I found Lewin where I had left him, seated beside the windows at his little table, reading a tome and making notes. The sage looked up from his work and nodded, but didn't speak. He couldn't; I'd ordered him never to speak to me unless I spoke directly to him. It was a petulant order, but Lewin tended to prattle, and I'd grown tired of it. Now, however, I needed his wisdom.

"So, Lewin, she was telling the truth. Invoking her talent *is* taxing." I sat at my desk and pointed to my empty blackbrew cup. A hovering servant filled it from an insulated pot and added the exact amount of milk that I preferred.

"Could you tell me how the talent manifested when it was invoked, your ladyship?" The light of interest glowed in Lewin's eyes.

"It was...interesting. At first, I thought she was having some kind of fit or putting on a show. Her eyes rolled back until only white showed, she went rigid all over and arched like some kind of spasm took her over, then answered my question in a voice that was so unlike hers, I was startled."

"My goodness!" He looked concerned. "Is she all right?"

"Unconscious." I sipped my blackbrew and consulted my notes. "She said she'd be out for half a day. Without any solid references on the subject, we have to assume that she's told us the truth about how often we can invoke her talent. If I can only ask one question every fourth day, that's going to slow down my schedule, but there is plenty to keep us busy in the interim."

"Certainly, your ladyship. And crafting your next question should be of paramount concern. The mysteries of the *world* are at your fingertips!"

I almost laughed at his excitement. I'd heard this lecture before. "I understand your enthusiasm, Lewin, but we have more immediate concerns than solving esoteric discussions of historical accuracy. We have a world to conquer."

"Of course, your ladyship." He went back to work.

"Summon Doctor Yiv," I told a servant.

"Yes, your ladyship." She hurried out.

I returned to my work, but my mind was inexorably drawn to the long list of questions I wanted answers for. Finally putting aside the mundane tasks, I pulled out the list and considered it. Referring to my calendar, I started putting dates next to them. The highest priority question should be who next to enslave. The truthsayer's magic could penetrate all the layers of deceit, lies, disguises, and politics unknown to me, and provide me with a direct answer. Wording that question might be tricky, and finding out why that choice would be wisest might require another question, but it was a foolproof strategy.

Then there are questions about the scourge itself...

The answers from Preel perfectly matched the information that Kevril had given me, but I'd long ago learned to mistrust perfection. *The truth or a carefully concocted lie?* The latter seemed too contrived. Besides, Preel must know the actual truth or my question would have invoked her talent. *But did she* tell *me the truth?*

In the end, I decided to put credence only in the answers that resulted from her talent. Also, I intended to carefully condition her so she would *want* to tell me the truth. Experience had taught me that no matter how many layers of commands I put into a knowing slave, they were always looking for a way to rebel. Ty-lee was just about the only exception; he'd served me unwaveringly from the beginning.

I found my fingers caressing the haft of the scourge, a nervous habit that I couldn't break, a sure sign that something was bothering me. But what? I had won. I had everything at my fingertips. All I had to do was ask.

But *what* to ask? I was already second-guessing my priorities. Could I possibly ask Preel what question I should next ask? The circular reasoning was giving me a headache.

A knock interrupted my musing, and Doctor Yiv entered with her usual surly mien. "You summoned me, your ladyship?"

"Yes. I'd like you to examine Preel again. She's unconscious as a result of invoking her talent, and I want to make sure she's okay."

One of her dark eyebrows arched. "Now?"

"Yes. Is there a problem with that?"

She shrugged. "No, your ladyship. I simply need to know when you want my report."

"Within the hour will be fine, and I have another task for you once you finish."

Her lips pursed into a frown. "Of course you do."

My temper flared. "I *could* order you to cut off your own lips and sew your surly mouth shut, Yiv, so keep a civil tongue in your head!"

The muscles at her jaw tensed. "Yes, your ladyship. What task do you have for me?"

"I want you to research different drugs. I'd like something that's undetectable in food or drink that will...ease a person's nervousness, make them calmer without interfering with coordination or thinking. If such a drug exists, I want you to procure it and figure out the proper dosage for Preel. She's...distraught."

"If I may ask, mistress, why not simply *order* her to calm down? I assume you *have* taken control of her."

I glanced up sharply—Yiv hadn't been in the room when I'd pricked Preel—then relaxed. It was an easy assumption for someone who knew me as she did. "Of course I have, but I want to keep her ignorant of that for now. After all, you attract more flies with honey than with vinegar."

"Bees, your ladyship. If you use honey, you'll get bees. For flies, try shit."

I barked a laugh. "I may just have to coin a new adage! More flies with bullshit than honey!"

The corner of her mouth twitched, Yiv's equivalent of a smile. "Is that all, your ladyship?"

"Yes, you can go."

She started toward the door, but then turned back. "Can I offer medical advice, your ladyship?"

"Of course, Yiv. It's your job, after all."

"Yes, it is." She pursed her lips again, then said, "You need sleep. Your eyes are red, sunken, and rimmed with dark circles. Your hands are shaking with fatigue. I prescribe a sleeping draught and eight hours in bed."

I bristled. "I'm *fine*, Yiv. I don't have *time* to sleep right now. You're dismissed."

"Yes, your ladyship." She turned away, but continued to speak on her way to the door. "But if you don't rest soon, you'll collapse. Your judgment is already impaired by fatigue, which is dangerous. If you continue at this pace, your avarice will kill you."

The door closed behind her. I stared at it for a while. Yiv couldn't lie to me, and I'd ordered her to tend to my health to the best of her abilities. I had to trust her advice.

Maybe I should get some rest, I thought. Preel would be unconscious for some time, and I had to be sharp when I spoke with her. Glaring at the pile of work on my desk, I swore under my breath.

Another knock, and Ty-lee entered, bowed, and said, "Your orders have been carried out, your ladyship."

"Good." I stood and rounded my desk. "Give me your honest opinion. How do I look?"

"You look tired, thin, and somewhat disheveled, your ladyship."

"Shit."

"I wouldn't go that far, your ladyship."

I glared at him. "Watch your tongue, Ty-lee!"

"Yes, your ladyship!" He withdrew a small folding pocket mirror, opened it, stuck out his tongue, and stared into the glass.

"Oh, stop that! You know what I meant!" I was tired, my temper was short, and I wasn't being careful with my commands. Was Ty-lee being flippant or just literal? With Yiv, I'd have said flippant, but Ty-Lee... He was one of my indispensable core of long-time servants. I'd conditioned him so well that he never failed to follow my orders to the letter and tell me the truth, even when I didn't want to hear it. "So, I look exhausted, do I?"

"I wouldn't say exhausted, but you haven't yet slept this night, and not much the night before."

"Fine." I found it difficult to sleep when there was so much to do, but I didn't want to wake groggy from one of Yiv's draughts. There was one other thing, however, that I knew would put me to sleep. "Pick out a few of my favorite bedmates and send them to my chambers at once. Wake me in six hours."

"Yes, your ladyship!" He smiled and bowed as I strode past him. "Any particular preferences?"

"No. I just need sleep."

"I understand perfectly, your ladyship." His grin widened, but I didn't care.

I went to my chambers and pulled the heavy drapes. By the time I had my boots off, three of my loveliest slaves were there to help me with the rest. I lay back and immersed myself in the sensations of warm hands, lips, tongues. In the midst of their enthusiasm, I realized that I still clutched the haft of the scourge in one hand. I told myself to let it go, to release it, to let myself enjoy this, but I could not.

I really am a slave, I thought, even as my attendants coaxed me into throes of ecstasy. *I'll never be free of it...and I don't want to be.* I gripped the haft of the scourge with white-knuckled ferocity and lashed out. My slaves cried out in pleasure as the lash tasted their flesh...because I'd ordered them to.

Chapter Twelve
Alternatives

A winning strategy often involves dire sacrifice.
The Lessons of Quen Lau Ush

From the dairy of Kevril Longbright –
My greatest fault is my temper. I've known this since I was a boy. Anger interferes with my reasoning, and I make bad decisions. Consequently, I've surrounded myself with people who aren't afraid to tell me when I'm being stupid. They've saved me from myself many times.

While the others secured Hemp to a chair, Miko pulled me aside. "Sir, you're exhausted." She made a vague gesture. "With what happened at the club, that gas, the crack on the head, you're not thinking clearly. And losing Preel has you too emotional to be pragmatic about this. You need some sleep before we can work out a plan."

I gritted my teeth and shook off her hand. "I'm getting her *back*, Miko. You can take your bullshit diagnosis and fuck off."

"Kevril," she said to me, her voice low and hard. Turning, she promptly ordered everyone else out of the cabin. "I need to talk to the captain in private."

They all looked at her as if she was committing mutiny, but I knew she wasn't. Miko rarely called me by my given name; when she did, it was important. There were things, personal things, Miko would only say to me alone. Besides, despite my raging temper, I knew she was right.

I nodded. "All right. Everyone out. Kivan, tell Wix what happened here and to continue his search of the crew; we need to know if Hemp is the only one she got to. Anyone found with whip marks is to be restrained, but not hurt. Also, set double watches around the clock. Bert, tend Hemp's wound. The rest of you help her tie Hemp into his hammock and stow him in the guest cabin, then get some sleep."

They filed out, Quibly and Quiff simply lifting the chair Hemp was tied to and hauling him out. When the door closed, I turned to Miko.

"Okay, out with it."

"I want you to remember something, Kevril." She went to my cabinet and poured two stout drinks. "I want you to remember what Preel asked you to do if Jhavika tried to take her." She turned and held out a glass to me.

I stared at the glass in her hand, but didn't take it. "I'm not going to kill her, Miko. I can't."

"Can't, or won't?" She glared at me. "You're being selfish."

"*Selfish?*" Now it was my turn to glare.

"Yes. Preel knew what would happen if Jhavika ever got her hands on a truthsayer. She'll take the whole fucking *world*. We'll *all* either end up her slaves or dead. With a truthsayer *and* the scourge, she's unstoppable."

"No, she's not." I took the glass and bolted down the spiced rum. "And I'll have *you* remember what I told Preel after that request."

"You said you would."

"I also said I'd fight like a dragon before I let that happen."

"It's *already* happened! Jhavika's got her, probably already lashed her with the scourge. Who *knows* what she's commanded her to do, to think, to *feel*?" She sipped her drink and shook her head sadly. "She's already gone, sir."

I stepped forward until our noses were barely a handspan apart. "No, she's not!"

Miko fearlessly stared me down. "She's in the hands of the most ruthless, avaricious, sadistic woman either of us have ever known, Captain. Think of what Jhavika did to *you* right here in this cabin!" She pointed to the bunk. "Not because she needed to, but because she *wanted* to! Jhavika's a spiteful control freak, and what you did— breaking her control—pissed her off. What do *you* think she'll do to Preel?"

I'd been thinking of little else since awakening in the *Folly*, but one thing kept coming back to my mind. "Jhavika's not stupid, Miko, and like you said, she's avaricious." I stepped around her to my cabinet and reached for the bottle of rum. "Preel can her get everything she wants, but not if she's...damaged."

"Not if she's *physically* damaged, you mean." She held out her glass as I filled mine, and I topped it up. "Even if we *could* rescue her somehow, she won't be the Preel you know anymore. Jhavika could order her to hate you, to live only to serve her, to kill or maim herself if anyone ever took her away. It'd be a kinder fate to kill her."

I shook my head and started to pace. "But killing Preel is no easier than killing Jhavika."

"Isn't it?" Miko nodded to the door. "Assaulting the keep is impossible, sure, but you heard what Bert said. I'd wager Jhavika's paranoid about her own food, but she can't have the whole keep's bread tested for poison."

I cringed at the thought of murdering everyone in Jhavika's keep. "It's too unsure. There's no guarantee. We have to be more specific than that. If we kill Jhavika, *all* of her slaves will be free."

"There's no way we can know that!" Miko sounded vexed with me. "We know that Captain Kohl's control over the crew didn't transfer to Jhavika when she took the scourge, but we don't know if the commands given by its master continue to be enforced after the master's death."

"Bugger!" Another question I could have asked Preel and hadn't. "So, what the hell are we supposed do, just sail away? I can't just leave Preel in Jhavika's hands!"

Miko raised a hand in a calming gesture. "I agree. Sailing away won't solve anything, and will probably just make us targets. Jhavika's already convinced the Council that recruiting a privateer navy is a good idea. If we run, we'll be their first quarry."

I huffed in frustration. "So, we're back to either killing Jhavika or destroying the scourge. The former isn't impossible, but nearly so, and the latter we don't even know how to do. With Preel, we might figure out how, but..."

Miko snapped her fingers. "That's something!"

"What?"

"Look, like you said, Jhavika's not stupid. She doesn't want to hurt Preel, she wants to use her. But you said Jhavika didn't like the notion that the scourge was controlling her. Maybe we can offer her something that'll serve us both."

"To destroy the scourge? That's Jhavika's entire power base. She'd never agree."

"Maybe not, but it's a bug to put in her brain. With Preel, she can find out *how* to destroy the scourge, and we can help her. I'm guessing it can't be done here in Haven. Once Jhavika's free of the thing, she'll be a lot easier to deal with. We'd need to push the benefits; she'll still be rich, powerful, and on the Council, but her avarice won't be driving her day and night to take the whole world. She won't be a slave to the scourge!"

I wasn't convinced. "She would still have Preel."

"But I'm betting that if the *scourge* is destroyed, all her slaves *will* be free."

"Don't tell Jhavika that! Talk about a deadly mutiny..."

"True." Miko sipped her rum and frowned. "It won't hurt to pitch it to Jhavika, though. It'll show her you're not going to do anything rash."

"Like walking in there with my pockets full of those gas bombs, gassing the whole keep, and slaughtering everyone?"

Miko snorted a laugh. "Yeah, like that."

"It's worth a try, I guess, and it might buy us some time." Convincing Jhavika that I wasn't going to storm her keep in a futile attempt to rescue Preel wouldn't hurt. "I'll send her a message requesting an audience."

"That'll be a tense meeting." She furrowed her brow. "You should make sure it'll be against Jhavika's best interest to capture or kill you. Just because you're free of the scourge's power doesn't mean she can't lash you with it again."

"She already knows I'll die before I let that happen, but yes, I'll make that clear in my message."

"And if she agrees to meet with you, you've got to keep a level head." Miko cocked an eyebrow at me. "No more shit like you tried to pull in the *Folly*."

"That was different," I assured her. "A momentary lapse of reason."

"Momentary?" Miko snorted and downed her rum. "You're in *love*, Kevril. That's like a life-long lapse of reason."

"Yeah, well, you should talk. I saw the way you and Illian looked at each other."

"Fair enough." Miko put her glass on the table and started for the door, then stopped. "Oh, and might I suggest we warp back out into the bay? If Jhavika decides to attack us, it'd make it harder."

"Good idea, but wait for first light." I downed my rum and sighed. "Thank you, Miko."

"All part of the service, sir." Grinning, she snapped a salute and left me alone in my cabin.

Alone... I stared at the bunk, the bed Preel and I had shared every night for half a year, and my heart shattered in my chest.

Chapter Thirteen
Embracing Despair

Sometimes the only choice that remains is between survival and death.
The Lessons of Quen Lau Ush

From the dairy of Preel Longbright –
With four children, one of them cursed but valuable, I cannot blame my parents for selling me into slavery. I remember learning what it meant to be a slave, being instructed in exacting detail that I no longer had free will. I remember trying to take my own life, and failing, being denied even that release. This is my lot in life. I am cursed. I must live with that knowledge, for I cannot even escape in death.

I woke in the same plush bed, in the same comfortable room, wearing the same soft robe. The only thing that had changed was in my mind, the memory of my answer to Jhavika's question.

Kevril wasn't planning to take me back.

Despair...my oldest friend. The pain was exquisite, a familiar ache that suffused me from the inside out. I was alone, abandoned, sold, an object, a tool to be used by the powerful. I was beyond tears, beyond wanting, beyond hope. Hope was a lie that only hurt worse when revealed.

I rolled out of bed and found Nala standing patiently by my bedroom door. Had she stood there all the while I slept? What did it matter? She opened the door and told her brother that I was awake, and I heard the outer door close. Shuffling to the window, I looked out through the bars at an incongruously beautiful day. Sunlight on the sea, colorful awnings on rooftops, the masts of ships...

Kevril...

Snapping closed the drapes to hide the world I was no longer a part of, I went to the bathroom to relieve myself. When I was finished, Nala met me at the bathroom door and gestured toward the table. It was set for two with gleaming crystal and porcelain. Evidently, I would have company. I didn't want company, but what slaves want and don't want never really goes into the equation.

I sat down.

Nala poured water into a glass, then reached out to tap the silken gag, her question clear in her eyes.

I considered refusing, then nodded. It wasn't worth fighting, rebelling, refusing. I knew what would happen if I did, and I was already in enough pain for a lifetime. Nala removed the gag and lay it beside my plate. I sipped the water to wash the sleep out of my mouth. It was flavored with lemon.

Again, I considered the glass as a potential weapon. I couldn't fight two armed guards with it, but if I was swift, I might take my own life. I looked at my wrists. *Not there, not again.* It was too unsure, too slow, and the flow could be stopped with a simple tourniquet. Putting the glass down, I inconspicuously felt for the pulse at my throat. Could I do it?

Yes, I decided, *but not yet.* My despair flared into hatred. I wanted to look into Jhavika's eyes when I stole victory from her grasp. Cold resolve settled in me like a chill blanket.

Soon enough, the door opened and she entered, flanked by Binsh, her two guards, and half a dozen servants wheeling two trollies heavily laden with covered silver platters, carafes, pots, and pans. The aroma of food wafted through the room.

"Good morning, Preel. I trust you slept well." Jhavika wore a silk blouse of dark burgundy and snug pants with soft leather boots. She looked ebullient, sharp, invigorated. The scourge hung from her belt, her hand never far from it. "I hope you don't mind that I arranged a late lunch for the two of us. I think it's important that we get to know one another better." Sitting, she motioned the attendants to begin serving.

I stared at her across the table, savoring the pain that filled me, yet curious. "Why?"

"Why get to know each other?" Her brow knitted.

"No. Why all this?" I waved a hand at the table, the servants, the opulent room. I'd been afraid to ask her last night, afraid to provoke her into using the scourge on me, but that didn't matter anymore. *Kevril's not coming...* "Why are you being so...solicitous? You could lash me with your scourge and command me as you wish, or not and still employ my talent. It's not voluntary. I can't refuse or rebel." Well, I could, which she would soon learn, but I wanted to know her motives first.

"We're going to be working together quite closely for a very long time, Preel. Your willing cooperation will be a thousand times more useful than the scourge's coercion. It'll be easier if we're familiar." She indicated the servants. "I'm not a monster, no matter what Kevril told you about me. I've ordered my people not to speak to you for your own safety, but if you wish, I can change those orders so Nala and Binsh can answer your questions about me. As long as they don't *ask* you anything, that would work."

"They would lie. You could have commanded them to lie."

"I can also command them to tell the truth. Would that suit?"

She was playing with me, and it piqued my temper. "I'm not a *fool*, Jhavika. You can supersede anything you say in my presence with an overlying set of commands. I can't trust anything that anyone here says to me, including you."

"You're certainly *not* a fool, which is another reason I want your willing cooperation." Jhavika lifted a crystal goblet of light wine and sampled it. "I could have done exactly as you said, though I haven't. The facts that your truthsayer talent isn't voluntary, and that I need nothing *else* from you, are precisely why I have no *reason* to enslave you. Consider, however, that I have every motivation to make you as comfortable, happy, and safe as possible here. If I mistreated you, you'd eventually find some way to escape or take your own life. That's the *last* thing I want."

Little did she know that I'd already found my only possible escape.

I lifted my wineglass, toasted my captor, and dashed the fine crystal against the edge of the table. The glass rang like a bell, and was halfway to my throat before I realized that it hadn't broken. I tried again, smashing it as hard as I could onto the edge of my fine porcelain plate. Both plate and glass rang with the impact, but neither broke.

"Preel, please!" Jhavika's guards hadn't moved, but Nala was already at my side, dabbing up the spilled wine with a cloth. "The glass and porcelain are enchanted not to break, and the utensils are similarly enspelled to never pierce living flesh. You can't hurt yourself with anything here."

I lurched up from my seat and whirled toward the window. In five long strides I could build up enough momentum to dash my brains out on the iron bars. I only made it one step before Binsh intercepted me, his strong arms enfolding me gently, not grasping, only intervening. I lashed upward, the heel of my palm striking the point of his chin—*rising sun sheds darkness.* The blow sent him reeling back, but two more attendants were there to take his place, the rest moving to intervene.

I whirled to glare at Jhavika. "Let me *go!*"

"I can't do that, Preel." She sipped her wine, unperturbed. Flanked by her guards, there was no way I could reach her. "I can offer you anything else you desire, but I can't let you go, and I won't allow you to hurt yourself."

"You *already* hurt me!" I raged, allowing the pain to rise up and fill me. "You took the only thing in this world that I ever cared about!"

"I didn't take anything from you, Preel. You were already a slave."

"You took *Kevril* from me!" I smashed my fists down on the table, clattering the dishes. "I thought he *loved* me!"

"I'm...sorry, Preel. I didn't realize..." Jhavika looked genuinely troubled, as if she'd just discovered a grave error. "I needed to know if he was planning to attack my home. Besides, I told you he was never in love with you. He loves only himself."

I clenched my eyes closed at the crushing pain of the truth, wishing I could end it all. But I couldn't. Even the relief of death was denied me.

"Please, Preel, sit down and have some wine, eat a meal with me. I'm not the monster Kevril said I was, and you have to admit that your quarters here are much more comfortable than that wretched ship."

I dashed the tears from my face and heaved a breath. I hated Jhavika Keshmir with every fiber of my being, not for what she was, not for her ambition, her greed, or her ruthlessness; I hated her for telling me the truth about the man I loved.

A truthsayer devastated by the truth... The irony almost made me laugh.

I sat down, picked up my newly filled wineglass, and drained it. The crisp vintage washed the lump from my throat. When I put the glass back down, the attendant was there with the carafe to refill it. I sat there hating the woman across the table, letting my rage cauterize my shattered heart. Hatred, too, was an old friend. I had hated every master I'd ever had, taken strength from it. That, at least, could not be denied me. I ate the food they served without tasting it, drank glass after glass of wine without feeling it, and hated Jhavika Keshmir.

She told me of the care she'd taken to ensure that everything— my rooms, my attendants, the food, wine, literature, and other amenities—was the best she could bestow, and encouraged me to enjoy them to the fullest. If she thought for one second that I was going to thank her, she was delusional.

"I want to make you *happy* here, Preel, I assure you." Jhavika sighed despondently at my refusal to respond. "Nala and Binsh have been instructed to watch over you and keep you from harm, so please don't try to hurt yourself again. And let me assure you that escape is impossible. You needn't wear the gag at all if you don't wish to. If you want conversation, I can rescind my order to your attendants not to speak to you. They're from Fornice, you know. I thought you might like a taste of home."

My home was aboard *Scourge*, with Kevril, and she'd destroyed it. I hated her a little more.

"I'm sorry for your pain, Preel, honestly. If I could take it away, I would."

"You can," I told her, savoring the surprise in her eyes.

"By freeing you? I already said, I can't do that."

"No, with that *thing* on your hip. Lash me with it and command me to feel nothing: no pain, no love, no loss, no hate. You can take it all away, make me numb." I downed yet another glass of wine; I'd lost count of how many, and my head was swimming.

"I know you don't mean that, Preel."

"You don't know *what* I'm feeling right now. You *can't* know."

"Can't I?" Jhavika frowned and swirled her wineglass, staring down at the amber liquid, the legs of the wine tracing down the inside of the enchanted glass. "You would be surprised."

"How can you possibly?"

She sighed and put the glass down, waving the attendants over to clear the table. "The reason I know so much about Kevril—how he thinks, how manipulative he really is—is because he did the same to me as he did to you."

"What?"

"When we were lieutenants together aboard *Scourge*, we...I thought we were in love. Kevril convinced me we were. Then, after Captain Kohl fell, he tried to kill me. It was only luck and *this* that saved me." Jhavika pulled the scourge from her hip and laid it on the white linen tablecloth before her, caressing the haft like a beloved pet. "I lashed him to save myself, though I didn't understand the power of it at first. By the time I did, I was ashore with a few trusted shipmates at my side...safe. It took me a long time to trust anyone again. He lied to me, just as he lied to you. That was why I did what I did to him later, why I commanded him to...make love to me, to *want* to. I wanted to humiliate him, possess him." She shrugged. "But thanks to you, he broke free. Now the tables are turned once again."

"I don't believe you." But in my core, gods help me, I did.

"He's a pirate to the bone, Preel. You were nothing but a piece of plunder to him." Jhavika stood, hung the gleaming length of dragon flesh on her hip, and started for the door, then stopped and turned back. "Nala, Binsh, you can speak to Preel. Ask her no questions whatsoever. Tell her everything about me that she wishes to know. This order supersedes all other orders I've given to you previously that restrict what you can and can't say to her."

"Yes, your ladyship," they both chimed, bowing at the waist.

"You should probably lie down, Preel; you've drunk a lot of wine. I'll be by later to check on you." Jhavika then left my rooms, taking all but my two attendants with her.

I sat there staring at the bare table for some time, feeling the pain ebb and flow like waves wetting a beach, savoring my hatred of the impossible truth. So many memories confounded my wine-addled mind, but one in particular plagued my thoughts—Kevril handing me the jewel-hilted dagger, telling me I was free, that if I didn't know why he had rescued me from Brekka, to sheathe that dagger in his heart. Would he have stopped me? Was it just a ploy, a manipulation? I would never know.

I *did* know that I had loved him. Whether that was still true or not, I had no idea.

"Lady?"

I turned, surprised to find Nala and Binsh standing there, attentive as ever. I realized I was crying. Embarrassed, I wiped my eyes and looked away. "What do you want?"

"Your pain grieves me, lady," Nala said. "Tell me, please, how we can help you."

"Don't call me lady. I'm a slave, like you. Call me Preel. And I don't want you to help me."

"As you wish, Preel, but..." Her delicate hand touched my hair, much disheveled from sleeping on it wet. "I could brush your hair, if you wish."

I recalled Kevril's hands stroking my hair while I sat astride his lap on our narrow bunk aboard *Scourge*, weaving to and fro with the motion of the ship as we coupled slowly, deliciously, endlessly, until I couldn't tell where he ended and I began. How could that have been a lie?

"No, thank you, Nala. I'm...not feeling well." Truth be told, I was very drunk and too full. "I think I should lie down." I tried to stand and wobbled.

Firm hands grasped me. "Let us help you to bed."

I let them.

The three of us staggered into the bedroom, and Nala helped me out of my robe and tucked me into bed. I lay there wondering, as the room spun beyond my closed eyelids, if I was truly a slave in the same respect as my two attendants. I'd found no injuries that might suggest Jhavika had used the scourge on me, but she was smart and devious. Why she would do it covertly, I had no idea. My only clue was the deep confusion that assailed my mind, as if my memories rivaled the truth at every turn.

I blinked my eyes open to stop the room's spinning and found Nala standing beside the bed, her dark eyes reflecting the crimson light of the setting sun through the gauzy drapes. I must have slept, but my mind still spun. *So many questions...*

"Did Jhavika lash you with her scourge?"

"Yes," she said, her voice emotionless. "Once."

"What does it feel like?"

"It hurts, like any whip might. I'd been lashed before, but never since."

I blinked in confusion, then understood. For one so skilled in crafting questions, I was fumbling here. The wine, no doubt. "No, not the scourge itself. What does it feel like for her to have control over you like that? Unable to disobey any command she gives."

"Much like being a slave feels. There's no pain. She's not malicious about her commands."

"She told you to hit your brother, and you did it."

"Yes, but that was to make a point to you."

I was still confused and drunk, but curious. Could I trust Nala to tell me the truth? *Jhavika can't have ordered her to lie about everything,* I reasoned. "How long have you been Jhavika's slave?"

"About six months."

"And you're really brother and sister?"

"Yes. We were dancers in Fornice, performers. But we spoke out against the pasha and were arrested for blasphemy, auctioned off to slavers." She tugged down the hem of her loose-fitting pants and showed me the brand on her hip. "We were sold together, at least. Serving Lady Keshmir is...less difficult than some of our previous masters."

I had no doubt that was true. "And she ordered you to do whatever I say."

"Yes. Anything you wish."

It can't be this easy... "Kill me."

"I can't, and I truly believe that you don't want me to."

"You're wrong."

She shrugged. "I could try to make you feel better. A massage, a bath, or...whatever you wish. Or Binsh could, if you prefer."

The notion revolted me, and I turned away. "No, Nala. I'll never ask you to do that. I'm a slave, too, remember?"

"I know, but we've been commanded to please you, Preel. I can see that you're in pain, and it...hurts me. We *want* to make you happy."

"No, you don't. You've been *commanded* to want to. That's not you, it's the scourge."

"As you say." There was no remorse in Nala's voice, only obedience.

It sickened me.

I lay there staring into the deepening dark, wanting, despite my reticence, to ask Nala to just lie next to me, hold me, but knowing if she did, it would be just another lie.

Chapter Fourteen
Victory Conditions

The spoils of war are often bitter.
The Lessons of Quen Lau Ush

From the journal of Jhavika Keshmir –
Seeing Kevril brought low gave me far less satisfaction than I
thought it would. I knew he was in pain, I could see it in his
eyes, but it gave me no solace. I had won. He wasn't there to
beg, but to discuss the terms of our resolved conflict. I loved
the arrogant bastard as much as I hated him then.

Kevril strode into my office like he owned the place. His message
had been terse bordering on belligerent, but cognizant and to the
point. He wanted Preel back, but knew there was no chance of me
handing her over. He wanted to discuss business, our "new
arrangement," and said he had something to offer me. He also warned
me that any acts of aggression against *Scourge*, or attempts to abduct or
enslave him, would end poorly for me. I had little doubt that he was
telling me the truth on that score.

I stood from behind my desk and walked around to the front, just to show that I wasn't afraid of him. "Kevril. I'm glad to see you're being rational about this."

His glare smoldered, muscles playing beneath the scars I'd given him. "Fuck you, Jhavika."

I laughed, waving off my nervous guards. "No, thank you. I've got people to attend to that sort of thing. People far better at it than you ever were."

"Slaves."

"Yes, Kevril, they're slaves, which doesn't mean they don't love me and would sooner eviscerate themselves than see me hurt." I sighed and leaned back on my desk, fondling my scourge. "Tell me why you're here."

"I want to see Preel."

"No. She's...recovering."

"From what?"

"From my first question. Perhaps I'll let you see her at a later date, when she's feeling better and you're not so emotional." And when I had her fully conditioned. Yesterday's conversation couldn't have gone better; my subtle commands and lies had sown the seeds of doubt in her mind. They needed time to grow and blossom before I let Kevril see her.

"I'll *never* not be emotional about this, Jhavika. You took the woman I love away from me and have probably already lashed her with that fucking scourge. I want her back!"

"You can't have her back, and I haven't, in fact, used the scourge on her. I have no need to." Sighing, I folded my arms. "Please consider something; she's safer and will be *happier* here than she could ever be aboard *Scourge*. You were putting an invaluable resource in danger. Having her in your bed isn't worth putting such a treasure at risk. You took her out in *public*, in *Haven*! That was foolish. You're lucky *I* was the one who took her instead of Balshi or Fa Chen."

"She's a person, not a thing."

"She's a *truthsayer*, Kevril, which makes her an invaluable asset, just like you're a capable pirate captain, also an invaluable asset. In fact, that's the only reason my nokitu didn't kill you when they took Preel. I don't waste assets or put them in danger unnecessarily." I gave him my most placating smile. "Preel will stay here and serve me. If you can't agree to that, you may as well sail away right now."

Kevril's fists clenched and a vein in his forehead throbbed. "If I sail out of this harbor without seeing Preel first, I'll make sure that every pirate in the Blood Sea will be set dead against you in a fortnight, Jhavika. Kill me or try to take me, and Miko will do the same. There's not a ship in Haven that can match *Scourge* on the open sea."

I frowned at him. "I don't like threats, Kevril." And this was a credible one.

"Then let me see her."

I nodded in acquiescence. "As soon as she's fully recovered, I'll arrange something."

"I'm not going to do any more work for you or the Council until I know she's safe."

"Very well. Consider yourself on a short vacation. My plans can wait a while."

"And if you try to take *Scourge*, everyone in Haven will know about *your* scourge and your slaves on the Council."

This was a threat I'd prepared for.

"I'm not a fool, Kevril, but let me assure you that spreading the word about my secret would only result in a great deal of unnecessary bloodshed. I'm not quite ready to take over the Council yet, but I have enough people placed in key positions to assassinate all but two of them with a single word." It was four, actually, but he had no way to know the truth. Not anymore. I let my smile go cold. "And remember, I *do* have Preel." I pulled the scourge from my hip and let the barbed thongs dangle. "It might be entertaining to watch her beg my entire barracks to fuck her."

Kevril's face flushed crimson, and his hand blanched white on the hilt of his cutlass. He didn't, however, do anything stupid. He'd always had masterful self-control in that regard.

"I have one more thing to offer you, Jhavika."

"You do?" I laughed and hooked the scourge to my belt. "You've already given me a truthsayer. What *else* do you have hidden away aboard *Scourge*, a dragon hatchling?"

"No. I can offer you freedom."

"Freedom?" I barked another scornful laugh. "From what?"

"From that coil of dragonhide and magic on your hip that's turned you into a monster. It'll get you killed eventually. Maybe not by me, but someone's going to figure out what you're up to and put an end to you before you can enslave the whole world. With Preel and me, you have the means to destroy it."

"Destroy the scourge?" I stared at him like he'd told me to cut off my own legs. "How?"

"I don't know, but all you have to do is ask Preel. I'll help you any way I can."

I narrowed my eyes at him suspiciously. "Why would you want me to destroy the scourge, Kevril? It'll make me queen of the world, and you'll be admiral of the greatest navy ever to sail the Western Sea."

"Because there are some things that outshine gold and power, Jhavika." He pointed to the scourge, his tone as hard and cold as chilled steel. "That has blinded you to human emotions like love, trust, and honest friendship. Destroying it might give you those things back, the chance to be a human being again."

"That's *ridiculous*, Kevril." My hand ached, I gripped the scourge so tightly. "It's just a bit of magic. The scourge isn't controlling me. It's making me greater, not less."

He shrugged and turned away. "Keep telling yourself that if you like. When someone finally kills you, and I'm betting that'll be sooner rather than later, Preel will be free again."

I stared at the door for a long time after he'd left. I flexed my hand to alleviate the ache, but kept it on the scourge. Even if it *could* be destroyed without killing me in the process, I didn't want to let it go. Without it, I was nothing but a petty crime lord, just like the rest of Haven's council.

Though I'd never admit it to Kevril, the scourge *had* made me into something I wasn't sure I liked. The constant need for more—more control, more power, more riches, more *everything*—surged like a drug through my veins, day and night. Perhaps I wasn't quite a slave, but I was certainly addicted to my own avarice.

Forcing my hand off the leather haft, I folded my arms and glared at the door. *May all the gods of the heavens and hells curse you, Kevril Longbright.* I damned him to the Nine Hells and beyond for offering me the one thing I couldn't take on my own.

Freedom.

Chapter Fifteen
The Subtle Approach

There is no gift from an enemy quite like a moment's respite.
The Lessons of Quen Lau Ush

From the diary of Kevril Longbright –
I saw not only the longing for freedom in Jhavika's eyes, but also that she could never relinquish the scourge. If not for Preel, I would have felt sorry for her. I realized then that there was no other way to save all I loved. Jhavika had to die. I had only two weapons: a faithful crew who felt as I do, and Jhavika's own avarice.

I reconvened my inner circle as soon as I got back to the ship. This time, I included Wix. If there was to be killing involved, his would be a valuable opinion. The only person absent was Hemp, who'd begged to be excluded. Any mention of Jhavika in his presence plagued him with the desire to cut his throat again, and I didn't want to risk his life. The aft cabin was barely large enough to accommodate everyone, but we made do.

"Ladies and gents, my bar is at your disposal." I poured a finger of whiskey into a tumbler and waved to the bottles and carafes arrayed on my navigation table. "This is a council of war. I'm convinced that the only way to get out of this is to kill Jhavika Keshmir. That'll be no simple task. So you all know, Preel once asked me to kill her rather than allow Jhavika to take her. There are three reasons I'm not willing to do that." I counted them off on my fingers. "Killing Preel would be no easier than killing Jhavika, doing so would bring Jhavika's wrath down on us like a hurricane, and...I love Preel."

My assemblage of pirates all traded worried looks. I couldn't blame them.

"The trouble with killing Jhavika is twofold." Miko broke the ice by filling a glass for herself and offering to serve the rest. She poured as she spoke. "First, she rarely leaves her keep, and when she does, it's under heavy guard. Second, we don't know if the commands she's given her slaves continue to be enforced after her death."

"I'll tell you one thing straight up, sir. That keep's a right fooker." Wix accepted a glass of rum from Miko, bolted the entire thing past his tusks, then smacked the glass onto the table and shook his head. "We ain't equipped for a siege, and I'd bet my left nut that swingin' bridge that accesses the upper floors is rigged to drop."

"There's got to be a service entrance," Quibly said.

"Aye, I doubt they take provisions in through the gatehouse," Bert agreed.

I shook my head. "The only one I know of is a postern door beside the portcullis. There might be another somewhere that was walled up when the place was renovated."

Boxley waved off the offer of a drink, her young features screwed up into a frown. "Then we wait until she leaves the keep and put a knife in her gut."

I started to pace. "Exactly my plan, if we can get through her guards, but there are problems with that, too. We have no idea when she might go out, and the longer we wait, the more likely it is that Preel won't be the same person even if we *can* get her back."

Kivan accepted a glass of wine from Miko, her brow knitted. "And Jhavika could have given orders for her slaves to kill Preel or sink *Scourge* if she ever comes to harm."

"Those are distinct possibilities, yes."

"So, if we *do* manage to kill Jhavika, we gotta rescue Miss Preel and sail away before they can...um...react." Quiff sipped whiskey and cleared his throat. "I don't see how we can do all three at once."

"Ain't *nothin'* impossible when it comes to war, lad," Wix said with a horrible grin.

My bosun's vehemence didn't surprise me, and I nodded my thanks. "One thing's certain: a direct attack on the keep is suicide."

"Maybe not, sir." Kivan swirled her wine, her eyes bright. "We could use ballistae to fire grapples and scale the walls."

"And face a hundred soldiers on the inside." I shook my head. "No, we have to be subtle about this and assume that Jhavika's watching us."

Bert snorted in disgust. "Can't watch everybody. You and the other officers, sure, but not every swab and ship's brat."

Miko perked up, cocking an eyebrow at me. "That's true enough, sir. It might allow us to put out our own spies or recruit some allies."

"Dangerous duty for whoever we send out. Jhavika's got spies everywhere."

"Or so she *says*." Boxley's frown deepened. "She could be lyin' about that, too."

"I don't think so, but you're right, Boxley. We have no way to know how many spies she has or who they are."

"Or even if there are more aboard *Scourge*," Kivan agreed.

They all exchanged looks. Hemp had been the only one we'd found, even after an exhaustive search, but I still saw suspicion in their eyes. "We can't start suspecting each other. I know Jhavika. If she has any more spies aboard, they've probably got orders similar to Hemp's. Just sitting here discussing how to kill her would drive them to suicide."

"We searched everybody and asked enough questions to flush out any spies." Wix reached for the bottle and refilled his glass. "But if we can't kill Jhavika without risking Preel *and* the ship, we're fooked."

Miko topped up her own glass. "If we kill Jhavika and rescue Preel *simultaneously*, we might be able to get aboard *Scourge* and sail away before her people can respond."

"That means getting someone inside her keep, which, *again*, is all but impossible." I sighed and rubbed my eyes.

"And whoever puts a knife in her's likely as good as dead," Quiff added.

"Maybe, maybe not." Bert's chins doubled in number. "We could thin out her troops easy enough with poison in their food or grog. I know a few alchemists who could mix up something lethal."

"I thought about that, Bert, but poisoning the whole keep is just too—"

"Alchemists!" Wix's eyes widened. "Bugger, me, sir, that's it!"

I stared at my bosun in puzzlement. "*What's* it?"

"Remember how that witch, Brekka, mixed up a potion so those Serpent's Children of hers could look pretty? She used one on herself, too!"

"Yeah, so?" It was rare that Wix's train of thought left me flummoxed, but I was at a loss here.

"So, Jhavika's people all know each other, right? Whammy up a potion so some of us can look like her guards, and we're in her keep slicker'n a merchant's conscience!"

"Sonofabitch." I looked to Miko. "Could that work?"

"Don't look at me, I'm not an alchemist." She nodded to Bert.

"I can ask next time I go ashore," she assured me. "Ain't nobody follows a ship's cook around town."

A flicker of hope energized me. "Do that. Not right away, but soon. The problem is, we don't know who we'll be impersonating. We'll need something we can mix up at the last minute."

Bert frowned, but nodded.

"Okay, so we can maybe get someone into the keep. Do we go in to kill Jhavika and rescue Preel at the same time?" Miko sipped her rum. "That'd cut down on the complexity of the operation, but whoever went in would be spread thin. Once Jhavika's dead, all hell's going to break loose. Getting Preel out alive would be tough."

"True. It would be safer for Preel if we lured Jhavika out somehow and killed her away from the keep. That'd give the people inside more time to get Preel out."

"But how? Who does she trust?" Miko asked.

"Nobody." I tapped my lips with a finger. "But she's on the Council now. If they say frog, she jumps."

"When's their next meeting?" Quibly asked. "Maybe I could whip up a forged invitation to one?"

"That's a thought, but dangerous. If she discovered a forgery before she's out of the keep, she'd know someone was planning something."

"So, we set up a *real* council meeting!" Miko countered. "Jhavika's not the only member you know personally."

"True." I didn't like to recall the night I'd met Ursilla Roque and Getashi Temuso. "But neither of them owes me any favors, and they're both Jhavika's slaves."

Miko wagged a finger. "I'd be willing to bet that neither of them *knows* they're her slaves yet, just like you didn't. That's one hell of a bargaining chip! For their help, you offer to free them from Jhavika's scourge!"

"But would they believe me?" I rubbed my eyes again and sighed. "And I can't very well just walk up to their keeps and ask for audiences. Bert might be able to come and go without anyone taking notice, but I can't." I was intentionally playing devil's advocate. If there was a way this could go wrong, I needed to know before we started the ball rolling.

"If you can set up a secret meeting, we can smuggle you off the ship somehow," Quibly offered. "Cargo comes and goes easy enough. We could put you in a barrel. We water up regular anyway."

"And you don't have to set up the meeting yourself, sir," Kivan added. "We could send someone out dressed like a scullery swab or a ship's brat."

"Send me, sir!" Boxley piped up. "I know Haven's streets and can take a message anywhere you say!"

The plan had merit. I hated to put Boxley in danger, but it wouldn't be the first time. I had to admit, I didn't know a thing about how council meetings were convened, and an ally on the inside would be invaluable. "All right, now the question is, who do I approach: Ursilla Roque or Getashi Temuso?"

"Roque owns *Fancy's Folly*," Miko pointed out. "After what happened there, she might be willing to meet with you."

"Pardon me, sir, but I think that's a bad idea," Quibly said.

"Why?"

"Because Roque will already be spitting nails about the attack on the *Folly*. Jhavika's going to be watching her."

"Bugger." I hadn't thought of that, but he was right. "That leaves Temuso." I didn't relish renewing my acquaintance with him, but, considering his enthusiasm during Jhavika's intimate get-together, I suspected he'd take me up on my invitation for a clandestine meeting. "I'll draft a letter for you to take to Temuso, Boxley."

"Aye, sir!" She grinned with the enthusiasm of a young colt.

"You'll dress down like a ship's brat and go ashore with Bert tomorrow. Wix, rewater two barrels tomorrow, too, so it won't be strange to see more going back and forth."

"Aye, sir."

"Bert, you've got the hardest task of anyone. You know what we need, but we can't allow any rumors to start spreading around town that you're asking about potions. Go to someone you trust first, someone you think can do the job. Money's no object, but this *has* to be kept on the sly."

"I know someone, sir. Discreet's his middle name. If he can't do it, he'll know who can."

"Great." It felt good to have some kind of a plan, but it also made me nervous. "Thank you all. You've given me hope. I want you all to think hard on this. If anyone can think of something that can go wrong, for Odea's sake, speak up. We've got to be subtle with every phase of this plan. One leak to Jhavika, and we're sunk."

They all nodded and drank up. Miko stayed behind and helped put the bottles and glasses back in my cabinet. When we were through, she gave me one of her looks.

"How are you?"

"Worried." I stared out the stern gallery windows. "I can't stop imagining what might be happening to Preel."

"Jhavika won't hurt her, sir. She's not stupid."

"No, but she's got a vindictive streak. She might lash Preel just to turn her against me."

"But she can't wipe out her memories. Preel knows how you feel about her."

I turned to face her and shook my head. "All Jhavika has to do is command her to hate me. If that command is still in effect after I kill Jhavika, I...don't know what I'll do."

"There's only one thing *to* do. Destroy the scourge."

"Which we don't know *how* to do."

"But with Preel, we can *learn* how!" Miko furrowed her brow at me. "Why are you looking for ways to fail, sir?"

"I'm not. I just need to prepare myself for the worst. Quiff was absolutely right about one thing: Whoever puts a knife in Jhavika Keshmir isn't likely to survive."

"And I suppose you're dead set on that person being you."

"Dead set..." I barked a laugh. "Yes, *exactly* that."

"So, maybe a poor choice of words." She chuckled, then sobered. "Don't worry so much, okay? We'll make this work somehow."

"Thanks, Miko." I sat down at my navigation table and nodded to the door. "Now get out of here. I've got to write a love letter to Getashi Temuso, and I'm not sure where to start."

"Well, I can't help you there." She opened the door and looked back at me. "Just don't get too mushy. He won't believe it."

"Yeah, I figured that." I sharpened a quill with my dagger and picked out a sheet of parchment. "I'll let you read it before I send it."

"Aye, sir." The door closed.

I dipped my pen and started to write.

Chapter Sixteen
The Elusive Truth

Truth and lies are sometimes two sides of the same coin.
The Lessons of Quen Lau Ush

From the journal of Preel Longbright –
Never in my life have I wished more to be able to invoke my own talent. Not only would the answers give me solace, but the question itself would release me from this madness.

Deft hands kneaded the muscles of my back, shoulders, and legs, working fragrant oil into my skin. Nala and Binsh had been relentless in their pleas to comfort me; yesterday afternoon, I'd finally relented. At first it was just to get them to shut up, but I had to admit that their ministrations were not unwelcome. It's hard to be miserable when you're getting a massage, a bath, having your hair brushed, listening to poetry, or even watching them dance. Their grace calmed me in ways I didn't know anything could. Never had a slave received such pampering.

But despite the treatment, confusion and doubt continued to plague my mind, my memories battling against Jhavika's version of Kevril. My captor visited me daily, sometimes taking a meal with me, other times just to check on my condition. Solicitous, kind, and forthcoming, she answered every question I posed with what seemed like frank honesty. Try as I might, I couldn't break past the simple conundrum of what was truth and what were lies. Jhavika had no realistic reason to lie to me about Kevril. It didn't hurt him, and hurting me gained her nothing but my enmity. My own answer to her question confirmed that he didn't intend to rescue me, but I also couldn't trust her to tell me the truth.

The scourge made her as avaricious and ruthless as a dragon. What that truly meant in human terms, I couldn't fathom. Nala and Binsh answered my every question, but I couldn't trust their words either. They assured me that Jhavika's scourge had never touched me, but my suspicion lingered. Why else would I take Jhavika's word for anything?

Because it makes a twisted kind of sense.

She had known Kevril much longer than I, and he'd admitted to me that they'd had an intimate relationship, though their two versions of that relationship clashed. If someone had asked me a week ago who I would believe, Kevril or Jhavika, my answer would have been certain. Now, I simply didn't know.

Taking solace in the sensation of my every muscle being reduced to jelly, I remembered Kevril's touch. Oil-slick hands gliding over my skin reminded me of Brekka's enchanted oil that I spread over every inch of him. All his tenderness came back to me, and I knew that I loved him. But can we ever truly know the heart of another? Alas, the questions I couldn't ask myself hung over my head like a thundercloud.

Does Kevril love me?

Has Jhavika enslaved me with the scourge?

The former, I had no way to know for certain. The latter, I might be able to find out. All I had to do was trick Jhavika into giving me a command, then try to disobey. Jhavika visited me daily, but had not yet directly ordered me to do anything. Today, the fourth day after her last question, I had little doubt that she would invoke my talent. I planned my rebellion carefully and waited for her arrival.

When the door to my chambers opened and the guards clattered in, I didn't stir, but lay there with my face pillowed on a rolled towel, continuing to enjoy the sensation of the deep massage.

"So, you've finally decided to avail yourself of the amenities. I'm glad."

From the sound of Jhavika's voice, she stood only feet away. I didn't respond, concentrating on my silence, my resolve. *Don't answer her. Don't move. Make her insist.*

"Binsh tells me you were doing some type of exercise this morning."

Be silent. Hate her. Refuse to answer.

"Fine. If you don't want to speak to me, it's no skin off my nose. I'll be asking you another question that'll invoke your talent now, so you may want to use the washroom first."

Don't move. Just lie here until she orders you to get up.

"Petulance doesn't suit you, Preel, but if you insist on silence, I can ask my question right here and now. Nala, Binsh, stop what you're doing and step away from her."

Damn... I rose up onto my elbows and turned my head to look at her.

She smiled sweetly at me. "Would you like to use the washroom or not?"

I wanted nothing more at that moment than to wipe that smile off her face, but curses and invective hadn't goaded her before. Silence also hadn't worked. I considered a physical attack, but her two guards flanked her. I wouldn't be able to lay a hand on her. There was only one other thing I could think of that might provoke her to command me.

I steeled my nerves and rolled up from the table. The towel that draped my backside fell away, but I made no move to retrieve it or to cover myself. Jhavika's eyes widened and her mouth opened, but she didn't speak. Her guards' faces flushed, and they looked away.

Say it! Order me to cover up!

Jhavika didn't say a word, but only blinked and barked a laugh.

I glared at her, strode to the sideboard, and poured myself a glass of wine.

"If you're trying to shock me, you'll have to do better than that, Preel, and if you're trying to *seduce* me, save yourself the trouble. I've got expert personal attendants far better than you could ever hope to be."

I downed my wine at one swallow and reached for the carafe. Jhavika continued to stare at me as I poured another and went to the window. *Order me away from the window.* I stared through the bars out at the city, the distant masts of ships over the tops of the buildings, and wondered which one was *Scourge.*

"Are you *sure* you wouldn't like to put on a robe, Preel?"

Not a command, but a question. Was she intentionally taking care with her words? If she was avoiding orders, that could mean she had already used the scourge to enslave me and wanted to keep me ignorant of the fact. Still, I couldn't be sure. Perhaps I could trick her.

I glared over my shoulder at her. "If you don't like the view, close the drapes."

One eyebrow arched slowly, her eyes roving down and back up my oil-slicked body. "You're a lovely young woman, Preel. Nudity doesn't offend me in the slightest, but I'm not particularly impressed either." She flicked a dismissive hand. "Wear whatever you like or nothing at all if you wish."

Bugger! In a fit of sheer petulance, I poured my wine onto the floor, dropped the glass, and walked right through the puddle to retrieve my robe.

"Nala, clean that up."

"Nala, leave it." I flung on my robe, but didn't tie it.

The poor woman froze for a moment, caught between the conflicting commands.

Jhavika sighed as if bored. "Nala, you will follow my orders in precedence to Preel's. Clean up the wine."

Nala hurried to comply, and I immediately felt bad for making extra work for her. I closed my robe and cinched the tie tight, wondering at my failed ploy. Jhavika certainly seemed to be intentionally avoiding giving me commands. Unfortunately, I still couldn't be sure. I folded my arms and leveled another cold stare at my captor.

"Preel, you're trying to anger me. Do you think that wise? You know I can make your life a living hell with one lash of my scourge." Jhavika's hand caressed the haft of braided leather at her hip.

"A slave has little power. My talent makes me too valuable for you to damage me. You *hurt* me. Why should I make this easy for you?"

"You've attempted suicide before, so I thought to create an environment pleasing enough that you wouldn't try it again. If you're going to continue being belligerent, I *can* punish you without causing permanent damage." She pulled the lash from her hip and shook out the thongs. The dragon-claw tips gleamed hungrily. "How would you like to entertain my entire barracks for a few days? One lash and I can have you begging on your knees to fulfill their every wish."

Fear and revulsion roiled in my gut. "No, thank you."

"Then perhaps you should cease to be such a pain in my ass."

Still not a command. "You can invoke my talent any time you wish, Jhavika. I have no control over it. You can't make me *happy* about being your slave."

"Actually, I can." She flicked her wrist, and the scourge's thongs snapped like willow switches. "I can make you anything I want."

I swallowed my fear of those barbed thongs. "So, why haven't you?"

The malicious gleam in her eyes dimmed. "I...don't exactly know. Like you said, your usefulness as a truthsayer isn't dependent on your cooperation, but I feel...I thought it would be...different to have someone to talk to who wasn't under the scourge's enchantment."

I gaped at her. "You're *kidding* me!"

Jhavika's face flushed, and I knew I'd scored. Her eyes narrowed dangerously. "You're a *slave*, Preel. You've been a slave your entire adult life. Have you never craved honest companionship, someone to talk to who wasn't another slave or your master?"

"I *had* that. You *stole* it from me." I gritted my teeth against the tirade I wanted to scream at her. Antagonizing her further would only earn me pain. "I'm not about to thank you for that. I was *happy* with Kevril. Even if you do lash me with that thing, you can't take that memory away from me."

"That happiness was a lie, Preel. I'm *sorry* it was a lie. You're safer here than you were with him. You'll never fall into the hands of some rapacious pirate again; I promise you that." Jhavika hung the scourge on her hip. "Now, I'm giving you an honest choice in your future. You can continue to be a belligerent bitch, in which case I'll lash you with the scourge and command you to be civil, or you can voluntarily be civil. What'll it be?"

"That's not much of a choice."

"It's more than most slaves get." She nodded to Nala and Binsh in emphasis. "More than they had."

That irrefutable fact made my choice for me. "I'll be civil."

"Good!" She gestured to the bathroom. "Now, would you like to bathe and eat a meal with me before I ask a question that'll put you unconscious for twelve hours?"

"Yes."

She cocked an eyebrow again, and her hand clenched on the haft of the scourge.

I gritted my teeth again. "Yes, *please*."

"Good. Nala, help Preel bathe. Binsh, bring hot water and tell the chef to have dinner for two here in thirty minutes." Binsh bowed and hurried out, and Nala escorted me to the bathroom.

Warm water, scented soaps, and Nala's tender care eased my tense nerves. I couldn't fight Jhavika, and I couldn't goad her without risking punishment worse than death. Whether she would follow through with her vile threat or not, I had no way to know. I'd been violated before, but the thought of her commanding me to beg for it, to want it, even to *enjoy* it, as she had done with Kevril, revolted me. I couldn't risk that if I hoped to remain sane.

But she had revealed one chink in her armor: Jhavika Keshmir was lonely. I'd seen the truth in her reaction.

Throughout our cordial dinner, I thought long and hard about how I might use that loneliness as a weapon, play her, manipulate her. I went through the motions of dining, chatting, discussing my talent and everything I knew about the scourge, being civil and honest, all the while letting my hate for her smolder in my gut. If she longed for someone to talk to who wasn't under the enchantment of the scourge, I could be that person.

At least on the surface.

Acting like her friend might not earn me freedom, but it might keep the scourge from tasting my flesh. If it hadn't already.

When we were done with dinner, Jhavika escorted me into my bedroom and ordered Nala to help me to bed. When I was comfortable, warm, sated, and already a bit sleepy from the wine, she asked her question.

"Is there any way to destroy the scourge without harming the weapon's master?"

The answer blazed in my mind as the familiar convulsion took me, seizing my muscles and filling my chest with a single word. "Yes."

Darkness took me down, but as I fell, I knew that I had found one more weapon I could use against Jhavika Keshmir.

Chapter Seventeen
Sparring with the Truth

Never underestimate the human capacity for cruelty.
The Lessons of Quen Lau Ush

From the journal of Jhavika Keshmir –
Having Preel as my slave, but refraining from exerting my control farther than the simple command to believe me, sparring with her, threatening to do what I'd already done, seducing her into believing she was free, felt like nothing else I've experienced.

I stared down at my truthsayer for a time, considering her answer, what it meant. I could be free of the scourge. Two or three more questions to nail down the specifics, then, with Kevril's promised help, I could be free of it.

But what would that really mean?

Every person I'd enslaved would be freed. Destroying the scourge would undoubtedly end their enchantment, sever my control, allow them to rebel. My loyal garrison of soldiers, my nokitu, all of my spies, and my pawns on the Council of Lords... They would murder me.

I shook my head irritably. Destroying the scourge was out of the question, a fantasy I couldn't afford to entertain. And I'd just wasted four days to satisfy my own curiosity. It wouldn't mean much in the end game, but I abhorred delays.

So why did you ask? The answer, of course, was Kevril. I'd beaten him, and still he plagued me. Well, I had his truthsayer now, and slowly, she was coming over to my side. By the time I finally allowed him to see her, she would be my best friend.

"Your ladyship?"

I glanced up to find Nala and Binsh looking at me with concern. How long I had stood there staring at Preel, I didn't know, but their scrutiny unnerved me.

"Both of you, leave the room and close the door."

Surprise crossed their features for an instant before they bowed and complied. The latch clicked, and I returned my gaze to my truthsayer.

If you don't like the view, close the drapes.

Her petulance in the face of such dire punishment had impressed me. But was this rebellion or something more? I'd been careful with my words, but had begun to think that Preel might suspect I'd used the scourge on her. She seemed to have been testing that suspicion by goading me, hoping I'd command her to be civil. *No fool indeed.* Her courage and intelligence intrigued me. Sparring with her had been stimulating, her bravery and audacity invigorating.

And when she asked me why I hadn't used the scourge on her, I hadn't exactly lied. I found the urges of the scourge, the need to have everything and to use any means to attain it, both distasteful and infuriating. It was a one-trick pony, and I was tired of that trick. Denying the power at my fingertips might be the only free will I could exert.

Besides, I *was* tired of interacting with slaves. I never thought I'd crave honest human contact, but the need was real.

Or is the scourge just making me want it?

I found my hand on the leather haft, caressing it like a lover. Pulling it free of the hook on my belt, I held it up to examine the dark braided leather. Dragon flesh, Kevril had said. The ruthlessness and avarice of a great wyrm ran through my veins, according to Preel. The compulsion to take the whole world for my own, even if I had to burn it down in the process.

Everything...

I looked down at Preel and wondered if holding back my control over her wasn't just more of the scourge's influence. Great dragons were said to take prisoners to keep them company. Was this the same? The avarice of a dragon? The desire for someone pretty to keep me company?

Kevril had taunted me with the one thing the scourge couldn't provide. *Honest friendship...*

A sudden sadness washed over me, long-forgotten memories of my childhood. I recalled my sister, Anjice. We'd been close, so close, best friends, inseparable. I'd never been happier in my life. Was that what I wanted from Preel? With the scourge I could take whoever I wanted, command them to want me, to love me, to fulfill me, and I had, but I knew it was all magic, just lies.

Preel could be different. I'd already given her the command to believe me, but if I refrained from ordering her any further, if I held back, resisting the urge to reforge her emotions, I might be able to achieve what Kevril had said I couldn't. A willing companion, a genuine partner... A friend, of her own free will.

Someone like Anjice...

Could I ever have that again?

I hung the scourge once more at my hip and looked down at my truthsayer, vowing to myself to refrain from invoking its magic, refusing the easy path. Preel would be special. A true companion. That was what I wanted, what I needed, and I both hated and reveled in that need. Maybe it was just the scourge wanting more, or maybe it was my free will exerting itself. Could the scourge make me *want* free will? Was that part of wanting everything?

The circular logic plagued me for a moment, but I shook it off. *You're just chasing your tail, Jhavika.* I brushed Preel's full lips with a fingertip, then turned away. I had work to do and a world to conquer. And with Preel at my side, I had the power to take it.

Maybe, when I finally had it all, I'd be sated. Only then would I be truly free.

Chapter Eighteen
A Curious Meeting

Keep your friends close, and your enemies closer.
The Lessons of Quen Lau Ush

From the diary of Kevril Longbright –
Never had I met anyone in combat with more trepidation than the day I sat down for drinks with Getashi Temuso. I had no way to know what commands Jhavika had given him, or even if he knew he was a slave. Then, of course, there was the issue of our first encounter. Dredging up my memories of that evening felt like scouring an open wound.

Lord Temuso stood as I entered the inn's private room, his expression intrigued yet cautious. His bodyguard, a dark-skinned man with the facial scars and bone piercings of a Shattered Isle cannibal, stepped between us, one hand on the kukri at his belt.

The islander's dark eyes covered me from head to toe, his lips curling back from teeth filed to points as he growled, "No weapons, Captain."

I didn't look like a captain at the moment, and I wondered how the bodyguard had recognized me. To my knowledge, I'd never met him. This didn't bode well.

"Forgive the precaution, Kevril," Temuso said with a casual smile and a flick of one hand. "Utake is ever concerned for my safety."

"And he obviously knows who I am." I kept my tone cordial but firm, my displeasure clear. "I asked you not to tell anyone."

"Utake isn't just *anyone*. He's...special. He knows everything about me. I owe him my life and my soul, and he owes me his. We're closer than family. I hope you can understand that kind of bond."

Not the rebuttal I expected, but I saw the truth of it in Utake's eyes. "I understand completely." I unbuckled my sword belt, and handed it over with my two daggers. "I'm just here to have a drink with your lord, Utake." My eyes slipped sideways to Temuso, and I arched an eyebrow. "A *private* drink."

"So your missive stated." Temuso patted Utake on the arm. "Wait outside. Kevril and I are well acquainted."

"As you wish, milord." The man bowed and left the room.

"I can't say how surprised I was to get your note, Kevril." Temuso turned to a table arrayed with decanters.

"It took you long enough to answer. I was wondering if you would." The two-day wait for a response to my carefully constructed plea had tested my every nerve. I'd expected a boarding party of Jhavika's soldiers every hour of every night. When Temuso's brief response finally arrived—The Hyacinth Inn, Room 5, 8 pm, Tomorrow—with no further explanation, I'd been suspicious, but I'd had no choice.

"I'm a careful man, Kevril. I had to make sure this wasn't some kind of trap." He lifted a bottle. "Wine, or something stronger?"

"Whatever you're having, Getashi." Truth be told, I needed a drink to calm my nerves. Riding ashore cooped up in a water barrel hadn't helped my mood. My disguise was paper thin—dressed like a common seaman with a broad hat and a five-day growth of beard hiding my distinctive scars—but I felt sure I'd evaded Jhavika's spies. "Thank you for agreeing to see me in private."

"It's my pleasure." He held out two crystal glasses of blood-red wine, allowing me to choose which one to take. "Or at least I *hope* it will be. You seem...uncomfortable with this."

I took a glass and raised it to him. "I am, but not for the reason you think."

Temuso touched his glass to mine with a musical note. "Then pray tell me the root of your unease, Captain." He drank, and I followed suit. "You obviously didn't ask me to meet you for a *romantic* liaison. It's been half a *year* since our previous and *only* encounter, much to my regret. Since little else connects our interests, this must be about Jhavika."

I nearly spit wine. "Gods and devils, man! How the hell did you figure *that* out?" I coughed and wheezed while he chuckled and clapped me on the back.

"Oh, you're adorable, Kevril. Simple deduction. We have *nothing* else in common besides Jhavika. Please, take a chair before you fall down." He guided me to a comfortable armchair and sat in the one beside it. "Now, tell me what this is about. I'm positively on pins and needles."

I sipped my wine and cleared my throat, considering Temuso's deduction. Had my invitation been so transparent? I hadn't liked him when we first met. He'd struck me as pampered, entitled, and ingratiating, but the man was clearly no fool. "You're not going to like it, even if you *do* believe me."

"There are many ugly truths in the world, Kevril. I've found that it's better to know them than to remain ignorant." He sipped his wine and leaned forward, his attention rapt. "Now, what's this about?"

"You were right; it's about Jhavika. But before I get down to the crux of this issue, I want to ask you a few questions. I don't really need answers as much as I need you to reflect." I'd thought long and hard about how to convince Temuso of the truth. I'd been hard enough to convince that I was a slave to Jhavika's every whim, and I'd had a truthsayer's help. "Haven is a nest of liars and spies, so I ask you only to believe your own memories. How good are your recollections of the night we met?"

Temuso's eyebrows rose and a sly smile curved his lips. "My memories of that night are exquisite."

"We were all more than a little drunk, Getashi. Are you sure?"

His smile thinned. "Let me assure you, I remember every word, every note of the music, every touch, and every detail. The ability is both a gift and a curse."

"That's good!" I downed my wine and stood to retrieve the decanter from the table. I'd tried very hard to banish my own memories of that night. I needed fortification to recall the details. Bringing the decanter back to the smaller table, I filled our glasses and sat down. "When the dance performance began, you sat with Ursilla Roque, and I sat with Jhavika. You recall?"

"I remember that you wore a jacket of deep blue brocade, highly polished boots with silver buckles, two daggers with ruby pommels in your boots, a dress cutlass with a gold filigree guard, and trousers with silk strips down the sides." He smiled thinly. "Would you like me to describe what the ladies wore, the lattice of scars on your back, the mole on Lady Roque's inner thigh? I remember *everything*, Kevril."

"Then your memory's better than mine, and for that I'm grateful." I drank more wine. "Remember, then, during the performance, when I first got up from the divan. What did I say?"

His brow furrowed. "Jhavika asked you where you thought you were going, and you said you were leaving."

"Do you remember *exactly* what I said?"

He blinked and considered. "Something about this not being your type of entertainment."

"Yes. Then she told me to sit down and enjoy it." I downed my wine, gritting my teeth against my recollection of that utter helplessness. "And I did."

"Yes. So?" Temuso's brow remained furrowed.

"So, I'm asking you to recall that entire night in detail." I refilled my glass. "Remember everything Jhavika said to me, when she said it, *how* she said it, and how I responded."

He frowned and regarded me with suspicion. "All right. At the time, I thought she was being a bit of a control freak, to tell the truth, ordering you around, but you didn't seem to be complaining. In fact, you seemed downright enthusiastic when the play escalated."

"I was." I drank and cleared my throat. "I was *enthusiastic* because Jhavika commanded me to be so."

"Well, you *are* her subordinate, despite all that wish-wash about being partners."

"No, that's not what I mean, Getashi." I gritted my teeth and laid it out. "I did what she commanded me to do, right down to bending over and begging you to fuck me up the ass, even *enjoyed* it, because she *commanded* me to, because I had no *choice*."

His face fell. "What?"

"I was controlled by magic, Getashi." I put down my glass and traced three fingers down the scars that marred my face. "Jhavika gave me these with that scourge she wears the day we fought over the captaincy of my ship. Neither of us knew it then, but that whip, the cat-o'-nine-tails she took from our former captain, is enchanted. From that day, I could refuse no command she gave me."

"But, you..." His eyes widened with the implications of my claim. "But she... She lashed *me* with that thing!"

"Yes, she did. And Ursilla, too. The entire night—the slaves' performance, her commanding me like a fuck-puppet, the alcohol, the music—was all a pretext to lash you and Ursilla with that scourge." I looked at him with real pity. "You're her slave, Getashi."

"Bullshit!" He lurched to his feet and downed his wine, glaring at me. "I'm *nobody's* slave!"

"Not knowingly, and certainly not *willingly*." I stood and held out my hands, open and empty. "I know it's hard to believe, and I don't expect you to take my word alone, but it's the truth. I didn't want to do any of the things she commanded me to do that night, but I did. I did everything because I couldn't disobey. That was when I realized that I was under her complete control."

"I don't believe it! This is something she's put you up to!" He whirled to the table and filled his wineglass with amber liquid from another decanter.

"I wish that was so, Getashi, but it's not. You're her slave, just as I was."

"Was?" He knocked back half of the liquor in his glass. "So, if you were ensorcelled, how are you not anymore?"

"I found an alchemist on Valaka who mixed a potion to break the spell."

"Oh, how *convenient!*" His tone dripped derision.

"No, it actually wasn't, but I don't expect you to believe me."

"Then why tell me this?"

"Because I want to offer you the chance to free yourself from this enchantment, Getashi."

"Oh? And how can I do that?"

Once again, it was time to lay it out. If Getashi had received surreptitious orders from Jhavika to kill himself if anyone ever suggested this, I'd have a lot of explaining to do to his bodyguard. "Help me kill Jhavika."

His mouth fell open, then closed. "Motherless son of a..." He downed his glass and reached for the decanter. "You can't *possibly* be serious."

"I am, Getashi, *deadly* serious, but I know you're not going to act on my word alone." I emptied my glass and joined him at the table. I needed something stronger than wine, too. "That's why I need you to verify what I've told you. The only way I can think for you to do that is to remember something Jhavika told you to do, or even something she told you *not* to do, and try to do the opposite. If she told you to vote for her inclusion on the Council, go talk to your peers and try to tell them she's unfit. If she told you to wear a blue coat, try to wear a red one. Whatever you can remember, try to do the opposite. When you can't, you'll know I'm telling you the truth."

The muscles bunched and relaxed rhythmically beneath his soft, fleshy cheeks, as if chewing on every word I'd said. His eyes scanned my face, undoubtedly searching for hints of a lie. I met his scrutinizing gaze with my most sincere. I'd said all I could to convince him, but he was an intelligent man, shrewd and successful. He would confirm my claim for himself.

"If this is true, Kevril..." Temuso raised a hand and put it gently on my arm. "...then I'm sorry for what happened to you that night. I wouldn't have...done what I did if I didn't believe you wanted me to."

His seemingly honest apology took me by the lee. "You had no way to know."

"But still, I'm sorry." He removed his hand and reached for the decanter, his eyes cast down. "I've never...forced myself on anyone, Kevril. I find that the most repugnant form of violation in the world." He poured his glass half full, then raised the decanter with a questioning look. "I apologize."

"It wasn't you, Getashi." I held my glass for him to fill, honestly touched by his sentiment. "It was Jhavika. She ordered me to ask you, to beg you, to want it, and I did, so you didn't do anything I didn't want you to do, really."

"And you've waited so long for your revenge on her?" His brow furrowed. "Why?"

"It was always too dangerous. After I broke the enchantment, I considered killing her, and even had the chance, but I would never have gotten out of her estate alive." I shrugged and sipped the sweet liquor. "Besides, riding her coattails *has* been profitable."

"Your restraint astonishes me." He still seemed skeptical. "So why now? What's changed in your relationship with Jhavika?"

I'd burn in all Nine Hells before I told him about Preel's talent, but rumors had already spread from that night at the Folly. I had to tell him something, and I'd had time to prepare. "Actually, I'm surprised you hadn't heard through Ursula."

"Heard?" Temuso was either very good at dissembling or honestly hadn't heard.

"Jhavika used the scourge on my steward so she could spy on me. Then, when my lady and I went out to *Fancy's Folly*, she had my wife abducted."

"Your *wife*?" Temuso looked stunned. "Wait! That was *you*? I'd heard there was a breach of security and some kind of scuffle, but..." His eyes narrowed. "That seems foolish of Jhavika. Why would she do that? Why provoke you?"

"She's holding my wife to pressure me into helping recruit a privateer armada. She wants a navy so she can take the whole Blood Sea." At another skeptical look, I tried to explain. "The scourge is affecting *her*, as well, Getashi. It makes her greedy to the point of mania. Jhavika won't stop until she rules the whole world. Riding her coattails is no longer a...viable future. She stepped over the line. I want my wife back, and the only way to accomplish that is to kill Jhavika."

"Hells and demons, man." Temuso sipped his drink and began to pace the small room. "If this is true, which I *do* intend to verify for myself, it would certainly explain Jhavika's meteoric rise to the Council. Aside from myself and Lady Roque, do you know if any other council members are under her sway?"

"One other, at least, I think, but I don't know who. She also made it clear to me recently that she has people poised to remove her competition. I don't know if I believe her, but she could have assassins placed in key positions, waiting for her command to act. For all I know, my steward was one, ready to slit my throat one night. Telling *anyone* what I've told you here could be deadly."

"Yes, I've considered that." He pursed his lips in thought. "Have you any plan how to eliminate her without getting killed?"

Truth be told, killing Jhavika was likely to end in my death. If I could take her life and die knowing Preel was free, I'd call that a win. But Temuso didn't need to know that. "That's where I need your help. Breaching her keep is suicide, and I don't know her private itinerary. A council meeting might be the best opportunity, but I don't know when the next one's scheduled."

"Not for weeks, and there's always considerable security. Lord Balshi's keep is a fortress, and we all have our own people present as well. Also, unless your people are capable of taking down a squad of armored cavalry to get to her, attacking Jhavika in transit would be impossible."

"Bugger!" I downed my drink and put the glass aside. I was starting to feel the effects of the liquor, and I needed my head clear.

"Don't despair, Captain. There's always another way." Temuso leveled a smile at me. "It would be best if we arranged for you to be present as a matter of Council business."

"Could you invite me to a meeting? You could convene a meeting to discuss this plan for a privateer navy and bring me in as a consultant."

"Hmm, that's possible, but I think there would be less security at a social engagement. After all, we were alone with her the night we first met, aside from a few footmen. Any one of us could have murdered her *that* night."

That spurred an idea. "She was just appointed to the Council! A celebratory dinner or a party in her honor wouldn't be suspicious."

"Precisely the opportunity we need." The lord grinned at me and winked. "I could bring you as my guest. And you could wear that beautiful jacket and those lovely trousers again."

"I'm afraid I burned those clothes, Getashi. But I don't think I could go as your escort anyway. Jhavika knows how I feel about...what happened."

"Well, *that's* unfortunate." Temuso sighed and pressed a finger to his lips. "However, what you've told me gives me some insight into Jhavika's mind. If I can arrange a celebration, I'll ask her if she minds if I invite you to accompany me. If she's as covetous as you say, she'll bring you along herself just to spite me."

"And if she doesn't?"

"Then I *will* invite you, and you'll accept to spite *her*. She *must* know you're not happy about what she did to you."

"Oh, she most *definitely* knows I'm not happy with her."

"Then this should work." Temuso smiled wolfishly. "And I must say that I would delight in having you on my arm."

"Just remember, if we pull this off, I'm there to murder Jhavika Keshmir. There are likely to be repercussions."

"But once she's dead, the enchantment will end, won't it?"

"Well, she won't be able to give any *more* commands, of course, but I don't know if her standing orders will still be in effect or not. We may have to destroy the scourge itself to wipe out the effect completely."

His eyes narrowed. "And there's always the danger of someone else picking it up."

Shit! I hadn't considered that, what with all my other concerns. If I killed Jhavika in the middle of a ballroom full of council members, the fight over the enchanted scourge would be vicious. *Except...* "You and I, and perhaps a few of Jhavika's slaves, will be the only ones there who know about the scourge's power. If I'm not slaughtered outright by her guards, I'll take the scourge to be destroyed." With Preel's help I could do it; it was just a matter of time and questions.

Temuso's eyebrows rose. "And you ask me to trust you not to claim it for your own and take over Jhavika's army?"

"Yes, I do ask that. Just like I'm trusting you not to tell anyone of this. I don't *want* the scourge, Getashi. I know what it does to whoever claims it."

"And what is that?"

"It imbues its master with the avarice and ruthlessness of a dragon, and will never *ever* let them go." I shivered just thinking about what that vile thing would turn me into. "It enslaves the wielder, Getashi. It pushes them to take everything, the whole world. Jhavika *knows* what it's doing to her, and *still* she can't give it up!"

"Well!" Temuso looked a little stunned at my vehemence. "Very well, then, Kevril, I'll verify this and send you my answer. If it's true, I'll set up a congratulatory ball in Jhavika's honor. It may take a week or so to settle the details."

"Thank you, Getashi." I stepped up and held out a hand. "I'm in your debt."

"Not yet, you're not, but if this is true, and you *do* manage to kill Jhavika, it's I who will be in *your* debt!" He shook my hand firmly and grinned. "And if you're looking for a new business partner after this is over, I'm sure we can reach a mutually beneficial arrangement."

"If we both survive this, I'll consider it." I released his hand and nodded my thanks. I hadn't liked him when we first met, and less after the intimate encounter, but I found myself appreciating his willingness to believe me and to apologize for what happened, even though it wasn't his fault. "Send your messages to East End Provisioners and address them to my ship's cook, Bert Cutworthy. She's trustworthy and will bring me your answer. And be careful how you phrase your message. If it gets intercepted, it can't implicate either of us in a plot against Jhavika."

"Oh, I'll be careful; you can be sure of that, Captain." Temuso stepped past me to the table and poured a finger of liquor into two glasses, then turned to hand me one. "To our success."

"I'll drink to that!" I took the glass, touched his, and we drank. "Just don't let word of this slip or we're both dead."

He barked a short laugh. "Rest assured, Kevril, when there's a woman out there who can command me to fall on my sword, my lips are sealed."

"Good." I nodded my thanks and left the room, retrieving my cutlass and daggers from Utake in passing. He handed them over without a word, and I wondered how much he might have overheard. I also wondered if he was one of Jhavika's slaves, and hoped that was only my growing paranoia.

I pulled my hat low and left the cozy little inn. I had to get back to the ship before dawn, and the only way to do it without one of Jhavika's spies spotting me was to work my way out to one of the headlands and swim for it. If I didn't get sick from the foul water of the bay, I'd consider myself lucky.

Chapter Nineteen
The Elusive Truth

Capitulation is often strategy in the guise of weakness.
The Lessons of Quen Lau Ush

From the journal of Preel Longbright –
I have had many cruel masters, but none so subtle in their cruelty, so manipulative, as Jhavika. For someone under an enchantment that made her ruthless, she showed remarkable restraint. Or, perhaps, she was simply lonely.

I woke with the memories of my failed ploy to trick Jhavika and my hopeful answer to her question playing a game of chase and catch in my mind. Her question had surprised me; with all the things she could have asked to further her conquest, to sate the desire to take the entire world for her own, she asked if it would be possible to free herself of that very desire. A new truth dawned in my mind as real as the growing light that tinged the drapes a light pink. *Jhavika hates the scourge.*

That revelation bore thinking on.

I was stiff from so long abed and stretched under the crisp sheets. I could usually gauge how taxing the invocation of my talent had been by how long I slept. This answer had cost me. My door opened, and the light from the sitting room illuminated Binsh standing there.

He leaned out the door and said, "She's awake."

He and his sister standing shifts to watch me sleep sent a shiver down my spine, but they were under orders. They couldn't disobey, and also couldn't hurt me, so I had no choice but to tolerate their undivided attention. I slipped out of bed to retrieve my robe, and Binsh was there to help me.

"Breakfast will be ready in a few minutes, Preel. I could draw you like a bath before, if you like."

"No, thank you. I just need to freshen up."

"Of course." He escorted me to the bathroom, but allowed me my privacy.

Unused to such avid and constant attention, I took a moment's comfort in seeing to my own needs. A quick rinse of face and hands woke me up, and I brushed and braided my hair. The lassitude from so long in bed began to ebb, and my stiff muscles eased after some slow stretches. When I heard the outer door open, I ventured out to find servants setting the table for one. Evidently, I would breakfast alone, which suited me fine. The last thing I wanted this morning was Jhavika's company. I needed time to think.

The food, of course, was excellent, though I missed Bert's attention to spice and flavor. The blackbrew I found watery after the jolting stuff Hemp brewed. And, of course, I missed Kevril.

Forcing my thoughts away from the spiraling depths of self-pity, I focused on the problem at hand: Jhavika Keshmir.

What a curious mix of avaricious control freak and insecure loner she was. Her question about destroying the scourge told me she wanted to be free of it, but I doubted she'd ever be able to relinquish that power. Her entire position here depended on it. Jhavika had built a house of cards with razor edges. Without the scourge's magic, those cards would fall and cut her to pieces.

The situation prompted many questions. Why hadn't she used the scourge's magic to control me? Or had she? And if so, why was she not exerting it? Was she really being careful not to overtly command me, or was I just being paranoid? Was her need for companionship genuine, a ploy to manipulate me, or the scourge exerting its will upon her?

My thoughts were spiraling again, so I pushed my plate away and went to my bedroom to change. Dismissing Binsh and Nala's help, I donned my accustomed pantaloons and a loose-fitting shirt. I emerged into the sitting room to find the table cleared and the furniture moved to provide enough space for my exercises. Only five days, and my attendants knew my schedule. I ignored them and did some slow stretches to prepare myself for yamshi. This simple discipline, more than anything, centered my thoughts and brought me some measure of comfort. I started with the basic routine: *greeting the sun, embracing the morning, willow in wind, tree reaches sky...*

My body and mind became one, my thoughts centered on every move, every twist, every placement of hand and foot. In the midst of the discipline, there was no room for my mind to wander, to dwell on those things over which I had no control, spiral into despair, miss the ones I loved.

Solace...

By the time I completed the routine, I was breathing deeply, a light sheen of sweat dampening my shirt, my mind at peace, my muscles loose and warm.

"Water, Preel?"

I accepted a glass of water from Nala and drank half of it. "Thank you."

"I'm curious about these exercises that you do."

"It's called yamshi. It was developed by Chen monks." I drained the glass and handed it back.

"It's very graceful." She took the empty glass.

"Less so than your dance, Nala, but it exercises my mind as much as my body. I could teach you, if you like."

"Perhaps, if you wish to, but—"

"Her ladyship wouldn't approve," Binsh cut in. "We're here to see to *your* needs, Preel, not for you to see to ours."

"But I..." Then I saw the trepidation in his eyes. He was afraid of something, and that fear was suddenly mirrored in his sister. If they didn't do as they were ordered, Jhavika would punish them, though they likely couldn't admit it. "I understand."

I went through another more advanced routine, then allowed them to give me a massage. I really didn't need one, but it fulfilled their need to care for me and, truth be told, felt wonderful. After a warm bath to wash off the scented oils, I selected a book from the shelf and sat down by the window to read. Binsh left the room, but Nala stayed to watch over me.

The book was less than gripping—an esoteric history of the Toki dynasties, conquest, avarice, and magic—and my mind slipped sideways into a consideration of my situation. Twice I found my jaw clenched, and forced myself to relax. With only Nala in the room, I could probably hurt myself, possibly even kill myself, before she could stop me. But despite my initial trepidation, the last few days had convinced me that Jhavika was telling the truth about one thing at least: I was safe and comfortable here. I wasn't being abused. A slave, yes, but a pampered one.

You're not suffering, Preel. It could be a thousand times worse... I recalled saying that very thing to Kevril when he was fretting in Valaka, and my heart ached anew.

But he's not coming to rescue me this time, I reminded myself.

Jhavika's words came to haunt me. "He's a pirate, Preel. He loves no one but himself."

Bugger it! I slammed down the book and stood to stare out the window at the distant masts on the bay. Most of my memories clashed against this new image of Kevril, but others plagued me like a flock of screeching harpies. Valaka especially. He had traded me to Brekka for the potion that would free him. Yes, he'd stolen me back, but had he rescued me because he loved me or because I was a truthsayer? Had his ploy with the dagger been genuine or just another lie?

I gripped the cold iron bars of my prison and glared my anguish out at the world. *I'm the dove that lays diamond eggs, and I live in a gilded cage...*

The door opened, and armor clattered. I knew it was Jhavika, but I didn't turn.

"How are you feeling today, Preel?" she asked.

"I'm fine."

"Binsh tells me you're exercising a lot. Some Chen discipline."

"Yes. It's called yamshi. I've done it for years. It...helps me cope."

"I walk in the gardens for the same reason. Would you like to walk there with me?"

I turned to her and opened my mouth to say that I'd sooner jump off a cliff, but stopped. Her mien seemed sincere, concerned for my wellbeing. Whether she truly was or not, I didn't know, and it really didn't matter. Antagonizing her would do me no good, and a walk in the sunshine would be welcome. "Yes, please."

A smile flashed. "Good. You may want some shoes."

Binsh proffered a pair of sandals, and I sat to allow him to put them on my feet. Then I accompanied Jhavika on a stroll through the keep to her gardens, followed by four of her guards, Nala, and Binsh. On the way, she introduced me to several of her staff. Her butler, a smiling Toki man named Ty-lee, bowed deeply, but said not a word. The hulking captain of her guard, Vakna, who sported two short tusks from his lower jaw that reminded me of Wix, nodded silently. I met several others, but not one said a word to me.

"Just a precaution, you understand. I can't risk your safety, and that binding you wore is inconvenient." Jhavika paused at the steps down to her lush gardens to smell the tiny white flowers of a vine trained to the balustrade. She urged me to do the same.

I did, and the heady scent of jasmine overwhelmed my senses.

"These gardens are my pride and joy," Jhavika explained as we descended into them. "The one place I can go to find beauty and peace without commanding anyone to serve me."

"I know *exactly* how you feel."

"Do you?" She looked at me sidelong, a skeptical smile on her lips. "I don't see how you can *possibly* understand how I feel."

"We're not so different, Jhavika." I paused to smell a rose, the thorns pressing into my fingertips as I pulled the stem close. "We're both slaves."

"I'm *not* a slave to the scourge, Preel." The smile vanished, her tone edged toward anger. "Do I need to caution you again about being petulant?"

"I'm not being petulant." I gave her my most sincere look. "You asked me yesterday if it was possible to destroy the scourge without harming you. You obviously want to be free of it." It wasn't petulance, but I knew my words pricked like the thorns on the roses. "If you really want someone's honest opinion, you have to be willing to listen without taking offense."

She stared at me for a moment, then nodded. "I do want to be free of its influence, Preel, you're right, but that doesn't make me a slave." She walked on, one hand resting on the coil of dragon flesh at her hip, the other waving to encompass the estate. "It's given me all this. How can that be slavery?"

"You've placed me in luxurious surroundings, Jhavika. That doesn't make me less a slave." I walked with her, placing my feet among the foliage with great care and choosing my words with even more. "Merchants are slaves to gold, soldiers are slaves to steel, rulers are slaves to power, and farmers are slaves to the soil. No one is truly free."

Jhavika shot me a skeptical scowl. "A philosopher as well as a truthsayer?"

I gave her a sardonic smile. "I read a lot."

She barked a laugh and nodded. "Philosophy and poetry. I wondered about those books in Kevril's cabin. They were yours, then."

Pain... "No, they were his. He loaned them to me."

"Another illusion of freedom." She shook her head and continued strolling. "He really is a master of manipulation."

I didn't comment, but followed along, nurturing my hatred of her beneath a placid façade.

"So, if that philosophy holds true, Preel, what do you think a pirate a slave to? 'Free and beholden to none' is their motto."

"That's simple. They're slaves to their own freedom."

Jhavika barked another laugh and strode on. "Oh, you really are a treasure, Preel."

"A priceless treasure..." Kevril's words stabbed me like a hail of daggers.

"What's that?" Jhavika turned back to stare at me.

"Just something one of my previous masters said. He compared me to the old story about the dove who laid diamond eggs." I wasn't about to tell her who that master had been.

"Huh, interesting. That story didn't end well for the dove, if memory serves."

"No, it didn't." I considered for a moment, and added, "Or any of the dove's successive owners, if you recall. Each murdered their predecessor, until the last killed the dove, only to find no diamonds inside."

"True enough. Such treasures draw the greedy like carrion draws crows. We'll have to make sure that the same doesn't happen to us, won't we?"

I considered that, and couldn't disagree. I wasn't suffering here, and I'd suffered in the past from cruel masters. Who knew what would happen if someone killed Jhavika and took me? But still, my hatred for her smoldered.

We suspended our subtle sparring and continued our stroll in contemplative silence, ending up on the patio that overlooked the garden. "I've got to get back to work, Preel. Thank you for walking with me. It was a nice departure from the norm."

"It *was* nice. Thank you." It wasn't a lie, but I wondered once again about her motives, if this was genuine or an elaborate lie. I could think of no motive for the latter. *Perhaps she is simply lonely.*

"Nala and Binsh will escort you back to your rooms." Jhavika motioned them forward along with my two door guards. "If there's anything at all you want—books, food, companionship—just ask them. Anything at all."

Revulsion roiled in my gut. "If by companionship you mean sex, no, thank you."

She looked at me like I'd said something ridiculous.

"As a slave, I've been on the receiving end of that kind of abuse too many times to command others to submit to it."

Jhavika shook her head sharply. "This isn't like that, Preel. I've commanded them to take pleasure in serving your every need. They *want* to please you."

"It's *exactly* like that, Jhavika." I wasn't being petulant, just pointing out the truth. She was so used to solving her every problem, sating her every desire, with the scourge's magic, that she saw the whole world through that lens. "You can command them to feel anything you wish, but it doesn't make those feelings real. They can still remember who they are, or who they *were* before they were changed by the scourge. They might want to serve me, might even take pleasure in it, but they know deep down it's a lie, and they'll hate me for it."

Jhavika looked a little shocked. "I could command them to love you. Would *that* suffice?"

I remembered the night Kevril returned from the party where Jhavika had manipulated him like a puppet, forcing him to pleasure her guests, to want it, to even enjoy it. I remembered the next day, after she'd forced him to pleasure her in the bed I slept in, and the pit of hate in my gut widened, deepened, and filled. Jhavika saw no problem with what she was doing to people. It sickened me. I couldn't risk her seeing that hatred, however.

"Please, Jhavika, no. That would be worse."

Again, she looked mildly surprised. "Whatever you wish, Preel. I just want you to be as happy as you can be."

I clenched my jaw against a cutting remark and forced a smile. "Thank you."

Jhavika nodded and strode away. I watched her go, noting her hand resting on the haft of the scourge. The weapon never left her side, and I wondered fleetingly if she slept and bathed with the thing. I indulged a fleeting fantasy of strangling her with it.

"We should return to your rooms, Preel," Binsh said, snapping me out of my musing.

"Of course." I waved him on, dwelling on my murderous fantasy as I followed, wondering if I could possibly make it come true.

While Jhavika never took off the scourge, she rarely wore any other weapon. She'd worn a dagger once, but not since. Her guards were always close by, too, which would foil anything but an immediately lethal attempt. Unfortunately, that meant that plucking the scourge from her hip and strangling her with it wouldn't work.

Could I even do it? I wondered. My stomach clenched when I remembered the would-be thief falling from the bridge. His death had been unintentional, but had pierced me to my very soul. Deliberately murdering someone would be an entirely different matter.

But he'd just been a petty thief. Jhavika is an ensorcelled maniac. She took me from the only man I ever loved... Putting the situation into that perspective eased my conscience and hardened my resolve.

I thought about my studies into the martial ancestry of yamshi, the deadly strikes and kicks, and wondered if I could physically do it. I hadn't the strength or focus of a warrior monk, but my blow to Binsh's chin had staggered him. I reviewed in my mind the strikes to throat and neck, the twists and turns derived from moves originally conceived to fracture bones.

I might have a chance, but I'd have to get close.

But what would happen if I succeeded? Would her guards kill me? Would I fall victim to all the horrors she'd threatened me with? And, even if I managed to escape, where would I go? The only logical place was back to Kevril, but now I wasn't sure whether he had ever truly loved me or simply wanted a truthsayer in his bed.

We arrived at my chambers, and I allowed my attendants to unbraid my hair and brush it out. I let my eyes close, enjoying the sensation, the comfort, the safety. Yes, I could end up in a much worse situation than a pampered lifetime as Jhavika's truthsayer.

That didn't diminish my hatred for her, but it was something to think about.

Chapter Twenty
Looking Death in the Eye

When one doesn't know the enemy's forces, attack is suicide.
The Lessons of Quen Lau Ush

From the diary of Kevril Longbright —
How much of Jhavika's belligerence was calculated avarice,
and how much was sheer spite, I'll probably never know. I do
know that I hated her a bit more every day she kept me from
seeing Preel.

I stood on the deck in the rain watching the launch row back from
shore. The weather had turned foul, the downpour beating Snomish
Bay flat. The monsoon season was upon us, and the deluge matched
my mood perfectly. Two days since my conversation with Temuso and
no answer yet, Jhavika still refused to let me see Preel, and Bert's
inquiries to alchemists had so far yielded nothing. It seemed that all
the practitioners with any real talent had already been scooped up by
the Council of Lords, either enslaved, blackmailed into servitude, or
contracted as their full-time attendants. The first rule of Haven, after
all, was money and power. Wield both, and you gain more of both.
Wield neither, and you're nothing.

Rauley barked at the deck crew to bring the launch alongside, and Bert came up the boarding ladder with amazing alacrity for a woman of her size.

"News?" I asked her, fighting to keep my anticipation under control. I'd had it dashed too many times already.

"Aye, *finally* some bloody news." She sniffed against the damp. "Mind if we get outta the rain first? I'm about drowned."

I waved her toward the sterncastle. "At least you didn't have to *swim* back to the ship!" I'd had a nasty bout of the flux after my dip in the bay and was still recovering. "Let's get a cuppa."

"Bloody fine!"

We shook out our weather cloaks and hats, hung them in the wet locker, and I followed Bert to the galley. She bustled in, and the scullery swabs scattered like a gaggle of ducklings fleeing a raging goose. Pronouncing the pot of blackbrew that had been on the stove for hours as unfit to drink, she put the simmering kettle on the hottest part of the stove and ordered her swabs to grind fresh beans. Then she turned to face me.

"First things first. Here!" Bert withdrew a waxed canvas envelope from under her tunic and handed it over. "Got a little crumpled, but it's dry. Dunno who it's from, but it was waitin' for me at East End."

"Temuso." I snatched the packet and withdrew a letter sealed with wax, but without any impressed marking. I broke it open and read.

K,

You were correct. I apologize for doubting you.
I hope to see you at the aforementioned social gathering within a week's time. You'll receive an invitation, one way or another.

With sincerest thanks and affection,

GT

"Well, I'll be a son of a..." I read it again, just to make sure I wasn't hallucinating.

"Good news?" Miko asked from the door.

"Yes, from Temuso. He's evidently confirmed what I told him about the scourge and is arranging a congratulatory ball in Jhavika's honor." I handed her the cryptic note. "If Jhavika doesn't invite me as her escort, he will."

"Perfect!" She read the note and chuckled. "It'd probably be easier if you went with Temuso. If Jhavika asks you, you'll have to play hard to get. She knows you're pissed at her."

"True." I scratched my thick stubble. "Either way, I'll need a shave." I missed my steward in more respects than one.

"Oh, let it grow! You look more piratical every day!" Miko never stopped trying to cheer me up, and the news from Temuso helped as much as her humor.

"Here you are, Captain!" Bert handed over a cup brimming with fresh blackbrew and another for Miko, then poured one for herself. "Can we have a sit-down for the rest, sir? My feet are killin' me from all the walkin' 'round town."

"Sure." I sipped the scalding brew and headed for my cabin. The place was uncharacteristically cluttered without Hemp's constant care; the swab he'd approved as my temporary steward had no notion of cleanliness. I kicked off my damp boots and gestured to the navigation table. "Have a seat."

"Thank you, sir." Bert sat and sighed, her round face pinched. "I swear, some days I think I'd rather cut off both feet and hobble around on a pair of pegs!"

"If you don't tell me what you found out today, I may just help you with that." I scowled at her and forced myself to sit down.

Miko took a chair and gave me a sour look. "There's an old adage about not killing the messenger, isn't there?"

"Miko..."

"No worries, sir, I know yer in a state." Bert sipped her blackbrew and ran a pudgy hand over her florid features. "So, I finally found an alchemist who says she can mix up yer potion. I know it took too damn long, but I had to be careful. It won't be cheap, but it should do the job."

"Money I've got. What's her name?"

"Tewhirke Kettleblack, a gnome, in case her name wasn't hint enough. She's old, cantankerous, and won't take any crap from anybody, but she's talented and honest as far as her abilities go. She said it'd be harder to make it the way you wanted—addin' somethin' from whoever you want to look like as the last ingredient—but it can be done."

"Excellent!" I sipped my blackbrew and felt the knot in my chest unclench. "Can she have it within a week's time?"

She nodded. "Five days, but she wants half the payment up front. Twenty-two hundred crowns."

I gaped at her. "That's *half* the payment?"

"Aye, and I haggled like a dwarven gem merchant to get *that* price. Rushin' it cost a bit." She sipped noisily and nodded to Miko. "The potion'll last about six hours, or half that time split between two people. She'll make it so you add a dram of blood from whoever you wanna look like right before you take it. She said she'll get started, but wants the advance money tomorrow mornin'."

"Fine. I'll send it with Quibly. He does the ship's banking anyway." I had that much ready cash stowed away aboard *Scourge*, but would have to convert some baubles to gold for the rest. I looked to Miko. "Now all we have to decide is who to knock on the head, and who to send after Preel."

"I know you don't—"

"Excuse me, sir." Bert downed her blackbrew and lurched up. "I best not know all yer plans. What I don't know I can't spill if psychobitch spanks me with that bloody lash. Already know too much, and it's got me nervous as a long-tailed cat in a room full of rockin' chairs."

"Of course." I stood. "I'm sorry for putting you in the middle of this, Bert. You didn't sign up to be a spy."

"No, I bloody didn't, but I'll help as I can." She rubbed her hands together and bustled for the door. "And don't think for a second that I'm doin' it fer *you*, you bloody pirate! I'm doin' it for Preel! That lass has been through hell already. She don't deserve this."

"I couldn't agree more. Thank you, Bert."

My cook turned and frowned at me. "Just get her the hell out of there, Captain, and you'll never hear another cross word out of my mouth."

I forced a piratical grin. "Don't make promises you can't keep, Bert."

She snorted a laugh and left the cabin, bawling orders for the scullery swabs to bring her something she could chop, pound, and mince into submission. From the sound of it, I'd be eating hash for dinner.

"So, as I was saying..." Miko got up and went to my cabinet. "I know you don't want me to go, but you need someone who can think on their feet. This requires more than brawn, Kevril." The cork came out of a bottle of spiced rum with a resonant pop.

"Wix is the obvious choice, and he's no fool." I turned to face the stern gallery windows, not in the mood to argue.

"Not arguing on that score, but three hours is plenty of time. We should send two people in. It'll double our chances."

I shot her a glare. "I'm not risking my first mate *and* my bosun on the same mission. If *none* of us comes back, *Scourge* will be adrift."

"So, advance Kivan and Quiff to lieutenant. You know they're both ready." She poured a measure of rum into both our blackbrew cups and offered me one.

"Kivan, maybe, but Quiff's still a laggard." I took my cup and sipped the heady brew.

"Advancing him will give him the impetus to work harder. Responsibility does that to people, especially with what's going on." Joining me in staring out the transom windows, Miko changed the subject. "The other question is who to knock on the head and impersonate."

"My first choice would be Ty-lee. He virtually *runs* Jhavika's household. Even the guards follow his orders."

"That would be nice, but is he likely to accompany Jhavika to this party? Whoever we knock on the head has to be *outside* the keep."

I shook my head. "Ty-Lee won't accompany her, but Jhavika *will* have a phalanx of cavalry as well as personal guards."

Miko looked at me sidelong. "And *you'll* be her escort? You step aboard a carriage surrounded by her soldiers, you'll never come out again."

"I don't think she'd allow that anyway. It'd be the perfect opportunity to put a dagger in her heart." I sipped my fortified blackbrew and stared out the windows at the rain. "No, if I'm her escort, I'll hire a carriage and bring along my own guards."

"So, you go in, we hang back, knock a couple of her guards on the head, take some of their blood, and hightail it back to Jhavika's keep." Miko cleared her throat. "What if they have passwords?"

I let the 'we' portion of her comment slide for now. "That's one reason I wanted Ty-lee. Nobody would question him, and, even if they did, he could order them out of his way."

"But he'll be *inside* the keep. How do we..." She turned to me, wide-eyed. "How about this; we impersonate *one* of Jhavika's escort, get back to her keep, call for Ty-lee, and tell him there's been an incident at the party and Jhavika wants him there. Then we impersonate him, too, and we're in."

"Think he'll buy the ruse?"

"Maybe not, but I'd bet a galleon full of Fornician silks that he's been conditioned to jump when she needs him."

"Good point." I nodded. "I like that plan except for one detail; you're going to tell me *you* should be the one to impersonate Ty-lee."

She grinned. "Hey, I thought *I* was the one who read *your* mind!"

I growled at her through clenched teeth. "I don't like risking you *and* Wix, Miko."

"Why not? You've risked us both before during dozens of boarding actions."

"Not like this. Not to Jhavika. If the two of you were captured, she could take *Scourge* and enslave the whole crew."

Miko gave me her most stubborn glare. "Not gonna happen, sir. Jhavika'll be dead, and, even if everything goes bad and we come back spoutin' all kinds of nonsense, you can just sew us in our hammocks like you did Hemp."

I had to make her see the reality of this situation. "Miko, you *know* my chances of getting out of there alive are miniscule. Even if I do manage to kill Jhavika, between her guards and the other council members, I'm as good as dead."

"Which is why you need *me* on the inside of Jhavika's keep."

I shook my head. "I'm not following you."

My first mate downed the rest of her rum-laced blackbrew and whirled to snatch the bottle off my chart table. "Seriously, Kevril, who do you think has a better chance than me and Wix of getting Preel out of there?"

"Okay, I admit that the two of you together have the best chance, but I can't risk—"

"Bullshit." She whirled on me, bottle in hand. For a moment I thought she might throw it at me. "You're not even *planning* to fucking survive this, are you?"

"I'm not suicidal, Miko, just realistic."

"So am I, and me and Wix together are the best chance for Preel. And you knowing Preel is safe is the best chance for you to survive."

"What?" I was flummoxed again. "I don't see how Preel being safe helps my chances."

"Because you're in *love* with her, you twit!" Miko stepped up and poured rum into first my cup, then her own. "Knowing she's safe gives you something to live for!"

I opened my mouth to protest, but could find no argument with her logic. Killing Jhavika wasn't about me—my hating her, or getting revenge, or something as foolish as honor—it was about Preel. Killing Jhavika was her only chance to be free again.

But if I could be with Preel when this was all over, if we could have our lives back...

I downed the rum, letting it burn the lump from my throat, and nodded to my first mate. "All right, Miko. You and Wix. He impersonates one of Jhavika's guards, you impersonate Ty-Lee, and you get Preel out." I took the bottle from her grasp and poured a hearty measure into my cup. "I'll agree to that under one condition."

"And that is?" She looked at me suspiciously.

"If I don't come back, you sail for the horizon with Preel and never look back."

Miko opened her mouth, then closed it and nodded. "Aye, Captain."

Chapter Twenty One
The Weapon at Hand

A true warrior has no favorite weapon.
The Lessons of Quen Lau Ush

From the journal of Jhavika Keshmir –
How curious it is to me that my visits to Preel have become the highlights of my days. Watching her slowly accept her situation, my friendship, the subtle web of lies reinforced by a command she doesn't even realize I've given, fulfills me. This is how I will win her over. Then I will let Kevril see what she's become.

I stared down at the diagram of my spy network with a mixture of pride and trepidation. "Do you think it's getting unwieldy, Ty-lee?"

"Unwieldy?" He frowned and shrugged. "Perhaps, but armies are unwieldy things. Establishing your command structure as you have gives you the ability to wield utter control with minimal effort."

"True, but I wonder if I've lost touch with the bigger picture."

I traced a finger down the pyramid of names, over a thousand, reflecting on the chains of command and obedience I'd forged with the scourge. Many of my new slaves occupied key positions, but the vast majority were nothing but common spies. Some of them I'd only met once, just long enough to lash them, establish the base indoctrination that ensured their loyal servitude, and tell them who they would answer to. All of the lines of command led back to me, of course, but I couldn't track every spy and assassin, every soldier and servant, every street urchin and whore under my control. I couldn't even remember who half of these people were. And some, before I'd truly understood the power of the scourge and its limitations, had long since fled. One of those had even tried to kill me.

Since that attempt, I'd become more careful with my indoctrinations, covering every conceivable contingency to avoid problems. I relied on my network of subordinates, most of whom I controlled through Ty-lee, Captain Vakna, and a few others. I gave these few a great deal of autonomy, for they were so indoctrinated that they literally lived to serve me. Still, it was hard to keep track.

"The bigger picture, your ladyship?" Ty-lee looked at me askance. "I don't understand."

"I'm beginning to think that enslaving the unwashed masses isn't worth the effort. I should be starting at the top, not working my way up from the bottom."

"You control three council members and currently have plans to remove or replace all but four of the others." He tapped a shorter list to the side of the complex schematic, those I deemed most critical to either control or eliminate. "When you have six under your control, you'll have a voting majority. Now, with Preel, you can discern where best to exert the scourge's control."

"True..." I caressed the scourge and considered the question I would ask her this afternoon. The four-day wait between questions vexed me, but I didn't dare risk pushing the time limit and killing my precious truthsayer. In fact, Preel had come a long way, even helping me craft the wording of the inquiries. Apparently, ambiguous questions yielded ambiguous answers. Fortunately, I had plenty of work to keep me busy. I waved Ty-lee away and considered my list of potential slaves on the Council. Tori Blackbriar had been next on my list, but, now that I had Preel, I was rethinking my strategy.

Balshi I could eliminate with a single word to his sister Brilla. Fa-Chen I could also have murdered at any time, but I wanted his ships, and killing him now wouldn't get them for me. Lord Malchi would soon be caught in my web, courtesy of Ursilla Roque's affair with the lord's young son, Maurice. I planned to invite them both to a social gathering, apply the scourge to the boy's backside, and plant a cuckoo in his father's nest. Once the older Malchi brothers met with lethal accidents, I'd be one heartbeat from controlling yet another house. Hells, with a stroke of luck, I'd even penetrated Lady Hatsu's inner circle.

My biggest worries now were Nahli Twince and Hashi Severn. Putting one of the god-emperor's truthseekers on to Twince without hinting at my own magic would be tricky. If word of my scourge or Preel leaked back to Toki, I'd be their next target. The problem with Severn was, quite literally, a two-edged blade. The legends Master Lewin had recently dug up regarding Soul Drinker terrified me. I didn't want to be anywhere near her or it.

Unless I can somehow take Soul Drinker for my own...

I clenched the haft of the scourge and considered how I might make that happen. Yet another question to pose to my truthsayer.

"Your ladyship?"

I turned to find Ty-lee proffering two letters on a silver salver. I picked up the envelope bearing the insignia of the Council of Lords and swore softly. "*Another* damned council meeting?" Truth be told, I dreaded attending because my plan to recruit a navy of pirates had stalled, Kevril flatly refusing to leave port until I allowed him to see Preel. The man was utterly smitten with her. His pain gave me no end of satisfaction, but I had to get him back on the job. He was the linchpin of the plan that would establish my naval power in the Blood Sea.

I tore open the missive and stopped at the first line. "What in the name of..."

"Your ladyship?" Ty-lee sounded distressed, but my eyes wouldn't leave the letter. "Is there something wrong?"

"Um... I'm not sure." I read the invitation again, pins and needles of suspicion pricking up my spine. "It's an invitation to a ball in my honor at Balshi's keep." I handed it to him, my mind racing.

"Oh, your ladyship, that's wonderful! You're finally being honored by the Council!"

I leveled a scathing stare at him. "Balshi hates me, Ty-lee. Why would he host a ball in my honor?"

"Perhaps he's trying to mend fences, or Lady Brilla might have suggested it."

"Brilla..." I hadn't considered that possibility. Her conditioning was at a delicate stage; she was enamored with me, but didn't know of her slavery. "Well, it's six days hence. That'll give us time to look into this. Draft an acceptance letter to Lord Balshi and make preparations. Take every precaution you can think of."

"Yes, your ladyship." He handed over the next letter, this one embossed with Temuso's seal. I received regular correspondence from my thralls on the Council, so this was no surprise.

I opened it and started reading, then barked a laugh. "So *that's* it! Temuso set this up!"

"Of course." Ty-lee beamed at the explanation. "He's consolidating support for you, just as you suggested he should."

"So it would..." I stopped as the last paragraph caught my eye.

And if you have not yet asked your dashing pirate, Captain Longbright, to be your escort, I would love the opportunity to have the good captain on my arm.

"Oh, *interesting*!" I handed the letter to Ty-lee. "He wants to ask Kevril to accompany him as his escort."

"Well, Lord Temuso *has* expressed an interest in Captain Longbright." He looked concerned. "Do you think it's a good idea for the two of them to spend time together?"

"Probably not, and Kevril would never go with him anyway. He doesn't particularly *like* Temuso."

"But Captain Longbright is still wroth with you over the loss of his truthsayer," Ty-lee pointed out. "Might he accompany Temuso out of spite, or even use the invitation as an opportunity to tell him about the scourge?"

I squeezed the scourge's haft, and a tingle of danger tickled the back of my mind. Temuso was valuable to me, but he knew nothing of his slavery. Even if Kevril did tell him of the scourge, I doubted Temuso would believe him. I also held Preel, which deterred Kevril from exposing me. The pirate did have a vengeful streak, however, and betraying me to Temuso might be too tempting for him to resist. No, I couldn't risk that.

"Damn Balshi for insisting we bring escorts anyway!" I whirled away to glare out the windows at my rain-soaked gardens. "Draft a letter to Temuso. Thank him for arranging the ball in my honor, and tell him sorry, but *I'll* be bringing Kevril as my escort."

"You *will*?" Ty-lee's voice cracked, betraying his concern. "Your ladyship, the captain is a dangerous man, and he's *angry* with you. He probably won't agree to accompany you, but, if he does, having him on your arm will be extremely dangerous."

"And if I *don't* ask him, Temuso will, and, as you pointed out, Kevril might accept just to spite me. One word to Temuso about the scourge, and I've got a bigger problem."

"And if Captain Longbright refuses your invitation?"

"Then I'll *convince* him." I turned to smile at him. "I've got the perfect lever to manipulate him with."

"Preel?"

"Yes. He's been hounding me to see her. I think she might be ready soon. Perhaps not tomorrow—I've got to ask her a question this afternoon, and she'll be fatigued in the morning—but soon." I tapped a finger to my lips, reconsidering my pending question. According to Preel, I couldn't ask about people's future intentions or how they would react if given an opportunity, but I might ask who would be best to bring as my escort. I waved a dismissive hand. That would be a horrible waste of Preel's talents. I had Kevril wrapped around my finger, and using Preel to manipulate him would be such poetic justice. "Draft the letter to Temuso, and another to Kevril. Invite the good captain to meet with me here the day after tomorrow to...discuss his request. That's all for now."

"*All*, your ladyship? You're *cancelling* the acceptance to Lord Balshi?"

I gritted my teeth, annoyed, but unable to be angry with Ty-Lee's literal obedience to my every word. At least he was intelligent enough to remind me when I faltered. "No, of course not. Draft a response thanking him for the invitation and assuring him that I'll attend."

Ty-lee smiled and bowed. "Yes, your ladyship."

I stared out the windows at my sodden gardens, lamenting the coming of monsoon season. The rains did wonders for the plants, but I loathed the damp. Walking through my gardens in the sunshine was one of my few refuges, and the company of Preel on those walks had become an added treat. The illusion of freedom made her happy, and when she was happy, she was compliant, helpful, and civil.

As I'd planned, her anger with me was waning. Soon, she'd be ready to face Kevril.

The rain lashing against the windows couldn't fully dampen my spirits. Things were moving forward nicely, and Preel's answer this afternoon would tell me what I'd longed to know most—who I should next enslave. I had spies, assassins, sages, physicians, lackeys, soldiers, attendants, and a plethora of lovely bedmates. It was time to aim higher, but who would serve my purposes best?

To that end, I checked the time. Barely mid-afternoon, and I was champing at the bit to visit Preel and ask my question. Girding my enthusiasm tested my self-control, but the payoff shone like a pot of gold at the end of a rainbow. *Patience...* I reminded myself. Every secret in the world lay at my fingertips, but I had to be patient.

I forced myself to sit and work for a few more hours. Immersing myself in the endless details of running my growing empire—myriad small businesses, loan sharks, guild influences, and an increasingly lucrative protection racket—time flew by. Finally, a servant interrupted me.

"Your ladyship, you requested to be told when dinner was near to being ready. Chef estimates half an hour."

"Good." I stood and stretched, the joints of my back and shoulders popping and cracking. Sitting stooped over a desk always left me stiff. "Arrange dinner for two in Preel's quarters when it's ready."

"Yes, your ladyship."

I went to my chambers, donned a fresh shirt, and proceeded to Preel's rooms. She sat in a comfortable chair by the window reading. Looking up with a curiously downcast expression, she closed her book.

"Did you have a good day, Preel?" I couldn't have cared less, but convincing her that I did care about her well-being was crucial to manipulating her.

"As good as could be, I suppose." She waved a hand at the window as she stood. "The weather reminds me of...things. No walk in the gardens today, either."

"I know *exactly* how you feel." I gestured to the sideboard. "Something to drink? Dinner will be up presently."

"So late already?" She sighed and touched the book she'd put on the chairside table. "I lost track of time, I guess."

"Well, a glass of wine, some good food, and a bit of conversation will perk you up." I motioned Binsh to attend. "Red or white?"

She sighed again and flicked a dismissive hand. "Red, I suppose."

"You seem downcast, Preel. Is something bothering you?"

Her dark eyes snapped up, then she looked away. "I...tend to dwell on things, sometimes, when I know my...talent is going to be invoked soon. It reminds me of what I am, I guess."

I accepted my wine, and Preel hers. "Really? I would think you'd be looking forward to a good night's sleep!" I sipped and kept my expression pleasant as her obsidian-dark eyes drilled into me. "I'm

186

serious, Preel. You answer a question and get twelve hours of uninterrupted rest. I can't *remember* the last time I had a decent night's sleep!"

Realization dawned on her features. "Of course. The scourge won't let you rest."

"I prefer to think that it *motivates* me." I joined her at the window, staring out at the rain. The book on the table was one of philosophy. "Gods, no *wonder* you're depressed reading this drivel!" I picked it up and opened it to a random entry. "'That which we gain too easily, we esteem too lightly.' Really? Ha! Written by someone who never had to risk life and limb to achieve anything, I'd wager."

"Probably true." Preel took a deep swallow from her glass and stared out the window.

I longed to simply command her to cheer up, but that was out of the question. "I could get some more cheerful books if you like. Bawdy tales of daring and romance? Tomes of arcane lore? Or how about a bard to perform for you? Elvish ballads, dwarvish drinking songs, Toki tea ceremonies? Whatever you like."

Preel looked at me sidelong. "You know what I would like?"

"You know I can't let you go, Preel."

"Not that. I know you can't."

"Then what?"

"Stop trying to cheer me up." She downed her wine and handed the empty glass to Binsh. "I'm your slave, Jhavika. I'll be civil and help you ask the right questions, but I was free for too long. It'll take me some time to...get used to this again."

I considered her request and realized that I'd been overdoing it. Preel knew my attempts to make her happy were self-motivated, even if she thought it was only to have someone not enslaved by the scourge to talk to.

"Very well, I'll ease up on the cheer. Truth be told, the weather depresses the shit out of me, too. I was hoping we could cheer each other up."

"Sometimes it helps me to concentrate on how my situation could be worse, not on how I can make myself happy. Ironically, that improves my mood." Preel accepted her refilled glass of wine from Binsh and raised it to me. "I just keep telling myself that things could be a thousand times worse. I'm not exactly *suffering* here, after all." She drank deeply.

"That's an interesting outlook." I sipped my wine more carefully.

"It's a slave's outlook." A pained smile tugged at the corners of Preel's mouth, and she raised her glass to me again. "And the wine helps."

"Ha! Wine *always* helps." We drank, and I changed the subject. "Do you mind if I ask you a question about your exercises?"

"Not at all."

"Where did you learn them?"

"Chen. My second master insisted I keep fit, so he brought in an instructor to teach me. Initially, he punished me if I didn't practice, but then I began to...enjoy it." She shrugged.

"You said they help you cope. How?" Not that I really cared, but it focused her attention on something positive.

"It's difficult to explain." She drank more wine and sighed. "It's like walking in your garden. The beauty there—the scents, colors, even the springy feel of the grass under your feet—occupies your mind so fully that you can't dwell on anything else. Yamshi synchronizes the mind and body. During the routine, every thought is directed to the placement of your hands and feet, the tilt of your hips, the angle of your spine, the positioning of fingers and toes, even your breathing as you move from one position to the next. There's no room in your mind for anything else. It's...peaceful."

"Huh." I was intrigued despite myself. "Would you mind if I watched you sometime?"

"No. It won't bother me." Preel glanced over as the door opened and servants entered with dinner. "Nala and Binsh watch me every morning. I think they're afraid I'm going to hurt myself."

"Good, it's their job." I gestured to the table, and we sat. "When do you exercise?"

"Usually after breakfast. I can send word."

"Perfect. Thank you, Preel." One more step toward honest friendship, and I did it without invoking the control of the scourge. A thrill of victory warmed my stomach.

She looked at me with a curious expression. "You're welcome."

We chatted a little during dinner, mostly about the discipline of yamshi and its various forms, and finally about her talent and the pending question. We refined the wording some more as we finished desert and sipped a sweet port. When we stood, she wobbled a little, but Nala was there to steady her.

"Too much to drink?" I asked.

"Not too much, but certainly enough." The truthsayer smiled then for the first time that evening, though the look in her eyes was wistful. "Enough to make me happy."

"Good."

"I should use the washroom before you ask me your question."

"Of course." I gestured, and Nala helped her.

I waved the attendants to clear the table and poured myself one more glass of the port. When Preel emerged from the bathroom, she wore a robe over a long silk nightgown, and her hair was down. She looked very different with her face framed by those onyx waves—younger, more fragile, like a young girl. *Like Anjice...*

I downed my port and cleared my throat, banishing the silly sentimentality. "Ready?"

"Yes." Preel accepted Nala's help getting into bed. When she was tucked in, she nodded and closed her eyes. "I'm ready."

"I'll see you in the morning, Preel. Rest well." I recalled the question we'd crafted, and stifled the worry that it wasn't the right one. I'd been through this a thousand times. It was time to move forward, not spin in circles. "Who in Haven should I enslave next with the scourge to most expediently facilitate my rise to Queen of Haven?"

Preel's eyes flung wide and rolled up. She arched back and drew a deep, ragged breath. "Tewhirke Kettleblack."

"What?" I didn't know that name. It wasn't on my list at all. "Who the hell is—"

"Your *ladyship*!" Nala's scream brought me around. "Please, no questions! You endanger Preel's life!"

I blinked at her, stunned by her outburst. Then I saw the stark terror in her eyes, and I knew she was right. My careless question could have killed my truthsayer.

"Gods and devils!" I stepped back from the bed, checking to make sure Preel was still breathing. The blankets rose and fell in a steady cadence. She was safe.

"See to her wellbeing." I strode out, leaving Nala and Binsh to care for their charge, silently thanking Odea that I'd ordered them to protect her.

Back in my office, I summoned Ty-lee and sent another servant after a pot of blackbrew. When both arrived, I had a list of orders already prepared.

"I need information on someone named Tewhirke Kettleblack. Probably a gnome, from the name, but all I know for certain is that they live here in Haven. I want to know everything you can find out about this person by morning. This is priority one, Ty-lee."

"They shouldn't be hard to find, your ladyship. I'll get right on it!"

"Good. Go!" I waved him out and sipped my blackbrew. I had my answer, but it wasn't what I'd expected. I had no idea who this person was or why they were vital to my plans, but Preel couldn't be wrong.

There was only one thing I knew for certain: I'd know who this person was by morning.

Chapter Twenty Two
The Double-Edged Sword

There is no such thing as a simple question.
The Lessons of Quen Lau Ush

From the journal of Preel Longbright –
Yes, I am a slave. Yes, the only thing I truly cared about has
been torn from me. But I'm not without weapons in this fight.
My talent is not my only strength. Manipulating Jhavika into
asking questions that limit my usefulness is dangerous, but I
know my limitations better than she.

As I swam up from the depths of slumber, I recalled my answer
and wondered, *Who the hell is Tewhirke Kettleblack?*
It wasn't the answer I'd hoped for.
If I had said "Preel Longbright," it would have confirmed that I
wasn't already under the scourge's enchantment. That I wasn't the
answer, however, didn't tell me anything; I was already Jhavika's slave
whether I'd been enchanted or not. The name I'd given Jhavika was
unknown to me. *Not one of the council members, anyway.* I wondered if
Jhavika had found and enslaved this person yet, and what they could
do to further her conquest.

I blinked my eyes open to darkness. It was early, pre-dawn. Not even twelve hours had passed; evidently this hadn't been a very taxing question.

I considered lying in bed a little longer, but my bladder insisted I get up. As I pulled the blankets aside and rolled up, a dull ache behind my eyes blossomed into a raging headache. *Too much wine.* I rubbed my eyes and massaged my temples, trying to scour away the pain.

"Preel? Are you all right?"

I started and muttered a curse. "Fine, Binsh. Just a headache. Can you light the—"

White light blossomed from the wall-mounted glow crystal beside the door. I winced and shaded my eyes from the glare that seemed intent on drilling into my eye sockets. Binsh was beside the bed in a flash with my robe, apologizing for the light.

"Never mind. I'll survive." He guided me to the bathroom and left me alone, thank the gods. After relieving myself and washing up, I considered going right back to bed, but my back ached already and my stomach growled. I'd slept long enough.

"Breakfast, Preel?" Binsh asked as I stepped into the sitting room. "It's early, but cook can have something up in about half an hour."

"Yes, please. And a kettle of warm water to wash up with." I went to my bedroom to find Nala laying out clothes, her hair disheveled and eyes bleary. I immediately felt guilty for waking them up early. "You don't have to do that, Nala."

She gave me a tired smile. "I *do*, Preel. Lady Keshmir ordered me to help you be comfortable any way I can."

"Nala, *please*." I put a hand on her shoulder. "I'm a slave. I know what servitude is. I'm used to doing these things myself. You doing everything for me doesn't make me comfortable, it makes me *uncomfortable*. Please, stop." I forgave myself the lie. In truth, Hemp usually insisted on doing all those little chores, but then, he was paid for his work. He wasn't a slave.

Nala froze, staring at me. "I... There must be *something* I can do to help you."

I rubbed my aching head and chuckled. "There is. Next time I start to drink too much wine, tell me to stop. My head is killing me."

Her smile flashed white. "I *will*, but I know how to help your headache, too."

"Oh?"

"Yes. Drink water and let me massage your pressure points."

More pampering... "I don't feel like a massage right now, Nala. Maybe after my exercises."

"No, not like that." She gently touched my temples, my scalp, and the nape of my neck. "These spots only. You can sit at the table."

She did have deft fingers, and if she could alleviate my headache... "Very well."

Nala beamed with such pleasure that I felt a little ill. The scourge was forcing her to want this, to enjoy it. To renege would be punishment she didn't deserve. So I sat at the table and let her press into those spots, her fingers working in tiny circles, coaxing the small muscles into passivity. At first, it just hurt, but my muscles began to respond in moments. My ears popped, and the pressure behind my forehead began to ease. I closed my eyes and breathed with each minute release, concentrating on relaxing, letting her do her work.

"Where does a *dancer* learn such techniques?" I asked.

"Binsh and I have been taught many skills in the years since we were branded," she said. "In Fornice, then Toki, and finally Chen. I bless the day we were sold to Lady Keshmir."

"You do?" I found that hard to believe.

"Yes." She didn't elaborate.

"But you said she used the scourge on you. How can you..."

"Preel, please relax. You're tensing." Her fingers pressed into my temples, massaging away the pain. "I'll tell you, though I don't know if you'll understand."

I took a deep breath and let it out, willing my tension away. "Tell me."

"The scourge's power is unique. Though being a slave is...unpleasant in the broader sense, the way Lady Keshmir employs the magic of the scourge is a mercy."

"You're right. I don't understand."

"If she commands me to enjoy my work, I do. If she tells me I will feel physical pleasure from serving her, or *you*, I do. I love to dance, but I've not known absolute rapture from performing until she commanded me to. It's..." Her fingers paused for a moment before resuming their soothing movements. "...the most fulfilling thing I've ever experienced."

"She can actually command what you *feel?* Dictate your emotions?" I recalled Kevril's account of the night he was commanded to please Jhavika's guests, to enjoy it, to *want* it, and shivered.

"Yes. It's discomforting at first, but if you simply embrace it..." Nala sighed as pressed her thumbs into the tiny muscles at the base of my skull to ease the tension across my scalp. "It's quite wonderful."

I tried to imagine such a rapturous enslavement, and failed. It seemed abhorrent to me, not only slavery of the body, but of the mind as well. All the times I'd been abused, violated, punished for the simplest infraction, I had always told myself that pain was only of the body, that my mind was my own. With Jhavika, that wasn't true. She could turn pain into pleasure or pleasure into pain, force her slaves to crave debasement or long for nothing but to serve her every whim.

The door opened, and the aromas of breakfast filled the room, interrupting my disturbing thoughts. My mouth watered, and I realized that my headache was much diminished. As the servants started to lay out a delicate omelet, fried peppers and potatoes, toast, juice, and steaming blackbrew, I patted Nala's hand and thanked her. Binsh came in bearing a steaming kettle as if on cue.

What Nala's ministrations had begun, a quick wash of face and hands with warm water and a fine meal finished. When I pushed my plate away, the last remnants of my hangover had been banished.

I stood from the table and stretched. The muscles of my back and legs protested; I needed exercise. The sky outside had just begun to lighten, and I felt a malicious little twist in my gut.

"Binsh, I'm going to exercise. Jhavika said she wanted to observe."

"Yes. I'll inform her ladyship at once." He nodded and hurried out.

I changed into my simple pantaloons and halter combination, and started my stretches in earnest. The servants had cleared the floor for me, even rolling up the sumptuous rug for surer footing. After learning to do my yamshi routine in the confines of Kevril's cabin, even chained to his bunk before he freed me, so much space was a luxury. I finished my stretches, but Jhavika had not yet arrived.

Well, I wasn't going to wait for her.

Facing the window, I placed my feet, and lifted my arms into the first position, *greeting the sun.* When I was about ten postures into the sequence, my mind and body settled into the familiar synergy, the door opened, and Jhavika entered.

"You're up early this morning," she said spritely.

I paused, holding my current pose, *water flows over stones*, and glanced at her. She looked fresh and awake, eyes bright, dressed in her usual comfortable blouse, trousers, and boots, the scourge at her hip as always. Servants behind her carried a blackbrew service. She settled into one of the comfortable chairs and accepted a steaming cup from her footman.

"Yes." I moved into the next position. "I can begin the routine again if you want to see the start."

"No. Just continue as you normally would. I'll observe, and we'll talk after."

I nodded and continued, easily slipping back into the meditative cadence. Yamshi isn't performance art, like dance, but it's pleasing to watch. Kevril used to sit on his bunk while I exercised, watching me. In fact, his observations that the postures resembled martial stances had stimulated my research into the discipline. I wondered if Jhavika would make the same connection.

I caught her reflection in the window, sitting comfortably, sipping her cup of blackbrew, watching my every move. I couldn't help but wonder at her motives here. Was this just Jhavika being solicitous, or did she think she could make me uncomfortable as some subtle manipulation?

I finished the first routine in less than a quarter hour, barely breaking a sweat, and accepted a glass of water from Nala.

"That was very interesting." Jhavika stood and regarded me with an expression that might have been amusement or appreciation. "And you do this every day?"

"I try to." I handed the glass back to Nala. "I generally do more than one sequence. If you'd like to talk, I can continue later."

"No, I don't want to interrupt your usual practice. I'd like to ask you about your answer from last night, but there's no rush."

"You must be busy. I don't want to—"

"No, please." Jhavika waved to the leaden sky out the window. "With this weather, I won't get my usual walk in the gardens. This will be my guilty pleasure for today, my indulgence."

"Watching *me* exercise?" I stifled a sardonic laugh and an urge to tell her she needed to get out more.

"Yes. It's...soothing, graceful." She shrugged. "If you don't mind."

She seemed sincere. "I don't mind. The next routine takes about twenty minutes."

"Then I'll relax and watch." Jhavika sat back down and accepted another cup of blackbrew from her footman.

Still suspicious of her motives, I positioned myself to be able to watch her watching me, and started my second routine. The basic routine, *ton-chi,* is simple, a warm-up to prepare the muscles for the more challenging sequences. I chose *gie-wa,* a routine that would truly press me. It begins the same as *ton-chi,* but quickly diverges into a series of poses that twist the spine and limbs into demanding contortions. It requires a great deal of concentration, which is why I find it soothing. However, while I'd never been bothered by Kevril watching me, Jhavika's scrutiny felt like something cold crawling up my spine. When

I assumed the pose *serpent climbs tree*, I caught Jhavika's look of open-mouthed awe and nearly lost my balance.

She wasn't feigning interest. This was genuine.

I continued, but my mind wandered. A slave has few weapons, and I'd use any I could put my hands on. If Jhavika truly was interested in yamshi, maybe I could use that to manipulate her. If she longed for genuine interaction with someone not enslaved by the scourge, giving her that might give *me* an edge. If I could teach her yamshi, the interaction would strengthen the bond between us. It might also allow me to get close enough to kill her.

I put the thought aside long enough to finish the routine. Making a blunder would be disastrous at this point. With the last pose—my breathing deep and regular, my muscles warm, my mind at peace—I considered the implications of Jhavika's interest. I had another weapon.

"That was *amazing*, Preel!" She stood again with a look of open admiration. "Truly beautiful."

"Thank you," I accepted another glass of cool water from Nala and drank it down, quenching the heat that had risen to my face.

"And it obviously keeps you fit." Jhavika looked me up and down. "Do you know how long you've been doing these exercises?"

I shrugged, appreciating the careful wording of her question. "Ten years, perhaps." I traded the empty glass for a towel. Binsh and another servant were moving the table near the windows and draping it with cushions and towels for my massage. "But it helps my mind as much as keeps me fit. It's a calming ritual."

"So you said." She looked introspective, perhaps intrigued.

I seized the opening. "I could teach you, if you wish."

Surprise flashed across Jhavika's face for a moment, then she waved me to the table. "I may take you up on that offer, Preel, but go ahead with your massage. You don't want to catch a chill." She turned away, accepting yet another cup of blackbrew from her footman. "We can talk while Nala and Binsh work."

"All right." It wasn't like she hadn't seen me unclothed before, but I turned away anyway just to be polite; I didn't want her to think I was being petulant again. Nala even draped a robe over my shoulders while I peeled out of my sweat-damped clothes. I lay on the table, my face pillowed on a cushion, and Nala placed a towel over my backside, then applied a light, fragrant oil to my skin. Her strong hands began to knead my warm muscles, reducing every tense fiber to flaccid bliss. I would have preferred to simply enjoy the sensation, but Jhavika had other ideas. "You want to talk about my answer to your question?"

"Yes. The answer surprised me. I'd never heard of Tewhirke Kettleblack before, but my people made some inquiries overnight. She's a gnomish alchemist here in Haven."

"An alchemist?" I immediately thought of Brekka.

"Yes. I already have my own, and I wondered if you might have any idea why this particular alchemist might be so important."

"None, unless she can mix up a potion that'll release you from the scourge."

"I thought you might say that. You said Kevril broke the scourge's enchantment with a potion."

"Well, it was an oil, actually. He said the alchemist told him it would draw the poison of the scourge from his blood."

"Poison?" She sounded startled.

"That's what she told him, yes." I turned my head to look at her. "If you want to know what this alchemist can do for you, I can help you craft a question to find out. Unless you've already enslaved her?"

Jhavika frowned. "Not yet. I don't like to act without a precise plan. I've got people asking questions, so I'll know more by this afternoon."

"Why are you being so cautious? Why not just walk into her shop and lash her with the scourge? Then you can ask her what she can do for you."

Her frown morphed into a thin smile. "Because caution is key, Preel. I'm not so powerful yet that I can use the scourge openly. If word got out that I've got an army enthralled by magic, there would be repercussions."

So much for provoking her into rash action, I thought. "Well, if you want to ask me what this gnome can specifically do to advance your position here in Haven, then you'll know, but you can't ask for another three days."

Jhavika nodded and began to pace. "Yes, I know, but there's another question I might need to ask first. I'll find out as much as I can about this alchemist, then perhaps offer her gainful employment."

"Whatever you like." I rolled back and let the sensation of the massage sooth me.

"And about your offer..."

"Offer?" I looked back at Jhavika, hiding my surge of hope with a look of puzzlement. "What offer?"

"To teach me yamshi."

"Oh, yes."

"Would tomorrow morning be too soon to begin?"

"Not at all." I tried to sound unconcerned, but couldn't help wondering if I might be given the opportunity I'd fantasized about. Her guards had stopped standing at her shoulders constantly when she visited me, and they certainly couldn't flank her while we exercised. I put my head back down. "Wear something comfortable, nothing restricting. Those pants are too tight."

"All right. What time?"

"I generally begin right after breakfast, but whenever you like is fine."

"Just send Binsh to fetch me." I heard her turn away, then stop. "Thank you, Preel."

I looked up again, my brow furrowed. "For what?"

"For the offer to teach me." She looked a little embarrassed. "It...means a lot coming from...someone who's not under my control."

"Oh." I searched for some hint of slyness in her expression, but saw only sincerity. "Sure."

A tiny smile flicked across Jhavika's face, and she left the room.

I settled back down and let Nala and Binsh knead my muscles into warm passivity while my mind circled my conversation with Jhavika like a shark scenting blood. The question at the core of my mental maelstrom was what opportunity I might be afforded while teaching yamshi to Jhavika.

Could I strangle her with the scourge before her guards cut me down? If they'd been ordered never to hurt me, that might give me an edge. If I killed her and lashed them with the scourge, that would make me its—and their—master, but that was a path straight to the Nine Hells.

I'd rather die than become a monster.

Chapter Twenty Three
Unwelcome Scrutiny

A warrior unwitting of his enemy's spies is doomed.
The Lessons of Quen Lau Ush

From the diary of Kevril Longbright –
One of the hardest lessons I had to learn when I took command of *Scourge* was to measure risks versus benefits. Risking human lives for gold seems heartless, but I'm not forcing any of my crew to leap into danger. They do it willingly. Some, in fact, love the thrill of danger so much it's hard to restrain them. I wish sometimes that I did.

With a welcome break in the rain, I took the opportunity to get some needed exercise and sword practice. My crew sparred regularly, but when the captain came on deck with a blunted cutlass in hand, everyone else gave way. I chose Wix for my practice today, not because I didn't think Miko was up to a bout—she was healing quickly and practiced with the midshipmen daily—but because I needed some mayhem to release my pent-up nerves. Wix was more than willing to oblige.

"Any particular flavor of pain you interested in today, sir?" He grinned and pulled a pair of bolt pins from the rail for simulated daggers.

"This party's going to be crowded with council members and their escorts. If Jhavika gets the chance to yell for help, all Nine Hells are going to break loose." I doffed my jacket and pulled a bolt pin for my off-hand. "She's got slaves on the Council, and there'll probably be a few more in the room, too. I could be facing several blades before the job's done. Why don't you have a couple of your mates join in?"

"Never needed any help kickin' yer arse alone before, sir, but it's yer skin." Wix called for Tansy and Foist to draw bolt pins.

"And I've never tried to assassinate a council member in the middle of a party, either." I stretched my shoulders and twisted my back. "Just don't break any bones."

"There ya go makin' rules again, sir." He hawked and spat over the rail. "Takes all the fun out of a knife fight, it does."

I glared at him and flourished my practice sword. "*So* sorry to spoil your fun."

"Not yet, you ain't, sir." The bosun grinned evilly and advanced on me. "But you will be."

I needed the practice, and Wix and his mates pressed me hard. He marked me half a dozen times, twice hard enough to bruise, quipping "Dead," each time. I barely marked Wix once, not a killing strike, but enough to surprise him.

I grinned and quipped, "Wounded."

Wix just laughed. "Nah, sir, just enough ta piss me off."

I took some solace in the fact that neither Tansy nor Foist managed to touch me once, even when they took to standing well out of my reach and flinging bolt pins at my head.

"On deck there! Launch is comin' back from shore!"

I disengaged and turned to look.

Wix swore and rapped me hard in the stomach with a bolt pin. "Dead again!"

"Gods damn it, Wix! I disengaged!" I rubbed the sore spot and glared at him.

"Aye, and I stepped up and cut yer liver out. You think one of them fancy fooks at this party'll give you pause if you ask for it?"

"Good point. Now, stand down. I want to talk to Bert when she comes aboard."

"Aye, sir." Wix touched his forehead with one of his bolt pins and put them away, nodding for Tansy and Foist to do the same.

I put up my bolt pin, handed the practice sword over to a crewman, and climbed the steps to the quarterdeck, trying not to wince at my battered ribs. Quiff was on watch and handed me a spyglass before I even asked for it. There might be hope for the lad yet.

I focused the glass on the launch, but Bert was facing aft so I couldn't learn anything from her expression. *Patience...* A hundred sea engagements should have taught me how to remain calm in situations like this, but while I could sip tea and take a nap during a chase at sea, in port I tended to fret. Forcing down my nervousness, I handed the glass back to Quiff. He had the good sense to remain silent.

I paced.

"Mister Rauley, bring the launch alongside," Quiff finally ordered.

I descended to the middle deck and stood out of the way until Bert clambered aboard. She barely glanced at me, but her face was pinched. I opened my mouth to ask her how her meeting with the alchemist went, but she cut me off.

"Don't, sir! Not on deck." She bustled past me, headed for the sterncastle. "Mayhap we got eyes on us."

"Bugger." I understood immediately and feigned interest in the launch. She'd spotted someone watching *Scourge*, and that meant Jhavika. If I took interest in Bert every time she came back from shore, someone might notice. I inspected some of the cargo being brought aboard and took my time ambling aft. Once inside, however, my semblance of boredom shattered. I hustled to the galley to find my cook standing at her chopping block reducing cheese and hard sausage into slices with a cleaver. She looked up when I came in and I could see on her face that we had a problem.

"Tell me," I said without preamble.

"Ain't as bad as all that, sir, but we gotta be more careful." She started arranging the morsels on a platter with the deft precision of a card sharp. "You should thank Tewhirke Kettleblack if you ever get the chance. She's got more friends lookin' out for her than you got hairs on yer head. One of 'em told her there's been all kinda folks askin' questions about her. She's a cautious one, she is."

"Jhavika." I hissed her name like a curse.

"Aye, and she's bold as brass about it. Sent Tewhirke a fancy note this very afternoon askin' if she'd come talk about workin' for her. Offered her coin just to come visit whether she said yay or nay."

"It's a trap! If she walks into Jhavika's estate, she'll never walk out again, and we're sunk. We've got to warn her!"

"Oh, she's warned all right." Bert cleaned and racked her cleaver and grinned at me. "I told her about the scourge."

"You..." I swallowed hard. That was dangerous, but I had to admit, it would put genuine fear into the gnome. "What did she say?"

"Dunno. Most of it was in gnomish, but it sounded like curses. She ain't too happy with us, neither, but she'll stick to our deal." Bert drew a pot of ale from a keg, picked up the platter and bustled past me. "What's more worrisome is how in hell Jhavika figured out we asked Tewhirke to brew up a potion for us. Can't believe she's got spies followin' *me*."

"She might have." I followed her to the wardroom where she put the platter and ale down. "She's got spies all over the city. She could have everyone coming or going from the ship followed."

"Seems a waste of time, and she ain't followed Boxley or Quibly, or we'd be up to our arses in trouble by now."

Of course, Jhavika *did* have a truthsayer... *What the hell kind of question would she have asked to get Tewhirke Kettleblack's name?* I had no idea, but it reminded me that we were working blind here. I'd gotten so accustomed to asking questions of Preel that I'd gotten lazy.

Bert struck the iron triangle hanging from the overhead with the back of a butter knife three times, the traditional summons for the midshipmen and warrant officers to afternoon nibbles. I heard the rumble of footsteps.

My stomach growled. I traditionally took my nibble in my cabin or on deck, though not recently. I never thought I'd admit it, but I missed my steward a lot. Hemp had been released from his hammock, but remained confined to the guest cabin under guard. As long as nobody mentioned Jhavika in his presence, he was fine. He'd even been mending and polishing my things to keep busy, but without access to my cabin, he couldn't tidy, sweep, scrub, and generally pamper me to his heart's content. I scratched my unshaven face and cursed Jhavika under my breath.

As I nicked a slice of cheese and a biscuit, Kivan, Boxley, Quibly, Rauley, and Wix rumbled into the wardroom, leaving barely enough room for Bert and myself.

"I'll go relieve Quiff," I told Bert around the cheese and biscuit. "I'm still worried about Tewhirke. I'd like to make sure she's safe." The gnome was the linchpin to our entire plan.

"Oh, no worries there, sir." Bert grinned as she poured ale into cups for my ravenous crew. "She's survived Haven long enough to learn how to defend herself."

"I thought you said she was old."

"Oh, aye, she's old and mean as a dragon with a toothache. Besides, her dead husband used to smith locks." She winked at me. "Ain't nobody gettin' into her shop without a pot of acid on their head."

"Trapped?" Gnomes loved traps like dwarves love ale.

"Aye, and a sign right above her door in plain speak and pictures for those who can't read to tell everybody so."

"Well, we picked the right alchemist, then."

"That we did, sir."

I went up on deck and relieved my midshipman, who hurried below to snag his share of the nibbles. My shirt was damp under my jacket, clammy against my skin. Hemp would have never let me put on a clean jacket over a sweaty shirt. Damn me, but I missed him. I missed Preel more. My bed seemed to have suddenly gotten too large, and I often woke reaching for her. I stared ashore and wondered if she might be looking down from a window of Jhavika's estate.

The rain started again, the first sheets slashing across the bay, battering the rippled surface to flat satin. I flipped up my collar, pulled my hat down low, and watched the deluge advance. Crew scrambled to secure hatches, but I just stood there admiring the coming squall, the sound of the rain on the water like ripping cloth, each drop forming a tiny bubble that instantly popped with a flashing sparkle, a diamond for an instant in time.

The dove that laid diamond eggs...

Tansy ran up the steps to the quarterdeck with a weather cloak in hand. "Best batten down, sir."

"Thank you." I took the cloak and pulled it on just as the rain hit. I squinted up the hill toward Jhavika's estate again, but I couldn't see anything through the downpour.

Chapter Twenty Four
A Touch of Solace

Love and war have much in common.
The Lessons of Quen Lau Ush

From the journal of Jhavika Keshmir –
I never thought I would be so moved by another's touch, and
I've been touched by some of the deftest hands in the world.
Was it her willingness that thrilled me so, or my need for
honest companionship? I refuse to let my suspicions spoil this
new sensation.

When Binsh came to fetch me for my first yamshi session with
Preel, I considered canceling. I was in a foul mood and feared I
wouldn't have the patience to deal with her. My invitation to Tewhirke
Kettleblack had been answered by a polite "Bugger off!" In response,
I'd sent my nokitu on a nighttime mission to break into the gnome's
abode and abduct her. Even knowing the place was trapped, they'd
fallen prey to Kettleblack's defenses. I now had only six nokitu instead
of the eight I'd had yesterday, and the alchemist remained ensconced.

And still, I didn't know why I needed the damned gnome in the
first place.

I opened my mouth to tell Binsh to give Preel my regrets, but then recalled what she'd said about her exercises. The routines helped her cope, settled her mind, gave her peace. The creak of leather reached my ears, and I realized I was squeezing the scourge so hard my knuckles ached. Right now, I needed peace of mind more than anything.

"I'll be right along. I've got to change."

"Yes, your ladyship." Binsh bowed and hurried off.

I went to my chambers and picked out a pair of drawstring pajamas with matching top that I rarely wore. The silk felt good, and they were baggy enough to let me move freely. The eyes of the guards stationed at Preel's door widened at my attire, but they didn't say anything. They obviously didn't feel like cutting out their own tongues today.

"Come in with me and stand by the door," I told them.

They followed me in and took their stations.

Preel was stretching, but looked up when I entered. One eyebrow twitched. "I wondered if you'd changed your mind."

"I almost did." I stopped a long stride from her and folded my arms. "I'll warn you up front, I'm in a mood this morning."

"Then you need this more than I do." She motioned me to stand beside her. "Here, just a few light stretches first. Don't push hard, just enough to loosen up."

The stretching didn't help my mood at all. My flexibility came nowhere near matching hers. I rarely exercised, other than some light sparring to keep my sword arm in trim. Preel assured me that it didn't matter. The basic yamshi routine wouldn't push my limits.

"The first pose is called *greeting the sun*, but first you have to learn how to stand. Put your feet shoulder width apart, your knees slightly bent, hips rotated to neutral, spine straight, shoulders relaxed." She faced me and assumed the stance as she spoke.

I refrained from telling her that I'd been standing my entire life, and tried to mirror her posture.

"Um..." Preel pursed her lips. "You're too stiff, and your hips are tilted." She stepped beside me and examined me in profile. "Your back is swayed."

I stifled the urge to snap back at her. If I was going to convince Preel that I trusted her, wanted her true friendship, then I had to expect her criticisms. I tried to straighten my posture.

Preel made a noncommittal sound and shook her head. "Your back's still swayed. Relax, rotate your hips, and pull your stomach in. Don't bend your knees so much. Distribute your weight evenly between the heel and ball of your foot. Concentrate on the position; put your mind in your feet, your knees, your hips, your back. Feel for the balance. Breathe from your stomach, not your chest."

I tried, but it didn't come easily—it took five minutes of Preel's criticisms before she was satisfied with my stance—and it felt anything but comfortable. "And this is supposed to be *relaxing*?"

Preel stepped back. "Okay, tell me this. What have you been thinking about for the last few minutes?"

I flicked a glare at her. "How to *stand* to your satisfaction."

"Precisely. And all the things that put you in a *mood*? Were you thinking about those?"

"No." I took a breath and let it out. "Okay. I get it." I wondered again at my motives for asking her to teach me this exercise. I'd thought of it as a way to show her my sincerity, take an interest in her interests, another subtle step in her conditioning. Maybe it was the scourge urging me to manipulate her, to own her, but maybe I *did* need this. "Continue, please."

"Good." She resumed her position in front of me. "So, elbows slightly bent, raise your arms slowly..."

As Preel assumed the first pose, *greeting the sun*, I followed, trying to mirror her every move. Her commentary continued into the second pose, and I adjusted as she directed, rotating the toe of my right foot, the heel of my left, and sweeping my arms into a cupping motion as she did. *Receive the morning.* It wasn't nearly as easy as she made it look. I concentrated on every placement, every nuance, every position of my feet, toes, knees, hips, spine, shoulders, arms, hands, and fingers. It was exhausting, but my mind could do nothing but focus on the progression of positions.

After only ten postures, my knees shook and sweat beaded on my stomach and back. The silk pajamas didn't breathe at all, and the fabric stuck to my skin. Preel looked as fresh as a daisy, damn her.

"Stop and relax." My truthsayer looked at me with a subtly surprised expression. "You're doing well!"

"I feel like a pig on ice," I admitted.

Preel smiled briefly, one of the few I'd seen from her since her abduction. "Let's go through it again from the beginning. Assume the first posture and just breathe. Close your eyes. Feel the balance."

I tried. It seemed easier this time, less strained. Then her hand touched my stomach and I jerked, snapping open my eyes and glaring at her.

"Sorry. I didn't mean to startle you." Her mouth quirked into an impish smile. Two in one day—a record.

She was enjoying this. I didn't know whether to feel angry or triumphant. I wasn't used to people touching me without commanding them to. "Just warn me next time."

"Okay. I'm going to touch you again. Now, just relax and breathe here." Preel put her hand on my stomach again, her other settling on my lower back. "Rotate your hips, and feel your tummy push against my palm as you inhale. Concentrate. Feel the air come in, and imagine your stress leaving with each exhalation."

I did, though it was difficult to relax with her hands on me. Her touch felt dangerous, electrifying, new. Why would the touch of someone not under my absolute control be so thrilling? It wasn't like it had never happened before. Memories of my childhood flashed into my mind again: Anjice and me cuddling for warmth, giggling at boys as we walked arm in arm, braiding each other's hair... Gods, how I missed the simple touch of an honest hand, a warm embrace, a thoughtful word. I breathed deep, pushing my tummy against her palm, straightening my spine as her other hand pressed forward. I exhaled, imagining all my stress leaving me with the expelled air. Balance settled into my bones, my shoulders dropping slightly. I breathed again and let the world disappear.

Yes...I need this. Some dark corner of my mind fought back. *Or it is the scourge that needs this?* I banished the thought with another breath, let the suspicion and confusion flow out of me. *Just...be...*

"Good. Now..." Preel stepped behind me, her fingers guiding my arms, "...*greet the sun.*"

I lifted my arms, yielding to the gentle pressure of her hands. Preel's breath brushed my neck like a soft whisper, her body a warm comfort at my back. Another flash of memory: Anjice spooning at my back in our narrow bed, her breath warm, her arm draped over me, a deep feeling of comfort, safety, home. *An honest touch, not compelled by magic. Who would have thought...*

"Elbows slightly bent, thumbs up, palms cupped. Good. Hold that for three breaths... Now, slowly, rotate heel and toe, turn one quarter, and move your arms into *receive the morning.*"

I rotated the ball of my right foot and the heel of my left outward, turning my hips and bringing my arms down into the cupping posture.

"Very good. Concentrate on breathing through the changes." Preel's hands moved to my hips, adjusting my rotation slightly. "Keep your posture aligned with the rotation of your feet."

I felt a tug at my hip, the poke of the metal hook looped over the drawstring of my pajamas. *The scourge!*

I jerked away from Preel, snapping around, my hand on the weapon. "What the *hell* are you doing?" My breath came in ragged gasps, my knuckles cracking with my iron grip on the whip's haft.

Preel looked terrified, as well she should, but there was confusion mixed with her fear. "What do you mean? I'm teaching you yamshi."

"You tried to take the scourge from me!"

"*What?*" Her eyes flicked down to my hip, then back up, wide with shock. "I didn't even realize it was *there*, Jhavika. I barely brushed the thing. And please be careful with your questions unless you don't want a truthsayer any longer."

The reminder took me aback. I hadn't even realized I'd asked her a question. I straightened, but kept my hand on the scourge. My guards had taken a step from their positions, hands on their weapons, but I waved them back. Had I been mistaken? Was this just paranoia, a simple accident, or had Preel really tried to take the scourge? There was only one way to be sure it would never happen again.

"Never touch the scourge again, Preel."

Her expression melted from shock and fear to derision. "Then don't wear the damned thing when we're exercising. Put it aside." She flicked a hand at the nearby table. "Or does it have such control over you that you must wear it all the time?"

"I can put it down whenever I like."

"Then *do*." Preel put her hands on her hips and gave me a look of sheer disgust. "I don't want to risk my life because *you're* paranoid about someone stealing your precious scourge."

Gritting my teeth, I took four strides to the table and slammed the scourge down onto it. Whirling away, despising the wrenching feeling of its loss as I strode back to her. "Now, are we going to do this, or are you going to be a pain in my ass again?"

Preel's eyebrows rose, and she smiled. "Honestly, I didn't think you *could* put it down. I was wondering if you bathed with it."

"I wear it out of habit, not necessity, Preel." I tried to take up the first pose again, breathe away my singing nerves. It had been a simple accident and wouldn't—couldn't—happen again. "Besides, it's a *ridiculously* powerful magical artifact. Leaving it lying around would just be foolish."

"Well, I understand that." Preel sighed and squinted at my posture. "You're tilting your hips again."

"Am not." I thrust my hips forward just to prove it. "There. Better?"

"Yes." She strolled over and stood behind me again. "Now, don't be startled. I'm going to guide your posture with my hands. Breathe and *greet the sun*."

I did, and the comforting warmth of her hands settled on my hips. I relaxed into the pose, my shoulders down, my spine straight, breathing. *Peace...*

"Good. Hold, breathe, and now, turn and *receive the morning.*"

I proceeded through the first ten postures slowly and methodically, concentrating and accommodating Preel's subtle adjustments, basking in the relaxing warmth of her touch as we proceeded through the moves. She wasn't doing this under compulsion, but because she wanted to. In wondering why, I came to a simple realization; Preel was as lonely as I when it came to honest companionship. She needed this as much as I did.

I finished the ten moves feeling less taxed than the first time, and Preel complimented me.

"Very good. You take to it quickly. It'll get easier with practice."

"Thank you." I breathed deep and accepted a glass of water from Nala. "Can we do more?"

"Of course." Preel handed her own glass back to Binsh and gestured. "Let's start with *water flows over stones*, and see if we can get in the next ten postures."

I'd watched her yesterday, but hadn't counted the poses. "How many are there in the whole routine?"

"One hundred four, but it's best to learn a few at a time." She assumed the pose, and I mirrored her. "Just remember to breathe, concentrate, and follow me."

I gave her a warm smile and a nod. *A slave commanding her master, how bizarre.*

"Now, settle your weight on your back leg and lift your front foot with your toe pointed. Now, raise your arms back, wrists curved forward, fingers pointed. This is *swans retreat from serpent.*"

I tried to emulate her, wobbling on my back leg. Preel waited patiently until I settled into the stance. I felt silly, but steady.

"Very good, now lower your foot to the side, rotate to your right as you did before, and slowly lunge out over your front foot, arms extended like this." She did it, and I tried to follow. "*Tiger in hiding.*"

I teetered for a moment, then settled into the posture.

Preel took me through the ten new poses, then we repeated them with her behind me, guiding my arms, legs, hips, and spine. Her touch felt more natural this time, still new, but comforting instead of dangerous. When we were finished, she took me through the whole twenty poses once again, this time side by side.

When we were finished, I was dripping sweat under my pajamas, and Prell's dusky skin shone like freshly oiled teak. She stood straight and smiled at me, clasping her hands with index fingers pointed, and bowed.

"What was that for?"

"For a job well done." Preel took a glass of water from Binsh, and I took one from Nala. "You did well. How do you feel?"

"Good." Surprisingly, it was true. My foul mood was gone, and my muscles felt languid and warm. "Thank you, Preel. Truly, I feel better."

"You're welcome. I think that's all you should do today. More and you'll be too fatigued to learn properly."

"What about you? Are you going to do more?"

"Yes." She handed her glass back to Binsh. "Teaching isn't the same as doing. I need to focus on myself, not you. You understand, don't you?"

"Of course." I wanted to stay and watch her, but I needed a bath, and knew my sweaty silks would chill into a clammy mess before she was done. "I'll just go then." I picked up the scourge and started for the door, but paused there to look back. "If it's not raining this afternoon, maybe you'd like a walk through the gardens?"

"If you have the time, thank you."

"Even if I'm busy, I can arrange an escort for you." I smiled and opened the door. "Enjoy yourself, Preel. I just want you to be happy."

I glanced back past the guards to find a curious look of puzzlement on the truthsayer's features. "Thank you."

Chapter Twenty Five
The Hawk and the Dove

Trust and friendship are not necessarily analogous.
The Lessons of Quen Lau Ush

From the journal of Preel Longbright –
Keeping my hatred of Jhavika hidden has become
challenging. As she demands more from me—civility,
warmth, companionship—I feel like I'm being slowly driven
insane. She's so sincere, so obviously lonely. How can this be
a lie?

The idea of murdering Jhavika was a non-starter. She was simply
too wary, too paranoid, too much the coiled dragon waiting to strike.
Her response when I barely touched the scourge, just to see if I could,
frightened me. She was like two people: the dragon and the woman. I
dared not antagonize the former, and manipulating the latter with my
new strategy of civility and kindness was stretching my nerves to the
breaking point.

Every time I touched her, I had to suppress the urge to wrap my
arms around her throat and twist.

I stretched slowly as I waited for Jhavika's arrival for our second yamshi session, and recalled our first. Jhavika had given me three commands that I could discern: never touch the scourge again, warn her the next time I touched her, and enjoy myself. The first, well, I'd had no other opportunity to touch the scourge, but that might be one way to find out if she'd already used it on me. I resolved to try to touch it if I had the chance. The second, I had done, but more out of self-preservation than any compulsion. The third...

After Jhavika had gone, I went through two full sessions of yamshi, the basic and the more advanced *teh-wa* sequence, then had a full body massage from my attendants, and a warm bath with Nala washing my hair. I'd sat on the divan reading a book while she brushed it dry and braided it, and ate a light lunch. Later, when the sun peeked out from between the clouds, I walked through Jhavika's delightful gardens, my feet wet in the damp grass, the air full of the scent of blossoms. I spent the rest of the afternoon reading, enjoyed a delicious dinner, then watched Nala and Binsh perform a complex and graceful dance routine.

I *had* enjoyed the day, but not out of any compulsion. How could I not, with all these amenities at my fingertips? A gilded cage, indeed.

The door opened, and Jhavika entered wearing the same black silk pajamas as the day before, the scourge again her only accessory. I refrained from telling her she looked ridiculous.

"Good morning, Preel." She positively beamed, eyes bright, step bouncy, a far cry from the moody, temperamental, paranoid crime lord who had walked through my door yesterday.

"You look to be in a better mood." I straightened from my stretch and forced a casual smile. "Something must have gone right."

"Not really." Jhavika sighed and strode to the table, placing the scourge carefully there before joining me for stretches. "I still haven't the *foggiest* idea why Tewhirke Kettleblack would be of any use to me, and she's virtually unassailable, so I can't ask her."

"Well, you can certainly ask *me*." It might doom the poor gnome, but asking for specific intents or future possibilities often yielded cryptic answers. That wouldn't help Jhavika much. The longer I could string her along, the better chance that someone would come along and murder her. Whether that would improve or worsen my position was moot; arresting Jhavika's ascension to omnipotence was my all-consuming goal.

"Which actually brings up a question." Jhavika winced as she performed a leg stretch, the previous day's exertions obviously having taxed her muscles. "Do you think it would be useful to ask you what would be the best question to ask you?"

I barked a laugh and shook my head. Jhavika was overthinking the confounding logic behind the truthsayer ability. "Not a good Idea. First, my talent has problems delving magical things, and I am, by definition, a magical thing. Second, remember that I can't see the future. The best question to ask me now might be different than the best one to ask me four days from now."

"Buggered again!" She barked a sardonic laugh. "But enough shop talk. We're here for yamshi!"

"That we are."

When Jhavika was done stretching, I took her through the first twenty postures as a warm up and review. She did remarkably well; I only had to correct her stance a few times. Then I slowly showed her the next ten moves and went through them a second time guiding her by hand. This was the most trying part of our sessions, for I had to remind myself not to slip into *serpent strangles tiger* every time my hands neared her throat. I glanced at the scourge a few times when she was occupied, wondering if I could contrive to touch it, but the table was four strides away. There was no way I could make that look like a casual mistake. And one of our observers—Nala, Binsh, or the guards—would warn her if I made one wrong move.

We progressed through ten more postures twice, then did the second twenty together. Jhavika was breathing deeply when we finished, sweat dampening her silks, but she insisted we continue.

"I'm fine, really! I want to do more." She gulped down a glass of water and assumed the last position she'd learned. "I need someone to push me, Preel, and you're the only one I can trust to do it."

Trust? I hid my surprise at that. I could barely believe that she trusted me in any respect, but then, she'd allowed me to touch her. Was that trust, or was she simply confident that her guards could save her life if I tried to murder her?

"All right, but if your form starts to suffer, we'll stop." I mirrored her posture, *swan takes flight*, and settled my nerves. "Doing yamshi wrong is worse than not at all. You could actually hurt yourself."

"You're a good teacher, Preel. You won't let me hurt myself." She flashed me a smile.

No, I'd much rather hurt you myself. I forced a smile and a nod. "Okay then. Rotate your right foot one quarter to the left and shift your weight..."

I took her through the next ten moves, then again guided her through them by hand. Resting my fingers on her neck to position her head tested my resolve, but I chided myself for the violent impulse. I had no desire to invent a new pose, *dove pecks hawk and gets torn apart for her stupidity.* Jhavika was a pirate, a warrior; I wasn't.

As I guided her stance into the low crouch of *serpent in grass*, I wondered if I might try pushing this budding friendship into something more. Did her guards watch over her while she had sex? If I could get her in bed, vulnerable, I might be able to silently strangle her. The notion revolted me, and I remembered what she'd said about any attempt to seduce her. Jhavika probably had a bevy of the most adept sex slaves in the world, all conditioned to pleasure her in ways I could never imagine. That, too, was a non-starter.

I would have to settle for providing simple companionship. That was what she craved most, after all, and the one thing I could provide, other than my truthsaying, that none other could. What advantage that would get me, besides avoiding punishment, I didn't know, but it was the only advantage I had at the moment.

We went through the last ten positions together once again, then I took Jhavika through the whole fifty that she'd learned thus far. She confused the sequence a few times, which is typical for beginners, but she recovered quickly and finished the exercise in remarkably good form.

"That was exhilarating!" Jhavika stood up straight from the last pose, grinning and streaming sweat. Nala handed us both towels.

"You did well. I'm impressed." I bowed with hands pressed together, index fingers pointed. The move meant nothing—I'd made it up—but she didn't know that. "You're an apt pupil."

"And you're an *amazing* instructor." She accepted a glass of water from Binsh and drained it. "And you still look fresh! Gods, I don't know how you do it."

I shrugged and forced myself to match her ebullience. "Practice. But there's plenty that I *can't* do. Kevril tried to teach me how to fight with daggers, and I was horrible at it."

"He did?" She looked shocked. "*Another* manipulation. That man never ceases to amaze me."

I shrugged again, remembering his laughter at my ineptitude. Had that been a subtle exertion of control, a reminder that he was better than me? But I'd laughed at his attempts at yamshi, too, albeit out of affection, not spite.

"Speaking of Kevril, I need to ask you a favor."

Danger slithered up my spine like a chill serpent. "A favor about Kevril?" Was this why she was being so solicitous, so accommodating, so infuriatingly friendly? "What favor?"

"He's being very stubborn." Jhavika frowned and shook her head as if lamenting the behavior of a recalcitrant child. "He's refused to do anything for me or the Council until I allow him to see you."

My heart pounded against my ribs, whether from longing or trepidation, I didn't know. "I'm...not sure that's a good idea."

"Oh, it's most certainly *not* a good idea to let him see you, Preel, but I need him to do his job." She sighed in frustration. "He'll undoubtedly try to manipulate you, but I've got a plan that will hobble his efforts."

Suspicion and dread vied for space in my throat. I struggled to keep both from my voice. "What plan?"

"This." Jhavika strode to the bookshelf and retrieved my long-disused silken gag. "I'll only agree to let him see you if he wears this. That way, he can't speak, but *you* can."

I bit back an acerbic reply. Kevril speaking wasn't the problem. Just seeing him would be a sword through my heart. "I wouldn't know what to say to him."

"That's simple. Just tell him the truth, that you're safer here with me than you were with him, more comfortable, better cared for, and content." She stepped over to me and put a hand on my shoulder in a most disconcertingly familiar gesture. "I've *proven* to you that I'm not the monster he's painted me to be, Preel, and I think we've both grown to realize that we're good for each other. I'm the only person you can trust to tell you the truth, and you're the only one I can trust to give me honest feedback."

"I..." I quashed the impulse to knock her hand away. Somehow her touching me was even worse than me touching her. *Don't provoke her. Just agree...* "Yes, that's true."

"Good, then it's settled." She gave my shoulder a squeeze and beamed happily.

"When?"

"Tomorrow, late morning." Jhavika tucked the gag in her belt and went to the table to pick up the scourge. I'd forgotten it lay there. "That'll give you time to prepare after our morning yamshi session. You should pick out something nice to wear, just to show him that you're not being kept chained to a wall in a dungeon."

"All right." I wanted to scream that it didn't matter what the hell I wore to meet with Kevril. He knew me like no other and would see through any façade. He had seen my soul laid bare, delved its deepest, darkest corners, and embraced both it *and* me. Seeing him now, not knowing if all his tenderness had been truth or lies, would be a torture even Jhavika's scourge couldn't match.

"I don't want you to fret about this too much, Preel." Jhavika looked concerned, had undoubtedly seen the trepidation on my face. "It'll be fine."

No, it won't be fucking fine! I wanted to scream, but instead I nodded. "I won't fret. It's just...hard."

"It's always hard to face someone who's abused us, Preel. Show him that you're *stronger* than he thought you were, that you've come to realize that he's nothing but a vile pirate."

A rapacious scoundrel... Kevril's words tore at me like claws. I swallowed my anguish and nodded. "I'll try."

"That's all I can ask." Jhavika smiled once more and left the room, taking the guards with her.

I went to the window and stared out at Haven, the ships' masts beyond the roofs of the buildings, the pennants flying from the mastheads. I couldn't see the flags clearly from here; there was no way to tell which was *Scourge*.

Or was there?

"Binsh, ask Jhavika if I might be allowed to have a spyglass. I enjoy looking at the scenery."

"Yes, Preel." He hurried out.

"You should continue your yamshi before your muscles cool, Preel." Nala stood very close behind me, probably worried that I would do something drastic.

"No, Nala. I need to think."

I felt like doing something drastic, screaming and flailing and dashing my brains out against the bars of my gilded cage. Of course, that would be worse than futile, ruining all my careful deceptions, all my posturing as the calm, resigned, helpful companion. Breathing deep, I struggled to calm my mind. I would meet with Kevril and show him that I was not being abused, that I was safe and comfortable here. I would convince him, not because Jhavika wanted me to, but for the sake of those aboard *Scourge* for whom I felt honest affection. Kevril had risked his entire crew to rescue me from Brekka, perhaps out of avarice rather than love, but he had done it. Hemp, Bert, Miko, Boxley, even Wix; these were my friends, and they were the ones who would suffer if Kevril declared war against Jhavika.

I had to convince him that I didn't love him anymore, that it would be better for everyone if I stayed with Jhavika. *Leave the dove in the cage... Don't die trying to free it.*

My door opened, and Binsh's voice interrupted my tryst with misery. "Preel? I've brought you a spyglass."

I turned and accepted the fine brass instrument he held out to me. "Thank you, Binsh. I'm going to enjoy the view for a while. I don't feel like exercising any more today. I'll have a bath in an hour or so."

"Yes, Preel." He bowed and backed away, obedient, compelled by the scourge.

I raised the glass to peer at the distant harbor, bringing into focus the mastheads and the pennants snapping in the breeze. It only took me a moment to find the familiar dragon skull and crossed scourges. *Kevril...* I would see him tomorrow. My gut churned with uncertainty.

Do I still love him? I wondered. There was only one answer. On the morrow, I would find out.

Chapter Twenty Six
Love and Lies

Even the greatest sages do not know why we hurt the ones we love the most.
The Lessons of Quen Lau Ush

From the diary of Kevril Longbright –
Never in my life have I experienced such pain without actual physical injury. I know firsthand the agony of being stabbed in the chest, the fear you're about to die, then that wonder when you don't.

The invitation from Jhavika to meet at her keep came as no surprise, but still set my nerves on edge. I didn't sleep at all that night, but paced my cabin with a thousand different scenarios whirling through my mind. If I had the opportunity, should I try to kill Jhavika then and there? If I saw Preel, which was my secret hope and greatest dread, should I try to take her life as I'd promised to? Logic told me the answer to both of these questions was "No." My heart, however, tried to convince me otherwise. It all depended how the cards fell.

My audience was set for late morning. At first light, when my temporary steward—a scullery swab named Whinn, whom I couldn't decide if I liked or not—came into the cabin to find me fully clothed and pacing, he stopped cold in terror.

"Um...breakfast, sir?"

223

"Blackbrew first." I pointed to my bunk where I'd laid out the clothes and weapons I'd chosen for my meeting with Jhavika. "Take all that to Hemp and tell him I want everything spit and polish and the blades shaving-sharp by midmorning."

"Aye, sir!" He dashed to my bunk, gathered everything up, started for the door, dropped a boot, picked it up, and dashed out.

I paced.

Whinn returned with a blackbrew service and managed to put it on my chart table without dropping it. "Um...breakfast in a quarter glass."

"I'm not hungry." I poured blackbrew into a cup, an action that Hemp would have done for me, and sipped.

"Um...sorry sir, but Bert said you'd say that and...um..." His lower lip trembled.

"And she said I'd bloody well eat breakfast or she'd come in here, sit on my chest, and shovel it down my gullet." I sipped again and decided the kid knew how to make blackbrew.

His eyes widened. "How'd you know, sir?"

I snorted a cold laugh. "It's a common theme. Tell *Lady* Roberta that, as much as I am stimulated by the image of her sitting astride my chest, I'll eat breakfast."

He blushed, still terrified, though probably more of Bert than me. "Aye, sir."

I paced until the food arrived. To my surprise, Bert delivered the meal herself, balancing the huge tray easily.

"Worried that worthless Whinn would drop it." She put it on the table and started setting two places.

"I'm having a guest?" I finished my blackbrew and refilled the cup.

"Yes," Miko said as she came in. "Considering your mood lately, I thought this might be my last chance to have a meal with you, so..."

Her sarcasm felt like a cold slap to the face. "I'm not in the mood, Miko."

"Which is exactly why I'm here." She sat down without invitation and started piling bacon, eggs, fried peppers and potatoes, and toasted bread onto her plate. "Preserving your life so that I don't have to take command of this ship full of lunatics is my job, so sit the hell down and eat."

Bert snorted a laugh and bustled out.

I glared at Miko, then sat down and started loading my plate. I hadn't lied, I wasn't hungry, but the aromas of Bert's cooking set an edge to my appetite that would have split a hair. I started eating.

"So, I was thinking we should have a password of some kind."

"Password?" I mumbled around a mouthful of toast smeared with tartberry jam.

"Yes, so, if Jhavika whips you with the scourge and commands you never to tell anyone she did it, you can say...um...tartberry jam, and I'll know you're compromised."

"Jhavika's smarter than that." I finished my toast and tried a bite of the eggs. My mouth exploded with the flavors of sharp cheese and spicy sausage.

"What do you mean?"

"She's learned how to...condition people, like she did Hemp. Her slaves can't betray her in any way. I've spoken to him about it, and he can't write or even nod yes or no without the urge to cut his throat again. If I'm compromised, I won't be able to let you know. It'd be better if you just tied me down when I came back and questioned me thoroughly."

"Okay, that'd work." My first mate looked at me skeptically. "So, you didn't sleep."

I scowled at her. "How'd you know?"

"Sunken eyes, dark circles, worn look. I've seen you after enough double watches to know what you look like when you're tired." She speared some potatoes and ate them. "Besides, the night watch said your light never went out."

I snorted in derision. "No bloody secrets aboard a ship, are there?"

"Not many." She cocked an eyebrow at me. "So, do you think you can hold it together?"

Miko knew me too well. "For Jhavika, yes. If I see Preel?" I sighed and drank more blackbrew. "That depends on her."

"You know Jhavika's used the scourge on her."

"I'll have to consider that, but think, Miko. There's really no reason for her to enslave her that way. Preel's talent isn't voluntary."

"But Jhavika's a maniacal control freak and would just *love* to see you squirm when Preel tells you to fuck off and die."

I choked on the bite I'd half-swallowed and glared at her. "I don't need you to tell me that, Miko. I've been having nightmares of what Preel's going through for weeks. What she could be if Jhavika's enslaved her."

"Good, then you're prepared for the worst." Miko put her fork down and poured blackbrew for us both. "It's gonna hurt like getting buggered with a red-hot poker, Kevril. You've got to hold it together. If you don't, if Jhavika thinks you're unstable, she won't take you to the party, and the whole plan falls apart."

"I know."

"Can you do it?"

"I won't know until it happens, Miko." I lifted my cup and downed the scalding contents. "How can I?"

"You want my advice or not?"

I looked at her squarely. There was no scorn in her face. "Yes."

"Hold this thought in your mind; this is the only chance in hell that you'll *ever* get Preel back. That's *if* our plan works. For it to work, you have to start by holding it together today. Convince Jhavika that she's won, that Preel is hers, that you've given up hope of ever getting her back."

I nodded, unable to speak. If anything, that thought would give me the fortitude I needed. We finished breakfast in companionable silence and I felt the fatigue of a sleepless night settle on me. I banished Miko, stripped to the skin, and went to my quarter gallery to clean up.

A dash of cold water woke me up, and a good scrub with a soapy cloth took away the days of funk that I hadn't cared about or even noticed. I rinsed and picked up my razor. One look in the mirror, however, stayed my hand.

A wraith stared back, eyes red and sunken, deep wrinkles at the corners. I'd also lost weight from not eating properly, my face not exactly gaunt, but harder, more angular. My untrimmed hair and a two-week growth of dark beard streaked with gray along my scars gave me the look of a vagabond. Losing Preel had destroyed me.

Defeated. Exactly what Jhavika needs to see.

I put down my razor. I'd bathe and dress in good clothes for my meeting with Jhavika, but I wouldn't disguise what losing Preel had done to me. I'd get no pity from Jhavika, but it might convince her that she'd won, that I'd given up. *And what if I see Preel?* I wondered. *What if she'd been enchanted by the scourge and commanded to hate me?* Well, then she would see what I'd become without her.

I pulled on a nightshirt and lay down on my bunk. The bedding had been washed, but I still caught the indelible scent of the woman I loved. Closing my eyes, I imagined her with me, fixating on the fact that I had only one chance to get her back.

Hold it together...

A hand on my shoulder snapped me awake. The lad Whinn stared down at me in terror.

"Mu...midmorning, sir. Time to get ready." He gestured to the table where all my things were laid out.

I'd slept.

"Thank you, Whinn." I rolled up and donned my clean clothes. My boots were polished to a brilliant shine, and the buckles of my belt and the hilts of my weapons gleamed. Two daggers, a cutlass, and a hold-out stiletto for my left sleeve were all sharp enough to shave a gnat's ass. Hemp had done a good job. Lastly, I went to my locker and opened the box where I kept my cufflinks and rings. From the padded interior I withdrew my last-ditch defense. A gift from Bert, she'd procured the tiny glass vial during one of her visits to the alchemy shops, assuring me that the poison was painless and quick. I tucked the vial into my cheek and looked into the mirror. With my growth of beard, the tiny bulge was invisible.

A knock sounded, and Miko ducked in. "Jhavika's carriage just pulled up on the quay."

"All right." I started for the door.

"No shave?" she asked with a curious look.

"Part of my strategy."

"Makes you look like a—" She stopped and then nodded. "Okay, I get it."

"Double watches while I'm gone, and make sure all goes well with Boxley." The midshipman was to retrieve the potion from Kettleblack while I was dealing with Jhavika. I slipped past my first mate and started down the passage.

"Everything's ready," Miko assured me. "How are you?"

"Better. Sharp. I got a catnap."

"Good."

I stepped on deck, thankful for a break in the weather. The afternoon promised more rain, but I might get to Jhavika's and back without getting soaked. "I'll see you in a few hours, Miko. Have everything ready for me."

"Aye, sir." She paused at the railing with me and held out a hand. "Into the breach, sir."

"Aye." I shook her hand. There was nothing else to say.

The launch took me ashore. The mountainous captain of Jhavika's guard nodded to me and held open the door to the carriage. I stepped aboard and settled back for the ride. The streets of Haven were relatively quiet at this hour; the seething dance of predators and prey didn't get fully underway until evening. Still, I was glad for the mounted escort and relieved that I didn't have to walk.

The squeal of the rising portcullis announced our arrival. The carriage stopped and I stepped down. Ty-lee stood at the main entrance, his gold-and-ivory smile intact.

"Good morning, Captain Longbright. I trust you're well."

"And I trust Lady Keshmir's at home." I despised the man, but there was no point in belligerence.

"She is." He bowed shortly. "Follow me, please."

I did, escorted by a contingent of soldiers, including Jhavika's captain. I'd expected no less. They took me to the morning room, where I found Jhavika at her desk, looking fresh and sharp. There were half a dozen more guards stationed around the periphery of the room, three of them with crossbows loaded and cocked.

"Ah, Kevril!" She looked up from her work as if pleasantly surprised at my arrival, but then her eyes narrowed at me. "Good gods, you look dreadful."

"Thank you for your opinion," I said with as little rancor as I could manage. "What do you want?"

She stood and rounded the desk. "I have a task for you."

Let the game begin, I thought, settling my nerves for the inevitable sparring. "And I told you, I'm not leaving Haven until I see Preel and know that she's all right."

"This task won't actually require you to leave." She leaned back on the edge of her desk, arms folded, one hand resting idly on the scourge. "Lord Balshi is throwing a ball in my honor to celebrate my ascension to the Council of Lords. I'd like you to attend as my escort."

I snorted in disgust, secretly relieved that our plan seemed to be working so far. "How nice for you, but why the hell ask *me*? I'm not your lapdog anymore, Jhavika. I won't be attending any balls with you."

"I'm asking you because your reputation among the council members has risen of late. I need you to be there, to be seen, and to answer questions about our plan to enlist the aid of the other Blood Sea pirates as privateers." She spread her hands in an accommodating gesture I'd not seen from her before. "I'm prepared to compensate you for your time."

"Compensate me?" I squinted at her suspiciously. "How?"

She smiled, and I caught a hint of cruelty there. "By letting you see Preel."

I let all the hope and pain I'd kept bottled up register on my face. "When?"

"Right now, if you agree to accompany me to this affair." She narrowed her eyes at me. "And to clean up properly. You look like you've been on a *binge*, Kevril!"

I glared at her. "Fine. I'll go with you. Let me see her."

"Excellent." She stood up and strode back around the desk, opening a drawer to retrieve something. "I have only one condition."

"I'm not disarming, Jhavika. I'm not stupid."

"Not that." She held out a swatch of white cloth. "You wear this, or you don't see her."

I recognized the enchanted cloth and chided myself for my lack of forethought. "You don't want me to ask her a question that'll invoke her talent."

"Yes, that, and I simply don't want you to upset her." Jhavika stepped closer and held out the cloth. "Yes or no."

"Why not put the gag on Preel? I only want to see her, Jhavika, not *interrogate* her." What I wanted more than anything was for her to hear my voice, to understand.

"No. You'll just plead your love or some bullshit and upset her. Besides, she has something she wants to say to you."

My heart raced, pounding against my ribs like the wings of a dove against the bars of its cage. "You've enslaved her, Jhavika. You've commanded her what to say to me."

"Actually, I have *not*, but I don't expect you to believe me." She held out the gag again. "Put this on and judge for yourself. If you refuse, you don't see Preel and you go back and sulk on your ship until *Scourge* rots out from under you. The Council has offered a letter of marque to Captain Tan and purchased *Golden Harlot* from Fa-Chen. You're not the only privateer in their armada anymore, Kevril."

I snorted in disgust. "Tan's a *merchant* captain, Jhavika. No Blood Sea pirate's going to give her the time of day. You need me. The *Council* needs me. Remember my promise; if I leave this estate without seeing Preel, I'll sail away and turn every single pirate within a ten-day sail dead against you. Kill me, and Miko will do the same. They'll all know about the scourge, and we'll blockade Haven until this whole fucking *city* starves to death. Those are *my* terms..." I gritted my teeth and clenched the hilt of my cutlass. I could probably kill her before her guards shot me down, but I'd die, and I didn't know what would happen to Preel. *Keep it together, Kevril, and follow through with the plan.* "But I'm willing to put that gag on if you'll let me see her."

"Good." She motioned, and Ty-lee stepped up to take the enchanted gag. She was being cautious.

"Afraid of me, Jhavika?" I grinned like a wolf at her. "You sure you want me as your escort to this party?"

"I'm *not* afraid of you, Kevril. I just didn't think you'd allow me to stand behind you with the scourge on my hip." She returned my grin as she caressed the coil of dragon flesh. "I know how you fear it."

"Remember, if I return to *Scourge* enchanted by that thing, Miko sails away to carry out my last orders." I stopped Ty-lee with a glare. "Do we understand each other?"

"I believe we do, Kevril." Jhavika pursed her lips. "I *do* need you, I admit it, and I know you've taken precautions to prevent me from enslaving you again. You have my word; you'll walk out of this estate a free man."

I nodded. "Very well." I stood still as Ty-lee affixed the band of enchanted silk over my mouth.

"Thank you, Kevril." Jhavika turned and gestured to her guards.

A door opened, and Preel entered the room.

My heart dropped to my stomach at the sight of her, a vision from my dreams. She wore a sari of deep blue with jewelry at her wrists and fingers, her hair framing her face in an onyx cascade. Her every feature—the curve of her jaw, her lips, her gait as she flowed forth—sent pangs of longing through me.

But her eyes...

Those bottomless pools of obsidian that I'd gazed into so many times, poured myself into, breathed my life into, stared at me with an utter lack of emotion, cold and lifeless, two chips of black ice.

Preel was gone.

I felt the blade slip between my ribs, pain so intense my knees almost folded. I actually raised a hand to my breast, expecting to feel cold steel piercing my flesh and the warm, sticky wetness of blood, but there was nothing there. I tried to speak, of course, but couldn't.

I could, however, work the tiny glass vial out from my cheek to between my teeth. I could end the pain with one clench of my jaws.

But what of Preel?

No, I couldn't abandon her. Enchanted or no, I loved her, and I would save her. I'd kill Jhavika and find a way to destroy the scourge, dragon magic be damned.

Preel stopped several steps away, flanked by two wary guards. Her lips pursed, the muscles of her jaw clenching and relaxing, her cold eyes taking me in. She saw my pain then, I know she did. She knew my soul better than anyone, and she recognized my agony.

Then her lips parted. "Hello, Kevril."

I flicked the vial of poison back into my cheek and embraced the pain.

Chapter Twenty Seven
The Dagger of Love

The human body can endure unending agony. The human soul, however, cannot.
The Lessons of Quen Lau Ush

From the journal of Preel Longbright –
If ever my hatred for Jhavika Keshmir reached its peak, it was
the moment I beheld the man I had once loved. I didn't know
if he had ever loved me, or even if I loved him still, but seeing
him so destroyed broke my heart. But was it Jhavika who had
destroyed Kevril, or was it me?

At first, I didn't recognize the man standing in the center of the
room surrounded by Jhavika's guards. The clothes, yes. The boots, the
cutlass at his hip, the ruby-pommel of the dagger at the top of his boot,
I knew. The hollow eyes, angular cheekbones, ragged beard streaked
with gray, I did not. Something within Kevril Longbright had changed
beyond my recognition. The only thing in his face that I did recognize
was pain.

I concentrated on keeping my poise, focusing on my inner
strength. I took position a step in front of Jhavika, but still far enough
from Kevril that the guards could intervene if he tried to murder me.
I'd asked him to, if ever Jhavika took me. I didn't think he would try.
I had to force myself to speak.

"Hello, Kevril." I cleared my throat and wet my lips, keeping my eyes on the band of silk girding his mouth. Anywhere but his eyes. "I didn't want to see you."

He shook his head. I didn't know what he was saying no to.

"I want you to know that I'm comfortable here. Jhavika is treating me well. Far better, in fact, than you did."

His brow furrowed, confusion. He didn't understand. I had to make him understand.

"I'm *safer* here than I was with you, Kevril. I have servants, guards, a whole *army* to protect me. I'm not free, but I never really was."

Another shake of his head, his eyes—gods, the pain in his eyes bore into me like daggers—registering confusion. *It's a lie*, I told myself. *He's manipulating me again.*

"You're a *pirate*, Kevril. You told me so yourself. Just because you didn't ravage me the moment you took me as a piece of plunder doesn't mean I wasn't ever anything more than your possession. You told me once that you weren't a rapacious scoundrel, but you *certainly* got your way with me eventually." Once again, memories of endless hours of tenderness clashed with what I had come to believe.

He shook his head emphatically, denying the cold, hard truth.

My careful composure crumbled away.

"You *never* loved me! You *seduced* me! You played a long game, tricking me into believing you'd free me just so you could have both a truthsayer *and* a slave you could *fuck* whenever you liked! A woman so enamored with you, so convinced that she loved you, that she'd *beg* you to take her." I gritted my teeth so hard my jaw ached, denying the anguished tears hot in my eyes. "Well, I'm *not* that woman anymore, Kevril! I'm *stronger* than that! I'm not free, but I'm safe here. Safe from *you!*"

The unfathomable anguish in Kevril's eyes almost undid me, but I clenched my fists at my sides against my emotions, digging my nails into my palms. Yes, I had loved him, but no more. If only for the sake of the people I cared for aboard *Scourge*, I had to convince him of that, even if I was still unsure.

"Leave me here, Kevril. Forget I exist. Jhavika and I are good for one another. She's not abusing me, and she's not the monster you told me she was." I took a deep breath and let the pain, his *and* mine, leave me with my exhalation. "Leave the dove in the cage where it's safe."

"That's enough, Preel." Jhavika's hand settled on my arm, and I found it less revolting than the first time. "You don't need to—"

Kevril bent down—at first, I thought he might be collapsing. Then he freed the ruby-pommeled dagger from his boot, and every guard in the room tensed. Steel whispered from scabbards and crossbows raised.

Jhavika pulled me back, stepping between us, but I knew it wasn't an attack.

Kevril straightened and dropped the dagger to the carpeted floor between us. The ruby pommel gleamed in the wan light.

"What the *hell*..." The suspicion in Jhavika's voice spoke volumes. She didn't understand the gesture.

I did.

I stepped around Jhavika, and the naked dagger lay at my feet. I relived that moment aboard *Scourge*, a lifetime ago. I sat again on Kevril's narrow bunk, only recently awakened, confused not to be in Brekka's clutches. Kevril dropped this same dagger in front of me, then stood with his shirt open, the tiny wound I'd inflicted only hours before still livid. *If you don't know why I came after you, Preel, then sheathe that blade in my heart and be done with it.* But it had been a lie then, and it was a lie now. He was a pirate. This was just another manipulation.

I glared down at the dagger, then up into his eyes, and I saw more there than pain. I saw freedom.

Did the dagger mean more now than it had then? If there was one thing I knew, it was questions and answers, multiple meanings. My mind raced and found three possible implications for his gesture: a reminder of his love for me, a plea to kill him if I didn't love him, or a chance of escape from my gilded cage.

I reached down to pick up the blade.

"Preel, don't!" Jhavika pulled me back again. "It's just another manipulation. He wants you to hurt yourself because he can't do it himself. If he can't have you, he wants you dead!"

It was truer than she knew; I'd asked him once to kill me rather than let Jhavika take me. Jhavika didn't see the other implications. I had to convince her that she was wrong. "No, it's not." I stepped back to her side and met Kevril's gaze, fighting to keep the pain in his eyes from touching me. "It's a plea."

"A *what?*" Jhavika stared at me in confusion.

"He wants me to kill him, but I won't." I eased Jhavika's hand off my arm. "It was a lie the first time, Kevril, and it's a lie now. I'm not yours anymore. You can't manipulate me." I breathed in all the pain radiating from him and expelled it in one horrible thrust. "I don't love you."

I had never seen defeat in Kevril Longbright's eyes before. Rage, yes. Pain, anguish, confusion, guilt, passion, perhaps even love, but never defeat. I saw it then, and it broke my heart.

I hurried out of the room without looking back. I'd hurt him enough. He would never want me now. My friends aboard *Scourge* were safe from his jealous wrath. I almost made it back to my room before the tears finally came.

Chapter Twenty Eight
A Question of Truth

Even the wisest can believe a convincing lie.
The Lessons of Quen Lau Ush

From the journal of Jhavika Keshmir –
The irony never ceases to amuse me. Lies from a truthsayer.
The tale of the dove who laid diamond eggs held true that day.

"Remove the gag, Ty-lee." I picked up the dagger as Ty-lee complied. Smiling at the anguished defeat in Kevril's eyes, content in the knowledge that I'd won this round, I tossed the weapon back to him. "Satisfied?"

He caught the dagger deftly and stared at it for a moment, probably trying to decide whether or not to throw it back blade first. Finally, he sheathed it and stared at me, all defiance, all pride gone from his haggard features.

"No, I'm not satisfied at all, but I'll stand by my word. You want an escort to this fancy ball, I'll go with you. I'll work for the *Council*, Jhavika, but not for you. Not anymore. I'm not your partner any longer."

I frowned, but then nodded. "Fair enough. I'll still recommend to the Council that you command our privateer navy. You're perfect for the job."

"Fine." Kevril was beaten and he knew it, but he wasn't a fool. He'd always followed the power, and he always would. "When is this party?"

"Tomorrow evening. I'll pick you up at the quay at sunset."

"I'll hire my own carriage and meet you at Balshi's estate. I'd rather not share a carriage with you." He wrinkled his nose in distaste, a petty insult.

"Suit yourself." I waved him out. "But *shave* at least, and wear your finest. This will be an elegant affair."

"Don't worry, Jhavika, I won't embarrass you in front of your slaves."

"They're not *all* my slaves, Kevril. Not yet." I smiled sweetly. "But they *will* be."

He was gone before I could interpret the look that crossed his features. No matter. I had accomplished exactly what I intended to. Kevril was back on the job, his impotent little strike crushed.

But Preel…

I fretted about her all the way to her rooms, and found her standing at her window with a glass of wine. Nala and Binsh flanked her, looking tense and worried. That didn't bode well.

I waved them aside and joined Preel. "Are you all right?" The last thing I wanted was her to spiral into a fit of depression. I swore by all the gods and devils that if she became petulant again, I'd simply command her to be happy and be done with it.

Then I reconsidered. *No*, I resolved. *I need her honesty, her friendship…*

"No, I'm not all right." Preel drained her glass and handed it off to Binsh. "But I will be." Turning, she gave me a wan smile, and I saw that she'd been crying. "I'm sorry, Jhavika, but that was…harder than I thought it would be."

"Don't be sorry, Preel. You were amazing! You showed him you're *stronger* than he is. You took all of his manipulations and threw

237

them right back in his face." It was true; she couldn't have done better, and I couldn't have hoped for more. Still, one thing niggled at my innate suspicion. "I still don't understand that business with the dagger."

"Oh, that." She flipped a dismissive hand and accepted a full glass of wine from Binsh. "You were right. It was another manipulation, but not the way you thought."

"Do you mind telling me about it?" I didn't trust any secret the two of them still shared, and that little demonstration had been more than just a simple test of wills.

"No, I don't mind." Preel sipped her wine and sighed. "Kevril bartered me for the potion that would release him from your enchantment. The alchemist evidently found out that Kevril had a truthsayer, and would accept nothing else in trade. I should have known then that he'd never loved me."

"But..." I was lost. *Bartered her?* "But he got you back later, obviously."

"Yes." Preel's eyes gleamed with the pain of the memory. "When he traded me for the potion, I tried to kill him. He'd given me a dagger, you see, showed me where to stab." Her fingers touched her abdomen just beneath her sternum. "He stopped me, caught my wrist and took away the dagger. I begged him not to trade me, but he just asked me if the potion Brekka had made would truly banish the scourge's enchantment. I answered him, then passed out."

"And he exchanged you for the potion. That heartless *bastard!*" Secretly, I marveled at Kevril's boldness. He'd risked everything—not only a truthsayer, but the love of the woman he obviously adored— and he'd still won. "But he got you back."

"Yes. While I was asleep, he and the crew assaulted Brekka's stronghold and rescued me. I woke up in his cabin aboard *Scourge*, confused and angry with him."

"And rightfully so!"

"He didn't blame me for being angry. But when I asked him why he rescued me, he just dropped that dagger, the same one with the ruby pommel, on the bed, and said that if I didn't know why he stole me back, then I should kill him. That I was free and could do whatever I wanted."

"Preel, he stole you back because you're a *truthsayer*."

She huffed a laugh and nodded, tears spilling down her cheeks. "I know that now, but...he obviously wanted more from me than my talent. I believed he loved me. That was...the first time...he touched me." She sniffed and downed her wine.

What a chance he'd taken, I thought in awe, wondering if he'd actually have let her kill him. Men have done far stupider things for love.

"I'm sorry for what he did to you, Preel. Truly." I sighed sadly, determined to convince Preel that the ploy with the dagger had been a lie. The more she hated Kevril, the more she'd turn to me. "I wish I could make you forget him."

"I wish you could, too." She handed the glass back to Binsh and waved him off. "Can I ask you a favor, Jhavika?"

I felt the warm rush of triumph. She wanted my help. "Of course! Anything you wish."

"Can you ask me your next question now?" She nodded toward the bedroom. "I...don't want to feel this way anymore. I know I'll wake up feeling better, and right now I just...I want to scream and cry and break things, and I know it won't do any good."

"I know exactly how you feel, but I'd planned to wait until tonight. That'll be four days since the last question. I don't want to endanger you." Never truer words passed my lips.

"I should be fine, Jhavika. The last question wasn't very taxing."

I wondered how she could know that, but had to trust her. This wasn't an attempt at suicide; if she had wanted to kill herself, she would have tried harder with Kevril's dagger. "Very well. Why don't you freshen up."

"Thank you." Preel went to the washroom and came out wearing her nightgown and robe. "I'm ready."

"Good." I followed her to her bedroom and waited while Nala tucked her in, all the while marveling at the strength it had taken for her to confront Kevril like she had. I wondered how much of it had been the impetus of the scourge and my subtle commands, and how much was her own force of will. It didn't really matter. She'd crested that hill of disbelief, severed all ties to Kevril. She was all mine now. "I'll see you in the morning, Preel. Maybe you can finish teaching me the whole first yamshi routine."

"I'd like that. Thank you, Jhavika."

Smiling, I brushed her hair back from her forehead. "Sleep well." I cleared my throat and asked the question we'd crafted. "What specific service can Tewhirke Kettleblack provide that would aid me in becoming Queen of Haven?"

Preel's eyes rolled back, and her body arched in the familiar spasm. "Nothing."

I gaped at her for a moment. "*Nothing?*" *What in the name of...* I gritted my teeth, suppressing the urge to slap the woman lying unconscious on the bed. Her last two answers had been completely contradictory. "Gods-damned *truth*sayer! Should be called a *bullshit* sayer!"

I forced down my frustration. This wasn't Preel's fault, it was just more complicated than I had bargained for. I needed to figure out better questions to ask to properly apply Preel's talent.

"See to her wellbeing!" Nala and Binsh quailed as I stalked out of Preel's chambers. Striding for my office, I muttered under my breath. I was wasting the most valuable weapon in the world with nonsense answers that got me nowhere, and I'd just wasted four more days.

Chapter Twenty Nine
To Free the Dove

There is no futility in denying weapons to your enemy.
The Lessons of Quen Lau Ush

From the diary of Kevril Longbright –
I told myself that Preel was under the scourge's enchantment,
that her words and feelings weren't her own. I told myself that
Jhavika had poisoned her mind against me. It did no good.
The truth, for once, was no consolation.

I managed to make it to the carriage before my emotions got the
better of me. In the dim confines, as we clattered through the mired
streets of Haven, I drew my ruby-pommeled dagger and considered
the deadly instrument in earnest.

I don't love you. The dagger would be far less painful than those
words.

But then Miko's words of encouragement, revisited me as well:
...something to live for. Swiping a sleeve across my eyes, I straightened my
shoulders and gazed at the blade with new resolve. I'd held it together
in front of Jhavika. I was going to the ball as her escort. We would

dance at least once. Then, I would plant this dagger in her black heart and end it for good.

I put the weapon away, then spat the vial of poison into my hand and pocketed it. Closing my eyes, I concentrated on calming my pounding heart and breathing the fetid air of Haven without being ill. To distract my mind from my recent torment, I envisioned various scenarios that might play out at Lord Balshi's ball, trying to consider all the things that could go wrong. I still doubted that I'd get out alive, but there was always a slim chance. If I could kill Jhavika *and* destroy the scourge, maybe Preel would be free to feel again. *Free to love again.*

After that, it would be up to her. If she truly didn't love me, if she still believed that I'd lied to her, seduced and manipulated her, then I'd take her wherever she wished to go and leave her there. I'd be free and beholden to none. My heart would be my own again.

The carriage jolted to a stop on the quay, and I got out. *Scourge*'s launch waited there for me, Kivan standing at the coxswain's position, her eyes intent upon me. I climbed down the iron rungs and stepped aboard without a word. I'd given orders to convey me to the ship in silence, for there was no way for them to know if I was enchanted or not. My faithful crew followed those orders to the letter, foregoing even the commands to ship oars and secure lines.

Miko and Wix met me at the boarding hatch, their faces as blank as sheets of slate.

I handed over my weapons one at a time. "Carry out your orders, Miko."

"This way, sir."

I followed her to my cabin, Wix, Tansy, and Foist at my heels. They were taking no chances. Good. Inside, Miko bade me sit in a stout chair, then applied manacles to my wrists and ankles. Wix stood behind me, his ham-hands on my shoulders. I tested my bonds and found that I could barely move.

"Need a drink?" Miko asked on her way to my cabinet.

"Like fish need water. Thanks."

Miko poured two tumblers half full and sat in another chair opposite me. One glass she handed to Tansy, and the other she sipped. "How'd it go?"

I sipped the malt whiskey without choking and nodded my thanks to Tansy. The lump in my throat eased, scoured away by liquid fire. "About as painful as you said it would be. Preel's...different."

"She's been enslaved by the scourge." Miko sipped again. "Are you?"

"No." I accepted another sip and cleared my throat. "Jhavika insisted I wear Preel's gag, so I couldn't speak to her. Preel did all the talking. It was pretty ugly."

"It wasn't her, Captain. You *know* that."

"Yeah, but I don't know if she'll ever be the same person, even if we do destroy the scourge." I shook my head at the offer of another sip of whiskey. I needed to think this through with a clear head. "She's convinced, or at least *seemed* to be convinced, that I never loved her, that I only manipulated her into falling in love with me so I could...have a truthsayer in my bed."

Wix muttered a curse behind me, one that involved Jhavika and an ogre, and was probably anatomically impossible.

Miko quaffed the last of her whiskey and shifted away from the painful subject. "So, you're going with Jhavika to this ball?"

"Yes, though I put up enough protests to make her believe that I didn't want to. She made no argument when I insisted on separate carriages, so you and Wix will be able to get into Balshi's estate without trouble." I nodded downward. "Mind unlocking these now?"

"Just a couple more questions first, sir." Miko scowled. "So, Jhavika didn't use the scourge on you, right?"

"No, she didn't."

"And she knows nothing about your plan to kill her?"

"Nothing. We're good to go."

"And she knows nothing about our plan to rescue Preel?"

I seriously considered that notion. "Not that I *know* of, but she does have a truthsayer. She could ask Preel that question tonight, and we'd be fucked."

Her eyebrows arched. "Very true. Okay, last question. Tell me how you're going to free Preel from Jhavika's influence."

"Kill Jhavika at the party, then steal the scourge *and* Preel, sail away, and use her talent to figure out how to destroy the fucking thing."

"Good." Miko nodded to Wix. "Unlock him."

"Good to have you back, sir," Wix rumbled as he unlocked the manacles.

"Thanks." I rubbed my wrists and accepted the tumbler from Tansy. Wix and his mates left my cabin. "Is Boxley back yet?"

"Yes, about half an hour ago." Miko went to my cabinet again, refilled her glass, then lifted up two brown bottles with waxed stoppers. "A dram of blood, a quick shake, and we look like whoever we want for three hours."

"Good. And Kivan's ready?" I got up and began to pace.

"She says so. Getting everything in place might be tight time-wise, but it should work. We won't go into Jhavika's estate until she's ready." Miko tucked the priceless potions away.

"That raises one worry I hadn't thought about until today, Miko." I sipped and paced. "If things go to hell at Balshi's party, and Jhavika lashes me with the scourge, she could command me to spill my guts." I grimaced at my choice of words. "Both literally *and* figuratively. I'd be forced to tell her all about the plan to rescue Preel."

"Then timing's going to be critical. You'll have to hold off killing Jhavika long enough for us to get Preel out."

"And likewise, if *you* fail, and word gets back to Jhavika before I have a chance to put a dagger in her heart, I'm buggered."

"True." She sipped whiskey and shrugged. "All we can do is plan accordingly."

"Too right you are."

A knock sounded at my door, and Whinn peeked in. "Lunch, sir. Your guests are waiting."

"By all means!" I waved him in.

Whinn was dressed in Hemps footman's jacket and breeches, a white cloth over one arm, and Miko's dress jacket over the other. The latter he handed to her, the former he spread on my table with a surprisingly smooth snap of his wrists. Bert followed bearing a huge silver platter laden with a whole suckling pig surrounded by mounds of vegetables. Lastly, my three midshipmen entered wearing their finest and looking a little terrified.

"Ladies and gentleman, please have a seat." I still wore my good jacket, and Miko donned her own. "This will be our final planning session before tomorrow night, though we can make some last-minute adjustments if the situation changes. First, I have an announcement to make." I carried a full decanter of my finest whiskey to the table and poured three tumblers half full. Kivan, Quiff, and Boxley looked up at me worriedly. "From this moment forward, Quiff and Kivan are promoted to the rank of second lieutenant." I raised my glass. "Welcome to the quarterdeck."

Their mouths dropped open. Boxley whooped in glee and grabbed a glass, crowing congratulations.

"Now raise your glasses *Lieutenant* Quiff and *Lieutenant* Kivan, and drink to our future."

They did. We all did. A warm swell of camaraderie displaced the agony in my chest.

Kivan cleared her throat and found her voice. "Pardon my boldness, sir, but why now?"

"Because killing Jhavika and rescuing Preel will risk both my life *and* Miko's." I sat and motioned Whinn to carve the pig. "And yours, too, to be honest, Kivan. Now, Quiff, you're senior by a few months, but I'm placing Kivan over you. I think you'll agree that she has a better grasp of navigation. She will, however, be off the ship tomorrow night, so if all goes badly and none of us come back from this mission, you'll be captain of *Scourge*. You understand everything that means, right?"

"Aye, sir." He sat a little taller in his chair. "And your orders, sir?"

"Well, if I'm dead my orders won't matter much, but I'd *advise* you to sail for the eastern horizon and not stop until you reach Tsing. If Jhavika survives, she'll hunt this ship relentlessly because she knows that the crew is privy to her secret. Change *Scourge*'s paint, the cut of her jib—Rauley and Wix can help you with that—rename her, whatever you can think of to keep her from finding you. Your lives depend upon it."

"Understood." Quiff sipped his whiskey. The hand that held the glass trembled, and he grinned nervously. "Please don't die, sir. I'm not ready to be captain."

I barked a laugh. "I'll do my best, and I'm glad you at least know your limitations. Your *job*, however, is to *exceed* those limitations if the need arises. You get me, Lieutenant?"

"I get you, sir."

"Good. Mister Boxley, you are now my senior and *only* midshipman." I glowered at her. "Don't let it go to your head."

She looked mortified. "Oh, *no*, sir!"

"I'll also want suggestions from you as to who from the lower deck might make the grade to join you in the wardroom. Get those suggestions to your captain, whoever that is, once this shitstorm has blown over. Clear?"

"Aye, sir."

"Good." I nodded to Whinn, who had done a passable job of reducing our piglet to slices. "Go ahead and serve, Whinn. We've got a lot of plans to work out today."

"Aye, sir!" He started with my plate and worked down the ranks.

"Oh, and when you have a chance, tell Hemp to hone his razor." I fingered my whiskers. "I'll need a shave tomorrow afternoon, and he's the only one I trust with a blade at my neck." I raised my glass to my officers. "Present company excepted."

That, at least, brought a gale of laughter from the table. We all drank and got down to the business of planning how best not to die on the morrow.

Chapter Thirty
The Reluctant Companion

No command can compel loyalty. That must be earned.
The Lessons of Quen Lau Ush

From the journal of Preel Longbright —
I thought I knew what it was to be a slave. I found that I had much to learn.

I slept until morning and woke to the urgent need to urinate and muscles so stiff that I could barely hobble to the washroom. Whether my long sleep was due to a particularly difficult question, the fact that it had been asked too soon, or my overall state of mind, I couldn't say. Memories of my confrontation with Kevril still plagued me, but the pain had dulled, as I knew it would after a night's rest. I had been cruel, intentionally so, but it had been necessary. I would never leave this estate unless some mishap befell Jhavika, and if that happened, who knew what my next master would be like.

Another rapacious scoundrel, mayhap.

After washing my face and hands in an attempt to wake up fully, I stretched to relieve my stiffness and thought about my answer to Jhavika's question. Better that than to dwell on Kevril.

Nothing.

The ambiguity of the answer brought a wry smile to my lips. Jhavika must have been fit to be flogged. I wondered if she'd spent the entire night working out all the possibilities of that answer's meaning. Would she see the simple explanation? Probably not.

Binsh met me in the common room with a gracious smile and a wave toward the table. A cup of blackbrew sat steaming in a saucer at my place. "Breakfast shortly, Miss Preel."

Miss... I'm no longer Lady Longbright. Not after what I said to Kevril. I banished the thought and sat down.

"Thank you, Binsh." I sipped my blackbrew and asked him for paper and pen.

I needed something to occupy my mind, and an analysis of Jhavika's question and my answer served that purpose and one other. I jotted down a list of possible interpretations, some so complex they were dizzying. The simplest, and what I thought the most likely, I listed near the end. To disregard it completely would be a glaring omission and put my motives in question, but I also didn't want it front and center, giving Jhavika something to latch onto. Mediating Jhavika's conquest, mollifying her aggression, and tempering her ruthlessness were now my primary goals. By becoming her confidant and companion, perhaps I could tame the dragon that had sunk its teeth into her soul.

By the time I'd finished my breakfast, I had two full pages of succinct, analytical, and confounding misdirection. I was proud of myself.

Jhavika burst into my rooms just as I finished my last sip of blackbrew, with a bright, "Good morning, Preel! I hope you feel better this morning." Her eyes gleamed with enthusiasm, not the frustration and despondency that I'd expected.

"I am, thank you." I stood and forced a grateful smile. "And thank you for indulging me yesterday. I needed the long rest."

"I was worried about you. Such a long sleep." Her ebullience devolved into a frown of concern. "You gave me a scare."

"I'm fine. Just a little stiff," I assured her. "Our yamshi session will cure that. Just let me change."

"Of course! No rush, I'm just champing at the bit." Her mood shifted again to enthusiasm. "I can't tell you how much these sessions are helping me. I feel like a new woman!"

"Good!" She hadn't yet mentioned my answer to her question, so I picked up my notes and handed them to her. "My answer yesterday was a little cryptic, so I spent the morning thinking about it and jotted down some notes. Go ahead and read them over while I get changed."

"Excellent! *Thank* you, Preel!" Jhavika took the pages, her eyes devouring the lines of notes.

"I hope they help." I hurried to my bedroom and changed into my accustomed pantaloons and wrap-around halter. I hustled back out to the main room, cinching the last tie at my back, to find Jhavika still poring over the notes, her brow furrowed. "Sorry if they're confusing, but answers like that one can take on many meanings."

"Yes, so I'm learning." She looked up at me and beamed. "These are *incredible*, Preel. I worked most of yesterday afternoon trying to figure out what the hell your answer meant. Here you have it all laid out like ducks in a row in an hour."

I shrugged. "I've been asked hundreds of questions. I'm used to interpreting ambiguous answers."

"So I see." She tapped the pages with a finger. "This first one seems pretty reasonable; we were confounded by time, so your answer, 'Nothing,' meant that the opportunity for Kettleblack to help me had already passed. Now, this one," Jhavika flipped over a page and tapped her finger again, "I like the sound of. Enslaving Kettleblack might have been to *prevent* her from doing something *against* me, rather than something *for* me."

Shit! Jhavika had hit upon the explanation I'd tried obscure. I hoped she wouldn't murder the poor gnome on that supposition. "It is a possibility, but what kind of a threat might an alchemist pose to you?"

Jhavika looked at me squarely. "An alchemist mixed the potion that freed Kevril, remember?"

"Yes…of course." I frowned and shook my head at the flood of memories. "But, can we please not mention *him* anymore?"

"Of course, Preel. I'm sorry." Jhavika gripped my arm warmly. "No more shop talk. I'm here to learn the rest of the yamshi routine today!"

"Right!" I forced a brightened countenance and patted her hand. "Some stretching first?"

"Stretching it is!" She put my notes and the scourge on the table and joined me in the warm-up routine, her enthusiasm bubbling forth in a prattling splurge. "I know we haven't been doing this long, but these sessions have truly helped me. Not only am I more flexible, but my frame of mind seems to have shifted. I'm so much more positive now. Setbacks don't bother me as much anymore."

"Good." I didn't really know what else to say, but that didn't stop Jhavika's gushing.

"I honestly don't know if it's the exercises or if it's you, Preel."

"What?" I girded my response.

"You said something yesterday that struck me like a lightning bolt, actually." The intensity of her gaze sent shivers up my spine. "You said we were good for each other. I truly feel that's correct, Preel. We *are* good for each other."

"I hope so." *Right, I keep you from becoming a monster, and you don't lash me with your scourge and force me into unspeakable acts of debauchery for your own sick entertainment.* "I'm trying to be…helpful." *Like helping you to not torture me.*

"You're being more than helpful, Preel. You're the one person whose opinion I can trust to be honest. It's like…" She straightened and her face took on a distant look. "Like when I was a girl."

"Oh?" I had difficulty picturing Jhavika as a girl.

"I had a sister, Anjice. We were…closer than family, more than friends." She smiled sadly. "Like peas in a pod."

"I...didn't know." I didn't want to know, either, but if she thought of me that way, all the better. The more highly she regarded me, the safer I'd be. I took the opening. "You say 'were'. What happened?"

Jhavika's expression darkened. "Raiders. We were scooped up with a few dozen others, but they didn't keep us together. I learned to fight to survive and eventually became a pirate. I don't know whatever happened to Anjice. I never saw her again."

"I'm so sorry, Jhavika." I really was, but not how she thought. *If she'd never become a pirate...* My mind spiraled down that path and I almost laughed. *I'd still be a truthsayer, and who knows who my master would be.* At least with Jhavika I didn't run the risk of being violated on a daily basis.

She shrugged. "Oh, don't worry. It happened years ago. It's just that...you remind me of her sometimes."

That revelation shocked me speechless, and it must have shown on my face.

"The way I'm spending time with you, learning yamshi with you, just talking, makes me feel...I don't know, nice, I guess."

"I'm glad I can make you feel that way, Jhavika." *No truer words...*

"Me, too." Jhavika beamed once again and barked a laugh. "Gods, listen to me getting all sentimental! If the members of the Council saw me like this, they'd die laughing!"

"Everyone needs someone, Jhavika." I stepped up and clasped her hands in mine. This was the tipping point I'd hoped for. If I truly reminded Jhavika of her long-lost sister, perhaps I *could* do some good, give her council, mediate her ruthlessness. "It's nothing to be ashamed of."

Jhavika smiled and squeezed my hands. "*Thank* you, Preel."

I squeezed back, then released her hands. "Now, let's go through what we've already covered, and see if you can master the last twenty poses today."

"Right!" She took the beginning stance with practiced ease and nodded. "I'm ready."

"Follow me, then, and *greet the sun.*"

Chris A Jackson

We progressed through the first eighty moves of the basic sequence with few faults; Jhavika really had a talent for yamshi. It had taken me a month to master the entire first sequence, but then, every time I faltered, I'd been punished and sometimes took a day to recover. Memories of those horrific times, the years before Kevril took me as his prize, made my current plight seem like paradise.

When we reached the last pose, I changed position to stand in front of Jhavika. "The next is *stork strikes sky*. Slide your right foot forward and deepen the lunge, extending your right arm, with fingers like so..."

"This reminds me of a fencing lunge, but without a sword," she commented as she complied with nearly perfect form.

"That's probably why you're so good at this. Yamshi has its roots in unarmed martial combat." I analyzed her stance. "Good, now turn both feet, then shift your weight to the left foot, reversing the stance into *serpent strikes sea*."

"I thought you said monks created this." Jhavika managed to make the change with little wobble.

Damn it! I hadn't meant to tell her about yamshi's martial origins. The last thing I wanted was for her to understand the potential violence of the moves. "They did. Warrior monks from the mountains of Chen." Again, I analyzed her stance and adjusted.

"Why do you think one of your masters would teach you a martial discipline?"

"Because he probably didn't know its origin, and yamshi isn't really martial anymore. Curve your fingers back more. Good."

"But if you learned to fight..."

"I didn't." I progressed her into the next pose, *tiger crouches low*, and continued. "I was only fifteen. I'd already tried to take my own life once. My master wanted something to make me less likely to do so again."

"He abused you?"

"Not as badly as my first," I said, grateful for her change of subject. I adjusted her hips and spine once again and moved us into

253

dragon takes flight. "He was more interested in magic than...anything else."

"What a bunch of fools they were," Jhavika said with a shake of her head that threw her balance off.

"Concentrate, please." I also didn't want to talk about my former masters; I knew where it would lead my thoughts. "Next, lower your arms in a cupping motion like *receive the morning,* but slide your right foot wide, toe pointed to touch the floor. This is *hold the dragon's egg.*"

"Sometimes I feel like...like I saved you, Preel."

"What?" Startled, I looked at Jhavika and saw her eyes glistening with tears. I opened my mouth, hesitated, and then said what I knew she wanted to hear. "I...think you did."

"And...I feel like maybe you're saving me, too."

I stopped the sequence and stood, my concentration shattered. Jhavika was opening up to me, admitting frailty, pleading for help. This was my chance. "I would like to save you, if you'd let me."

Jhavika straightened, blinking away unshed tears. "But from what? From myself or the scourge?"

"You can never let it go, Jhavika." I took her hands in mine, squeezing hard. "But maybe I can prevent it from making you into something you don't really want to be."

"A monster," she whispered.

"You're not a monster. I *know* you're not." I didn't know anything of the kind, but perhaps if I convinced her she wasn't, it might stop her from sliding further into power-hungry depravity. "I can help you. Let me."

"I'm trying." She smiled and sniffed, her underlying vulnerability and loneliness, the desire to be good, to be *human,* all laid bare.

It almost made me like her. Almost.

"Trying is all *any* of us can do. Now let's continue the routine."

"Yes." Jhavika resumed the previous pose. "Thank you, Preel, for listening."

"My pleasure." I flashed her a smile. "Now, less talk, more concentration."

She nodded, and I taught her the last of the moves. After I guided her through them once more as before, we performed all twenty together, finishing with the final pose of *sun low in sky*. I straightened and bowed to her with my fake little hand gesture.

"Well done."

"Thank you."

I accepted a glass of water from Nala. "How do you feel?"

"At peace." Jhavika shook her head, drank some water, and sighed. "Really, for the first time in...I can't remember."

"Good." I covertly watched Jhavika as I drained my glass and handed it back to Nala. Was she simply putting me on with a show of enthusiasm and closeness or was she being honest? I just couldn't tell. "We can do the whole routine together if you'd like."

Her eyes lit up. "I'd love that."

"So would I." Truly, I needed the concentration and the exercise, and I didn't want to think about Jhavika anymore. If I could pose as her friend and mediate her ruthlessness, I'd be content. A beneficent queen of the world wouldn't be so bad.

We went through the entire *ton-chi* routine with only minor prompts by me. It would take her time to commit the progression to memory, but that was less important than learning the discipline as a whole, experiencing the balance, the concentration, the peace. We finished, both of us breathing hard and dripping sweat.

"That was *amazing*!" She drank more water and accepted a towel.

"It saved my life," I told her honestly.

"And you're saving mine." She beamed at me, but then her smile faltered. "I want to ask you—"

"Careful, please," I cautioned her. Now was not the time to escape my gilded cage in death, not when I had Jhavika exactly where I wanted her.

"Oh, nothing that'll invoke your talent. Just..." She wiped her face and sighed. "I just don't know if any of this is real."

The statement stunned me. I'd thought I was being clever, but had she seen through my ruse? "Wha...what do you mean?"

"I mean, I can't trust my own feelings on this." Jhavika gestured vaguely to encompass the whole room. "I don't know if I'm actually enjoying your company, the yamshi, this whole thing, because *I* want it, or if it's just the scourge making me want it."

"The scourge making you want honest companionship?" That struck me as a 'tail wagging the dog' argument. Paranoia made Jhavika double-think everything. "No. That can't be."

"Why not?"

"Because it doesn't make sense. *You* chose to be here with me and learn yamshi because you *enjoy* it. It doesn't gain you anything but peace of mind. No riches, no conquest, no power." I handed my towel back to Nala. "It's free will, Jhavika. This is your *choice*. The scourge can't be forcing you to want free will. It's not possible."

Her brows arched in a comical look of surprise. "You really think so?"

"I *know* it, Jhavika." I gave her my most genuine smile. If I hoped to keep her from becoming something truly horrible, I had to convince her of this. "You're *not* a slave to the scourge in everything. *This* is real. It's *you*. You just needed a friend to show you the truth." *Even if it's a false friend.*

"Oh, Preel!" Two strides and she embraced me hard, her arms squeezing the breath out of me.

I would sooner have expected Jhavika Keshmir to spontaneously combust than exhibit such a genuine human emotion. Stifling my shock, I embraced her back, more out of self-defense than any sort of emotional reciprocation. If she could truly feel this, be human... *I've won*, I though smugly.

Jhavika sniffed in my ear and coughed a laugh. "You're like the best friend I lost, Preel. That's what's been missing in my life. I needed you so much!"

"I'm here, Jhavika." I patted her back, feeling uncomfortable, foolish, a liar. Guilt choked me at deceiving her so, but I swallowed it. This woman had enslaved hundreds, murdered, cheated, tortured, all for power. She would rule the world or die trying. I was the only thing keeping her from becoming a ruthless tyrant. "I'll help you. Don't worry."

She squeezed harder, crying softly on my shoulder. "You feel that way about me, don't you?"

"Of course, I do," I lied, clenching my teeth against the truth, the hatred.

"I love you like I did my sister Anjice. I never thought I could again." Jhavika sniffed again and laughed. "Love me like a sister, Preel, and we can take the whole world together."

"Yes, I..." My stomach plunged to my feet and a chill radiated outward along every nerve.

Everything changed.

My smoldering hatred for Jhavika, my plans to murder her, even my resentment at my lost happiness, all melted away in the blink of an eye. An irrepressible shudder shook me to my bones.

I loved Jhavika like a sister.

The scourge!

Realization struck like lightning through darkness, illuminating everything in stark clarity. All the things she'd said to me, the hidden commands and subtle manipulations—"Just relax. Enjoy yourself. Calm down. Be strong."—raged in a torrent through my mind. But the most horrific of all had been, "Believe me."

I had. I did. I couldn't hate Jhavika any longer. I loved her like a sister. It wasn't me—I knew that in my soul—but I couldn't change what I felt.

And so, I embraced my lost sister and silently cursed my existence. I was powerless to resist her every whim. I was her slave, body and soul.

Chapter Thirty One
The Moment of Truth

When faced with certain death, an act of defiance is sometimes the only option.
The Lessons of Quen Lau Ush

From the diary of Kevril Longbright –
I've had my ass kicked by the very best. My father, Captain
Kohl, and yes, Jhavika Keshmir. I am, however, still alive, still
fighting, still struggling to be free. Why? I honestly don't
know. Perhaps I was born a pirate after all.

I arrived at Lord Balshi's estate early, but only slightly. This, and
every step I'd taken this day, had been calculated. Arriving early would
allow Wix and Miko to position themselves with plenty of time and
without being noticed. They wore the same livery as my hired
coachman and guards, so they blended in perfectly.

As I stepped down, I caught Miko's eye. She was tying her mount
to the boot of the carriage, a swift, sturdy horse and my chosen means
of escape. Nodding subtly, I ascended the steps to Lord Balshi's
palace. You couldn't have called it anything else. It made Jhavika's
estate look like a summer house. In fact, with thousands of tiny
rainbows gleaming in the light cast from the towering windows, it

seemed a fairy palace. Mist from the waterfall beaded on everything. I couldn't imagine living with the constant roar and the unending damp, even in a place like this.

Where the hell do people get so much money? I wondered as the doorman bowed and asked my name.

"Captain Longbright. I'm escorting Lady Keshmir. We're in separate carriages, so I came early to walk her in."

"Of course, sir." He gestured to one side. "You may await her right over here. If there's anything I can get you, please ask."

"Thank you." I could think of nothing I needed short of a way to vanish into thin air after I murdered Jhavika. I didn't think he would be able to provide that.

I checked my pocket watch, stood with my hands clenched behind my back, and watched the other council members arrive. Most I didn't recognize, though I'd heard enough rumors to match names to faces. They were an eclectic group, garbed in everything from frills to formal kimonos. A fae woman, undoubtedly Lady Nahli Twince, glided past in a gown of white feathers that seemed to be affixed to her skin, two ebon-clad escorts wearing white fox masks at her flanks. Then I spotted a familiar face. Ursilla Roque ascended the stairs wearing a cunningly cut gown of turquoise satin that elegantly accommodated a rapier at her hip.

I nodded and smiled to her. "Good evening, Lady Roque."

"Why, Captain Longbright!" She greeted me with a two-handed clasp and a kiss to my cheek. I could hardly shy away; we'd been far more intimate at Jhavika's party. "You look positively *delicious* this evening!" She leaned in again to whisper, "Good enough to eat," and laughed.

"And *you*, Lady." I smiled at her, restraining a grimace at the memory of our previous acquaintance.

"I *love* the new look." She brushed my newly groomed beard with manicured fingertips. "Very piratical."

I'd indulged Hemp's creative suggestion on a whim. He'd done a passing fine job shaving me, but left moustache and a sharply trimmed goatee behind. I'd been surprisingly pleased by the new look and decided to keep it, if not out of vanity, then because it made me look different. I wanted Jhavika to realize, before I killed her, that I was not the pirate she thought she knew.

"I'm glad you approve." My eyes slid to the young man on her arm, and I stifled my surprise. "Young Lord Malchi! Well met...again." I extended a hand to the young man and cocked an eyebrow at Ursilla, thinking, *Really?* He was half her age, and had a near-legendary reputation with the ladies.

"Captain Longbright." Maurice shook my hand stiffly.

"You've met?" Ursilla looked from my face to his and back again.

"Only in passing. Ships in the night, you know," I assured her.

"It was *foggy*, if I remember, not night, but yes, it was a brief acquaintance." He smiled tightly and took Ursilla's arm.

"A good evening to you both." I stopped short of telling Ursilla not to hurt herself with her escort. There was no reason to be rude.

When I'd met Maurice Malchi aboard a ship I was pirating, he'd been in a compromising position...beneath the captain. Captain Tan had abandoned her paramour at my sudden entrance, snatching up a dagger that paled in comparison to the shaft she'd been impaling herself upon. My crew had told stories of his heroic dimensions for a month and more. Then I recalled the mention of Maurice Malchi at Jhavika's party, and how Ursilla had jested about seducing him to win over the young lord's father, also a council member. I wondered if Jhavika had commanded her to go through with it. It sounded like something my former partner would have done.

The next familiar face was a welcome one.

"Lord Temuso. Good to see you well."

"Kevril! I'm *so* glad you could come!" Temuso gripped my proffered hand and embraced me warmly, whispering in my ear. "I trust all is in readiness?"

"Yes, Getashi. Everything's as it should be." We separated and I saw that his bodyguard, Utake, accompanied him as his escort. The two made a sharp couple, both in black jackets with different, but coordinated, colors of waistcoats. Getashi wore the same dress katana I'd seen at Jhavika's party, while Utake wore twin kukri through a sash at his waist, the ivory hilts crossed. I feigned ignorance as I turned to the bodyguard. "And you are…"

"Utake, Captain." He bowed from the hips. "I am pleased to meet you. May the evening bring you all you wish."

I knew then that Getashi had told him my plan, and prayed to every god I knew that word hadn't gotten back to Jhavika. If it had, I would die before I could kill her. I was okay with after, just not before.

…something to live for.

"And where's the lady of honor?" Getashi asked, snapping me out of my reverie.

"Socially late, I hope." There were three more coaches pulling into the courtyard, and the last in line I recognized. "There she is."

"Good luck to you, then, Captain." Getashi bowed to me and allowed Utake to escort him into the palace.

I watched the last few carriages disgorge their passengers one by one. Two were surrounded by their own security entourages. The carriage right before Jhavika's was not. The woman who stepped from that coach could only have been Lady Hashi Severn. Tall, lithe, and dark, she reminded me of a hunting cat. She walked as if the rest of the world didn't exist. A short silver chain draped over one hand led to the collar of her escort, a tall man dressed all in black, his skin the hue of chalk, his expression blank. I wondered if he was alive or undead, a companion or mere pet. Severn wore a snug gown of black samite that shimmered with fine silver embroidery patterned in an eerie and anatomically accurate depiction of bones, her bones. The aspect shifted as she walked, as if I could see right through to her skeletal structure. A dagger, blade pointing upward between her breasts, was sewn right into the material. My skin prickled as she strode past.

Then Jhavika arrived, and my attention focused upon her with mind-numbing intensity. She wore a strapless gown of pure gold with matching elbow-length evening gloves, her figure pinched into an hourglass. Her eyes found me, and she smiled. Her squad of retainers stayed with the carriage save for the captain of her guard. The man towered over her, and probably quadrupled her weight. There was no way I would be able to clear a blade near her with him close. But when we danced...

As she climbed the steps, I looked for the scourge and didn't see it. I had no doubt it lurked somewhere on her person. She'd never come to a function so crowded with her enemies without it. If she'd hidden it under her gown, it would be hard to reach, which might save me.

"Lady Keshmir." I gave her a stiff half-bow, my hands away from my sword. The cutlass I wore was a beautiful piece, with a gold basket hilt shaped like a dragon. This drew her eye, exactly as I'd hoped; it was the ruby-pommeled dagger hidden in my frilly right sleeve that would pierce her heart.

"Captain Longbright." Her eyes raked me from head to foot. "Quite nice. Thank you for cleaning up. The sword's new, isn't it?"

"No. Actually, it's quite old. I inherited it from a pirate captain who thought he would take *Scourge* from me." I extended my arm for her to take. "His avarice killed him."

"Your tongue will be your undoing, Kevril." Jhavika laid a hand on my arm, and we entered Lord Balshi's palace. "Veiled threats to the woman who will one day be your queen are likely to be your end."

"No threat intended. It was merely the truth." I concentrated on keeping my hands clear of my weapons as we followed the other guests across the polished floor of the cavernous entry hall. The mountain of meat following us probably had orders to cut me down if I so much as touched a hilt. "You're familiar with the truth, I'm sure."

"Oh, I'm *intimately* familiar with the truth." She squeezed my arm. "Not quite as intimately as *you* were, but we've become fast friends."

I refused to rise to the bait. I had to keep my temper in check, and sparring with Jhavika wasn't the way to do it. I guided us up a sweeping stairway wide enough to sail a ship, and cast her a sidelong look.

"I'm here at your request, Jhavika. Can we not snipe at each other all evening, please? I find it boring."

"Very well. I'll be good if you'll be good." She met my eyes. "I hereby call a truce to hostilities."

I nodded. "Truce." Of course, truces were temporary, as she would find out, but I had to bide my time, give Miko and Wix the opportunity to rescue Preel before I struck.

At the top of the sweeping stair, we turned down a vaulted hallway as wide as *Scourge*'s middeck. House guards stood at intervals like statues, halberds gleaming in their hands, and I wondered how many were stationed throughout the estate. Considering the covert warfare waged incessantly among Haven's lords and ladies, I was mildly surprised that the council members came here without worrying that Balshi would have them all slaughtered. Of course, if he did, he'd be cutting his own throat, given certain retaliation by their heirs. Perhaps they actually *were* working toward a united Haven; odder things had happened.

"This is quite a place," I commented, simply to give my mouth something to do besides grind my teeth. "It doesn't look gnomish."

"No, it doesn't. I don't know its origin, honestly. Perhaps dwarves built it for the gnome king. It's certainly old." She sighed wistfully. "It's lovely, though."

"A bit overdone, if you ask me. All flash and gilt with little attention to comfort or function." The place seemed cold to me, lifeless, like a show sword that wouldn't hold an edge. "Of course, the private wings might be completely different."

"True. One never knows what lies behind a pretty façade." She chuckled and nudged my elbow. "You, for instance."

"Me?" I cast a glance at her, forcing myself not to glare. "You think I'm putting on a façade?"

"Don't take it personally, Kevril. It's a compliment." She raked her eyes up and down me once again. "You clean up beautifully and look quite dashing, lordly even. One would never know that a rapacious scoundrel lurked beneath the surface."

I stiffened. "So much for our *truce*, I guess."

"Oh, come *on*, Kevril. That wasn't an insult; it's true. You take what you want: ships, pretty swords, women. I certainly can't fault you for *that*!"

I gritted my teeth against a cutting reply. I knew Jhavika had used 'rapacious scoundrel' deliberately, purloining the phrase from Preel's outburst during our ill-fated meeting, a twist of the knife. Truth be told, when I first found Preel, I *had* taken her as plunder; her truthsayer talent made her a priceless treasure. I had not, however, taken her person without her consent. Jhavika would never believe that I honestly loved Preel or anyone else, probably because I had spurned her advances. I wondered if the scourge imparted the *ego* of a dragon as well.

At the end of the corridor loomed the entry to the grand ballroom. Through the portal, a towering lattice of glass and gold arched overhead, glittering glow-crystal chandeliers twinkling in a million tiny rainbows. Ivory-clad servants hefting silver platters of food and drink lined the glass walls, awaiting their master's order to circulate and serve. Before us, twin rows of council members and their entourages stepped back, creating an aisle for us to walk. It seemed a gauntlet to me, but their faces, most of them anyway, were alight with pleasure, even welcoming. As we passed the portal, the entire chamber erupted in applause.

I nearly balked.

I don't know why, but in all my imagined scenarios of this affair, none had included Jhavika and me parading through a crowd of applauding nobles. I don't know why I hadn't expected it. The ball was in Jhavika's honor, after all.

I glanced at her and grasped Temuso's genius. Jhavika's face glowed with pleasure as she soaked up the adoration like a tree soaks up the sun. She would never have turned down the chance to attend a ball in her honor; the scourge wouldn't let her. Jhavika wanted it all, everything the world could offer, and this was part of it.

She wants the entire world enthralled with her, I thought, swallowing my revulsion.

Forcing a smile, I accompanied her toward a low dais at the end of the ballroom. Behind the dais towered a massive stained-glass window. It must have been spectacular during the day, illuminated by the sun. Even now, in the light of the glow crystals, it refracted rainbows into the mists outside. Standing on the dais, also applauding, stood a man in resplendent garb and two women in matching gowns: Lord Balshi, his wife, and his sister, whom I had made a widow. Brilla Balshi didn't look to be grieving for her murdered husband. In fact, of the three on the dais, hers seemed the most genuine expression of adoration. Her eyes sparkled and her face flushed with pleasure as she gazed at the woman on my arm and ardently clapped her hands. Her brother and sister-in-law seemed less enthusiastic, Lord Balshi's smile bordering on a sneer of loathing.

What's up with that little triangle? I wondered, but only fleetingly. Politics and Jhavika's conquests wouldn't matter by the end of this evening. She'd be dead, and so, probably, would I. There were too many guards and too damn many people here for me to slay the guest of honor and escape alive, even if I did have something to live for.

The applause faded and stilled as we stopped at the foot of the dais. Jhavika curtsied, and I bowed.

"Welcome to my home, Jhavika, and let me be the first to formally offer you my heartfelt congratulations." Lord Balshi bowed from the waist and spread his arms wide. "The Council of Lords honors you this night!"

Applause erupted again, and I took my cue to release Jhavika's arm, step away, and join in the ovation. She turned a slow circle, beaming with pleasure and nodding her thanks to her peers.

Then I saw it.

As Jhavika turned her back to me, I spotted the scourge. It nestled at the small of her back like a coiled viper, the haft at her spine, the nine barbed thongs draping over the curve of her ass like nine clawed tails. I should have known; I'd seen her wear it thus before. There was little doubt in my mind that it had tasted Preel's flesh, that Jhavika completely controlled her. I couldn't fault Preel for what she'd said to me; I knew that helplessness, the inability to feel what I knew I should, instead of what I had been commanded to feel. It revolted me.

The applause stilled, Lord Balshi gestured, and the servants bustled forward with trays of crystal glasses filled with sparkling wine. I took two and handed one to Jhavika, wishing I could poison it.

Lord Balshi made a little speech, then toasted Jhavika, the guest of honor. I raised my glass with the others and sipped the wine without tasting it. Then, to my surprise, I caught my name being spoken.

"...and a toast to our most honorable Captain Longbright, soon to become *Admiral* Longbright." Lord Balshi raised his glass to me. "May his defense of our city, and I daresay our budding *empire*, meet with continued success."

I bowed to hide my grimace and gritted teeth as cheers and applause rang out. *We'll see how they feel about me at the end of the night.*

The speeches and toasts continued, Lord Balshi lavishing praise upon many of the other council members. I ceased to pay attention, lost in my own thoughts, applauding and raising my glass when appropriate. Finally, it was done, and the ball started in earnest.

"Well, *that* was a little embarrassing, wasn't it?" Jhavika sighed and exchanged her empty glass for a full one, still glowing from the adoration.

I gave her a sardonic look. "Oh, don't try to feed me that bilge water. You loved it and you know it." I exchanged my own glass, but sipped carefully. The last thing I needed was to be drunk.

Jhavika gave me a knowing look. "Fair enough. I can't say that I honestly dislike praise, and neither can you...Admiral."

"Don't throw that title around prematurely, please." I had to put her at ease, and pretending like I'd follow through with her plans to recruit a privateer navy seemed a good way to do that. "There's a lot of work to be done before we have a real fleet."

"True, but I know you're up to the task, and I'm not just blowing sunshine up your skirts." She raised her glass to me. "It's our first step to creating an empire, Kevril, and you're a key element in that future."

I really didn't want any part of Jhavika's future, but nodded in acquiescence.

A few of the lords and ladies approached to congratulate Jhavika in person, shaking her hand and smiling. I gauged them out of habit. Lady Twince seemed utterly without emotion, her golden eyes expressionless. Lady Severn smiled like a predator as she extended a hand to Jhavika. Jhavika hesitated a bare second before shaking it, from reluctance or fear, I wasn't sure. I logged that in the back of my mind.

Lord Balshi finally approached us, his wife on his arm and his sister at his other elbow. He shook Jhavika's hand, then mine, prattling on in that pompous voice of his. I nodded and smiled like I knew I should. Brilla surprised me by embracing Jhavika with gusto, planting a kiss on her cheek, her eyes alight with glee. Jhavika beamed back at the woman and clutched her hands warmly, leaning in to whisper in Brilla's ear.

Brilla's her slave, I realized, glancing at Lord Balshi, who watched the exchange with a poorly hidden sneer of distaste. *Perhaps if I told him the truth...*

But no. I had a plan and I had to follow through with it. I played my part, shaking hands, smiling, carrying on banal conversations with people I didn't know or trust. Ursilla Roque came by, of course, showing off her dashing young escort like a new toy, which is exactly what he was. I wonder what his father thought of his son's dalliance with a fellow council member. Jhavika embraced Ursilla and the two exchanged giggling whispers. If young Maurice wasn't already Jhavika's slave, I guessed he would be soon.

No, he won't, I told myself, *because Jhavika's going to die tonight.* I looked around as if searching for a footman, gauging my surroundings with a tactical eye. Jhavika's captain still loomed nearby, too close. I would have to wait. Accepting a tidbit from a silver tray, I surreptitiously checked my watch again. Barely half an hour had passed since our arrival. Not nearly enough time before I could make my move.

A string quartet started playing, and people edged away from the center of the room to clear a space for dancing. Couples began gliding out to move with the music. I watched them, noting the lack of bodyguards on the dancefloor. *There, Jhavika,* I thought. *That is where you will die.*

"Might I have the first dance?"

I recognized Temuso's voice before I turned, and wondered why in the world he would be asking Jhavika to dance. Then I found him staring at me, not her, his hand extended.

I gaped for a moment, wondering at his motive, but his countenance seemed sincere.

"Oh, come now, Getashi." Jhavika stepped up and put a hand on Temuso's arm. "I don't think Kevril wants to—"

"Nonsense." I suddenly needed to dance with him simply to shock her. I grasped Temuso's proffered hand and gave him a sincere smile and a short bow. "I'd very *much* like to dance with you, Lord Temuso, if Utake doesn't mind." I slid my gaze over to Jhavika. "And if Lady Keshmir won't be too lonely in my absence."

Jhavika laughed a little too loudly for it to be genuine and flicked a dismissive hand. "By all means, dance! You never cease to amaze me, Kevril!"

You want a surprise? Wait for it, I thought, girding my vengeance and bowing to her graciously. I walked with Getashi onto the floor, and he extended his hand for me to lead.

"Well, *that* rattled her cage," he whispered with a smile as we glided along.

"It did." And anything that put Jhavika off balance tonight was to my benefit. "Thank you."

"Don't thank me yet, Kevril. I truly just wanted to dance with you." He pulled me close. "And ask you something."

"Ask away." As we circled, I spotted Jhavika chatting with Utake.

"Do you think you'll get your lady back from her?"

I met his eyes and found only sincerity there. ...*something to live for.* "I hope to, yes."

"Good." He smiled sincerely. "That means you plan to survive the evening, though I don't know how you're going to manage it."

"I'm not sure yet either, Getashi, but I'm going to try my damnedest. I have something to live for, and I'm *very* good at staying alive."

"Oh, I have no doubt." The lord's countenance sobered. "I wanted to tell you that I've...taken precautions, should things go awry."

"Precautions?" That didn't sound good.

"Yes, Kevril." His smile returned, but it was sad now. "I'll never be anyone's slave, you see."

"I understand completely," I said, comprehending the implication. "I hope it doesn't come to that."

"So do I, dear Kevril. For if it does, it means you'll have failed and will probably be lying dead right here on this floor."

"Yes, it does." I squeezed his hand tight, pulled him close, and gave him my best piratical grin. "Good thing I'm a pirate."

He barked a laugh and held me tight. "Oh, you *scoundrel!*"

"That, too."

The music stopped and we glided to a halt. He bowed to me then. "You dance divinely, Captain Longbright."

"And you, Lord Temuso."

As we strode back to our escorts, I snatched two glasses of wine from a passing waiter and handed one to Getashi. Jhavika watched us approach with amusement writ large on her face.

"I never thought I'd say it, Kevril, but you dance well with another man."

"Why should that surprise you, Jhavika?" I raised my glass to Getashi, and we toasted each other.

She furrowed her brow. "Well, after your first encounter, I thought..."

"Oh, that was just too much to drink and the randy entertainment you arranged, Jhavika!" Getashi sipped his wine and took Utake's arm. "No hard feelings at all, I'm sure."

I raised my glass to him. "None at all, Getashi."

"Well, before you two lovebirds trundle off to some secluded corner, perhaps, Captain Longbright, you'd deign to dance with your *escort*." Jhavika's words pricked like the barbs of her scourge. I'd embarrassed her, and she was angry.

I didn't care. She was giving me the opportunity I needed.

"Of course." I downed my wine and passed the glass off to a waiter before taking Jhavika's arm and guiding her onto the floor. "Angry with me?"

"A little." She took my hand and put her other on my shoulder. "You did it just to gall me."

"Not really. Just to show you that you don't know me as well as you think you do." I settled my other hand on her hip, well away from the scourge that coiled up her spine.

Jhavika snorted in disgust. "I know you better than you know yourself, Kevril."

I smiled at her. "You really don't."

"Oh, I really *do*." Her smile turned sickly sweet. "Preel's told me all *sorts* of tales."

I stiffened and missed a step. "Don't go there, Jhavika."

She laughed musically. "Why shouldn't I? She's *mine*, Kevril, my very closest companion, my dearest friend. We're like sisters. She's going to help me take the world. First Haven, then the Obsidian Isles, then Hyko and Sariff and Mati. Then all of Tira, and Toki, and finally Chen. It'll all be mine, and Preel will stand at my side, my devoted companion."

"You're very sure of yourself, Jhavika." I gauged the time and deemed it close enough. Near an hour had passed. Miko and Wix should have been inside Jhavika's keep by now, and either Preel was free or they were all dead. It was time.

"I *am* sure." She beamed at me. "I have everything I need. I'll take it all or burn it to the ground."

"Or you'll die trying."

Jhavika laughed again. "Well, there is—"

I interrupted her quip by pulling my hand from hers and snapping my wrist to slide the hidden dagger into my palm. Jhavika had only time to widen her eyes in shock before I drove the point into her stomach, just below her sternum, angled up at the precise angle to pierce her heart.

Immediately, I knew I'd been foiled. My thrust met stiff resistance instead of soft flesh. She folded over the blow, the air leaving her lungs as if she'd been punched, not stabbed. Her corset was armored.

Fuck!

Snatching back the dagger, I thrust again, intending to drive the blade into Jhavika's neck, but she twisted away, gasping for breath. The tip of my dagger passed an inch from her throat. A snap cut the air as she spun around, and the barbed thongs of the scourge lashed out. I blocked reflexively, the clawed tips raking the back of my hand.

I stared for a heartbeat at the shallow wounds, a heartbeat too long.

"Stop, Kevril!" Jhavika croaked, still struggling to breathe.

I froze, dagger poised to strike, every muscle trembling, my hand and forearm tingling like a hail of nettles.

Like the ripples from a pebble thrown into a pond, the guests around us reacted. Lords and ladies gasped in shock, ceased their dancing, and backed away. The music sputtered and died, the very air seeming to vibrate with tension.

Jhavika caught her breath and stood straight, her features contorting into a vengeful rictus. "Kevril Longbright, cut your own throat. Cut it to the *bone!*"

The dagger in my hand rose as of its own volition, the nettles in my arm stinging hot and cold. I strained to resist, knowing I couldn't. The razor-edged blade reflected the light of a thousand enchanted crystals as it neared my throat.

I'm sorry, Preel. Strange how, as death neared, my thoughts were for those I'd leave behind, those I'd failed. *Sorry, Miko, Wix, everyone...*

Then…my arm tingled no more.

Chapter Thirty Two
Reluctantly Rescued

There are times when love is the enemy.
The Lessons of Quen Lau Ush

From the journal of Preel Longbright —
Never in my life have my heart and my mind been so at odds.
My memories of Kevril and the life I had loved aboard *Scourge*
battled with the truth I now accepted. My remembered hatred
of Jhavika vied with my new love for her, my dear sister. I had
no choice in what I felt. I could only embrace my new life or
go insane.

I snapped out of a fitful slumber to the unmistakable cacophony
of mayhem. Months aboard a pirate ship had well-acquainted me with
the clash of steel, cries of agony, and splintering of wood.

By the time I vaulted out of bed and grabbed my robe, Nala had
already reached the bedroom door. The room flooded with light as
she touched the wall sconce and hazarded a peek into the sitting room.
Another cry rang out, Binsh's voice, and something heavy hit the wall.
Nala slammed the door and braced her back against it, her eyes wide
with panic.

"What is it?" I pulled on my robe and cast about for a weapon, but, of course, there wasn't so much as a candlestick. Jhavika had seen to that.

"A guard and Ty-lee have..." Nala shook her head. "I don't understand what could be—"

The door slammed open against Nala's back, flinging her across the room like a ragdoll and wrenching a scream from her throat. She hit the bed hard and tumbled across it, striking the headboard.

I stared in terror as a large guard in Jhavika's livery burst into the room, followed by Ty-lee. The guard gripped two daggers, their wide bronze guards studded with long, blood-stained spikes. Ty-lee wielded a fine katana, its blade also dark with blood.

Something was very wrong.

"What the hell..."

"Preel!" Ty-lee rushed forward, blade lowering, but Nala launched herself off the bed at him like a wildcat, her hands like claws. Ty-lee pivoted and sent Nala flying into the guard's grasp.

"Stupid fook!" The guard raised one of the daggers.

My heart leapt in my throat. "NO! Please, don't kill her. She's just a slave ordered to protect me. She has no *choice*!" I started forward.

Ty-lee intercepted me, his blade held carefully aside. Over his shoulder, he said, "Wix, don't kill her. She's just following Jhavika's orders."

"Bloody fookin' nuisance!" The guard brought the pommel of his dagger down on Nala's head, and she collapsed.

"*Wix?*" I stared at the big guard. He looked nothing like Wix, but the daggers I suddenly recognized. I shifted my gaze to Ty-lee. "Who are *you*?"

"It's Miko, Preel. We took potions to get inside the estate. We've come to take you out of here."

"What?" I stared at Ty-lee—*Miko?*—as he wiped his katana on my bedspread and sheathed it. "No!"

"No isn't going to be a part of this discussion, Preel." Ty-lee—*no, it was Miko*—cast a glance around the room. "No time to change clothes. All Nine Hells are going to break loose in about two minutes. Do you know where your gag is?"

"Yes, but..." My eyes darted involuntarily to the outer room. "I...I'm not going with you, Miko! I can't!"

"You are, and you can, whether you want to or not." She grabbed for my wrist, but I twisted free. "Preel, you *have* to come with us! Guards are coming!"

Something smashed into the outer door, and Wix swore. "Guards are bloody here, sir. Get a move on!" He turned to the main room.

My mind reeled, and I backed away. "You should go, Miko! Leave me here! I told Kevril the *truth*! I'm *safer* here. Jhavika's not a monster!"

"Yeah, Kevril said you'd say that." She advanced. "It's the scourge, Preel. Jhavika's controlling you with the scourge."

"I *know* that! It doesn't change anything!"

"It changes *everything*! Now come along!" Miko grabbed for me, arms wide.

"NO!" I blocked and ducked, but she was far stronger than me, and just as quick. I squeaked a scream as she pinned my arms to my sides and lifted me bodily. I kicked and screamed, but couldn't break free. Another impact struck the outer door as Miko hauled me into the sitting room and flung me down to the carpet.

I tried to jump up, but she landed on my back, forcing me down. I screamed bloody murder, howled for help, and two more impacts rattled the door. A stout chair had been wedged up under the latch, but the wood was beginning to splinter.

Miko grabbed my arm and snapped something metallic onto my wrist: a golden manacle.

I groaned. "Miko, don't..."

"It's for your own good, Preel. We don't want you to hurt yourself." She snapped the second manacle onto my other wrist. "The gag, Wix!"

"Bloody lookin' for it."

"Let me *go*!" I screamed. "Miko, *please*! Don't do this. I don't want to go with you. I need to stay here!" She shifted and started binding my legs at the knee and ankle despite my struggles. "Stop it, you goddamned pirate! I need to stay with Jhavika! I'm *good* for her! I help her!"

"Because she's lashed you with the bloody scourge, Preel. You don't know what you're saying."

"I fucking *DO* know what I'm saying! I *know* I'm under the control of the scourge, but it doesn't change anything. I *love* her! I have to stay with her! If I don't, she'll become a monster!"

"Bloody hells!" Miko cursed a blue streak and wrenched me to my feet. I tried to struggle, but hobbled as I was, it was futile.

"Got it!" Wix approached with the silken gag.

"NO!" I fought them, shaking my head back and forth. Miko ended my struggles by grasping my hair, and Wix tied the gag.

"I'm sorry, Preel, but we're taking you. It doesn't matter what Jhavika wants anymore. She's dead."

Dead? The news struck me like a blow to the gut. I could no longer protest, but I could still struggle. I writhed like a snake in Miko's grasp, bucking and lashing out as best I could, my mind reeling with grief and rage, my vision blurred with tears. *Murderers! They killed my sister!*

"Preel, stop it!" Miko flung me onto a divan and whipped another line between my bound ankles and wrists, completely immobilizing me, then let go. "Come on, Wix. The table!"

"Aye, sir!"

Still I struggled, wrenching my legs down until the manacles at my wrists bit cruelly. I pitched off the divan and landed hard on my shoulder. Wincing at the pain, I blinked away tears to see Wix and Miko lifting the heavy table like a battering ram. They smashed it sideways into the iron bars on the window—once, twice, and a third time—finally knocking them away into a bent and twisted heap. Beside my bedroom door lay Binsh, a bloody gash across his forehead. Thank the gods, his chest still rose and fell. The two guards who had stood at my door and a man in servant's livery lay sprawled with bloody wounds, likely dead.

Murderers, pirates... Please no. They can't have killed Jhavika.

276

"Get her, Wix!" Miko commanded, leaning out the window to wave and whistle a sharp note.

"Sorry, Lady Preel. For your own good." Wix hauled me up and over his shoulder like a sack of grain.

"Incoming!" Miko ducked away from the window.

An iron-tipped ballista bolt shot through the opening and smashed into the ceiling, wedging deep at a steep angle. The wrist-thick shaft trailed a rope that quickly twanged tight.

Another impact smashed into the door, splintering more wood. Shouts from the hall rang out.

"No time, Wix!" Miko pulled two short lengths of chain from her belt and handed one to the bosun. "You first!"

"Aye, sir!" I couldn't see what he was doing, but the chain rattled, and we were at the window, then through it and racing through the air.

I would have screamed if I'd been able.

We struck something hard, and I found myself flung down onto a soft bundle in the bed of a wagon. Familiar faces surrounded me: Kivan, Tansy, Foist... Wix whirled around in time to catch Miko or, at least, soften her landing.

The rope parted with a slash from Miko's blade, and she bellowed, "Go!"

A whip cracked and we tore off through the night, a cordon of mounted pirates around the wagon waving bared steel. I lay there screaming my anguish within my own mind, tears streaming, my thoughts reeling. *Dead...my sister...dear Jhavika...please no.* And yet my memories of hating her clashed again with the adoration and grief. My head pounded as I tried to reconcile the contradiction. *It's the scourge. You don't really love her.*

But I did, and it was tearing me apart.

Chapter Thirty Three
The Curse of the Scourge

Defeat is often snatched from the jaws of victory.
The Lessons of Quen Lau Ush

From the journal of Jhavika Keshmir —
I will curse the name of Kevril Longbright until my dying day
and beyond. May all the devils in all the Nine Hells feast on
his entrails for eternity.

The leather haft of the scourge warmed my hand, the intoxicating
thrill of satisfaction as it once again tasted Kevril's flesh. With a grin
of triumph, I watched my enslaved pirate raise the blade to his throat.
He had tried to murder me and had to pay the price. My plans, my
perfect strategy to unite the pirates of the Blood Sea, to carefully
enslave their captains, to ravage shipping from Mati to Hyko to Tira
and Chen with my own pirate navy, to conquer one city-state after
another until the entire region was mine, would have to be altered. A
necessity, for my pirate admiral, Kevril Longbright, had to die.

Then…the blade quivered to a halt at his neck. Kevril's eyes
widened from horror to surprise, then narrowed. I'd seen that look
before. It was victory.

The dagger flipped in his hand, then flashed end over end at my face. Only the reflexes honed by a hundred boarding actions saved me. I jerked my head aside, but the razor edge sliced a gash across my cheek. My hand came away from my face bloody.

I stared at him in shock. "How..."

"I'm *immune*," he growled through clenched teeth as he drew cutlass and dagger. "And you're *dead*!"

Kevril advanced, and I backed away, lashing furiously at him with the scourge to keep him at bay. His blades stabbed and slashed, the impervious thongs of the scourge entangling, raking at his wrists, its barbed tips scraping along steel. The scourge tasted his blood; it dripped onto the marble floor from his ravaged hands. But Kevril had spoken truly; he apparently could resist its magic.

I was in trouble.

"Vakna!" My hulking captain had one job—to protect me—and if ever I needed protection, it was now. I dared a glance, and my heart sunk to see Vakna halfway across the ballroom, fighting through the mass of milling council members, escorts, and attendants between us. Even with his broadsword out and flailing to make a lane, he wouldn't arrive in time.

I needed help. Suddenly I realized that I had help all around me; all I need do was command it.

"Help me! He's gone mad!" I slashed again, and the thongs of the scourge clashed against Kevril's cutlass. "Friends! To my aid! Save me!"

Kevril lunged, but it was a feint. I'd sparred with him for years and knew his tricks. I dodged and lashed out with the scourge to block his next move, a low dagger thrust. But that thrust never came. Instead, he dropped his dagger and caught the thongs of the scourge, wrapping them around his hand even as the barbed tips bit into his flesh.

He jerked hard, trying to take it from me, but I wouldn't let go, couldn't release my grip on my weapon, my soul. At the edge of my vision I glimpsed my slaves rushing to my aid, but they were still too far. Kevril raised his cutlass. Panic hazing my fury, I hauled back; never would I release the scourge to him. The fine edge of his sword fell.

I sprawled backward onto the floor, the impact sending a jolt up my spine from tailbone to skull, stunning me for a moment. Reaching back, I tried to lever myself to my feet, but my hand slipped on something, and I went down again, cracking my elbow hard. Then I saw...

I had no right hand.

I stared in horror at the blood, my blood, spurting from my truncated wrist. *Where...* Then I saw it; my severed hand still clung to the haft of the scourge dangling from Kevril's grip. He grinned and lunged with his cutlass, and I was helpless to defend myself.

A thin rapier and a gleaming katana crossed before me to intercept that deadly stroke. Ursula and Getashi stared agape at their own blades; my faithful slaves had finally come to my rescue. I clenched the bleeding stump of my wrist and spat out my revenge.

"Kill him!"

Steel flashed, Kevril's cutlass parrying masterfully as Ursilla's longer blade and Getashi's katana flicked and slashed. He backed, unable to reach me. From around the hall, several of my other slaves closed in.

Then Getashi Temuso surprised me. "Kevril! Run!"

And, to my astonishment, he did.

Screaming vengeful curses, I struggled to my feet as Kevril dodged and weaved, parried and slashed his way across the ballroom. Even Balshi's guards moved to impede him—he had attacked a council member, after all, their master's guest of honor—their halberds crossing in his path. Kevril dropped and slid under the deadly blades, parrying and rolling up to dash on. Where he intended to go, I had no idea. I smiled grimly as I tucked my bleeding stump against my side, trying to staunch the flow. There was nowhere for him to run.

I was wrong.

With the desperation of a pirate fighting across the deck of a burning ship, Kevril Longbright vaulted from the raised dais at the end of the room, soared over a row of stunned guards, and smashed through the stained glass out onto the balcony.

"Kill him!" I screamed.

"Shoot him down!" Brilla cried out, and the Balshi guards responded.

But, even as their crossbows twanged, I saw Kevril leap to the balcony railing and launch himself into the night, my scourge still in hand. If he survived the hundred-foot drop to the lake below, he might even escape alive.

Over my dead body... I almost laughed at the irony of that oath. Kevril had tried to kill me, and failed. He wouldn't get a second chance.

But this was no time to hesitate. My secret was out. Every single member of the Council had seen me command others, and had watched them obey. Every slave now knew of their slavery. I had to martial my forces and catch the goddamned pirate. Plans be damned, it was time to pull out all the stops, to take control of Haven, and to hell with the consequences. Gripping my bleeding wrist, I gritted my teeth and took command.

"All my allies, protect me! Brilla, your time is now! Take your place! The Queen of Haven commands her vassals to carry out their final orders! Strike down your lords and come to me!"

Pandemonium and blood swept through the ballroom.

Brilla stepped up behind her brother, reached around to pull a dagger from his belt, and drew the edge across his throat. Even as he fell and his lady screamed in horror, my sweet slave buried Balshi's blade in his widow's breast. The Balshi guards stared at her in horror, unsure what to do.

Getashi, Ursilla, Captain Vakna, and a late-arriving Tambris Matesh formed a cordon around me, blades facing outward. One of Lady Hatsu's two komei bodyguards swept the head off his comrade in a lightning stroke, then split his charge from crown to crotch. Lord Fa-Chen collapsed wide-eyed as a trusted retainer stabbed him in the back. The gnomish lord, Blinth Tinworthy, and his round little wife went down in a hail of steel as their guards revolted. Ingrid Brickhammer and Tori Blackbriar fared better, fending off their would-be assassins with hammer and dueling sword, fighting back to back toward the exit with their armed escorts. Lord Malchi called his panicked son to his side and cowered behind a wedge of loyal retainers who formed a spearhead to escape. No matter; I would deal with them later.

Nahli Twince clapped her hands once overhead and transformed into a great white eagle. As their lady soared aloft, her two retainers doffed their fox masks to reveal canine faces beneath. They covered her escape, drawing steel to slash and stab with feral ferocity.

Only Hashi Severn stood calmly in the middle of the chaos, gazing around at the blood and mayhem as if vaguely amused.

My eyes fixed upon the smoldering black blade at her breast, and avarice gripped me. My scourge was gone. I needed a weapon fit for the deluge of blood that was to come.

"Vakna, kill Lady Severn and bring me Soul Drinker."

"Yes, your ladyship!" Vakna, gripping his broadsword in two massive hands, stalked toward Severn and her pale companion.

Severn watched him come, quirked a little smile, and released the chain that bound her escort. The pale man strode forth without a command from his mistress, the chained pet turned protector. Though weaponless, the figure curled his hands like ivory claws tipped with shards of obsidian. Pitiless eyes stared steadily at my advancing captain as pale lips drew back from ragged black teeth.

Not for a second did my enslaved captain falter. Vakna struck like a charging bull, sweeping his sword in an arc that should have cut his foe in half. Any normal foe, that is, but Hashi's protector deflected the stroke with a swat from one pale hand, black nails ringing like steel against Vakna's sword. The fell creature's other hand raked across Vakna's face, tearing flesh from bone. Despite the horrible wound, my captain spun with the impact and slashed low. The force of his blow would have felled a tree, and indeed, did sever his foe's legs. The thing fell in a welter of black blood, but the presumably mortal wounds proved only an inconvenience. Without even a cry of anguish, it clawed at Vakna's legs. My battle-hardened captain sidestepped the attack, raised his sword high, and brought it down. The stroke severed the creature's head, and the pale, hairless orb bounced twice before settling on the marble floor. And yet, still, it didn't die. The teeth gnashed, the legs quivered, and the arms stretched out, clawed fingers scrabbling at the floor as it pulled its body forward, black nails cutting furrows in the marble.

The power of Soul Drinker, I realized. *What an army such creatures would make!*

Captain Vakna kicked the thrashing torso aside and strode toward Lady Severn.

Finally, casually, she plucked Soul Drinker from its sheath. Hoarfrost formed on the obsidian blade, but Hashi Severn didn't raise the fell weapon to strike. She merely lifted her other hand to intercept the deadly stroke of Vakna's broadsword.

My captain's fine blade disintegrated into a cloud of rust at her touch.

I caught my breath in horror as Vakna stumbled. Soul Drinker flashed out like a black viper. Though the dagger barely nicked my captain's shoulder, it pulled from the wound a trail of white mist. The mist thickened and pulsed as it flowed from Vakna's flesh and curled around the blade, drawn into the solid obsidian, absorbed by the weapon. With a high-pitched keen, my captain collapsed to his knees. His limbs trembled, then stilled as the last of the trailing mist was drawn into Soul Drinker. His skin now the hue of winter, Vakna yet remained upright, mouth agape, eyes wide. The fell blade had consumed his soul and frozen his flesh to the bone.

Hashi shoved aside the pillar of ice that had been my captain. It hit the floor with a sickening crack, shattering into shards of blue-white flesh.

Then she pointed Soul Drinker at me and arched one dark eyebrow. "Do not vex me, Jhavika."

I opened my mouth to reply, but Brilla's shrill cry surprised me. "Say the word, my love, and I'll have the witch riddled with arrows!"

I looked to find Brilla standing on the dais surrounded not only by the corpses of her brother and sister-in-law, but by a cordon of house guards, their halberds and crossbows at the ready. I considered giving the order, or perhaps commanding Lady Hatsu's komei warrior to kill her, then thought better of it. Arrows would likely fare no better than Vakna's sword against Hashi's fell power, and I dared not risk the komei. I had more pressing matters to attend to.

"No. Let her go. I have no need of her."

Hashi Severn's smile chilled my blood, and she strode from the hall as if she cared not whether anyone lived or died. Perhaps she didn't.

Later, I thought, *when I've consolidated my power and have the scourge back, I'll find you.*

My wrist hurt abominably, but the blood no longer flowed so freely. I took a moment to assess my post-coup situation. I now controlled five houses, and three more would be mine by morning, giving me well more than half the might of Haven. But that triumph paled next to the loss of my scourge.

I'll have it back before the sun rises over Snomish Bay, I swore to myself.

"Brilla! Call your healer to attend me, and send your guards after Kevril Longbright. If he survived the fall to the lake, bring him to me. Above all, bring me my scourge!" I turned to my remaining guardians. Any hope of maintaining the secrecy of their slavery had been destroyed—*Damn you, Kevril!*—so there was no need to prolong the charade. I did, however, have to establish the basic rules; a more thorough conditioning could wait until later. "Ursilla, Getashi, you will never harm me in any way. You will command your houses to serve me. You will—"

Getashi interrupted me with a peal of gibberish. "Utake! Wiera bah nuik!"

I opened my mouth to tell him to shut up, but it was too late. Tesumo's islander bodyguard stepped up to his master, his face solemn, a gleaming kukri in one hand.

"NO!" But I had no way to stop him; he wasn't under my control. Getashi stood perfectly still as his bodyguard thrust the curved blade. The islander twisted the kukri, thrusting his other hand forward. Getashi jerked, shuddered, and fell to the floor. The islander stood there with a bloody blade in one hand, and Getashi's pulsing heart in his other. To my horror, he raised the quivering organ to his mouth.

"Ursilla, kill him!"

Ursilla Roque lunged, her form perfect despite the baffled look on her face, the tip of her rapier piercing the islander's chest. Utake didn't even try to block the thrust, but just fell, his master's heart still clenched between his pointed teeth. I hissed in frustration. Getashi had denied me control of his house, robbing me of one fifth of my forces. He'd been prepared for this, commanded Utake to kill him.

But why would he have been prepared to die tonight?

Suddenly, all the pieces fell into place. Getashi had arranged this entire affair, had given Kevril the opportunity to murder me, had saved Kevril's life by telling him to run. Kevril must have convinced Getashi that he was my slave.

That still didn't explain everything. Kevril had to have known what would happen to Preel, even if he succeeded in killing me. His precious truthsayer would endure atrocities that would make her lifetime of slavery pale by comparison.

But Kevril's not stupid, I realized. *And he's crazy in love with her.* Another piece of the puzzle clicked into place. Kevril would try to take Preel from me. Against all reason, all logic, all the threats of damnation that I could bring down on him, he would try to rescue the woman he loved.

Preel...

The dove that laid diamond eggs. The tale was coming true. *Except this master hasn't been murdered.*

"Everyone, marshal your forces! Call out your guards, your armies, your spies and assassins! Find Kevril Longbright. Take his ship, the *Scourge*! Kill every pirate aboard!" I strode for my coach, even as Brilla's healer struggled to bind my bleeding wrist. The pain stoked my rage like a furnace. "And bring me that fucking pirate's head!"

Chapter Thirty Four
Pirate's Luck

Never discount the tenacity of the truly desperate warrior.
The Lessons of Quen Lau Ush

From the diary of Kevril Longbright –
That I escaped Lord Balshi's estate with my skin at least
somewhat intact astonished me. My mission had failed, but
only in part. Jhavika had survived, but the scourge was mine.
If I could only destroy it, her entire house of cards would fall
apart. That thought, more than anything, kept me alive.

I hit the icy water first, hard enough to numb my legs and
drive the breath from my body. I plunged deep into the darkness, the
snow-melt water from the mountain peaks painfully cold. But I was
alive, and I still clutched my cutlass and the scourge. I still had a
chance.

Kicking off my boots, I fought my way upward, guided only by
the shimmering light on the surface. Pain lanced through my right leg,
perhaps some injury I hadn't noticed during my flight. I blessed
Getashi Temuso for telling me to run; I honestly hadn't considered it

until he told me to. I wondered if he was alive and still a slave, or if he'd escaped the only other way possible.

I broke the surface, and the pounding of White Rock Falls, muted underwater, nearly deafened me. The roar would, however, cover my gasping breaths from any within earshot. The current was already taking me downstream, beyond the lights of Balshi's palace. Darkness was my ally now, for there would be soldiers hunting me. But as the roar of the falls diminished, another grew. There were deadly rapids at the egress of Mirror Lake. I had to reach shore before I was tumbled to death in the flow.

Sheathing my cutlass, I felt for the source of the pain in my leg and found the fletching of a crossbow bolt. Touching it sent jolts of agony through me, but I couldn't swim and certainly couldn't run with it embedded in my flesh. I felt around to the front of my leg and touched the bulge of the bolt's head, not quite protruding from the skin.

Shit!

There was no other way. I slammed my palm into the fletched end of the arrow, screaming my agony into the water. Fumbling my fingers around to the front again, I gripped the barbed head of the bolt and jerked the whole thing free from my leg.

I thanked the gods for the numbing chill, as the waves of pain subsided. Now if I could just make it to shore before I froze to death.

Shuddering with the cold, I swam as best I could for the southern shore. I would have to get through Haven on foot, injured and without boots, before Jhavika could marshal her army to find me. With any luck, she'd soon discover that Preel was gone. I wondered which would enrage her more, the loss of the scourge, her hand, or her truthsayer. I also wondered how that rage would manifest.

Her wrath would be terrible. I had to get the hell out of Haven.

I clawed my way ashore fifty feet from the rapids and certain death. Cursing the pain in my leg, I pulled my last dagger and split my pant leg to tie it around the wound. I could stand and walk, but I needed to run. It was perhaps half a mile to the city proper by the road, but there would be carriages and soldiers there. The beeline route would be rougher, but faster on foot. I lamented the loss of my boots and started off at my best speed, which wasn't very good.

Exercise and the warmth of the sultry night banished the chill of the lake, and my pace increased, but between my injured leg and the sharp rocks beneath my bare feet, I didn't know if I would make it. I considered cutting my jacket into rags and wrapping my feet, but I didn't have time to spare. My need for haste superseded comfort.

I blessed the first smooth cobbles my ravaged feet encountered, but I knew what still lay before me: the filthy streets of Haven and the dregs of a society bereft of laws. Ruthless cutthroats lurked in every alley, and they'd certainly murder me for my shiny weapons and fancy jacket. Well, if they tried it, they were in for a surprise.

I drew my cutlass and limbered up Jhavika's scourge. I doubted its magic would work for me, but it had a longer reach than a dagger and would better dissuade any assault. I didn't meet any resistance for the first few blocks, probably because I passed the cowering wretches before they could respond; bare feet at least made me silent.

Then my luck ran out.

A group of thugs—about ten by my quick count—blocked my path. It was hard to tell in the darkness, but I could make out an assortment of weapons: broken boards studded with nails, daggers, cleavers, and clubs. They were filthy, starving, and desperate. I would have bet that my desperation matched theirs, but I couldn't fight so many.

I stopped and brandished my weapons. "Nobody's got to die here. Leave off."

"Can't take us all with one sword and that whip," one of them said as they all crept forward and fanned out. "Whips don't hurt none anyways."

"Maybe I can't take all of you, but I'll wager half of you will lie dead on the street before I fall. Any volunteers to go first?" This gave them pause, long enough for me to think. "But nobody has to die at all, and I can offer you something worth far more than my sword and jacket."

"Like what?" The grim man in the fore edged into the wan light of a second-floor window. His face was deeply pitted from pox, his hair patchy and sparse, but he held his spiked club in a wiry strong fist.

"I'm Captain Kevril Longbright of the pirate corsair *Scourge*." I stood up straight and leveled my cutlass at him. "Get me through the city to the quay, and I swear by all I hold dear that I'll take you on as members of my crew. That means three meals a day, a dry place to sleep, a sword in your hand, and training in seamanship."

That really brought them up short. Muttered curses, oaths, and exclamations of disbelief rattled through them like hail on a tin roof.

"How do we know we can trust you?"

"Because I'm a dead man if I don't get to the quay, and you're a dead man if you try to stop me." I flourished my cutlass again. "I don't have time to fuck around here. Make your decision." If they decided a bird in the hand was worth a whole flock in the bush, I'd have to cut and run. I was in bad shape, but I was healthy and well-fed. They were starving and wretched.

They muttered amongst themselves for a moment, but need won out over caution, and their spokesman nodded.

"All right, Captain Longcock, we're yer escort through the perils of Haven." He brandished his club. "Double-cross us, and you die."

"It's Long*bright*," I countered with a snort of grim laughter. "And I won't double-cross you. I need you as much as you need me. Now, to the quay as quick as you can!"

I followed my grimy escort at their best speed. Mine would have been faster, but I wasn't about to complain; they got the job done. The other shadows cowered in their holes as we passed. Evidently, this mob garnered some respect in the cesspool of Haven's streets.

"What's your name?" I asked their apparent leader after a few blocks.

"What's it matter?" he shot back with a scowl.

"I've got to call you *something* aboard ship."

290

"Call me Spike, then. I gave up my name when I killed my fucker of a father."

A pang of understanding—my own abusive father—smote me. "Spike, then. I hope the fucker deserved it."

He snorted and spat. "They all deserve it. You talk too much."

"Part of the job. Captains talk. It's called giving *orders*."

"Orders?" Another grimy figure snorted a laugh. "I used to take orders when I worked as a barmaid! Ha!"

That got more snorts of laughter, even one from me.

Miraculously, we made it to the waterfront without a fight and before Jhavika's forces arrived to cut us down. A longboat bobbed at the quay wall, four grim pirates standing in front of it onshore, loaded crossbows in hand. They raised their weapons, and I recognized Foist's deep-voiced warning.

"Leave off, you rabble, or we'll shoot you down."

"Stand down, Foist." I stepped to the fore. "Shooting your captain's called mutiny, and these *rabble* are my escort and our new shipmates."

"Captain? Gods and devils!" He waved their weapons down. "What the hells *happened* to you! And what's this mob?"

"This mob got me through the city without getting gutted for my clothes. I promised to take them on as crew, and I'm going to make good on that promise!" I waved my filthy escort forward. "Everyone aboard!"

"Oh, aye, sir, but..." Foist cringed away from the reeking vagabonds I'd just recruited. "But what happened at the party? Did you...um...kill her?"

"No, but I took her hand...and this." I raised the scourge for them to see. "Unfortunately, that makes her a wounded dragon now, so we've got to haul anchor and haul ass."

"Aye, sir!" We tumbled aboard the launch and Foist took an oar while I took the tiller. My escort of thugs looked nervous.

We were halfway to the ship when I asked the only question that really mattered to me. "And your mission, Foist?" That he was here

291

waiting for me meant that not everyone had been slaughtered, but not necessarily that it had been successful. *Please, dear Odea, please...* "Did you...get the prize?"

"Oh, aye, sir, and mad as a wet cat she is." Foist shook his head and bent his oar. "I'll let yer first mate tell the tale, but she's safe aboard."

My heart lifted in my chest, and all of my pains, injuries, and fatigue washed away in a torrent of relief. Preel was safe aboard *Scourge*. I might not have killed Jhavika, but we now had a chance for freedom...and each other.

Chapter Thirty Five
The Rapacious Scoundrel

Even compassion is suspect if offered from a hated hand.
The Lessons of Quen Lau Ush.

From the journal of Preel Longbright –
The familiar surroundings, the faces of my friends, the scent
of *him* on the sheets of the bed we so long shared, plagued me
like a taskmaster's lash. Lies and truth, love and hate,
unending hours of tenderness and the horrific violation if had
all been manipulation, all warred in my head. My memories
tortured me. If I could have deleted them then, I fear I would
have.

Despite my anger, I tolerated Bert's tender care. How could I not?
She had always been kind to me, nursed me, doted on me, pampered
me with her love. I couldn't reconcile my tender feelings for her with
the violent vengeance I harbored for Kevril. I wished Miko hadn't put
me here on the very bed I'd shared with him; it roused too may
conflicting memories. This was where he'd handed me a dagger and
bared his breast, told me to bury the blade in his heart if I didn't know

how he felt about me. Then, I had been so sure that I loved him. Now, I was equally sure that I no longer did.

He murdered my sister.

What would I do if offered that dagger again? I was afraid to find out.

"That should do, dear." Bert finished with the last bandage around my wrist and slipped the golden manacle back down over the soft linen. "I'm sorry for those damned things, but... Well, you know."

Yes, I knew. Miko had apologized a hundred times for kidnapping me against my will, binding me, enslaving me, chaining me to Kevril's bunk. I couldn't hate her or Wix or the rest of them; they were only following *his* orders. One of my friends, however, I hadn't yet seen, and Hemp's absence worried me. I wondered if Kevril might have finally killed him in a fit of rage.

Before Bert could pack up her things and leave me alone, I clapped my hands and pantomimed writing. The chains, strung from my wrists through an eye bolt in the bulkhead, clattered.

"I don't know if that's a good idea, Preel. The captain—"

I clapped my hands loudly, the chains clashing again, and made a pleading gesture.

"Oh, all right." Bert put down her bag and fetched a pen and paper from the table.

She held a pot of ink for me to wet the nib, and I wrote, "Where is Hemp?"

"Oh, he's confined to the guest cabin. He...um...tried to cut his own throat a while back. Seems Jhavika lashed him with that bloody whip of hers and ordered him to spy on you and the captain. Told him to cut his throat if anybody pressed him for anything about her." She chuckled. "He did, too, but not deep. He outfoxed her right enough." She took the pen and paper back. "Now, you rest here, Preel. You been through all Nine Hells. Captain'll be back soon enough."

The door closed, and I sat staring at it in dread. *Kevril. Gods, please no.* I may have loved him once, but not now. *Murderer... If he killed Jhavika, so help me...*

But under my anger, dread loomed. What would he do to me? I'd revealed his lies, told him I didn't love him. How would his wrath take form? I looked around at my familiar surroundings and imagined the worst. Why else would he command Miko to chain me here on his bed? If Kevril had seduced me, manipulated me, and now knew I had learned of his lies...

Please, Gods of Light and Darkness, not that. Not from him.

Shouts and thumps from overhead told me the crew was suddenly busy. Cries of "Topcrew aloft!" and "Waisters to the capstan!" meant that we were hauling anchor and getting underway. That could mean only one of two things: either Kevril was dead, or he had returned to the ship. The latter meant that Jhavika was dead. My heart and mind disagreed on which would be the more terrible news.

More rumbling footsteps and calls from overhead, and I tried to see in my mind's eye what was happening. I couldn't pick out any familiar voices save Wix's colorful obscenities. Flexing my hands, I girded my tortured nerves. I'd know soon enough.

The door to the cabin opened, and a ragged caricature of the man I had loved and now hated stood there staring at me. Kevril looked horrible: his shirt torn, his face gaunt and riddled with tiny cuts, the small beard making him look even thinner. His pants were torn, too, one blood-soaked leg bound around the thigh, more blood trailing down his shin. His feet were bare and filthy, and a stench of raw sewage wafted in with him.

"Gods above, Preel!" He strode forth, and I cringed back, but my eye caught two more details I'd missed before. A cutlass rode at his hip, the fancy one with the dragon guard, and a cat-o'-nine-tails hung from his belt.

Jhavika's scourge. There was no way that she would have relinquished it. The sight of it hanging from Kevril's belt told me the horrible truth: he'd murdered her.

Jhavika...my sister... Gods, please no.

Kevril knelt beside the bunk, reaching out to touch me. "I'm so sorry you had to—"

Murderer!

I lashed out with my foot—*serpent strikes low*—and the hard edge struck true. The blow had all the force of my leg behind it, and sent him sprawling to the cabin sole. Kevril heaved up, spitting blood. I may well have sealed my own fate with that one kick, but death at his hands would be less painful than enduring the torment of his touch.

But when Kevril looked at me, his chin dripping blood, there was only shock and pain on his face, not rage.

He whirled to the door, still unsteady, and opened it. "Bert! I need you in here!"

"Two shakes, Captain!"

Kevril closed the door and limped to his cabinet without looking at me. Glass clinked, and he downed a glass of amber liquid. I could smell the spiced rum. He swallowed and hissed in pain, then poured another.

The door opened, and Bert came in again with her bag, fresh bandages, and a bucket of steaming water that smelled of lye. She took one look at Kevril and stopped short. "Miko said you took an arrow in the leg and your feet were cut up, but not that you got hit in the face."

"I didn't." Kevril accepted a cloth to wipe the blood from his chin and looked at me again, distress clear on his face. "Preel kicked me."

"She..." Bert stared at me in shock.

I tapped the gag, intent on fighting him the only way I could.

"Go ahead and take it off, Bert." Kevril sat down and eased his grimy feet into the bucket, hissing again in pain.

"You sure, sir? She don't seem quite right, if you know what I mean."

"She's not. She's been enslaved by the scourge and filled with lies that she's been forced to believe. I need to talk to her, to make her understand."

"Suit yourself." Bert leaned over me and untied the gag.

"*Murderer!*" I spat, venting all my anguish in that one word. "You killed my sister!"

"Your *sister*?" Kevril looked confused again. "I wouldn't even know where to *look* for your sister."

"*Jhavika* was my sister! You *murdered* her! Miko said so, and you've got her scourge!"

"Gods and devils preserve us." Bert made a warding sign before sitting down to unwrap the makeshift bandage from Kevril's thigh.

Kevril winced and downed another swallow of rum. "Preel, Jhavika's not your sister. You've been enslaved by the scourge. She lied to you. And, anyway, I didn't kill her."

I fell back against the headboard. *Truth or lie?* In Kevril's eyes I saw the truth. "You...*didn't* kill her?"

"No. I tried, I'll admit, but failed." He gritted his teeth as Bert probed the wound in his leg. "I took her hand and the scourge, but she was alive and kicking mad when last I saw her."

"Her *hand*?" My heart wrenched at the thought of Jhavika maimed. *But if she's alive...* "Take me back! I was *safe* with Jhavika! I was *good* for her! She's not a monster! I can *help* her!"

He stared at me, and I hated the sadness in his eyes. "She's filled you full of lies, love. It's the scourge talking, not—"

"Don't you *dare* call me that!" I jerked my wrists hard against the chains, longing to slap him, to hurt him, to maim him as he'd maimed Jhavika. "I love *her*, not you!"

"No, you don't, Preel. It's the *scourge*." The calm certitude in Kevril's voice stabbed me. He plucked the length of dragon flesh from his belt and threw it onto the table as if that explained everything. "It's this!"

"I *know* it's the scourge, you..." I bit off the curse and turned away, willing myself not to cry. "That means nothing."

"It means *everything*, love. She's turned you—"

"I *told* you to not fucking *call* me that, you gods-damned pirate!" I lurched forward, the manacles biting into my wrists and wrenching my shoulders. "You *lied* to me! You *seduced* me! You *never* loved me. You just wanted a truthsayer you could *fuck*!"

Bert gasped, her face flushing crimson. "Sir! Let me put that gag back on her. There's no point to lettin' her rave like this."

"No, Bert. Let her talk." Kevril's gaze settled on me again. "I need to know what she's been commanded to believe. I need her to trust me."

"*Trust* you! How can I trust anything you've ever done?" I raged. "For all I know you *sent* Giet into this cabin to ravage me just so you could play the gallant!"

"Sir, *please*!" Bert pleaded, disgust and anger contorting her face.

Bert obviously didn't believe that Kevril could have done such a thing, so why did I? I dug the heels of my hands into my eyes and fell back against the headboard again, assailed by confusion and love and hate and grief all at once. I clenched my teeth against the scream that fought to escape, fearing that my sanity would flee with it.

"No, Bert." Kevril growled curses as she started to scrub his lacerated feet. Bloody water dripped into the bucket. "I swore never again to put the gag on Preel unless she asked me to. I need to have her on my side if I'm going to have any hope of destroying the scourge."

His words struck me a blow. "What?" I dropped my hands and glared at him. "If you *what*?"

"I'm going to destroy the scourge, Preel." He lifted the vile thing from the table and squeezed the leather until it creaked. "This isn't about Jhavika, and it's not about revenge or pride. It's about *this*." He shook the scourge, then pitched it back down onto the table. "Once it's gone, you'll be free."

My mind raced.

Free... Another lie? No, it couldn't be. I knew the scourge had tasted my flesh, that Jhavika had used it to control me, but knowing that didn't change the way I felt; Jhavika had commanded me to love her, so I did. But if the enchantment was broken, if I could trust my feelings, I'd know what was real and what was a lie. That was the only thing that seemed logical, an answer to my plight.

"Yes."

"Yes?" Kevril looked at me askance. "Yes *what?*"

"I'll help you destroy it." The decision felt right, the first genuine sentiment I'd had in who knew how long. "The scourge can be destroyed without killing its master; Jhavika asked me that question. Once it's gone, I'll know my feelings are true, and Jhavika will be free of it."

Kevril straightened in his chair, some of the man I knew so very well—or thought I knew—returning to his face. "Good. How long until I can ask you a question that will invoke your talent without endangering your life?"

Of course, he can't risk my life, I thought venomously. *I am, quite literally, his fucking truthsayer.*

With that thought, the notion that I could escape this torment with a simple lie struck me. If he asked me a question that invoked my talent right now, the strain would likely kill me. I'd be truly free. *He'll expect that*, I realized. *Even if I lie, he won't believe me.*

But perhaps I could shame him into a bargain that would forestall any torment.

"I'll tell you, if you agree to one stipulation."

He looked surprised. "I can't free you from restraint, Preel. In your state of mind, I—"

"Not that."

"Okay, what then?"

"You don't *touch* me!" I gritted my teeth at the shock that crossed his face, and unloaded all of my loathsome terrors right into his lap. "Not even platonically. You either put me in another cabin or stay the hell out of here. I don't want to be in the same space or breathe the same *air* as you. The only time I'll even tolerate seeing you is when you ask a question that invokes my truthsayer talent."

The muscles beneath the scars that Jhavika had given him writhed. I'd hurt him, offended him. So be it.

Kevril looked away from me and nodded. "I agree to your terms, Preel. I'll arrange for separate accommodation as soon as I can."

"Good."

"So, how long must I wait to ask you a question?" Still he didn't look at me.

"Three days."

"Very well."

We fell into an uneasy silence, we three. Bert scrubbed Kevril's feet, applied a foul-smelling unguent, then wrapped them in clean linen. She anointed and bound his leg as well. Kevril swilled spiced rum. I averted my gaze as Bert cut off his pants and handed him a robe. I ignored the twinge in my heart; I'd given him that robe as a gift.

Tenderness... Love... Caring... The memories were real. I knew they were, but there were too many contradictory truths swirling around in my mind, impossible to ignore.

Bert finally finished her work, instructing Kevril not to walk on his injured feet unless he had to, and telling him she would change the bandages daily. He agreed, and she left without looking at me.

Kevril immediately stood and strode to his cabinet for another drink.

I opened my mouth to tell him he was breaking his word, then stopped myself. The impulse had come from nowhere, a reflex I no longer needed or wanted. I looked away, refusing to feel what I remembered feeling for him, but knew I was lying to myself.

Kevril returned to the bedside and placed a tumbler on the night table. "I thought you might need a drink."

"And I thought you were going to not *be* here," I spat.

"I will be shortly gone." He hobbled to the quarter gallery, and I heard the splashing of water and brushing of teeth through the closed door.

I turned and looked at the tumbler he'd left for me. *Probably drugged...* I felt ill as I considered what he might do to me if I fell unconscious.

I recollected the atrocities my former masters had committed upon me, then the peace and safety I had learned to expect aboard *Scourge*. Even before I was free, when I lay chained to this very bunk, save for the lone attack of a vengeful midshipman, nobody had ever touched me without my consent.

Once, a slave at the time, I had even kissed Kevril without *his* consent. I slumped as that sweet wine-addled memory came back to me. I had so wanted him to touch me, to hold me, to love me, but he had relentlessly refused. At the time, I had wondered if he preferred men. I'd learned later that this wasn't so, and I'd loved him all the more for his restraint.

My memories couldn't lie... *I'd loved him.*

I clenched my nails into my palms against the truth.

Kevril emerged from the quarter gallery clean-shaven and smelling of scented soap. He glanced at me, at the untouched drink, and sighed. Limping to his clothes locker, he began removing shirts, jackets, pants, and a pair of worn boots.

Finally, he spoke.

"I'll honor my agreement with you, Preel, because I know what you're going through." He looked at me, his eyes cold, then dropped his gaze. "I've *felt* what you're going through. I know that confusion, that helplessness, that...impotence."

I recalled the night he returned from Jhavika's party, the night he'd learned of his slavery. I remembered his impotent rage, his pain, and mine to see him so. "I remember."

"And that's all I'll ask from you." He gathered up his things and shuffled for the door, then paused, still not looking at me. "Just remember. Your memories are yours, they're true. No magic can alter them. You told me so. That alone, you can trust. Not what I tell you, not what Jhavika told you, not anything else. Just remember."

Before I could reply, he opened the door and was gone, leaving me alone to my thoughts and memories.

I sat still for a very long time...and remembered. Running my hand across the soft sheets, I recalled the very first night I lay on this bunk, utterly helpless, vulnerable, at the mercy of a pirate captain, fearing the worst.

Kevril had soothed my fears then—"You might have heard that pirates are rapacious scoundrels... I however, am not."—and I'd loved him for it.

And yet, I loved Jhavika, too, my dearest friend.

But I also remembered hating her after she'd kidnapped me, plotting to kill her, manipulating her, falsely befriending her to better my situation and temper her wrath, even teaching her yamshi. I recalled the first time she touched me, the revulsion I'd felt, the urge to draw away. And yet, I loved her. She was the family I'd lost, my sister. *Because she told me so.*

I took up the tumbler of spiced rum and knocked it back at one swallow. The fire burned the lump from my throat. I drew a deep breath and let it out, imagining all my thoughts, all my dreads, all my memories leaving me with that expelled breath.

It didn't work.

I lay down and clutched the pillow that smelled like the man I remembered loving, whom I now hated, and I wept myself to sleep.

Chapter Thirty Six
Wrath of the Dragon

A dragon in pain is a danger beyond reckoning.
The Lessons of Quen Lau Ush

From the journal of Jhavika Keshmir –
Perhaps I am insane. Perhaps the pain of losing the scourge, Preel, and my hand all in one night has driven me over the edge. If I am mad then, I have good reason. Woe to those who stand against my just wrath.

"Faster, gods damn it!" I screamed, pounding a fist on the carriage roof. I had to get back to my estate before they took my truthsayer.

Careening around a corner, one wheel struck something, and the whole conveyance lurched. I threw my arms out to steady myself, forgetting that one now ended in a stump. A scream escaped my throat at the agonizing jolt, even worse than the cauterizing. Brilla's healer had offered opium to dull the pain, but that would have also dulled my wits, which I couldn't allow. I would have to think to exact my revenge and get my scourge back.

"Damn you, Kevril!" The curse had become my mantra. I whispered it again and again as I clutched my arm and willed away the throbbing pain.

Even keener than the loss of my hand, however, was his theft of my scourge. Not a physical pain, but more visceral. A part of my soul had been torn away.

I'll get it back...and I'll mount Kevril's head on a fucking wall.

The carriage clattered to an abrupt halt. Shouts, cries, and the panicked neighing of horses rang out from behind as my entourage tried to stop without slamming into one another. Sticking my head out the window, I saw that the portcullis to my keep was down, the gates closed. The guards I had sent ahead milled about, still on horseback, while high atop the curtain wall, torches illuminated ranks of crossbowmen with weapons readied.

I stormed from my carriage. "What the hell's going on?"

"They won't let us in," said one of my personal guard.

"Use the gods-damned password!" I commanded.

He wheeled his mount and called out, "Dragon's Tears! Open the gate," but no one replied, and the gate remained closed. "I'm sorry, your ladyship. We've tried. They refused."

"Refused? What the hell is going on?" The knot of dread in my gut told me that something had happened. Something horrible. I strode forth and called up. "Lieutenant Yorish!"

"Who's there?" a voice called from above. I recognized the officer I'd left in charge in my absence.

"The woman who can command you to leap off the fucking parapet! Lady Keshmir! Now open the gods-damned gate!"

"Open the gate!" Yorish bellowed.

"About damned time!" I boarded my carriage as the portcullis rose, and we rolled into the courtyard. Stepping down, I watched as the other carriages stopped and my cohort of slaves piled out. I raised a hand to halt Ursilla and Tambris in their tracks. "Wait here for your forces to arrive, while I attend to a few things. Brilla, come with me."

Turing my face up to the wall, I bellowed, "Yorish! Get the hell down here!"

He hurried up a moment later, looking a little ill. "Here, your ladyship! I must tell you—"

"Wait! I need you to do something first. Yorish, you're my new captain of the guard. Vakna's dead." I showed him my bandaged wrist, and his eyes widened. "I was attacked by Kevril Longbright. I want you to mobilize every asset we have to find him, barring my personal house guard. They'll stay with me. Longbright's undoubtedly fleeing to his ship. Blockade the quay. I'll send reinforcements soon."

"At once, your ladyship!" Yorish barked orders, and soldiers scrambled to obey.

When he turned back to me, I demanded, "Now, tell me what the bloody hells happened here! Why did you not respond to the password?"

Yorish paled. "There was...an incident, your ladyship. A guard, one of your entourage tonight, came to the postern gate about an hour ago and asked to see Ty-lee. He said you needed him urgently at Lord Balshi's estate."

"What? Who? I sent no one!"

"The big fellow, Gerrard, your ladyship. He insisted you needed Ty-lee at once. They both left, but then they returned only minutes later, and..." He faltered, his lip quivering uncertainly.

My gut twisted. "*Tell* me!"

"They stole Preel."

"*Stole* her?" My darkest fears had come true. I clenched my remaining hand so hard it shook. I'd sent no messenger, and Ty-lee would never have taken Preel from the estate. This had to have been a deception by Kevril. *But how?* He'd been with me less than an hour ago. "Follow me and tell me *exactly* what happened!" I hurried across the foyer and mounted the steps toward Preel's room.

"Ty-lee...wasn't acting like himself, your ladyship. He ordered a footman to take him to Preel's room. Then, there was screaming from inside, but they'd blocked the door. When we finally broke it down, we found Preel's guards and the footman dead, her servants beaten unconscious, and...Preel was gone."

My heart pounded against my bruised ribs. Ty-lee asking for directions to Preel's rooms made no sense at all. Only a stranger in the keep would need directions. *A disguise?* Pain lanced up my leg as I turned a heel on the steps. I cursed my dress shoes, kicked them off at the first landing, and raced on. "How the hell did they get her out?"

"Out the window, it was smashed open," Yorish continued as he huffed along behind me.

"Fuck!" I raged as I dashed up the next flight, cursing myself for ever thinking that Kevril was beaten, that I'd won. He'd played me like a fiddle.

Two new guards stood by the doorway to Preel's rooms. Why the hell were they guarding an empty room? Ignoring them, I stepped over the splintered door, then stopped short. Two guards and a footman lay just inside, bloody and quite dead, one's face completely crushed in. The sitting room was a shambles, the table splintered, apparently used to smash away the bars on the window. A fathom-long ballista bolt pierced the ceiling, a stout line trailing from it out the window, their escape route.

The bedroom door had been smashed open, and I rushed inside. The bed sheets were rumpled, and Preel was conspicuously absent. *Stolen, right from under my nose!* Seething, I stalked back into the sitting room.

Nala and Binsh stood to one side, hands clasped before them, eyes down, obviously injured and miserable. My face grew hot and my entire body trembled. I'd ordered them to protect her with their lives, yet they lived.

"Nala! Tell me *exactly* what happened here!"

"Your ladyship!" Nala looked up, then to her brother, then at her feet. "Ty-lee and one of your personal guards killed the door guards, overpowered Binsh, and broke into Preel's bedroom. I tried to defend her, I swear, but they were too skilled and strong! I was knocked unconscious. When we awoke, Preel was gone."

"Ty-lee would *never* have done this!" I'd condition my steward far too well for him to even think of betraying me. "This was *not* Ty-lee!"

Nala cowered. "I know only that it looked like him, your ladyship. He wielded a katana I'd never seen him wear, and the guard with him, Wix, held two daggers with heavy spiked guards. He knocked me—"

"Wix?" The familiar name stabbed me like a lance. Now I understood Preel's answers to my last two questions. Tewhirke Kettleblack had nothing to do with me, and everything to do with one pirate captain. The alchemist had made him potions to disguise his crew so they could steal Preel from me. *Damn you, Kevril!* "Fucking FUCK!" I slammed my fist into the wall, forgetting my severed hand.

Pain exploded up my arm, tearing a scream from my throat. Nala and Binsh grabbed my elbows to keep me from collapsing as I cried out my anguish.

Preel...my companion, my friend, my sister...my truthsayer! This can't be fucking happening!

Bereft of both the scourge and my truthsayer, I was nothing. I struggled to breathe, but couldn't inhale. On the verge of panic, I realized the constriction around my chest was my corset. Though the fine mail sewn into the garment had saved my life from Kevril's dagger, it was now suffocating me.

Brilla hurried up, uttering soothing nonsense. I'd forgotten she was even there. Gasping, I commanded her, "Brilla! Cut these...gods-damned...corset laces! I can't...breathe!"

"Yes, Jhavika!"

She applied the very same dagger that had slain her brother, the bowstring-taut laces parting like a sail ripping in a hurricane. I drew a deep, cleansing breath, forcing away the darkness that threatened to close in. Though my arm throbbed to the beat of my racing heart, my legs steadied, and I tore myself free of Nala and Binsh's grasps. The world around me refused to burst into flames as I silently wished it would so that everyone would suffer as I was suffering.

Heaving in another breath, I exhaled slowly, releasing the tension that had my body wound as tight as a spring. *As Preel taught me.* Calm settled into me like an icy snowfall, chilling me to the bone, but leaving me able to think again. I had three tasks before me: rescue Preel, retrieve my scourge, and kill Kevril Longbright. I could do this.

But first, I needed to deal with my recalcitrant household staff.

"Guards!" The door guards were at my sides before the echo of my voice died. "Give me your belt daggers." I held out my left hand.

The two hilts smacked into my palm. I turned to Preel's failed protectors.

"Nala, Binsh, each of you take a dagger."

They did.

"Now, face one another and look into each other's eyes."

They complied, their faces streaked with tears. They knew something terrible was coming. I strived not to disappoint them.

"Do you know what the word 'eviscerate' means?"

"Yes, your ladyship," they both sobbed.

"Good. Now, when I leave this room, you will eviscerate each other. You will pull out each other's every last organ with your bare hands until your hearts cease to beat. Do you understand this command?"

"Yes, your ladyship," they both said, still staring into each other's eyes, still weeping.

"Jhavika." Brilla's hand touched my shoulder. "It wasn't their fault. They were overpowered."

I looked at this woman—this slave—who loved me above all other humans in the world, and asked, "Would you like to join them?"

Brilla looked shocked, then mortified. "N...no, my love. I live only to please you. But I don't want the pain of this...setback to destroy you. Please."

She cared for me, I knew she did, because I'd commanded her to. But I didn't need love right now. I needed obedience. "Please me, then, by following my orders, Brilla. You will stand here and watch these two slaves until they are both dead. You will take the greatest pleasure you have ever felt in watching them. You will revel in their pain. You will do this because you love me, and will perish of heartbreak if you don't follow my every command. When they are dead, you will attend me. Nod if you understand me."

Brilla nodded, her face drained of color.

As I turned and strode from the room, screams shrilled the air behind me, two in agony and one in ecstasy. The screams continued to echo through the halls as I marched toward my chambers. I wondered if Brilla would be sane when the evening was done, but it didn't really matter. I didn't need her sane. I needed her for her army, and she'd already ordered her officers to obey me.

"Guards, summon my physician, my alchemist, and my sage to my quarters at once. Also summon my personal attendants and my armorer. I must be garbed for war!"

Guards and attendants scattered like leaves on the wind to do my bidding.

I'm coming for you, Kevril Longbright, I vowed. How he'd outwitted me so far, I didn't know, but I had to prepare for the eventuality of him reaching Scourge and escaping Haven. *You might escape the city, but you won't escape me!*

But to catch him at sea, I needed one more thing.

"Send all unattached forces to the waterfront! I need *ships*! Every ship in harbor! I want them NOW!"

Chapter Thirty Seven
Flight from the Dragon

There is nothing more powerful in the world than hope.
The Lessons of Quen Lau Ush

From the diary of Kevril Longbright –
It seems ironic that, in my flight from Haven, my thoughts
went to the Council of Lords. I wondered what had happened
after my departure from Balshi's palace: who lived and who
perished, what would happen to the balance of power, and if
there would be a Haven to return to at all. I also entertained
many fantasies about what Jhavika's slaves would do to her
once I'd destroyed the scourge.

Sharing a cabin with Hemp was going to be problematic; the space
was tiny compared to the great cabin, and he snored. A lifetime at sea
had inured me to confined spaces and the sounds, smells, and quirks
of other sailors, however, and I found his presence oddly comforting.
It was reminiscent of my time as a midshipman.

That, unfortunately, brought back memories of Jhavika and our
time together under Captain Kohl.

There wasn't much joy to be had aboard *Scourge* in those days, so the officers and crew found it wherever we could. Jhavika and I found it in each other's pants. We were young, healthy, and as randy as year-old pups, but there was little emotion involved. I was promoted to lieutenant barely a month before her, which made us virtual equals, so there was no question of favoritism. I never loved her, but we enjoyed each other's company with abandon. I learned two things from her in those years. First, sex in a hammock is next to impossible. Second, to never trust her. That second lesson came only minutes after we escaped the trap that had killed Captain Kohl, when she'd tried to put a blade in my back.

Perhaps that was why I had the nightmare.

The dream started out predictably, considering the circumstances. I missed Preel horribly, and her blow to my ego, not to mention my face, left me bereft. I went to sleep wondering if we might have a life together when this was all over, if she could ever love me again. In my dream, my wishful thinking came true. The scourge was destroyed, and Preel's heart was mine once again. Together in my cabin, she told me that she loved me, that she wanted me to touch her again. Then, in the midst of the most wonderful lovemaking, she changed into Jhavika, smiled down at me, and plunged a dagger between my ribs.

In the dark cabin, I snapped awake, believing for a moment that it was real, that we had literally impaled one another, her implement steel and mine flesh. Then I felt the swing of my hammock and thought, *Sex in a hammock? No way.* I felt my ribs and found no blade, then lower, and discovered my typical morning condition.

My morning flagstaff, Preel used to call it.

Used to... Preel... A far more painful reality than my dream crashed down upon me.

"Bloody hells." I rolled out of the hammock and landed on my injured feet. Biting off a cry, I dropped to my knees, but that wasn't much better. The arrow injury in my thigh stabbed me as the muscle stretched.

"Sir? You all right?" Hemp thumped to the deck, and the lamp flared from a low glow to blinding white.

"Fine, Hemp." I wasn't, but I didn't want him fawning over me. "Just forgot my bloody feet."

"Here, sir." He helped me to the cabin's single chair. "Just put yer feet up on the desk here and let old Hemp have a look-see."

"I'm fine, Hemp, really." I bent my uninjured leg to look at the sole of one foot and grimaced. The greenish unguent that Bert had slathered on had soaked through the bandage, along with quite a lot of blood. Hemp muttered and placed a hand on the linen.

"Swole up, but it ain't hot yet."

"It'll do." I pointed to the clothes rack. "Pants and a shirt. The loose ones."

He helped me get dressed with minimal fawning, but balked when I asked for my boots.

"None of that, sir. You ain't never gonna get those feet in boots. Best to go without 'til they're healed."

"Bert said not to get my feet wet." I could tell by the motion of the ship that there was a sea running and we were beating, which meant wet decks. I could also tell from the light through the port that the sun would be up soon. "It's first light. I need to go on deck."

"Well, I could get a couple bosun's mates to haul you up in a chair."

"To hell with that!" I put slow pressure on my feet and stood. The pain was manageable, but I wouldn't be running any foot races. "I'll ask Bert which is the lesser of two evils, boots or wet feet."

"Fair enough, sir." Hemp helped me on with a jacket and knocked on the cabin door. The bolt clicked, and a crewman looked in. "Just the captain leavin', Getri. Fetch me a biscuit and a cuppa, would you?"

"Sure." Getri looked me up and down. "Need help, sir?"

"No. Just going to the galley. I'll have Bert send something for you, Hemp."

"Thank you, sir." Getri closed the door and threw the bolt.

I hobbled to the galley to find Bert working over the stove.

She glanced at me, kicked a stool in my direction, and snapped, "Sit!"

I sat. "Thanks. I need to go on deck, but you said no boots and to keep my feet dry. Choose which."

She frowned at me. "Boots, but only for a short while. And *loose* ones! You shouldn't be walkin' at all."

"No choice." I started to get up, then stopped. "Hemp's awake, so if you'll make up a tray for him, I'll take it. And I'm going to have to ask you to take care of Preel for me. She doesn't want me anywhere near her."

"After what she said to you, I'm surprised you ain't trailin' her behind the ship in an open boat!" Bert hadn't kept her displeasure with Preel a secret. She didn't understand.

"Please, Bert. I'm not ordering, I'm asking. She needs a kind hand."

"Needs a swift kick in the—"

"Bert! Please, listen to me. You have to understand that Jhavika *commanded* her to feel what she's feeling. She has no choice, and it's tearing her apart. Just like Hemp had no choice about cutting his own throat, and I had no choice about...any of the things she ordered me to do. They can't *resist* her commands."

Her face flushed deeper crimson. "I understand that, sir, but...she was just *cruel* to you. You never laid an unkind hand on her."

"No, I didn't, but she *believes* I did." I sighed and rubbed my eyes. I needed blackbrew and to be on deck. "Look, she believes that I lied to her, never loved her, that I seduced her and abused her the entire time we were together. How would you feel if someone did that to you?"

"If someone did that to me, I'd have their liver on toast!"

"Or maybe kick them in the teeth." I rubbed my jaw. It still hurt, and the inside of my mouth was cut to shreds. "In her mind, I deserved it."

Bert shook her head. "I'll feed her and tend her wounds, sir, and I won't be mean to her, but if you want someone to be *nice* to her, pick someone else."

"But there is no one—" I stopped dead. There *was* someone aboard who dearly loved Preel and understood her plight perfectly. "Hemp!"

Bert looked at me as if I'd ordered her to shinny up the mizzen mast naked. "You think that's safe, sir? I mean, with both of 'em half crazed by that damned scourge?"

"Misery loves company, Bert." I lurched to my feet. "And both of them are certainly miserable."

"Aye, ya got that right." She handed me a tray with a tin pot of blackbrew and half a dozen ship's biscuits.

I hobbled back to Hemp's door and nodded to Getri. "Open it." He threw the bolt and I stepped inside.

Hemp looked up from the chair, a needle and thread poised over one of my socks in his lap. "Thank you, sir."

I put the tray down on the desk. "Bert said boots, as long as they're loose and I don't walk too much." He vacated the chair and I sat. "And I've got a job for you."

"Job, sir." He nodded to my things and grabbed my freshly oiled boots. "Got a job. I'm still yer steward, ain't I?"

"You are, which means you care for the captain's things *and* the captain's cabin. Right now, I have a guest in that cabin who needs your tender care far more than I do."

He gaped at me. "Lady *Preel?*"

"Yes. I want you to take care of her, Hemp. I know you love her as much as I do, in your own way, and right now she hates me." I laid out the situation: what had happened to Preel, what she believed, what she'd said. The color drained from his face. "I don't need you to talk to her about it, or explain, or try to convince her she's not thinking clearly. I just need you to see to her needs. Clothes, food, books, whatever she wants. But we can't let her loose from the manacles. Even when she uses the quarter gallery or exercises, they're to remain

314

on her. I'll have the carpenter's mates put bars on the windows. I fear she'll try to escape if given the chance."

Hemp stared at me open-mouthed.

"Can you do it?"

"I..." His voice caught. He hiccupped, swallowed, and tried again. "Yes, sir. I'd be honored to take care of Lady Preel until we...solve this problem."

"Good man." He helped me into my boots and I stood. "I'll have Bert explain to her, and you can get to work."

"I will, sir! And thank you, sir, for your trust, I mean." He smiled and a tear spilled from his eye. He wiped it away and sniffed. "After what I done..."

"I know it wasn't you, Hemp, and there's no one I'd sooner trust." I clapped him on the shoulder and left the cabin.

I stopped by the galley to advise Bert of the situation, and asked her to warn Preel not to mention Jhavika in Hemp's presence, unless she wanted to watch him cut his throat. She grumbled assent, handed me a cup of blackbrew, and waved me out.

I drew on a weather cloak and hobbled on deck.

It was an ugly day at sea. The burgeoning sky promised squalls, and we were beating into a nasty head sea, short, steep swells with plunging tops. I ducked spray and made my way up to the quarterdeck.

Quiff snapped a salute, motioned me over beside the mizzenmast, and yelled over the wind. "Sir! I was just about to send for you."

"What's amiss?" I glanced aloft out of habit, but everything looked shipshape: yards braced hard fore and aft, sheets taut, trysails drawing smartly. I suspected Rauley had trimmed the sails himself, for Quiff hadn't such a deft hand.

"Nothing aloft, sir. Sailing south by southeast, making six knots." He handed me the watch spyglass and pointed aft. "The problem's back there."

I took the glass and moved into the shelter of the mizzenmast. Before I even put my eye to the lens, however, I spotted them. Sails all across the sea to the north, far closer than I'd hoped. Focusing on the nearest, a small galleon, I gauged the press of sail, their angle, and realized we were being chased.

I handed the glass back. "How many?"

"Lookout says seven in all, spread out northeast to southwest, but they all altered course at first light." Quiff tucked the glass away looking grim. "They're cracking on straight at us."

"Well, bugger!" It didn't take a stretch of intellect to figure out who was after us. "I didn't think Jhavika would be able to commandeer *one* ship before we were over the horizon, let alone *seven*!"

"Orders, sir?" Quiff asked, his face set in stone.

I considered. Few ships that had been in port the day before could match *Scourge* on the open sea. Jhavika, however, was a sailor and knew *Scourge*'s limitations as well as I did. I needed to know more about the ships chasing us, but the math was simple. We needed speed, and beating close-hauled into these steep seas was slowing us down.

"Fall off the wind a point or two and trim her smartly, Quiff. If she'll bear topgallants, fly them. We've got three days to lose them."

"Aye, sir, but why three days?"

"Because in three days, we'll have a destination." I glared at the pursuing ships. "In three days, I ask Preel where we need to go to destroy the scourge."

About the Author

Born and raised in Oregon, Chris meet his wife and soulmate, Anne, while attending graduate school in Texas. Since then they have been nigh inseparable: gaming together since 1985, sailing together since 1988, married since 1989, and writing together off and on throughout their relationship. Most astonishingly, they have not killed each other during the creation or editing of any of their stories...although it was close a few times. Since 2009, the couple has been sailing and writing full-time aboard their beloved sailboat, *Mr Mac*. They return to the US every summer for conventions, always happy to sign copies of their books and talk with fans.

Preview Chris' books and get updates on upcoming events at jaxbooks.com. Follow Chris and Anne's cruising adventures at www.sailmrmac.blogspot.com.

Novels by Chris A. Jackson

From Jaxbooks
A Soul for Tsing
Deathmask

Blood Sea Tales
The Pirate's Scourge
The Pirate's Truth
The Pirate's Curse (coming 2020)

Weapon of Flesh Series
Weapon of Flesh
Weapon of Blood
Weapon of Vengeance
Weapon of Fear *
Weapon of Pain *
Weapon of Mercy *
(* with Anne L. McMillen-Jackson)

The Cornerstones Trilogy
(with Anne L. McMillen-Jackson)
Zellohar
Nekdukarr
Jundag

The Cheese Runners Trilogy
(novellas – also on Audible)
Cheese Runners
Cheese Rustlers
Cheese Lords

From Dragon Moon Press
The Scimitar Seas Novels
Scimitar Moon
Scimitar Sun
Scimitar's Heir
Scimitar War

From Paizo Publishing
Pirate's Honor
Pirate's Promise
Pirate's Prophecy

From Privateer Press
Blood & Iron (ebook novella)
Watery Graves

From Fantasy Flight Games
The Deep Gate (hardcover novella)

From Falstaff Books
The Dragons of Boston Trilogy
Dragon Dreams
Dragon's Nemesis (Spring 2020)
Dragon's Legacy (Spring 2021)

Check out these and more at
JAXBOOKS.COM
Want to get an email about my next book release?
Sign up at http://eepurl.com/xnrUL

www.ingramcontent.com/pod-product-compliance
Lightning Source LLC
Chambersburg PA
CBHW071100250626
47159CB00002B/536